"Saramago's lovely and original questing story, in a lineage of others such as *Don Quixote* and Kipling's *Kim*, is a journey of the spirit told as a journey of the feet"

RICHARD EDER, *Los Angeles Times*

"A parable of cultural potency with a deliciously written account of the characters' geographical, philosophical and sexual pilgrimage to an unknown destination. Saramago has said the writer's job is to enlarge the world. He does" **PAUL HYLAND**, *European*

"José Saramago . . . is the García Márquez of Portugal, but he belongs to an utterly distinct culture and identity . . . This is the best new book I have read this year. Better still, it is an invitation to one of the richest bodies of work by a living writer"

AMANDA HOPKINSON, *New Statesman*

"Tremendous wit is always apparent in his imaginative conceits, comic digression and verbal and narrative games"

IAN CRITCHLEY, *Sunday Times*

"An engaging fantasy . . . this book can't be pinned down however, either as magic realism, Swiftian satire, or dystopian science fiction: in fact its concerns are largely philosophical . . . Pontiero's excellent translation preserves the strange, looping rhythms of José Saramago's prose, as well as his likeably self-referential humour and, most important of all, the sense of a deep and luminous intelligence which informs the whole enterprise"

JONATHAN COE, *Mail on Sunday*

JOSÉ SARAMAGO was born in Portugal in 1922. His oeuvre embraces plays, poetry, memoirs and several novels which have been translated into more than 40 languages. It was the publication in 1988 of *Baltasar & Blimunda* that first brought him to the attention of an English-speaking readership. This novel won the Portuguese PEN Club Award, as did his next, *The Year of the Death of Ricardo Reis*, which also won the *Independent* Foreign Fiction Award. His fiction has since established him as one of Europe's most influential living writers. In 1998 he was awarded the Nobel Prize for Literature.

GIOVANNI PONTIERO, formerly Reader in Latin-American Literature in the University of Manchester, was Saramago's regular English translator. His translation of *The Gospel according to Jesus Christ* was awarded the Teixeira-Gomes Prize for Portuguese translation. He was also the principal English translator of the works of Clarice Lispector. He died in 1996.

Also by José Saramago in English translation

Fiction

MANUAL OF PAINTING AND CALLIGRAPHY

BALTASAR & BLIMUNDA

THE YEAR OF THE DEATH OF RICARDO REIS

THE GOSPEL ACCORDING TO JESUS CHRIST

THE HISTORY OF THE SIEGE OF LISBON

BLINDNESS

ALL THE NAMES

———

THE TALE OF THE UNKNOWN ISLAND

Non fiction

JOURNEY TO PORTUGAL

José Saramago

THE STONE RAFT

Translated from the Portuguese by
Giovanni Pontiero

THE HARVILL PRESS
LONDON

First published in Portuguese with the title *A Jangada de Pedra* by
Editorial Caminho, Lisbon, 1986
First published in Great Britain in 1994 by Harvill
This paperback edition first published in 2000 by The Harvill Press

10

Copyright © José Saramago and Editorial Caminho, SARL, 1986
English translation copyright © Harcourt Brace , 1994

José Saramago asserts the moral right to be identified as the author of this work

This translation is published with the financial assistance of the Instituto de
Biblioteca Nacional e do Livro, Lisbon, which is gratefully acknowledged

The Harvill Press
Random House, 20 Vauxhall Bridge Road, London SW1V 2SA

www.randomhouse.co.uk

Addresses for companies within The Random House Group Limited can be found at:
www.randomhouse.co.uk/offices.htm

The Random House Group Limited Reg. No. 954009

A CIP catalogue record for this book
is available from the British Library

ISBN 9781860467219

Typeset in Linotron Fournier by Rowlands Photosetting Ltd, Bury St Edmonds, Suffolk

Half title illustration by Jeff Fisher

Penguin Random House is committed to a sustainable future for
our business, our readers and our planet. This book is made from
Forest Stewardship Council® certified paper.

Printed and bound in Great Britain by Clays Ltd, St Ives plc

Every future is fabulous

ALEJO CARPENTIER

TRANSLATOR'S NOTE

In *The Stone Raft*, as in all his other major novels, José Saramago restricts his punctuation to commas and full stops without any dashes, dots, colons, semicolons, interrogation or exclamation marks. This should not be seen as some perverse eccentricity. Citing the example of reputable medieval texts, Saramago insists that his prose style adheres to the basic principle that everything *said* is destined to be *heard*. Defining himself as an oral narrator whose words are meant to have the same impact as music, he claims to orchestrate rather than merely construct phrases and to write as if he were composing a score by concentrating on a pattern of sounds (loud or soft) and pauses (long or short). For him, commas and full stops suffice to create the necessary tension in prose, and he is adamant that any additional punctuation marks would inevitably destroy the sense of 'continuous flow' and hinder his experiments with timbre and resonance.

GIOVANNI PONTIERO

When Joana Carda scratched the ground with the elm branch all the dogs of Cerbère began to bark, throwing the inhabitants into panic and terror, because from time immemorial it was believed that, when these canine animals that had always been silent started barking, the entire universe was nearing its end. No one remembers any longer the origin of this deep-rooted superstition or firm conviction, which in many cases is the matching alternative expression, although by means of the familiar ploy of hearing the story and repeating it with fresh distortions, French grandmothers used to amuse their grandchildren with the fable that in mythological times of ancient Greece, here, in the district of Cerbère in the Eastern Pyrenees, a dog with three heads and the above-mentioned name of Cerberus had barked when summoned by its master, the ferryman Charon. We are equally unclear about the organic changes this legendary, howling canine must have undergone before acquiring the historically proven muteness of its degenerate one-headed offspring. However, and this is a point of doctrine known to almost everyone, especially if they are of the older generation, the dog Cerberus, as written and pronounced in English, guarded with ferocity the gates of hell, so that no soul would dare try to escape, and then, perhaps as one last act of mercy by the moribund gods, all the dogs thereafter fell silent for the rest of eternity, perhaps hoping their silence might erase the memory of the infernal regions. But since the everlasting does not last forever as the modern age has clearly shown us, it sufficed that a few days ago, hundreds of kilometres from Cerbère, at a place in Portugal, the name of which we shall remember anon, a woman named Joana Carda should scratch the ground with an elm branch for all the dogs to come out on to the streets howling, dogs, let me remind you, that never barked before. Were someone to ask Joana Carda what had possessed her to scratch the ground with an elm branch, more the gesture of a moonstruck adolescent than that of a mature woman, if she had not thought of the consequences of an act which seemed meaningless, and those, remember, are the most dangerous acts of all, perhaps she might reply, I don't know what came over me, the branch was lying on the ground, I picked it up and drew a line. She had no idea that it might be a magic wand. It seemed rather big for a magic wand, and I've always heard it said that magic wands are made of shimmering gold and crystal with a star on top, Did you know it was an elm branch, I know very little about trees, they told me afterwards that wych-elm is the same as wych-hazel, botanically known as *ulmus*, none of them having supernatural powers, even by changing their names, but in this case, I'm sure that a matchstick would have produced the same effect, Why do you say that, What must be, must be, is very powerful and cannot be resisted, I've heard it said a thousand times by older people, Do you believe in fate, I believe in what has to be.

In Paris they had a good laugh at the appeals made by the *maire*, who appeared to be telephoning from a kennel at the hour when they were feeding the dogs, and only at the insistent pleading of a member of parliament, born and bred in the commune, therefore familiar with local legends and tales, were two qualified veterinary surgeons of the Deuxième Bureau despatched to the south, with the special mission of investigating this unusual phenomenon and presenting a report and plan of action. Meanwhile, the desperate inhabitants, almost reduced to deafness, had scattered throughout the streets and squares of the agreeable resort transformed into a hell-hole, with dozens of poisoned meat pies, a method of supreme simplicity, whose effectiveness has been confirmed by experience in every age and latitude. As it happened, only one dog died, but the lesson was not lost on the survivors, who, yelping, barking and howling, soon disappeared into the surrounding fields, where, for no apparent reason, they fell silent within a few minutes. When the veterinary surgeons finally arrived, they were presented with the sad Medor, cold, swollen, so different from the contented animal who accompanied his mistress when she went shopping, and being old, liked sleeping out in the sun without a care in the world. However, since justice still has not entirely abandoned this world, God decided, poetically, that Medor should die from the meat pie cooked by his beloved mistress, who, let it be said, had left the pie out for a certain bitch of the neighbourhood who was never out of her garden. The older of the veterinary surgeons, confronted by that sad corpse, suggested, Let's hold an autopsy, which was pointless, for any inhabitant of Cerbère could, if he or she so wished, testify to the cause of death, but the hidden intention of the Faculty, as it was referred to in the jargon of that secret service, was to proceed in secrecy to an examination of the vocal cords of an animal which, between the quietude of death that was now definitive and its silence which seemed eternal, had finally enjoyed several hours of speech like any other dog. Their efforts were futile, Medor did not even have any vocal cords. The surgeons were amazed, but giving his official and judicious opinion, the *maire* said, That's not surprising, for centuries the dogs of Cerbère have not barked and their vocal cords have wasted away. Then, why the sudden change, I don't know, I'm not a veterinary surgeon, but our worries were over, the *chiens* disappeared, from wherever they are they cannot be heard, Medor, dissected and badly stitched up again, was delivered to his weeping mistress, as a living reproach, which is what reproaches are even after they are dead. On the way to the airport, where they were about to catch a plane to Paris, the veterinary surgeons agreed that they would omit from their report the curious episode about the missing vocal cords. And to all appearances definitive, for that same night there was Cerberus out prowling, an enormous dog as tall as a tree, with three heads but mute.

About the same time, perhaps before, perhaps after Joana Carda had scratched the ground with the elm branch, a man was strolling along the beach, it was towards evening, when the noise of the waves can scarcely be heard, brief and restrained like an unprovoked sigh, and that man, who will later say that his name is Joaquim Sassa, was walking above the tidemark that distinguishes the dry sands from the wet, and from time to time he bent down to pick up a shell, a crab's claw, a strand of green seaweed, we often while away the hours in this way, and this solitary passer-by was doing likewise. Since he had neither pockets nor sack to hoard his findings, he put the dead remains back in the water when his hands were full, let the sea have what belongs to the sea, let the earth remain with the earth. But every rule has its exceptions, and Joaquim Sassa picked up a stone he had seen ahead, beyond the reach of the tides. It was as large and heavy as a discus and irregular in shape, if it had been like the others, light, with smooth outlines, like those

3

stones which fit easily between the thumb and the index finger, then Joaquim Sassa would have thrown it on to the surface of the water, to watch it bounce, childishly satisfied with his own ability, and finally sink, the impetus gone, a stone that appeared to have its destiny traced out, dried by the sun, dampened only by the rain, and finally sinking into the dark depths to await a million years, until this sea evaporates, or upon receding brings the stone back to land for another million years, allowing sufficient time for another Joaquim Sassa to come down to the beach, who unwittingly will repeat the same gesture and movement, let no man say I shall not do it, for no stone is secure and firm.

On the southern shores, at this tepid hour, there is someone having one last bathe, swimming, playing with a ball, diving under the waves, or relaxing by floating on an air-mattress, or feeling on their skin the first waft of the evening breeze, or adjusting the position of their body to receive one last caress from the sun which is about to settle momentarily on the sea, the longest moment of all, for we look at the sun and the sun allows itself to be watched. But here, on this northern shore where Joaquim Sassa is carrying a stone, so heavy that his arms are already tiring, the breeze is chilly, the sun is already halfway down and there is not a seagull in sight flying over the waters. Joaquim Sassa threw the stone, expecting it to fall a few paces away, not much further than where he was standing, each of us is obliged to know our own strength, there were not even any witnesses there to mock the efforts of the frustrated discus-thrower, it was he who was prepared to laugh at himself, but things did not turn out as he expected, dark and heavy, the stone went up into the air, came down and hit the surface of the water, the impact sent it up again, with one great flight or leap, and down it came again, and then up, and finally sank at a distance, unless the whiteness we have just seen in the distance is not just the spume of a breaking wave. How did that happen, Joaquim Sassa mused in bewilderment, How could I, weak as I am, have thrown such a heavy stone so far, way out to that sea which is already darkening, and there is no one here to say, Well done, Joaquim Sassa, I'm your witness for the *Guinness Book of Records*, such a feat cannot be ignored, such rotten luck, if I were to tell people what has happened, they would call me a liar. A very high wave came in from the open sea, foaming and gushing, the stone finally dropped into the water, this is known from the rivers of childhood by anyone who had rivers in their childhood, the concentric undulation caused

4

by stones thrown into the water. Joaquim Sassa ran upshore, and the wave dispersed on the sand dragging shells, crab's claws, green algae but also other species, gulf-weed, coralline, sea-tangle and a small stone, light, of the type that can fit easily between the thumb and the index finger. How many years since it has seen any sunlight.

Writing is extremely difficult, it is an enormous responsibility, you need only think of the exhausting work involved in setting out events in chronological order, first this one, then that, or, if considered more convenient to achieve the right effect, today's event placed before yesterday's episode, and other no less risky acrobatics, the past treated as if it were new, the present as a continuous process without any present or ending, but, however hard writers might try, there is one feat they cannot achieve, that is to put into writing, in the same tense, two events which have occurred simultaneously. Some believe the difficulty can be solved by dividing the page into two columns, side by side, but this strategy is ingenuous, because the one was written first and the other afterwards, without forgetting that the reader will have to read this one first and then the other one, or vice versa, the people who come off best are the opera-singers, each with his or her own part to sing, three, four, five, six between tenors, basses, sopranos and baritones, all singing different words, for example, the cynic mocking, the ingénue pleading, the gallant lover slow in coming to her aid, what interests the opera-goer is the music, but the reader is not like this, he wants everything explained, syllable by syllable and one after the other, as they are shown here. That is why, having first spoken of Joaquim Sassa, only now will Pedro Orce be mentioned, when in fact Joaquim threw the stone into the sea and Pedro rose from his chair at the very same instant, although according to the clocks there was an hour's difference, because the latter happened to be in Spain and the former in Portugal.

It is common knowledge that every effect has its cause, and this is a universal truth, however, it is impossible to avoid certain errors of judgment, or of simple identification, for we might think that this effect comes from that cause, when after all it was some other cause, beyond any understanding we possess or knowledge we think we possess. For example, there appeared to be proof that if the dogs of Cerbère barked it was because Joana Carda scratched the ground with an elm branch, and yet only a very credulous child, if any child has survived from the golden decades of credulity, or an innocent one, if the holy name of innocence can thus be taken in vain, only a child capable of believing that by closing its hands it has trapped the sunlight inside, would believe that dogs could bark that had never barked before for reasons that are as much of a historical order as a physiological one. In these tens and tens of thousands of hamlets, villages, towns and cities, there are many people who would swear that they were the cause and causes, as much of the barking of the dogs as of all the rest to follow, because they slammed a door, or split a fingernail, or picked a fruit, or drew back the curtain, or lit a cigarette, or they died, or, not the same people, were born, these hypotheses about death and birth would be more difficult to concede, bearing in mind that we are the ones who would have to propose them, for no child comes out of its mother's womb speaking, just as no one speaks any more once they have entered the womb of the earth. And there is no point in adding that any one of us has plenty of reasons for judging himself the cause of all effects, the ones we have just mentioned as well as those which are our exclusive contribution to the functioning of the world, and I should dearly like to know what it will be like when there are no more people or the effects which they alone cause, best not to think of such an enormity, for it is enough to make one dizzy, now then, it will be quite sufficient for some tiny animals, some insects to survive for there still to be worlds, that of the ant and the cicada, they will not draw back curtains, they will not look at themselves in the mirror, and what does it matter, after all, the only great truth is that the world cannot die.

Pedro Orce would say, if he so dared, that what caused the earth to tremble were his feet hitting the floor when he rose from the chair, great presumption on his part, if not ours, since we are frivolously expressing doubt, if every person leaves at least one sign in the world, this could be that of Pedro Orce, which is why he declares, I put my feet on the ground and the earth shook. It was an extraordinary trembling, so much so that no one appeared to have felt it, and even now, after two minutes, as the wave on the beach began to recede and Joaquim Sassa said to himself, If I were to tell anyone they would call me a liar, the earth vibrates just as the chord continues to vibrate although it can no longer be heard, Pedro Orce can feel it in the soles of his feet, he continues to feel it as he leaves the pharmacy and steps out on to the street, and no one there notices a thing, it's like watching a star and saying, What lovely light, what a beautiful star, without knowing that it went out in mid-sentence, and their children and grandchildren will repeat those words, poor things, they speak of what is dead and say it is alive, this deception does not just happen in the science of astronomy. Here precisely the opposite happens, everyone would swear that the earth is firm and only Pedro Orce would say that it is trembling, just as well he kept his mouth shut and did not run away in terror, besides the walls are not swaying, the lamps hanging from the ceiling are as straight as a plumb line, and the little caged birds, who are usually the first to sound the alarm, doze peacefully on their perches with their head tucked under one wing, the needle of the seismograph has traced and continues to trace a straight horizontal line on the millimetric graph-paper.

Next morning, a man was crossing an uncultivated plain covered in brush and swampy pastures, he was making his way along paths and tracks between trees, as elevated as the name by which they are known, poplars and ash, and clumps of tamarisks, with their African scent, this man could not have chosen greater solitude or a loftier sky, and overhead, making the most incredible din, a flock of starlings followed him, so many of them that they formed a huge, dark cloud, like a prelude to a storm. Whenever he paused the starlings began to fly in a circle or swooped noisily on to a tree and disappeared amidst the branches until all the leaves were shaking, and the crown echoed with grating, strident sounds, giving the impression that some ferocious battle was being fought inside. José Anaiço started walking again, for that was his name, and the starlings took sudden flight, all at once, vruuuuuuuuuu. If we did not know this man, and started guessing, we might decide that he was a bird-catcher by trade or, like the snake, has the power to charm and entice, when, in fact, José Anaiço is as puzzled as we are about the reason for this winged festivity. What can these creatures desire of me, do not wonder at this obsolete expression, for there are days when one does not feel like using commonplace words.

The man was travelling from east to west, for this was the route or stroll he favoured, but, having been forced to skirt a great reservoir, he turned south as he took the bend, travelling alongside the edge. By late morning the temperature will soar, but meanwhile there is a fresh, clean breeze, what a pity one cannot store it in one's pocket and keep it there until it is needed once the heat builds up. José Anaiço was turning these thoughts over in his mind as he walked, vague and involuntary as if they did not belong to him,

7

when he suddenly became aware that the starlings had remained behind, were fluttering beyond, where the road curves, skirting the reservoir, their behaviour was quite extraordinary, but when all is said and done, whoever goes, goes, whoever remains, remains, goodbye little birds. José Anaiço had now circled the lake, an awkward journey which took nearly half an hour, amidst thistles and nettles, and he resumed the same route as before, in the direction which he had come from, east to west like the sun, when suddenly, vruuuu, the starlings reappeared, where had they been hiding. Well now, here's something for which there is no explanation. If a flock of starlings accompanies a man on his morning stroll, like a dog faithful to its master, and waits for him the time it takes to go round a reservoir and then follows him as it did before, one does not ask it to explain or check its motives, birds don't possess reasons but instincts, often vague and involuntary as if they were not part of us, we spoke about instincts, but also about reasons and motives. So let us not ask José Anaiço who he is and what he does for a living, where he comes from and where he is going, whatever we find out about him, we shall only find out from him, and this description, this sketchy information will also have to serve for Joana Carda and her elm branch, for Joaquim Sassa and the stone he threw into the sea, for Pedro Orce and the chair he got up from, life does not begin when people are born, if it were so, each day would be a day gained, life begins much later, and how often too late, not to mention those lives which have no sooner begun than they are over, which has led one poet to exclaim, Ah, who will write the history of what might have been.

And now this woman, called Maria Guavaira, such a strange name, who climbed up into the attic of the house and found an old sock, of the real old-fashioned kind that were used to keep money as safely as in any bank vault, symbolic hoardings, gratuitous savings, and upon finding the sock empty she set about undoing the stitches to amuse herself, having nothing else with which to occupy her hands. An hour passed and another and yet another, and the long strand of blue wool is still unwinding, yet the sock does not appear to get any smaller, the four enigmas already mentioned were not enough, which shows us at least on this occasion that the contents can be greater than the container. The sound of the seawaves does not reach this silent house, the shadow of passing birds does not darken the window, there must be dogs but they do not bark, the earth, if it trembled, trembles no more. At the feet of the woman

8

unravelling the thread is the mountain that goes on growing. Maria Guavaira is not called Ariadne, with this thread we shall not emerge from the labyrinth, perhaps it will help us to succeed at last in losing ourselves. Where is the end of this thread.

The first crack appeared in a large slab of natural stone, as smooth as the table of the winds, somewhere in these mountains of Alberes which, at the eastern end of the Pyrenees, slope gradually downwards to the sea and where the ill-starred dogs of Cerbère now rove, an allusion which is not inappropriate in time or place, for all these things, despite their appearances, are inter-connected. Excluded, as has been stated, from any domestic sustenance, and consequently forced by necessity to recall in its unconscious memory the skills of its predatory ancestors in order to catch some stray rabbit, one of those dogs, Ardent by name, must, thanks to the extremely sharp hearing with which the species is endowed, have heard the stone cracking and, although incapable of sniffing, the dog approached the stone, dilating his nostrils, his hairs bristling, as much out of curiosity as fear. The crack, ever so fine, would remind any human observer of a line drawn with the sharpened point of a pencil, altogether different from that other line made with a branch on hard soil or in the loose, soft dust, or in the mud, should we choose to waste our time on such daydreams. However, as the dog was approaching, the crack grew bigger, grew deeper and began to spread, splitting the stone up to the edges of the slab, and then all the way across, there was room to put a hand inside, a whole arm in width and length, had there been any man around with enough courage to cope with this phenomenon. The dog Ardent prowled around, agitated, yet unable to escape, attracted by the snake of which neither the head nor the tail could be seen, and suddenly he was lost, not knowing on which side to stay, whether in France, where he now found himself, or in Spain, no more than three spans away. But this dog, thanks be to God, is not one of those creatures who adapt to situations, the proof being that with one jump he leapt over the abyss, if you'll pardon the obvious exaggeration in this expression, and ended up on this side, he preferred the infernal regions, and we shall never know what longings influence a dog's soul, what dreams, what temptations.

The second crack, but for the world the first, appeared at a considerable distance, towards the Bay of Biscay, not far from a place called Roncesvalles, alas all too famous in the history of Charlemagne and his twelve Paladins, where Roland died when he blew on Oliphant, without Angelica or Durendal to come to his assistance. There, descending along the foot of the Sierra Abodi, through the north-eastern strip, runs the River Irati, which, originating in France, flows into the Spanish Erro, in its turn an affluent of the Aragón, which is a tributary of the Ebro, which will finally carry and deposit all their waters in the Mediterranean. At the bottom of the valley, on the edge of the Irati, there is a town, Orbaiceta by name, and upstream exists a dam or weir as it is called in those parts.

It is time to explain that what is reported here or may come to be reported is the truth and nothing but the truth, as you may verify on any map, provided it is sufficiently comprehensive to include certain details which might seem so insignificant, for that is the virtue of maps, they show what can be done with limited space, they foresee that everything can happen therein. And it does. We've already mentioned the rod of destiny, we've already proved that a stone, even if it be removed from the highest tidemark, can end up falling into the sea or make its way back to the shore, now it is the turn of Orbaiceta, where, after the salutary upheaval caused by the construction of the dam many years ago, calm had been restored, a city in the province of Navarre and dormant amidst mountains, now thrown into turmoil once more. For some days Orbaiceta became the nerve centre of Europe, if not of the world, invaded by government ministers, politicians, civil and military authorities, geologists and geographers, journalists and mineralogists, photographers, film and television crews, engineers of every kind, inspectors and sightseers. However, the fame of Orbaiceta will not last for long, a few fleeting days, not much longer than the roses of Malherbe, and how could the latter have lasted having been grown on poor soil, but we are talking about Orbaiceta, nothing else, until some more notable event is reported elsewhere, which is what happens with notable events.

In the history of rivers there has never been anything like it, water flowing eternally and suddenly it flows no more, like a tap which is abruptly turned off, for example, someone is washing his hands in a basin, removes the plug, has turned off the tap, the water drains away, goes down the pipe, disappears, what has remained in the enamelled basin will soon evaporate. To put it more aptly, the waters of the Irati retreated like the waves that ebb from the shore and vanish, leaving the riverbed exposed, nothing but pebbles, mud, slime, fishes that gasp as they leap and die, then sudden silence.

The engineers were not on the spot when this incredible event took place, but they noticed that something abnormal had occurred, the dials on the observation panels indicated that the river had stopped feeding the great aquatic basin. Three technicians set off in a jeep to investigate the intriguing development, they made their way along the edge of the weir, examined the different possible hypotheses, they had plenty of time to do so for they travelled almost five kilometres, and one of those hypotheses was that a subsidence or landslide on the mountain might have diverted the river's course, another was that it might be the work of the French, typical Gallic perfidy, notwithstanding the bilateral agreement about fluvial waters and their hydro-electric uses, yet another hypothesis, and the most radical of all, was that the source, the fountain-head, the spring, had dried up, the eternity that appeared to exist but did not exist after all. On this point, opinions were divided. One of the engineers, a quiet man, the thoughtful type, and someone who enjoyed life in Orbaiceta, feared that they might send him to some remote place, the others rubbed their hands with glee, perhaps they might be transferred to one of the dams on the Tagus, or closer to Madrid and the Gran Vía. Debating these personal worries they reached the far end of the reservoir, where they found a drainage ditch but no river, nothing but a thin trickle of water still seeping from the soft earth, a muddy swirl that would not have enough power to turn a toy water wheel. Where the devil can the river have got to, exclaimed the driver of the jeep, and he could not have been more forthright and explicit. Puzzled, amazed, uneasy and concerned, the engineers once more began discussing among themselves the various hypotheses mentioned earlier and when they saw that there was nothing to be gained from this discussion, they returned to the offices attached to the dam, then went on to Orbaiceta where the administrators awaited them, having already been informed of the river's mysterious disappearance. There were recriminations, exclamations of disbelief, telephone calls to Pamplona and Madrid, and the final outcome of these exhausting discussions was expressed in an order of the utmost simplicity, broken down into three successive and complementary stages, follow the course of the river upstream, find out what happened and say nothing to the French.

Next morning before sunrise, the expedition set out heading for the frontier, keeping alongside or in sight of the parched river, and when the inspectors wearily arrived there, they realized that there would be no more Irati. Through a crack that could not have been more than three metres wide, the waters rushed into the earth, roaring like a tiny Niagara. On the other side, the French had already started to gather, it would have been sublimely ingenuous to think that their neighbours, astute and Cartesian, would have failed to notice the phenomenon, but at least they showed themselves to be as amazed and dumbfounded as the Spaniards on this side, and all brothers in ignorance. The two sides got round to speaking, but the conversation was neither wide-ranging nor profitable, little more than exclamations of justified alarm, a tentative airing of new hypotheses on the part of the Spaniards, in short, a general atmosphere of irritation which could not find anyone on whom to turn, the French were soon smiling, after all they continued to be masters of the river down to the frontier, they would not need to modify their maps.

That afternoon, helicopters from both countries flew over the area, took photographs, using windlasses, observers were lowered and suspended over the cataract, they looked and saw nothing, only the black gaping hole and the curving line and the shining surface of the water. In order to make some useful progress, the municipal authorities of Orbaiceta on the Spanish side, and of Larrau on the French side, met near the river under a tent set up for the occasion and dominated by the three flags, the national bi-coloured and tri-coloured flags, alongside that of Navarre, with the intention of examining the tourist potential of a natural phenomenon that must certainly be unique in the world and how it might be exploited to their mutual advantage. Having considered the inadequacy and undoubtedly makeshift nature of the methods of analysis at their disposal, the gathering failed to draw up any document defining the obligations and rights of each party, so a joint commission was nominated and entrusted with preparing an agenda for another formal meeting, with all possible haste. At the last minute, however, a disturbing factor arose to upset the relative consensus they had reached, this was the almost simultaneous intervention in Madrid and Paris of the representatives of the two States on the permanent commission for settling boundary disputes. These gentlemen expressed grave doubts. First, let us see where the hole is opening up, whether it's towards the Spanish side or towards the French side. It seemed a trivial detail, but once the essentials had been explained, the delicacy of the matter became clear. It was clearly beyond question that from now on the Irati belonged entirely to France, under the jurisdiction of the district authorities in the Lower Pyrenees, but if the crack should open up entirely on the Spanish side, in the province of Navarre, the negotiations would require further discussions, since both countries, in one sense, would bear an equal share. If, on the other hand, the crack was also on the French side, then the problem was entirely theirs, just as the respective primary resources, the river and the gaping hole belonged to them. Faced with this new situation, the two authorities, concealing any mental reservations, agreed to keep in touch until some solution could be found to this crucial problem. In their turn, with a joint declaration which had been laboriously drafted, the Ministries for Foreign Affairs of both nations announced their intention of pursuing urgent talks within the scope of the aforesaid permanent commission for boundary matters, to be advised, as one would expect, by their respective teams of geodetic experts.

It was about this time that vast numbers of geologists from all over the world began to appear on the scene. Between Orbaiceta and Larrau there were already a considerable number of foreign geologists, if not quite as many as stated earlier. But now all the wise men of this and other lands began to arrive in force, the inspectors of landslides and natural disasters, erratic strata and blocks, carrying a tiny hammer in one hand, tapping on everything that so much as looked like stone. A French journalist and something of a wit, called Michel, quipped to a Spanish colleague, a serious fellow named Miguel, who had already reported to Madrid that the crack was de-fi-ni-te-ly Spanish, or, to speak in geographical and nationalist terms, Navarrese, Why don't you lot keep it, was what the insolent Frenchman said, if the crack gives you so much pleasure and you need it so badly, after all, in the Cirque de Gavarnie alone we have a waterfall four hundred and twenty metres high, we do not need artesian holes turned upside down. Miguel could have replied that on the Spanish side of the Pyrenees there were also plenty of waterfalls, and some of them very fine and high, but the problem there was different, a waterfall open to the sky presents no mystery, always looks the same, in full view of everyone, while in the case of the Irati, you can see where the crack originates, but no one knows where it ends, just like life itself. However, it was another journalist, a Galician, moreover, who was passing through, as often happens with Galicians, who raised the question that still needed to be asked. Where does this water go. This was at a time when geologists in both camps were engaged in scientific discussions, and the question, like that of a timid child, was barely heard by the person who is now putting it on record. Since the accent was Galician, therefore discreet and cautious, it was muffled by Gallic rapture and Castilian bluster, but then others arrived to repeat the question, proudly claiming to have thought of it first, but then no one pays any heed to tiny nations, this is not a persecution mania, but a historical fact. The debate among the wise men had become almost incomprehensible for the layman, yet notwithstanding, two basic theories emerged from their discussions, that of the monoglaciologists and that of the polyglaciologists, both inflexible, and soon in opposition, like two conflicting religions, the one monotheist, the other polytheist. Certain statements even sounded interesting, such as the one about deformations, certain deformations which might be due either to a tectonic elevation or to an isotonic compensation of erosion. All the more so, they added, since the examination of the actual forms of the cordillera allows us to conclude that it is not old, that is to say in geological terms. All this, probably, had something to do with the crack. After all, when a mountain is subjected to such play of traction and force, it is not surprising that there comes a day when it finds itself obliged to give way, to splinter, collapse, or, as in this instance, to crack open. This was not the case with the great slab, lying inert on the mountains of Alberes, but the geologists had not seen it, the slab was far away, in a remote spot, no one got near it, the dog Ardent chased after the rabbit and did not return.

After two days, the members of the commission for boundaries were engaged in field work, taking measurements with their theodolites, checking with their tables, calculating with their instruments, and comparing all these data against the aerial photographs, the French somewhat disgruntled because there was no longer any doubt that the crack was Spanish, as the journalist Miguel had been the first to argue, when suddenly there was news of another fracture.

No more was said about tranquil Orbaiceta nor about the River Irati which had been cut off, *sic transit gloria mundi* and that of Navarre. The journalists, some of whom were women, swarmed on to the Eastern Pyrenees, which marked the crucial region, fortunately endowed with excellent means of access, so many and so excellent that within a few hours everyone who mattered was assembled there, people had even come from as far away as Toulouse and Barcelona. The highways were congested, and by the time the police on both sides of the border intervened to divert the flow of traffic it was much too late, the cars stretched for kilometre after kilometre, mechanical chaos, it soon became necessary to take drastic measures, to make everyone turn back on the other lane of the motorway which meant pulling down barriers, jamming the sides of the road with cars, an inferno, the Greeks had good reason to locate hell in this region. Particularly useful in dealing with the crisis were the helicopters, those flying artefacts or airships capable of landing almost anywhere and, whenever it proves impossible to land, they imitate the hummingbird, draw close until they almost touch the flower, the passengers do not need a ladder, a little jump and that is all, they enter the corolla at once, amidst the stamens and pistils, breathing in the aroma, frequently that of naphtha and charred flesh. Heads lowered, they set off running, anxious to find out what has happened, some of them have come straight from the Irati, already experienced in structural geology, but not equipped to cope with anything quite like this.

The crack cuts across the road, the entire parking area, and runs on, thinning out on both sides, heading towards the valley, where it disappears from sight, winding up the mountain slope, until it finally vanishes among the bushes. We are standing right on the frontier, the real one, the line of separation in this nameless limbo between the stations of the two police forces, the *aduana* and the *douane, la bandera* and *le drapeau*. At a prudent distance, for one cannot rule out the possibility of a landslide if the edges of the ruptured area should cave in, technicians exchange phrases devoid of any meaning or purpose, one cannot refer to that babble of voices as dialogue and, to make matters worse, use loudspeakers to hear each other better, while the experts inside the pavilions speak on the telephone, one minute among themselves, the next with Madrid and Paris. No sooner had they landed than the journalists were off to discover what happened, and they all picked up the same story with some embroidered variants, which they were to embellish further with their imagination, but in simple language, the person who vouched for the occurrence was the motorist who, passing through as darkness fell, sensed his car give a sudden lurch, as if the wheels had bounced across a pothole in the middle of the road, and he got out to see what it was, thinking they might be resurfacing the road and had unwisely forgotten to put up a warning sign. By this time, the crack was half a span wide and some four metres long at most. The man, who was Portuguese, called Sousa, and travelling with his wife and parents-in-law, went back to the car and told them, It looks as if we're already in Portugal, would you believe it, there's an enormous pothole in the road, it's a miracle it didn't flatten the tyres or snap the axle. It was no pothole, nor was it enormous, but the words, as we have written them, have one real advantage, simply because they are exaggerated, they soon allay fears and calm nerves, why, because they dramatize. The wife, without paying much attention to what he said, replied, You'd better take a look, and he decided to heed her advice, although that was not her intention, the woman's words were more of an exclamation than an order, one of those exclamations that often serve as a reply, he got out of the car again and went to check the tyres, fortunately there was no apparent damage. Within the next few days, back in his native Portugal, he will become a hero, be interviewed on radio and television, make statements to the press. You were the first to see it happen, Senhor Sousa, give us your impression of that terrible moment. He will repeat his story countless times, and he always finishes off his embroidered version of events with an anxious, rhetorical question, calculated to make the listener shudder as he himself shudders with delicious ecstasy. Just think, if the hole had been bigger, as they say it now is, we would have fallen in, God knows how far down, and the Galician must have been thinking more or less the same when he asked, as you may recall, Where does that water go.

How far, there is the crucial question. The first practical step would be to examine the damage, to check the depth, and then to study, define, and put into operation the appropriate measures in order to fill in the breach, no word could be more precise, it is of French origin, after all, and one is tempted to believe that someone thought of it one day, or invented it, so that it could be fittingly invoked whenever the earth should crack open. The investigation once completed, registered little more than twenty metres, of no real significance, given the resources of modern engineering in carrying out public works. From Spain and from France, from near and afar, concrete mixers were brought in, those interesting machines which, with their simultaneous movements, remind one of earth in space, rotation, removal, and upon reaching the spot they poured out the concrete, torrential, quantified to achieve the right effect with large amounts of rough stones and fast-setting cement. The filling-up operation was well under way when one imaginative expert suggested that they should attach some clamps, a method once used to heal human wounds, large clamps made of steel, which would secure the edges, assisting, as it were, and speeding up the process of closing the breach. The idea was approved by the bilateral commission coping with the emergency, the Spanish and French metallurgists immediately began carrying out the necessary tests, checking the alloy, the thickness and the section of the material, the relationship between the size of the spike that would be driven into the ground and the space covered, in short, technical details intended for the specialist, and here mentioned somewhat superficially. The crack swallowed up the torrent of stones and grey sludge as if it were the River Irati pouring into the depths of the land, deep echoes could be heard coming from the earth, it was even suspected that there might be some gigantic hollow down below, a cavern, some kind of insatiable gorge, and if this is the case, there is no point in carrying on, you simply build a bridge over the gap, probably the easiest and most economical solution of all, and bring in the Italians, who have a great deal of experience when it comes to building viaducts. But, after pouring in God knows how many tons and cubic metres, the sounding line registered a depth of seventeen metres, then fifteen, then twelve, the level of the concrete went on rising, the battle was won. The technicians, labourers and policemen embraced each other, flags were waved, the television announcers, excited, read the latest bulletins and gave their own opinions, praising this titanic struggle, this collective victory, international solidarity in action, even from Portugal, that tiny country, a convoy of ten concrete mixers set out, there is a long journey ahead, more than one thousand five hundred kilometres, an extraordinary achievement, the cement they are carrying won't be necessary, but history will remember their symbolic gesture.

When the gap had finally been filled in, the general excitement exploded into wild euphoria as if this were another New Year's Eve, with fireworks and the bullfight of São Silvestre. The air vibrated with the horns of the motorists who had not budged from the spot even after the motorways had been cleared, the lorries let off the hoarse bellowing of their *avertisseurs* and *bocinas*, and the helicopters hovered triumphantly overhead, like seraphim endowed with powers that were probably far from celestial. The cameras clicked incessantly, the television crews drew near, overcoming their fears, and there, close to the edges of the crack which no longer existed, they filmed great layers of the rough concrete, the evidence of man's victory over the vagaries of nature. And this was how spectators, remote from the scene, in the comfort and safety of their own homes were able to see pictures transmitted directly from the Franco-Spanish frontier at Coll de Pertus, laughing and clapping their hands and celebrating the event as if they themselves had been responsible for its success, this was how they saw it, unable to believe their own eyes, the concrete surface which was still moist begin to move and descend, as if the enormous mass were about to be sucked under, slowly but surely, until the gaping breach became visible once more. The crack had not widened, and this could only mean one thing, namely that the depth of the hole was no longer twenty metres as before, but much deeper, God alone knows just how deep. The workers drew back in horror, but a sense of professional duty, which had become second nature, kept the cameras turning, tremulous of course, and the world could now see faces change their expression, the wild panic, shouting could be heard, cries of horror, there was a general stampede, within seconds the parking area was deserted, the concrete-mixers were abandoned, here and there some were still working, the drums turning, filled with concrete which three minutes ago ceased to be necessary and was now quite futile.

For the first time, a shudder of fear went through the Peninsula and nearby Europe. In Cerbère, not very far from there, the people, running impulsively on to the streets as their dogs before them, said to each other, It was written, whensoever they should bark, the world would end, but it was not quite like this, it had never been written, but great moments call for great words and it is difficult to say why this expression, It was written, figures so prominently in handbooks recording prophetic statements. With greater justification than anyone, the terror-stricken inhabitants of Cerbère began to abandon the town, migrating en masse on to firmer soil, in the hope that they would be safe there from the world's encroaching end. In Banyuls-sur-Mer, Port Vendres and Collioure, to mention only these villages and hamlets dotted along the coastline, there was not a living soul to be seen. The dead souls, having died, were left there, with that persistent indifference which distinguishes them from the rest of humanity, if anyone ever said otherwise, or suggested, for example, that Fernando Pessoa visited Ricardo Reis, the one being dead and the other alive, it was their foolish imagination and nothing else. But one of these dead men, in Collioure, stirred ever so slightly, as if hesitating, shall I or shan't I go, but never into France, he alone knew where, and perhaps one day we shall know too.

Amidst the thousand items of news, opinions, commentaries and round-table conferences which occupied the press, television and radio the following day, the brief statement by an orthodox seismologist passed almost unnoticed. What I should dearly like to know is why all this is happening without as much as an earth tremor, to which another seismologist, of the modern school, pragmatic and flexible, replied, All will be explained in due course. Now, in a village in southern Spain, a man, listening to these conflicting opinions, left his house and set off for the city of Granada, to tell the television men that he had felt an earth tremor more than a week ago, that he had not spoken up sooner because he feared that no one would believe him, and that he was now here in person, so that people could see how a simple man can be more sensitive than all the seismographers in the world put together. As luck would have it, a journalist listened to what he had to say, either out of heartfelt sympathy or because he was intrigued by the unusual occurrence, and this latest scoop was summed up in four lines and, although there were no pictures, the news was given on television that night, with a cautious smile. Next day, Portuguese television, lacking any material of their own, took up the man's story and developed it further by interviewing a specialist in psychic phenomena who, judging from his one important statement, could add nothing to what was already known on the subject, as in all situations of this kind, everything depends on one's sensibility.

Much has been said here about causes and effects, taking great care to weigh up the facts, proceed logically, be guided by common sense, and reserve any judgment, for it must be clear to all that you cannot make a silk purse out of a sow's ear. It is only natural and right, therefore, that we should doubt that the line drawn on the ground by Joana Carda with an elm branch was the direct cause of the Pyrenees cracking open, which is what has been insinuated from the beginning. But one cannot deny this other fact, which is entirely true, that Joaquim Sassa went off in search of Pedro Orce after having heard his name being mentioned in the evening news bulletin, and having listened to what he had to say.

A loving mother, Europe was saddened by the misfortune of her lands on the extreme west. Along the entire Pyrenean cordillera, the granite split open, the cracks multiplied, other roads appeared to have been severed, other streams and torrents sank to the bottom until they disappeared. Seen from the air, a continuous black line suddenly opened up on the snow-capped peaks like a trail of dust, where the snow was sliding and disappearing with the white sound of a tiny avalanche. The helicopters came and went incessantly, observed the summits and valleys swarming with experts and specialists of every kind who might prove to be useful, geologists, the latter in their own right, although their field of work was currently obstructed, seismologists, perplexed, because the earth insisted on remaining firm, without as much as a tremor, not even a vibration, and also volcanologists, secretly hopeful, despite the clear sky, free of any signs of smoke or fire, the perfect, blue glaze of an August sky. The trail of smoke was merely a comparison, and we should never take comparisons literally, this or any other, unless we learn to treat them with caution. Human strength could do nothing on behalf of a cordillera which was opening up like a pomegranate, without any apparent suffering, and simply, who are we to know, because it had matured and its time had come. Only forty-eight hours after Pedro Orce had said what he said on television, it was no longer possible to cross the frontier at any point from the Atlantic to the Mediterranean either on foot or by surface transport. And in the low-lying coastlands, the seas, each from its own side, began to find their way into new channels, mysterious unknown gorges, increasingly deeper, with those sheer walls, dropping vertically all the way, the clean cut exposing the arrangement of ancient and modern strata, the synclines, the intercalations of clay, the conglomerates, the extensive concretions of soft limestone and sandstone, the beds of shale, the black, siliceous rocks, the granites, and all the rest which cannot be listed here because of the narrator's lack of knowledge and time. Now we know what reply should have been given to the Galician who asked, Where does this water go. It ends up in the sea, we should tell him, transformed into the finest rain, into dust, into a waterfall, depending on the height from which it drops and on the amount of water, no, no we are not talking about the Irati, that is some distance away, but you can be sure that everything will end up by conforming to the laws of nature, as jets of water, even as a rainbow, once the sun is able to penetrate the sombre depths.

On both sides of the frontier, along a narrow belt stretching about a hundred kilometres, the population abandoned their homes and withdrew to the relative security of the interior, but matters were complicated in the case of Andorra, which we were inexcusably forgetting, that's what tends to happen to little countries, which could just as easily have turned out to be bigger. At the beginning, there was great uncertainty about the final outcome of the cracks, they existed on both sides, on the two frontiers, and also because some of the inhabitants were Spanish, others French, and yet others Andorrans, each of them gravitated to their native soil, so to speak, or were influenced by what seemed right or in their best interests at that moment, even if it meant breaking up families and other relationships, Finally, the continuous line of the fracture settled once and for all on the French border, several thousand French nationals were evacuated by air, in a brilliant rescue operation which was given the code name Mitre d'Evêque, a name which incurred the grave displeasure of the Bishop of Urgel, who unintentionally provided the inspiration, but this did not detract from his satisfaction when he realized that in future he would become the sole overlord of the principality, provided the latter, barely encircled by the Spanish side, did not end up in the sea. All that was left in this desert, created by the general evacuation, were some military detachments who went around with a prayer on their lips, under the constant surveillance of the helicopters hovering overhead, ready to pick up personnel at the slightest sign of any geological instability, and, as one might expect, those inevitable looters, generally alone, for catastrophes always bring snakes out of their lairs or eggs, and who, in this case, just like the soldiers who shot them without pity or remorse, also went around with a prayer on their lips, according to whichever faith they professed, every living being has the right to the love and protection of their god, bearing in mind, in allowance and defence of the robbers, that one could argue that those who have abandoned their homes do not deserve to live there and enjoy them, besides, as the proverb rightly says, All birds eat corn, only the sparrow pays, let each of you decide whether there is any connection to be found between the general principle and this particular case.

This might be the moment to express our regret that this true story is not the libretto of an opera, for if it were we would stage an ensemble the like of which has never been heard before, with twenty voices comprising lyric and dramatic sopranos of every timbre, one by one, or in chorus, in succession or simultaneously, trilling their parts, namely the joint sessions of the Spanish and Portuguese governments, the total disruption of the electric transport system, the declaration of the European Community, the stand taken by the North Atlantic Treaty Organization, the flight of tourists in panic, the attack on aeroplanes, the congestion of traffic on the roads, the meeting between Joaquim Sassa and José Anaiço, their encounter with Pedro Orce, the agitation of the bulls in Spain, the nervousness of the horses in Portugal, the disquiet on the coasts of the Mediterranean, the disturbance of tides, the flight of the rich and their fortunes, shortly there will be no singers left onstage. Those who are curious, not to say sceptical, will want to know what is causing all these serious developments, as if the simple breaking up of the Pyrenees were not enough for them, with rivers turning into waterfalls and tides advancing several kilometres inland, after a recession which has lasted millions of years. At this point the hand falters, how can it plausibly write the words that are about to follow, words which will inevitably throw everything into jeopardy, all the more so since it is becoming extremely difficult, should such a thing ever be possible in life, to separate truth from fantasy. The fact is, let us finish what remained in suspense, by striving to transform with words what can probably only be transformed with words, the moment has arrived, it has finally come, to reveal that the Iberian Peninsula has suddenly broken away, all in one uniform piece, leaving a gap of ten whole metres, who would believe it, the Pyrenees have opened up from top to bottom as if some invisible axe had descended from on high, penetrating the deep cracks, clawing stone and earth down into the sea. Now we

24

can certainly see the Irati dropping a thousand metres, falling head-long into infinity, the Irati opens to the wind and sun, a crystal fan or the tail of a bird of paradise, the first rainbow poised over the abyss, the first vertigo of the hawk hovering with drenched wings, tinged with seven colours. And we should also see the Visaurin, Monte Perdido, the peaks of the Perdiguere, and of Estats, two thousand metres, three thousand metres of steep slopes unbearable to watch, you cannot even see where they descend, because of the misty atmosphere in the distance, and then fresh clouds will appear as the gap widens, as certain as the existence of destiny itself.

Time passes, memories fade, we can scarcely perceive any longer the truth and truths, once so clear and defined, and then, wishing to confirm what we ambitiously call the accuracy of the facts, we consult the evidence relating to the period, the various documents, newspapers, films, video recordings, chronicles, private diaries, parchments, especially the palimpsests, we question survivors, with much good will on either side, we even succeed in believing what some old man claims to have seen and heard as a child, and from all of this we shall have to draw some conclusion, in the absence of any convincing certainties one has to pretend, but what appears to be beyond question is that until the electric cables burst apart there was no real fear in the Peninsula, although it has been stated to the contrary, of course there was some panic, but not fear, which is emotion of another order. Obviously there are many people who preserve a clear picture of the dramatic scenes at Coll de Pertus when the concrete disappeared from the sight of those who were shouting, We are winning, we are winning, but the episode only made an impression on those who were actually there, the others looked on from a distance, sitting at home before their own little stage, their television set, in that small rectangle of glass, that court-yard of miracles where an image sweeps away the previous one without trace, everything is on a reduced scale, even emotions. And those sensitive viewers, for they still exist, those viewers who start shedding tears on the slightest pretext and to disguise the lump in their throat did what they usually do when they cannot bear it any longer, confronted by famine in Africa and other such calamities, they turned their eyes away. Besides, we must not forget that vast areas of the Peninsula, in the heart of the countryside where news-papers do not arrive and the television reception is poor, there were millions, yes, millions of people who did not see what was happening, or had only a vague idea, formed from words whose

25

meaning they had only half digested, perhaps not even that, which was so unreliable that there really was not much difference between what some people thought they knew and what others did not.

But when all the lights in the Peninsula went out at the same time, a blackout they later referred to as *apagón* in Spain, *negrum* in a Portuguese village that still invents words, when five hundred and eighty-one square kilometres of land became invisible on the surface of the earth, then there was no longer any doubt, everything was coming to an end. It was just as well that the entire power-cut did not last more than fifteen minutes before emergency connections were restored which put domestic energy resources into action, scant at this time of the year, the height of summer, mid-August, dry, low reservoirs, a shortage of power stations, and these cursed nuclear installations, but the pandemonium was truly peninsular, demons on the loose, cold fear, bedlam, even an earthquake could not have had a worse effect on morale. It is night, the beginning of night, when most people have retired indoors, they are sitting watching television, in their kitchens the women are preparing dinner, one particularly patient father is helping to resolve, somewhat tentatively, an arithmetical problem, there does not appear to be much happiness, but it soon becomes clear just how much this terror means, this pitch darkness, this ink-stain which has dropped on to Iberia. Do not take away the light, oh Lord, let it return, and I promise you that until my dying day, I shall ask for nothing else, this is what penitent sinners are saying, but then they always exaggerate. Anyone living in a valley would have imagined themselves to be inside a covered well, anyone living higher up climbed to the top and, for many leagues around, could not see a single light, it was as if the world had changed orbit and was now travelling in a space without any sun. Trembling hands lit candles in the houses, torches, paraffin-lamps kept for an emergency, but not like this one, candlesticks in wrought silver, those in bronze which were only used as ornaments, brass candlesticks, long-forgotten oil-lamps, dim lights which filled the darkness with shadows and allowed one to catch a glimpse of startled faces, as distorted as reflections on the water. There were lots of women shouting, lots of men were shaking, as for the children, all one can say is that they were all crying their hearts out. After fifteen minutes, which, as the saying goes, seemed like fifteen centuries, although no one had lived the latter to be able to compare them with the former, the electric power came back, little by little, intermittent, the lamps were like sleepy eyes casting surly looks everywhere ready to fall asleep again, until they could finally stand the light and hold it there.

Half an hour later, radio and television stations resumed transmission, gave reports about the blackout, and so we learned that all the high-voltage cables between France and Spain had blown up, some pylons had collapsed, through some inexcusable oversight none of the engineers had remembered to disconnect the lines since it was impossible to cut them. Fortunately, the fireworks caused by the short-circuits did not claim any victims, a most selfish way of putting it, for while it is true that no human lives were lost, one wolf, at least, did not escape the fulmination and was reduced to smoking cinders. But the blowing up of the cables was only one half of the explanation for the blackout, the other half of the explanation, despite the garbled form in which it was deliberately expressed, soon became clear, each man spelling things out to his neighbour, What they don't want to admit is that it is not just the cracks in the ground, otherwise the cables wouldn't have broken. Then tell me, neighbour, what do you think happened, It's white and the hen lays it but this time it wasn't an egg, the cables broke because they were stretched, because the earth was pulled apart, that's what happened as sure as God is my Maker, You don't tell me, I'm telling you, I'm telling you, just you wait and see, they'll end up spilling the beans. And they did, but only the following day, when there were so many rumours flying about that one more, even if true, could not have added to the confusion, however they did not explain everything, or put it very clearly, they simply announced, and these were the exact words, that an alteration in the geological structure of the Pyrenean cordillera had resulted in a continuous rupture, in a disjunction of physical continuity, and for the moment all communications by road between France and the Peninsula were interrupted, the authorities were carefully monitoring the situation, air connections were being maintained, all airports were open and fully operational, and as from the morrow the number of daily flights was likely to be doubled.

And how badly they were needed. When it became clear and beyond question that the Iberian Peninsula had separated completely from Europe, as people began saying, The Peninsula has broken away, hundreds of thousands of tourists, for as we know this was the peak season, hastily left their hotels, *pousadas, paradores,* inns, hostels, pensions, rented houses and rooms, camping sites, tents and caravans without paying their bills, suddenly causing the most colossal traffic jams on the roads, which grew even worse when cars were left abandoned everywhere, it took some time but then it was like a fuse, people are generally slow in recognizing and accepting the seriousness of situations, for example, the futility of having a car once the roads to France were cut off. Littered around the airports, like a flood, stood masses of cars of all sizes, models, makes and colours, which obstructed the roads and approaches, all bunched up, completely disrupting the life of the local communities. The Spaniards and the Portuguese, having recovered from the frightening experience of finding themselves in a blackout, *apagón* or *negrum*, looked on in panic, thought it absurd, After all there has been no loss of life, ah, these foreigners, take them out of their routine and they lose control, that's the price they pay for being so advanced in science and technology, and after passing this damning judgment they went off to choose, from among the abandoned vehicles, the one that appealed to them most and matched up to their aspirations.

In the airports, the desks of the airline companies were assailed by the excited multitude, a furious Babel of gestures and shouting, bribes such as had never been known before were offered and accepted to secure a ticket, people were selling and buying everything, jewels, cameras, clothes, drugs, now being peddled quite openly, my car's outside, here are the keys and documents, if you can't get me a seat to Brussels I don't mind going to Istanbul, even to hell, this tourist was one of the distracted ones, he could not see the wood for the trees. Overloaded, with their plethoric memories, saturated, the computers wavered, mistakes were multiplied, until the entire system was jammed. Tickets were no longer sold, the planes were stormed, such ferocity, the men first because they were stronger, then the fragile women and innocent children, a great many women and children were left crushed between the terminal gate and the boarding steps, these were the first casualties, and then there was a second and third group of casualties when someone had the tragic idea of forcing their way through, brandishing a pistol only to be tackled and knocked to the ground by the police. There was shooting, there were other weapons in the crowd and they were fired, there is little point in stating in which airport the disaster occurred, an abominable affair repeated in several other places, although with less serious consequences, for eighteen people died there.

Suddenly someone remembered that you could also escape from

seaports, this sparked off another bid for salvation. The fugitives turned back, once more in search of their abandoned cars, sometimes they found them, sometimes they did not, but what did that matter, if there were no keys or they could not be used, one soon put two and two together, anyone who did not know quickly learned, Portugal and Spain were transformed into an earthly paradise for car thieves. When they arrived at the ports they went in search of a small boat or canoe to carry them, or, better still, a trawler, a tugboat, a gig, a sailboat, and in this way they abandoned their last possessions in this cursed land, they departed with the clothes they were wearing and little else, a grubby handkerchief to blow their noses, a lighter without value or gas, a tie no one had ever liked, it's not right that we should have profited so outrageously from the misfortune of others, we were like brigands from the coast robbing castaways of everything they possessed. The poor wretches disembarked wherever they could, wherever they were swept, and some were left in Ibiza, Majorca and Minorca, in Formentera, or in the islands of Cabrera and Conejera, in the hands of fate, the hapless creatures were stuck, in a manner of speaking, between the devil and the deep blue sea, so far there is no evidence that the islands have moved, but who can tell what tomorrow may bring, the Pyrenees appeared to be solid for all eternity, and look what happened. Thousands upon thousands of refugees ended up in Morocco, having fled from the Algarve or from the Spanish coast, the latter being those who were below the Cape of Palos, anyone who might have been north of the Cape preferred to be taken straight to Europe, if at all possible, and they would ask, How much do you want to take me to Europe, and the chief mate would cock his eyebrow, purse his lips, look the refugee up and down assessing his means, You know, Europe is a damn long way from here, it's right at the other end of the world, and there was no point in arguing. Such exaggeration, there are only ten metres of water, once when a Dutchman dared to use this sophism, and a Swede backed him up, they were cruelly told, Oh, so there are only ten metres, then why don't you swim them, so they were forced to apologize and pay twice as much. This barter flourished until the various countries jointly agreed to provide shuttle services for the mass transportation of their citizens, but, even after this humanitarian measure got under way, certain sailors and fishermen continued to make a fortune, one must not forget that not all travellers go in peace with the law, the latter were prepared to pay over the odds, nor had they any choice, for the naval forces of Portugal and Spain were patrolling the coasts assiduously, on full alert and under the discreet surveillance of the naval squadrons of the other powers.

Some tourists, however, decided not to leave, they accepted the geological fracture as an irreversible act of fate, saw it as an imperious sign of destiny, and wrote to their families, at least they showed some consideration, to say that they no longer thought about them, that their world had changed, and their way of life, they were not to blame, on the whole they were people with little willpower, the sort of people who cannot make up their mind, leave everything for tomorrow, tomorrow, but this does not mean that they do not cherish dreams and desires, the sad thing is that they die before achieving or knowing how to achieve even a small part of them. Others opted for silence, they simply disappeared, they forgot and allowed themselves to be forgotten, well now, any of these human episodes on its own could provide a novel, the story of how it turned out in the end, and, even if there is little or nothing to relate, no two human episodes are ever the same.

But there are those who carry heavier burdens on their shoulders, from which they cannot escape, so much so that when the nation's affairs are going badly we immediately start asking, Now then, you lot, what are you going to do about it, what are you waiting for, these outbursts of impatience are in some measure quite unjust, after all, poor things, they can't escape their destiny either, at best they can go to the President and tender their resignation, but not during a crisis, for that would bring them into dishonour, history would judge severely any man in public life who took such a decision at a time like this when, strictly speaking, everything is going under. On both sides of the frontier, in Portugal and in Spain, the governments began making reassuring statements, they have formally assured us that the situation does not give cause for any grave concern, a curious way of putting it, and that all the necessary steps are being taken to safeguard people and their property, finally, the heads of government appeared on television, and then, to pacify troubled minds, their King also appeared over there and our President over here, Friends, Romans, countrymen, lend me your ears, they said, and the Portuguese and Spaniards, gathered in their forums, replied with one voice, Of course, of course, words, words, nothing but words. Faced with the hostility of public opinion, the Prime Ministers of both nations met at a secret location, first on their own, then accompanied by members of their respective governments. Jointly and separately, they held two days of exhaustive talks, before finally deciding to set up a joint committee to cope with the crisis whose main objective would be to co-ordinate civil-defence operations in both countries to muster their mutual resources, both technical and human, and use every expedient in order to deal with this geological challenge which had distanced the Peninsula ten metres from Europe, If it doesn't get worse, people whispered in corridors, the matter won't be too serious, you could even say that it will be one in the eye for the Greeks, a channel bigger than that of Corinth, so widely renowned. Even so, we cannot ignore the fact that our problems of communication with Europe, already so complicated in years gone by, will become explosive. Well then, let's build some bridges, What worries me is that the channel will become so wide that ships will be able to navigate it, especially the oil-tankers, that would be a severe blow for Iberian ports, and with consequences just as important, *mutatis mutandis*, of course, like those which resulted from the opening of the Suez Canal, in other words, northern and southern Europe would have direct communications, and be able to avoid, as it were, the Cape route. And we end up watching the ships, a Portuguese commented, the others took him to mean the ships that would be passing through the new channel, but we Portuguese know perfectly well that the ships to which he was referring are altogether different, they carry a cargo of shadows, longings, frustrations, delusions and deceptions, their holds filled to the brim, Man overboard, they shouted, but no one went to his assistance.

During their meeting, as had been agreed beforehand, the European Community issued a solemn declaration, whereby it was made clear that the displacement of the Iberian countries towards the west would not jeopardize the agreements in force, all the more so since any separation was minimal, nothing more than a few metres, when compared with the distance that separates England from the Continent, not to mention Iceland or Greenland, which have so little in common with Europe. This declaration, with its clear objectives, was what resulted from a heated debate among the members of the Commission, during which some member states came close to displaying a certain detachment, there is no more precise adjective, even going so far as to suggest that if the Iberian Peninsula wished to go away then let it go, the mistake was to have allowed it to come in. Naturally, this was all said in fun, a joke, in these awkward international gatherings people also have to amuse themselves, there has to be more than just work, work, work, but the Portuguese and Spanish members strongly objected to this blatantly provocative remark, so anti-Community in spirit, each quoting in his own language the well-known Iberian proverb, A friend in need is a friend indeed. A declaration of Atlantic solidarity was also requested from the North Atlantic Treaty Organization, but the reply, without being negative, came to be summed up in an unpublishable phrase, Wait and see, words, moreover, which didn't quite express the whole truth, considering that the bases of Beja, Rota, Gibraltar, El Ferrol, Torrejón de Ardoz, Cartagena, and San Turjo de Valenzuela, not to mention smaller installations, had all been put on alert as a precautionary measure.

Then the Iberian Peninsula moved a little further, one metre, two metres, just to test its strength. The ropes which served as evidence, strung from one side to the other, as firemen do with walls that develop cracks and threaten to cave in, broke like ordinary string, some that were stronger uprooted the trees and posts to which they were tied. Then there was a pause, a great gust of air could be felt rushing through the air, like the first deep breathing of someone awakening, and the mass of stone and earth, covered with cities, villages, rivers, woodlands, factories, wild scrub, cultivated fields, with all their inhabitants and livestock, began to move, a ship drawing away from harbour and heading out to an unknown sea once more.

This olive tree is *cordovil*, or *cordovesa*, or *cordovia*, what does it matter, for these three names are used indifferently on Portuguese soil, and the fruit it produces, because of its size and beauty, would be referred to here as the queen of olives but not as cordoban, although we're closer to Cordoba than to the frontier beyond. These seem superfluous details of no real importance, melismatic vocalizations, the ornamental artifices of a plainsong that dreams of wings of sonorous melody, when it is much more important to speak of the three men seated beneath the olive tree, one of whom is Pedro Orce, the second Joaquim Sassa, the third José Anaiço, what prodigious events or deliberate manipulations could have brought them together in this place. But calling the olive tree *cordovil* will at least serve to show just how remiss the evangelists were when, for example, they confined themselves to writing that Jesus cursed the fig tree, this information should be enough for us but it isn't enough, no sir, after all, twenty centuries have passed and we still do not know whether the cursed tree produced white or black figs, early or late, of this or that variety, not that Christian science is likely to suffer because of this omission, but historical truth most certainly suffers. Anyhow, the olive tree is *cordovil*, and three men are sitting under it. Beyond these hills, and invisible from here, there is a village where Pedro Orce once lived, and by a strange coincidence, the first of them, if this is the first coincidence, both he and the village bear the same name, a fact which neither diminishes nor increases the verisimilitude of the story, a man can be called Metcalfe or Merryweather without being a butcher or a meteorologist. As we have already observed, these are coincidences and manipulations, but made in good faith.

They are sitting on the ground, in their midst can be heard the nasal twang of a radio which must have weak batteries, and the announcer is making the following statement, According to the latest measurements, the velocity of the Peninsula's dislocation has stabilized at around seven hundred and fifty metres per hour, more or less eighteen kilometres per day, that may not seem a lot, but if we work it out carefully, that means each minute we move away twelve and a half metres from Europe, and while we should avoid giving way to panic and despair, the situation is truly worrying. And it would be even more worrying if you were to say that we are talking about just two centimetres and a bit per second, remarked José Anaiço, who was quick at making mental calculations, but incapable of reducing the figures to tenths and hundredths, Joaquim Sassa asked him to be quiet, he wanted to listen to the announcer, and it was worth his while, According to the latest reports we have received, a great crack has appeared between La Línea and Gibraltar, therefore it is feared, bearing in mind the irreversible outcome of the fractures so far, that El Peñon may end up isolated in the middle of the sea, if this should happen there is no point in blaming the British, we are to blame, yes, Spain is to blame for not having known how to recover in good time this sacred piece of the fatherland, now it is too late, El Peñon itself is abandoning us. This man is an artist with words, said Pedro Orce, but the announcer had already changed his tone, had overcome his emotion. In Great Britain, the Prime Minister's office has issued a statement whereby the government of Her Sovereign Majesty reaffirms what they refer to as their rights over Gibraltar, which have now been confirmed, we are quoting, by the incontrovertible fact that El Peñon or The Rock has detached itself from Spain and so all the negotiations which were working towards an eventual, if somewhat problematic, transfer of sovereignty remain unilaterally and definitively suspended, There are still no signs of the British Empire coming to an end, quipped José Anaiço. In a statement to parliament, the opposition in Her Majesty's government demanded that the future north side of the island should be fortified without delay, so as to transform the steep rock all around its perimeters into an unassailable fortress, proudly isolated in the middle of the now widened Atlantic, as a symbol of the enduring power of Albion. They're mad, Pedro Orce muttered, contemplating the heights of the Sierra de Sagra rising before him. For its part, the government, attempting to reduce the political impact of any claim, replied that Gibraltar, in its new geostrategic conditions, would continue to be one of the jewels in the crown of Her Sovereign Majesty, a formula which like the Magna Carta has the magnificent virtue of satisfying everyone, this ironic conclusion was provided by the announcer, who took his leave by saying, We shall be back with more news in an hour's time unless there should be any unforeseen circumstances. A flock of starlings flew past like a hurricane passing over a bare mountain, vruuuuuuuuuu, Are they yours, asked Joaquim Sassa, and, without even turning round, José Anaiço replied, They're mine, he ought to know, for ever since that first day, amidst the green fields of Ribatejo, they have scarcely ever parted, only to eat and sleep, a man does not nourish himself on worms and scattered grains and a bird sleeps in the trees without any bedclothes. The flock flew round in a wide circle, fluttering, their wings trembling, beaks that drink in the air and sunlight, the few clouds, white and piled high, navigate through space like galleons, the men, they as well as all others, look at these different things, and, as usual, do not really understand them.

It certainly was not to listen to a transistor radio in each other's company that Pedro Orce, Joaquim Sassa and José Anaiço gathered here, having travelled from such different places. For the last three minutes we have known that Pedro Orce lives in the village which lies hidden behind these hills, we have known from the outset that Joaquim Sassa came from the shores of Northern Portugal, and José Anaiço, we now know for certain, was strolling through the fields of Ribatejo when he came across the starlings, and we should have guessed as much had we paid sufficient attention to the details of the landscape. What remains to be known is how the three men met each other and why they are hidden away here under an olive tree, unique in this spot, among rare and unruly dwarf trees that cling to the white soil, the sun is reflected on all the plains, the air shimmers, this is the heat of Andalusia, and although we are surrounded by mountains, we suddenly become conscious of these material things, we have entered the real world, or it has forced its way in.

If one thinks about it, there is no beginning for things and persons, everything that began one day has begun before, the history of this sheet of paper, for instance, just to take an example at hand, in order to be true and complete, would have to date back to the origins of the world, the plural has been used here deliberately instead of the singular, yet even so, we could ask whether those first origins were not simply points of transition, sliding ramps, this poor head of ours, subject to such exertions, an admirable head, notwithstanding, which for all sorts of reasons is capable of going mad, except for this one.

There is then, no beginning, but there was a moment when Joaquim Sassa left the spot where he found himself, on a beach in northern Portugal, perhaps Afife, that beach with the enigmatic stones, or better still A-Ver-o-Mar, which means Sea-view, in order to have the most perfect name imaginable for a beach, poets and novelists could not have invented anything better. From there came Joaquim Sassa having heard that a certain Pedro Orce from Spain could feel the ground shaking beneath his feet when there were no tremors, this is the natural curiosity of someone who threw a heavy stone into the sea with a strength he did not possess, all the more so since the Peninsula wrenched itself away from Europe without any shock or pain, like a hair quietly falling, simply because willed by God, as the saying goes. He set out on his way, in his old Deux Chevaux, he did not say goodbye to his family, alas, for he has no family, nor did he give any explanation to the manager of the office where he works. This is vacation time, you can come and go as you please, now they don't even ask to see your passport at the frontier, you simply show your identity card and the Peninsula is yours. On the seat, beside him, he carries a transistor radio, distracts himself by listening to music, the prattling of the announcers, sweet and soothing like an acoustic cradle, suddenly irritating, that was in normal times, now the ether is rippling with febrile words, the news coming in from the Pyrenees, the exodus, the crossing of the Red Sea, Napoleon's retreat. Here on the roads of the interior, there is little traffic, nothing when compared with the Algarve, all that bustle and turmoil, or with Lisbon, and the motorways going north and south, Portela airport looks now like a besieged stronghold, an invasion of ants, iron filings attracted by a magnet. Joaquim Sassa strolls peacefully through the shady lanes of La Beira, heading for a village called Orce, in the province of Granada, on Spanish soil, where the aforesaid man lives who spoke on television. I'm going there to see if there is any connection between what happened to me and that business of someone who can feel the ground shaking under his feet, once you start imagining things, you start putting two and two together, more often than not you were mistaken, sometimes you hit the nail on the head, a stone thrown into the sea, the earth shaking, a cordillera that has split open. Joaquim Sassa is also travelling amidst mountains, even if they can't be compared with those Titans, but suddenly he feels uneasy. Suppose the same thing were to happen here, suppose the Serra de Estrela were to crack, the Mondego were to sink into the bowels of the earth leaving the autumn poplars without a mirror in which to reflect themselves, his thoughts have become poetic, the danger has passed.

At this moment, the music stopped, the announcer began to read the news, there was nothing fresh to report, the only item of interest, however relative, was a bulletin from London, the Prime Minister went to the House of Commons to state, categorically, that British sovereignty over Gibraltar warrants no discussion, whatever the distance separating the Iberian Peninsula from Europe, to which the leader of the opposition added a formal guarantee promising the most loyal co-operation from our benches and party at this great moment in our history, but he then introduced a note of irony into his solemn speech which brought laughter from all the honourable members. The Prime Minister committed a serious mistake by speaking of a peninsula when referring to what is now unquestionably an island, although by no means as solid as our own, of course. The members of parliament cheered this closing remark and exchanged complacent grins with their opponents, and to be sure, there is nothing like the national interest for uniting politicians. Joaquim Sassa also grinned. Such a comedy, and suddenly he caught his breath, the announcer had spoken his name, Senhor Joaquim Sassa, who is travelling somewhere in the country, is kindly requested, we repeat, Senhor Joaquim Sassa is kindly requested, they were asking him kindly to present himself urgently to the nearest civil governor, in order to assist the authorities with their investigations into the causes of the geological fracture verified in the Pyrenees, for the competent bodies are convinced that the aforesaid Joaquim Sassa can give them information of national interest, we repeat our appeal, Senhor Joaquim Sassa is requested, but Senhor Joaquim Sassa was not listening, he had been obliged to stop the car in order to recover his composure, his sang-froid, so long as his hands continued to tremble like this he would not even be able to drive, his ears were buzzing like a shell, Good Heavens, how did they find out about the stone, there was not another soul on the beach, at least as far as I could see, and I did not say a word to anyone, for they would have called me a liar, but someone somewhere must have been watching me after all, although no one usually pays any attention to someone throwing stones into the water, yet they spotted me at once, tough luck, and then you know what happens, one person speaks to another and adds on what he thought he saw but could not have seen, when this story reached the ears of the authorities, the stone must have become as big as me, at the very least, and now what am I going to do. He would not answer the appeal, he would not present himself to any civil or military governor, just imagine what an absurd dialogue that would be, behind closed doors, the tape-recorder playing, Senhor Joaquim Sassa, did you throw a stone into the sea, I did, How much would you say it weighed, I don't know, perhaps two or three kilos, Or more, Yes, it could have been more, Here are some stones, try holding them, and tell me which one comes closest in weight to the stone you threw, This one, Let's weigh it, like so, now then, be so good as to check the weight with your own eyes, I'd never have thought it could weigh so much, five kilos and six hundred grammes, Now tell me, have you ever experienced anything like this before, Never, Are you certain, Absolutely, You don't suffer from any mental or nervous disorders, epilepsy, somnambulism, trances of any kind, No sir, Afterwards we'll take an electroencephalogram, for the moment try your strength on this machine over here, What is it, A dynamometer, put as much pressure on it as you can, I can't do any more, Is that all, I've never had much strength in my arms, Senhor Joaquim Sassa, you couldn't possibly have thrown that stone, I'm inclined to agree, but I did, We know that you threw it, there are witnesses, persons of the utmost credibility so you must tell us how you managed it, I've already explained, I was walking along the beach when I saw the stone, I picked it up and threw it, That's impossible, The witnesses can confirm it, True, but the witnesses cannot say where that strength came from, only you can tell us, I've already told you I don't know, The situation, Senhor Sassa, is very serious, I'd go so far as to say, most serious, the rupture of the Pyrenees cannot be explained by natural causes, otherwise we would be plunged into a planetary catastrophe, it was on the basis of this evidence that we began to investigate certain unusual happenings which have taken place during recent days, and yours is one of them, Surely throwing a stone into the water couldn't cause a continent to crack up, I have no desire to engage in idle philosophizing, but do you see any connection between a monkey descending from a tree twenty million years ago and the making of a nuclear bomb, The connection is, precisely, those twenty million years, Well answered, but now let's suppose that it might be possible to reduce to hours the time between a cause, which in this case would be the throwing of a stone, and an effect, such as the Peninsula's separation from Europe, in other words, let us suppose that, under normal conditions, that stone thrown into the sea would only produce any effect twenty million years hence, but that, under other conditions, precisely those of the phenomenon we are now investigating, the effect is verified some hours, or days, later, That's pure speculation, the cause might well be something else, Or a concurrent combination of the two, Then other unusual events would have to be investigated, That's what we're in the process of doing, and the Spaniards, too, as in the case of the man who can feel the earth shaking, By adopting this method, once you have examined the unusual events, you will have to proceed to the usual ones, The what ones, The usual ones, What do you mean by usual, Usual is the opposite of unusual, its antonym, If necessary, we shall pass from the unusual to the usual events, but we must discover the cause, You have a lot of investigating ahead of you, We're making a start, tell me where you found the strength. Joaquim Sassa made no reply, he silenced his imagination, all the more so since the dialogue was threatening to go round in circles, now he would have to repeat, I don't know, and the rest would be as before, with some minor variations, above all formal, yet this was precisely where he would have to be careful, because, as we know, through form one arrives at the substance, through the wrappings at the contents, through the sound of the word at its meaning.

He put Deux Chevaux into gear, into step, if such a thing might be said of a car, he wanted time to think, he needed to give the matter serious thought. He had ceased to be an ordinary traveller heading for the border, a simple man without any special qualities or importance, no longer, at this very moment they were probably printing posters with his picture and particulars Wanted in big, red letters, a manhunt. He looked into his rear-view mirror and saw a police patrol car, it was coming so quickly that it looked as if the car were about to come through the back window, They've caught up with me, he said, accelerated but quickly slowed down, without braking, all quite unnecessary, the patrol car overtook him in a flash, it must be rushing to some emergency, they did not so much as look at him, if only those speeding policemen knew who was driving along there, in fact, there are lots of Deux Chevaux on the road, that may sound like a mathematical contradiction, but it is not. Joaquim Sassa took another look in the rear-view mirror, this time to take a good look at himself, to acknowledge the relief in his eyes, the mirror reflected little else, a tiny bit of his face, which makes it difficult to know to whom the face belongs, to Joaquim Sassa, as we already know, but who is Joaquim Sassa, a man who is still young, in his thirties, closer to forty than thirty, the day inevitably comes, his eyebrows are black, his eyes brown like those of most Portuguese, his nose sharply outlined, his features really quite commonplace, we shall learn more about him when he turns towards us. For the moment, he thought to himself, It's only an appeal over the radio, the worst is yet to come at the frontier, and as if that weren't enough, there's this surname of mine, Sassa, which unfortunately means stone, when what I need right now is to be any old Sousa, like that other one from Coll de Petrus, one day he consulted the dictionary to see if the word existed, Sassa, not Sousa, and what did he find, he discovered that it was a massive tree from Nubia, a pretty name, the name of a woman, Nubia, near the Sudan, in West Africa, page ninety-three in the atlas, And tonight, where am I going to sleep, certainly not in a hotel, there the radio is always being switched on, by this time every hotel in Portugal must be looking out for hotel guests who request a room for one night, the refuge of the persecuted, you can imagine the scene, Let's see now, yes sir, we have an excellent room available, on the second floor, room two hundred and one, I say, Pimenta, show Senhor Sassa to his room, and no sooner is he resting on the bed, still fully clothed, than the manager, quite flustered, nervous, is on the telephone, The fellow's here, come quickly.

He parked Deux Chevaux at the side of the road, got out to stretch his legs and clear his mind which, instead of giving him good advice, came up with a dubious proposition, Stay in a more populated city, where there is plenty of nightlife, look for a brothel, spend the night with one of the prostitutes, you may rest assured that they won't ask for your identity card so long as you pay, and if you don't feel like gratifying your flesh with all this worry at least you'll be able to get some sleep, and you'll pay less than you would in a hotel, How ridiculous, said Joaquim Sassa in reply to this suggestion, the solution is to sleep in the car, in some quiet road off the beaten track. But suppose some vagrants, tramps or gypsies were to appear, they might attack and rob you, they might even murder you, It's peaceful in these parts, But suppose some arsonist or madman were to set the pine forests on fire, there are lots of them around these days, you would find yourself surrounded by flames, end up being burned to death, which must be the worst of all deaths, from what I've heard, just think of the martyrs of the Inquisition. How ridiculous, Joaquim Sassa repeated, I've made up my mind, I'm going to sleep in the car, and the thought was suppressed, easy enough when one is strong-willed. It was still early, he could cover some forty or fifty kilometres along these winding roads, he would camp near Tomar, or Santarém, in one of those dirt-roads that open on to cultivated fields, with those deep furrows once made by carts drawn by oxen and nowadays made by tractors, no one passes at night, Deux Chevaux can be hidden anywhere around here, I might even sleep out in the open, the night is so warm, his mind did not react to this idea and clearly disapproved.

He did not stop in Tomar, nor reach Santarém, he dined incognito in a town on the banks of the Tagus, the local inhabitants are inquisitive by nature, but not to the extent of asking the first traveller point-blank, Tell me, what's your name, but if he were to linger here, then certainly they would very soon be asking questions about his past life and his plans for the future. The television was switched on, as he ate his dinner Joaquim Sassa watched the last part of a film about underwater life, with numerous shoals of tiny fishes, undulating rays and sinuous moray eels, and an ancient anchor, then came the advertisements, some with striking, rapid montage, others deliberately slow like some voluptuous gesture drawn from experience, there were children's voices shouting loudly, the insecure voices of adolescents, or of women that were somewhat hoarse, all the men were baritones and sounded virile, at the back of the house the pig was grunting, fattened on slops and leftovers. At last they gave the news and Joaquim Sassa shuddered, he wouldn't stand a chance if they should show his photograph. The appeal was read out, but no photograph appeared, after all, they were not pursuing a criminal, they were simply requesting, with polite insistence, that he should report his whereabouts, and serve the supreme interest of the nation, no citizen worthy of the name would shrink from complying with such a simple duty by failing to appear before the authorities in order to make a statement. There were three other guests who were dining, an elderly couple and, at another table, the usual man sitting by himself of whom one always says, He must be a commercial traveller.

The conversations ceased when they heard the first news from the Pyrenees, the pig went on grunting but no one paid any atten-

41

tion, and, all this in an instant, the landlord got up on to a chair to increase the volume, the girl who waited at table stood there wide-eyed, the guests carefully rested their cutlery on the edge of their plate, and little wonder, on the screen they were showing a helicopter which was being filmed from another helicopter, both were entering the dreaded channel, and they showed the towering walls, so tall that the sky could scarcely be seen overhead, the merest thread of blue, Good heavens, it's enough to make you dizzy, the girl said, and the landlord snapped, Be quiet, now extremely powerful floodlights were showing the gaping hole, this is how the entrance to the hell of the Greeks must have looked, but where Cerberus would have barked, a pig is grunting, mythologies are not what they were. These dramatic pictures, the announcer reeled off, were taken under hazardous conditions putting lives at risk, the voice became husky, muffled, the two helicopters transformed themselves into four, the phantoms of phantoms, Blasted aerial, the landlord muttered.

By the time the sound and picture became stable and intelligible, the helicopters had disappeared and the announcer read the same old appeal, now addressed to the public at large, Anyone who may know of any strange events or inexplicable phenomena, which they believe to be suspicious, is requested to inform the nearest authorities at once. Prompted by these words addressed directly to her, the girl remembered how people had gossiped locally when a kid goat had been born with five legs, four black and one white, but the landlord rejoined, That was months ago, you fool, kid goats with five legs and chicks with two heads are nothing out of the ordinary, now what's really odd is this business of the teacher's starlings, What starlings, what teacher, Joaquim Sassa asked, The local teacher, his name is José Anaiço, for some days now, wherever he goes, he is followed by a flock of starlings, there's as many as two hundred of them, Or more, the commercial traveller corrected him, only this morning I saw them as I was arriving, they were circling above the school, and the racket they were making, flapping their wings and screeching, was unbelievable. At this point the elderly man interrupted, Unless I'm mistaken, we should inform the mayor about the starlings, He already knows, the landlord observed, He knows all right, but doesn't connect the one thing with the other, he can't tell his arse from his elbow, if you'll forgive the expression, Then what should we do, Let's go and talk to him tomorrow morning, besides it would be good publicity for the region if it were to

42

be announced on television, it would benefit our trade and industry, But let's keep it a secret among ourselves, tell no one, And that teacher, where does he live, Joaquim Sassa asked as if he were not really very interested in the answer, so the distracted landlord was not in time to prevent the girl from blurting out, He lives in the teacher's house right beside the school, there's always a light at the window well into the night, there seemed to be a note of sadness in her voice. Furious, the landlord railed at the poor girl, Shut your mouth, imbecile, you'd better go and see if the pig needs feeding, hard to imagine a more foolish command for pigs do not eat at this hour, they are normally asleep, perhaps the landlord's angry outburst was caused by worry, for here, too, in the stables and paddocks around the countryside, the mares neigh and shake their heads, nervous, restless, and in their impatience they scratch the loose gravel on the ground, tear at the straw. It must be the moon, in the opinion of the foreman.

Joaquim Sassa paid for his dinner, made his farewells, left a generous tip in recompense for the information the girl had given him, the landlord might pocket it, out of pique rather than greed, the generosity of people is no better than they themselves are, no less influenced by eclipses and contradictions, rarely constant, as in the case of this girl, scolded and abruptly dismissed, trying unsuccessfully to feed a pig which is not hungry, scratching its forehead between the eyes. The evening is pleasant, Deux Chevaux is resting beneath the plane trees, refreshing its wheels in the water that runs idly from the spring, and Joaquim Sassa lets it be, goes on foot to look for the school and the illuminated window, people cannot hide their secrets even though they may say they wish to keep them, a sudden shriek betrays them, the sudden softening of a vowel exposes them, any observer with experience of the human voice and human nature would have perceived at once that the girl at the inn is in love. The town is nothing but one large village, in less than half an hour you can walk past all the houses from start to finish, but Joaquim Sassa will not have to walk quite so far, he asks a little boy who is passing where the school is and could not have found a better-informed guide, You take that street there, when you come to a square you'll see a church, turn left, then keep to the right, you can't go wrong, you'll see the school at once, And does the teacher live there, Yes sir, he does, there's a light in the window, but there was no hint of love in any of those words, probably the lad is a bad pupil and the school is his first experience of purgatory, but his voice suddenly becomes cheerful, children are never resentful, that is their saving grace, And the starlings are always there, and they're always screeching, if the lad does not abandon his studies too soon, he will learn to construct sentences without sticking the same verbal forms so close together.

There is still a clear patch in one half of the sky, the other half has not completely darkened, the sky is blue as if dawn were about to break. But inside the houses the lights are already on, the tranquil voices of weary people can be heard, quiet sobbing from a cradle, truly people are so lacking in awareness, you put them out to sea on a raft and they go on living their lives as if they were on terra firma forever, babbling like Moses when he descended the Nile in a little basket made from rushes, playing with the butterflies, so blessed that even the crocodiles could not harm him. Situated at the end of the narrow street, surrounded by walls, is the school, had Joaquim Sassa not been warned he would have thought it was just a house like any other, at night they all look drab, by day some are still drab, meanwhile darkness has started falling, but there is some time to go before the streetlamps light up.

In order not to contradict the girl at the inn and the little boy who kept his feelings to himself, there is a light in the school window and Joaquim Sassa went and knocked there on the window-pane, after all, the starlings do not make that much noise, they are settling down for the night, with their habitual squabbling and neighbourly disputes, however it will not be long before they calm down beneath the enormous leaves of the fig tree where they have perched themselves, invisible, black amidst the inky darkness, only later will the moon rise, then some will awaken when touched by white fingers before going back to sleep, they do not know how far they have to travel. Inside the house, a man's voice enquired, Who is it, and Joaquim Sassa replied, If you please, magic words which substitute for any formal identification, language is full of these and other more perplexing enigmas. The window has opened, it is not easy to see who lives in this house, against the light like this, but, in compensation, Joaquim Sassa's face is perfectly clear, some of his features we described earlier, the rest conform, dark-brown hair, smooth, sunken cheeks, the nose quite commonplace, the lips become full only when he speaks, Forgive me for disturbing you at this hour, It isn't late, said the teacher, but he had to raise his voice because the starlings, having been disturbed, sent up a chorus of protest and alarm, It's really because of them that I'd like

44

to talk to you, Them, who, The starlings, Ah, And about a stone I threw into the sea, much heavier than my strength can take, What is your name, Joaquim Sassa, Are you the person they keep mentioning on radio and television, That's me, Do come in.

They have spoken about stones and starlings, now they are speaking about decisions taken. They are in the yard behind the house, José Anaiço is seated on the doorstep, Joaquim Sassa in a chair since he is a visitor, and because José Anaiço is sitting with his back to the kitchen where the light is coming from, we still do not know what he looks like, this man appears to be hiding himself, but this is not the case, how often we have shown ourselves as we really are, and we need not have bothered, there has been no one there to notice. José Anaiço poured a little more white wine into their glasses, they are drinking it at room temperature, which is how it should be drunk in the opinion of experts, rather than this modern fad of chilling the wine, something which is out of the question here because there is no fridge in the teacher's house. That's enough for me, said Joaquim Sassa, after the red wine I had with dinner, I've already passed my limit. Let's drink to the trip, replied José Anaiço, and he smiled, showing the whitest of teeth, a detail worth noting. It makes good sense to go off in search of Pedro Orce, for I'm still on vacation and free of any obligations, Me too, and for much longer, until the schools reopen at the beginning of October, I'm on my own, So am I, It wasn't my intention to come here to persuade you to accompany me, I didn't even know you, I'm the one who's asking you to take me along, if there's room in your car, but you've already agreed and you can't go back on your word now. Just imagine the commotion there will be when they discover you've gone, most likely they'll call the police at once, start thinking you're already dead and buried, hanging from some tree, or lying at the bottom of the river, obviously they'll suspect me, the stranger with incredible strength who turned up from nowhere, asked questions

46

and disappeared, it's all in the books, I'll leave a note on the door of the town hall saying that I had to leave unexpectedly for Lisbon, I hope no one remembers to go and ask at the station if anyone saw me buy a ticket.

For several moments they remained silent, then José Anaiço rose to his feet, took a few steps in the direction of the fig tree as he drank the rest of his wine, the starlings went on screeching and began to stir uneasily, some had woken up with the men's conversation, others were perhaps dreaming aloud, that terrible nightmare of the species, in which they feel themselves to be flying, all alone, disorientated, and separated from the flock, moving through an atmosphere which resists and impedes the flapping of their wings as if it were made of water, the same thing happens to men when they are dreaming and their will tells them to run and they cannot. We shall leave an hour before sunrise, José Anaiço said, and now we must get some sleep, Joaquim Sassa rose from his chair. I'll sleep in the car, and come to fetch you before dawn, Why don't you sleep here, I've only one bed but it's wide, there's plenty of room for both of us. It was a clear night, the sky all speckled with stars which seemed to be close as if invisibly suspended, glass dust, a snow-white veil, and the great constellations shone dramatically, the Morning Star, the Two Bears, the Pleiades, a fine shower of tiny crystals of light fell on to the upturned faces of the two men and clung to their skin, got caught in their hair, it was not the first time this phenomenon had occurred, but suddenly all the murmurings of the night fell silent, above the trees the first light of the moon appeared, now the stars must go out. Then Joaquim Sassa said, On a night like this, I might even sleep under the fig tree if you can lend me a blanket, I'll keep you company. They gathered and then spread enough straw for their beds, as one does for cattle, they spread out the blankets, lay down on one half and covered themselves with the other. The starlings watched their shadowy forms from the branches, Who can that be, beneath the tree, among the branches everything is wide awake and with a moon like this, getting to sleep is going to be very difficult. The moon is rising swiftly, the squat, rotund crown of the fig tree transforms itself into a black and white labyrinth, and José Anaiço remarks, These shadows are not what they were, The Peninsula has moved so little, a few metres, it can't have had much effect, Joaquim Sassa observed, pleased at having understood the remark, It has moved, and that was enough for all the shadows to change, there are branches there

47

which the moonlight is touching for the first time at this hour. Some minutes passed, the starlings began to settle down, and José Anaiço murmured, in a voice which sleep finally interrupted, each word waiting or searching for the next one, Once upon a time, our King, Dom João the Second, known as The Perfect King and in my opinion the perfect wit, made a certain nobleman a gift of an imaginary island, now tell me, do you know of any other nation where such a thing could happen, And the nobleman, what did the nobleman do, he set out to look for it, now, what I'd like to know is how you can find an imaginary island, That's something I can't tell you, but this other island, the Iberian one, which was a peninsula but not any longer, I find just as amusing, as if it had set out to sea in search of imaginary men. Nicely phrased, couldn't be more poetic. Well, let me assure you that I've never written a line of verse in my life, Worry not, if all men were to become poets, they would write no more verses. That phrase also has a certain charm, We've had too much to drink, I agree. Silence, calm, infinite harmony, and Joaquim Sassa murmured, as if he were dreaming, What will the starlings do tomorrow, will they stay or will they accompany us, When we leave we shall know, it's always the same, José Anaiço said, the moon is lost among the branches of the fig tree and will spend all night searching for a way out.

It was still dark when Joaquim Sassa rose from his bed of straw to go and look for Deux Chevaux, which had been parked under the plane trees in the square, right beside the fountain. To avoid being seen together by some early riser, of whom there are many in farming communities, they had agreed to meet on the outskirts of the village, at some distance from the last houses. José Anaiço would turn off the main road, take by-lanes and short cuts, keeping well out of sight, Joaquim Sassa, however, would discreetly take the main road used by everyone, he is one of those travellers who goes neither in debt nor fear, he sets out early to enjoy the fresh morning air and to make the most of the day, tourists who are out and about early are like this, at heart troubled and restless, unable to accept the inevitable shortness of life, late to bed and early to rise does not make one healthy, but it does prolong life. Deux Chevaux has a quiet engine, the starter is as smooth as silk, only the few inhabitants who could not sleep heard something, they thought they had finally fallen asleep and were dreaming, now you could barely hear the steady noise of a water-pump in the stillness of dawn. Joaquim Sassa left the village, passed the first bend, then the second, then brought Deux Chevaux to a halt and waited.

In the silvery depths of the olive grove the trunks started to become visible, there was already a touch of humidity in the air, the faintest hint of a breeze, as if the morning were emerging from a well of clouded water, and now a bird sang, or were his ears deceiving him, for not even the larks sing at this early hour. Time passed and Joaquim Sassa began muttering to himself, Perhaps he's thought it over and decided not to come, but he didn't strike me as being that sort, or perhaps he had to take a much more roundabout way than he imagined, that must be the explanation, and then he's carrying a heavy suitcase, that's something I overlooked, I could have carried it myself to the car. Then, from amidst the olive trees, emerged José Anaiço, surrounded by starlings, a frenzy of wings ruffling continuously, strident cries, whoever mentioned two hundred is unable to count, this reminds me more of a swarm of big, black bees, but what Joaquim Sassa obviously had in mind, were the birds in Hitchcock's classic film, albeit the latter were wicked assassins. José Anaiço approached the car with his garland of winged creatures, he comes smiling, which makes him look younger than Joaquim Sassa for, as everyone knows, a serious expression makes one look older, he has the whitest of teeth, as we discovered last night, and while there is nothing remarkable about any individual feature, there is a certain harmony in those sunken cheeks, besides, no one is obliged to be good-looking. He put his suitcase into the car, climbed in beside Joaquim Sassa, and before closing the door looked out to see the starlings, Let's go, I wondered what they would do, and you can see for yourself, If we had a rifle here and fired a few shots, two cartridges of lead pellets would finish them off, Are you a hunting man, No, I'm only repeating what I've heard others say, We don't have a rifle, Perhaps there might be another solution, I'll get Deux Chevaux moving, and the starlings will be left behind, they're a species with short wings and little stamina, Try. Deux Chevaux changed gear, accelerated on a long stretch of straight road and, taking advantage of the flat terrain, soon left the starlings behind. The morning light became tinged with contrasting shades of pale and bright pink, colours fallen from the sky, and the air turned blue, we repeat, the air and not the sky, as we also observed yesterday evening, these hours are much the same, the one beginning the day, the other ending it. Joaquim Sassa switched off his headlights, reduced his speed, he knows that Deux Chevaux was not destined for such bold exploits, it lacks pedigree, besides, the car has seen better days and the engine's tameness is nothing more than stoic resignation, Good, that's the end of the starlings, these were the words of José Anaiço but there was a note of regret in his voice.

Two hours later, in the province of Alentejo, they stopped for some light refreshment, coffee with milk, cinnamon-flavoured sponge cakes, then they returned to the car, discussing the same old worries, The worst thing that could happen won't be to find myself barred from Spain, it would be much worse if they were to keep me there, You haven't been accused of anything, They can invent some pretext, detain me for questioning. Don't worry, before we reach the frontier we're sure to find some means of getting on to the other side, this was their dialogue, which adds nothing to our understanding of the story, perhaps it was only put here so that we should know that Joaquim Sassa and José Anaiço are already on familiar terms, something they must have decided during the journey. Let's drop any formalities, one of them said, and the other replied, I was just about to make the same suggestion. Joaquim Sassa was on the point of opening the car door when the starlings reappeared, that enormous cloud, resembling more than ever some great swarm whirling overhead and making a deafening noise, one could see that they were angry, people down here on the ground stopped and looked up, pointed to the sky, someone declared, I've never seen so many birds together in my whole life, and judging from his appearance he was old enough to have had this experience and many others, There are more than a thousand of them, he added, and he's right, at least one thousand, two hundred and fifty birds had gathered on this occasion, They've finally caught up with us, said Joaquim Sassa, let them wear themselves out and we'll be rid of them for good. José Anaiço watched the starlings as they flew triumphantly in a great circle, he stood there transfixed, staring at them intently, Let's drive slowly, from now on we'll go slowly, Why, I don't know, it's just a premonition, for some reason these birds won't leave us alone, You could be right, so do me a favour and go slowly, and we'll see what happens.

How they crossed the Alentejo in this blazing heat, under a sky that is more white than blue, amidst shining stubble, with the occasional holm oak on the bare land and bundles of straw waiting to be gathered, beneath the incessant chirping of the cicadas, would make a whole story in itself, perhaps even more painstaking than that other one I narrated in an earlier novel. It is true that for kilometre after kilometre along this road there is not a living soul to be seen, but the corn has been cut, the grain threshed, and all these tasks required men and women, but on this occasion we shall learn nothing about the one or the other, all too true is the proverb that warns us, Don't count your chickens before they're hatched. The heat is oppressive, suffocating, but Deux Chevaux is in no hurry, is only too pleased to stop wherever there is some shade, then José Anaiço and Joaquim Sassa get out to scan the horizon, they wait as long as they have to, finally there it comes, the only cloud in the sky, these stops would not be necessary if the starlings knew how to fly in a straight line, but because there are so many of them, and all of them differently inclined, even if they are gregariously united, dispersions and distractions are inevitable, some would prefer to rest, others to drink water or to peck at some berries, and until their desires coincide, the flock will be dispersed and their itinerary upset. Along the route, in addition to the kites, solitary predators, and species of lesser congregation, other birds of the starling family have been sighted, but they do not join the flock, perhaps because they are not black, but speckled, or they have some other destiny in life. José Anaiço and Joaquim Sassa get into the car, Deux Chevaux resumes its journey, and so, starting and stopping, stopping and starting, they arrive at the frontier. Then Joaquim Sassa says, And now let's see if they'll allow me to pass, you follow, perhaps the starlings will help.

Just as in those tales about fairies, enchantments and knights of chivalry, or in those no less admirable homeric tales of adventure in which, through the bounty of the tree of fables or through some caprice of the gods or other such divinities, anything might happen contrary to custom, in some unnatural manner, it came about that Joaquim Sassa and José Anaiço stopped at the police lookout, frontier post in technical jargon, and God alone knows how anxious they must have felt as they presented their identity cards, when the next moment, like a sudden downpour of lashing rain or an irresistible cyclone, the starlings swooped down from the heavens, a black meteor, their bodies transformed into flashes of lightning, hissing, screeching, and at the height of the low roofs they scattered in all directions, no different from a whirlwind out of control, the terrified policemen waved their arms about, ran to take shelter, Joaquim Sassa saw his chance, got out of the car and retrieved the documents the policeman had dropped, there was no one to observe this infringement of customs regulations, and that was that, secret crossings had been made by many routes, but never like this. Hitchcock is applauding from the stalls, the applause of someone who is a master of the genre. The excellence of this method was soon confirmed, showing that the Spanish police, like their Portuguese counterparts, take these omens of birds and black starlings in all seriousness. The travellers passed without any difficulty, but dozens of birds remained on the spot, for at the customs post across the border there was a loaded shotgun, even a blind man would have been able to hit the target, all one had to do was to shoot into the air, and this was needless slaughter, because in Spain, as we know, no one is looking for Joaquim Sassa. Nor is it certain that this is the action the Andalusian guards would have taken, for the starlings were Portuguese by nationality, born and bred in the lands of Ribatejo, and they had come to die so far away, let us hope that these cruel guards will at least have the decency to invite their colleagues from Alentejo to share the feast of cooked starlings in an atmosphere of wholesome conviviality and comradeship.

Accompanied by the canopy of birds overhead, the travellers are already heading for Granada and the surrounding region, when they are obliged to seek assistance at the crossroads, for the map they are using does not indicate the village of Orce, how very inconsiderate on the part of those who designed the topography, I'll bet they never forgot to indicate their own birthplace, in future they should remember how vexing it is for someone to check out his birthplace on a map only to find a blank space, this has created the most serious problems in trying to establish personal and national identities. Along the route, they pass Seat cars and Pegaso trucks, they can be recognized immediately by their name and registration plates, and the villages through which Deux Chevaux passes have that sleepy air which is said to be characteristic of the south, the people here are accused of being indolent by northern tribes, facile and arrogant remarks of racial disparagement made by those who have never had to work with the sun beating down on them. But it is true that there are differences between one world and another, everybody knows that on Mars the inhabitants are green, while here on earth they are every colour except green.

From an inhabitant of the north we should never hear what we are about to hear, if we stop to ask the man who is passing there, astride a donkey, what he thinks about this extraordinary business of the Iberian Peninsula having separated from Europe, he will pull the donkey's reins, Whoa, and reply without mincing his words, The whole thing's a joke. Roque Lozano judges from appearances, they have helped him to form his own judgment which is easy to understand, behold the bucolic tranquillity of these fields, the serene sky, the harmony of the rocks, the mountains of Morena and Aracena which have remained unaltered since they were born, or, if not that long, since we were born, But television has shown worldwide how the Pyrenees have split open like a watermelon, let us say for argument's sake, using a metaphor within the grasp of rustic minds, I don't trust television, unless I can see things with these eyes of mine which the earth will devour up, I don't trust them, Roque Lozano replies without dismounting, So what are you going to do, I've left my family to look after my affairs and I'm off to see if it's true, With these eyes of yours which the earth will devour, With these eyes of mine which the earth hasn't devoured yet, And do you expect to arrive there riding a donkey, When it can't carry my weight any longer, we'll both travel on foot, What name does your donkey answer to, A donkey doesn't answer to anything, it's called by its master, So what do you call your donkey then, Platero, And we're both making the journey, Platero and I, Can you tell us where Orce is, No sir, I don't know, It would appear to be a little further on than Granada, Oh, in that case, you've still got some way to go, and I must bid you gentlemen from Portugal farewell, for my journey is much greater and I'm riding a donkey, Probably by the time you get there, you'll no longer be able to see Europe, If I don't see it, that'll be because the place never existed, Roque Lozano is absolutely right when all is said and done, because for things to exist there are two essential conditions, that a man should see them and be able to give them a name.

Joaquim Sassa and José Anaiço spent the night in Aracena, following in the footsteps of our King, Dom Afonso the Third, when he conquered the town from the Moors, but it was a sun of short duration, for those were the Dark Ages. The starlings disappeared into the various trees in the vicinity, because being so many, they could not stay together as a flock, as they would have preferred. In the hotel, already lying down, each in his own bed, José Anaiço and Joaquim Sassa discuss the threatening pictures and words they have seen and heard on television, Venice is in peril, and that appears to be true, St Mark's Square flooded at a time when the water is not normally high, a smooth, liquid surface which reflects in every detail the campanile and the façade of the Basilica, As the Iberian

Peninsula gradually moves away, the announcer said in solemn, measured tones, the damaging effect on tides is certain to worsen, grave consequences are predicted throughout the entire Mediterranean basin, the cradle of civilization, we must save Venice, that is our plea to humanity, even if it means making one less hydrogen bomb, one less nuclear submarine, if it is not too late. Joaquim Sassa, like Roque Lozano, had never seen the Pearl of the Adriatic, but José Anaiço could vouch for its existence, it is true that he had not given it either its name or surname, but he had seen it with his own living eyes, had touched it with his own living hands, What a terrible tragedy if Venice should be lost, he said, and these anguished words affected Joaquim Sassa more than the agitated waters in the canals, the tumultuous currents, the encroaching tide penetrating the ground floors of the palaces, the flooded quaysides, the awesome impression of seeing an entire city sink, an incomparable Atlantis, a submerged cathedral, the Moors, their eyes blinded by water, striking the bell with bronze hammers until the seaweed and barnacles paralyse the mechanism, liquid echoes, the Christ Pantocrator of the Basilica finally in theological conversation with the seagods subordinate to Jupiter, the Roman Neptune, the Greek Poseidon, and deliberately restored to the waters from where they emerged, Venus and Amphitrite. Only the God of Christians is without a wife. Perhaps I'm to blame, Joaquim Sassa murmured, Don't overestimate yourself to the point of thinking you're to blame for everything, I'm referring to Venice, the loss of Venice, If Venice should be lost, everyone will be to blame, and for past generations, the city has been declining for some time through neglect and speculation, I'm not speaking about those causes, the entire world has been destroyed on their account, I'm referring to what I did, I threw a stone into the sea and some people believe that caused the Peninsula to break away from Europe. If you should have a son one day, he will die because you were born, no one will absolve you from this crime, the hands that make and weave are the same hands that dismantle and undo, right engenders wrong, wrong produces right, Poor consolation for a man in distress, There is no consolation, sad friend, man is a creature beyond consoling.

Perhaps Joaquim Sassa, who voiced this opinion, is right, perhaps man is a creature who cannot and will not be consoled, but certain human actions, without any meaning other than that of being to all appearances meaningless, sustain the hope that man will one day come to weep on man's shoulder, probably when it is too late, when there is no longer time for anything else. The television announcer mentioned one of those actions in the news bulletin and tomorrow the newspapers will debate it further with detailed statements from historians, critics and poets, this was the secret landing in France, on a beach near Collioure, of a band of Spanish civilians and men of letters, who in the dead hours of the night, without fear of hooting owls or ghosts, burst into the cemetery where for many years the poet Antonio Machado had lain buried. They had a brush with the gendarmes who, alerted by some night-hawk, pursued the grave-robbers, but could not catch up with them. The sack containing the poet's mortal remains was thrown into a waiting launch on the beach with its engine running quietly, and within five minutes the pirate ship was out in the open sea, from the shore the gendarmes fired into the air, just to give vent to their annoyance, not because they felt bereft of those poetic bones. In an interview with *France-Presse*, the *maire* of Collioure tried to discredit the deed, even going so far as to insinuate that no one could be sure that they were the mortal remains of Antonio Machado after all this time, nor is it worth enquiring how many years have passed, only through some improbable oversight on the part of the administration would they still be found there, despite the particular reverence with which the bones of poets are usually handled.

The journalist, a man of much experience, and so lacking in scepticism that he did not even appear to be French, stated that in his opinion, the cult of relics only requires a suitable object, its authenticity is of no importance, and for the sake of verisimilitude one asks for nothing more than a mild resemblance, consider the Cathedral of Valencia where in times gone by, the faith was promoted with a collection of precious relics, namely, the chalice used by Our Lord during the Last Supper, the shirt He wore as a boy, some drops of Our Lady's milk, locks from her hair, fair in colour, and the comb she used, and also some fragments from the Holy Cross, some indefinable object that belonged to one of the Holy Innocents, two of those thirty pieces, made of silver after all, with which Judas allowed himself to be bought through no fault of his own, and, to end the list, one of St Christopher's teeth, four fingers in length and three in width, dimensions which are undoubtedly excessive, but will surprise only those who are unaware of the saint's gigantic proportions. Where will the Spaniards bury the poet now, asked Joaquim Sassa, who had never read Machado, and José Anaiço replied, If, despite the ups and downs of life and the reversals of fortune, everything has its place and every place claims what belongs to it, what remains of Antonio Machado today must be buried somewhere in the fields of Soria, beneath a holm oak, which in Castilian is called *encina*, without any cross or tombstone, nothing but a tiny mound of earth which doesn't even have to look like a stretched-out corpse, in the fullness of time, earth will turn to earth and all will be equal. And we Portuguese, what poet should we go and look for in France, if any of our poets ever stayed there, As far as I know, only Mário de Sá Carneiro, but in his case there's no point even trying, first of all, because he wouldn't have wanted to come, secondly, because the cemeteries in Paris are well protected, thirdly, because so many years have passed since he died, the administration of a capital city would not commit the errors of a provincial town, which also has the excuse of being Mediterranean, And besides, what purpose would it serve to remove him from one cemetery in order to put him in another, now that in Portugal it is forbidden to bury the dead in an unauthorized place or in the open air. Not even his bones would rest in peace if we were to leave him under the shade of an olive tree in the Parque Eduardo VII, But are there any olive trees left in the Parque Eduardo VII, That's a good question, but I can't give you an answer, and now let's get some sleep, for tomorrow we must go in search of Pedro Orce, the man who can feel the earth shaking. They switched off the light, lay there with open eyes waiting to drop off, but, before sleep arrived, Joaquim asked another question, And what about Venice, what's going to happen there, Believe me, the easiest of all the difficult tasks in this world would be to save Venice, all they would have to do would be to close the lagoon, and link the islands together so that the sea wouldn't be able to enter so readily, if the Italians aren't capable of carrying out the job on their own, let them send for the Dutch, they could dry out Venice in no time at all, We should help, we have certain responsibilities, We are no longer Europeans, well, perhaps that's not entirely true, For the time being you are still in territorial waters, interrupted an unknown voice.

In the morning, as they were paying their bill, the manager started to unburden himself of his worries, the hotel was almost empty at the height of the season, such a pity, Joaquim Sassa and José Anaiço, absorbed in their own affairs, had not even noticed that there were few guests. And the grottoes, no one is visiting the grottoes, the hotelier repeated in dismay, for no one to visit the grottoes was the worst of catastrophes. On the street there was great excitement, the children of Aracena had never seen so many starlings together, not even when they went bird-watching in the countryside, but the pleasure of this novelty did not last long, no sooner had the Portuguese Deux Chevaux started off in the direction of Seville, than the starlings took flight as if the entire flock were but one bird, they circled twice as if saying farewell or trying to get their bearings, and disappeared behind the castle of the Knights Templar. The morning is clear, you could touch the sky with your fingers, and today promises to be less hot than yesterday, but the journey is long, From here to Granada there are more than three hundred kilometres, and then we have to go in search of Orce, let's hope we're successful and we find the man, these were the words of José Anaiço, that they might not find the man was a possibility that only now came to mind, And if we should meet him, what are we going to say to him, now it was Joaquim Sassa's turn to be doubtful. Suddenly, because of the light of another day or as a result of night's evil counsel, he found all these events absurd, could it be true that a continent had divided simply because someone had thrown a stone into the sea, a stone that exceeded the strength of the person who threw it, yet there was no shadow of doubt that a stone had been thrown and the continent had divided, and a Spaniard swears that he can feel the earth shaking, and a flock of demented birds are following a Portuguese schoolmaster everywhere, and who knows what else has happened or is about to happen throughout that peninsula yonder, Let's talk about your stone and my starlings, and he will talk about the earth that shook or is still shaking, And then, Then, if there is nothing more to see, to experience and learn, we shall return home, you to your job, I to my school, pretend it was all a dream, and by the way, you still haven't told me what you do for a living, I work in an office, I also work in an office, I'm a teacher. They both laughed, and Deux Chevaux, ever prudent, pointed out on the dial that they were running out of petrol. They refilled the tank at the first petrol station they encountered, but they had to wait more than half an hour, the queue of vehicles stretched all along the road as everyone was anxious to have a full tank. They got back on to the road, Joaquim Sassa was now seriously worried, There's a run on petrol, very soon they'll close the pumps, and then what, We should have been prepared for this, petrol is a sensitive commodity, unstable, whenever there's a crisis it's the first indication, some years ago there was a ban here on supplies of petrol, I don't know if you can remember or even heard about it, utter chaos broke out, I'm beginning to think we'll never reach Orce, Don't be a pessimist, I'm a born pessimist.

They passed through Seville without stopping, but the starlings lingered for a few minutes to admire the Giralda which they had never seen before. Had there only been half a dozen of them they could have formed a diadem of black angels for the Statue of Faith, but because there were thousands of them, upon descending like an avalanche they covered the statue and transformed it into a indefinable figure, which could just as easily have been taken for the symbol of Doubt as the Statue of Faith. The metamorphosis was short-lived, José Anaiço is already speeding through this labyrinth of streets, let's follow him, winged species. Along the route, Deux Chevaux drank wherever possible, some petrol stations had notices saying Sold Out, but the pump attendants said *Mañana*, the latter are an optimistic lot, or perhaps they have simply learned how to make life tolerable. But the starlings had no lack of water, thank God, for Our Lord is much more concerned about birds than humans, nearby are the tributaries of the Guadalquivir, the lagoons, the reservoirs, more water than those tiny beaks could ever drink in a million years. It was already mid-afternoon when they arrived in Granada, Deux Chevaux was panting, shuddering after all that effort, while Joaquim Sassa and José Anaiço went off to investigate, as if they were carrying sealed orders and the moment had come to open them, now we shall know where destiny awaits us.

At the tourist office, an employee asked them if they were Portuguese archaeologists or anthropologists, that they were Portuguese could be seen at once, but why anthropologists and archaeologists, Because Orce is generally visited only by the latter, some years ago a discovery was made in nearby Venta Micena, the oldest human remains to be found in Europe, A whole skeleton, asked José Anaiço, Only a skull, but ancient, dating somewhere between one million three hundred thousand and one million four hundred thousand years, And do we know for certain they are human remains, Joaquim Sassa cautiously enquired, whereupon Maria Dolores replied with a knowing smile, Whenever human remains from ancient times are discovered, they always belong to some man, Cro-Magnon Man, Neanderthal Man, Swanscombe Man, Peking Man, Heidelberg Man, Java Man, at that time there were no women, Eve still hadn't been created, she was only created later, You're being ironic, No, I'm an anthropologist by training and a militant feminist by inclination, Well, we're journalists and we want to interview a certain Pedro

Orce, the one who felt the earth shaking. How does such news arrive in Portugal, Everything arrives in Portugal and we arrive everywhere, this part of the dialogue is conducted solely with José Anaiço, who always has an answer ready, undoubtedly because he's used to coping with school children. Joaquim Sassa had moved away to examine some illustrated posters of the Courtyard of the Lions, the Gardens of Generalife, the entombed effigies of the Catholic Kings, studying them he had to ask himself if there would be any point in visiting these places after having seen the photographs. Absorbed in these thoughts about perceptions of reality, he lost the drift of the conversation, what could José Anaiço have said to make Maria Dolores laugh so heartily, if the Dolores had not changed their name into Lolas, each of those guffaws would have been a scandal. The latter no longer showed the slightest hint of feminist aggression, perhaps because this Ribatejo Man was something more than just a mandible, a molar and a skullcap, and because there is plenty of evidence in this age in which we live that women do exist. Maria Dolores, who works in tourism because she cannot find employment as an anthropologist, draws the missing road on the map for José Anaiço, indicates the village of Orce with a black dot, and that of Venta Micena right beside it, now the travellers may proceed, the sorceress at the crossroads has shown them the way, It is like a lunar desert, but one can see in her eyes that she regrets not being able to accompany them, to practise her skills in the company of Portuguese journalists, especially that rather more discreet one who moved away to look at the posters, how often life has taught us not to judge by appearances, as Joaquim Sassa himself is now doing, his mistake, modest man that he is, If we were to stay here you would be having it off with the lady anthropologist, let us forgive him this vulgar expression, when men are together they engage in this coarse talk, and José Anaiço, presumptuous, but also fooled, replied, Who knows.

This world, we shall never tire of repeating, is a comedy of errors. Another proof of this maxim is that the name Orce Man should have been given to some old bones, not exactly in Orce but in Venta Micena, which would make a nice title for palaeontology, if it were not for that name Venta, which translates as Sale, the symbol and sign of inferior merchandise. The fate of words is truly strange. Unless Micena was a woman's name, before it became that of a man, like that celebrated Galician woman who gave her name to the town of Golegã in Portugal, perhaps some Greeks from Mycenae, in flight from the demented Atridae, arrived in these remote parts, and anxious to re-establish the name of their native region, they happened to choose this place, much further away than Cerbère, at the heart of hell, and never so remote as now, as we go sailing off. However difficult you may find it to believe.

The devil had his first abode in these parts, his were the hooves that scorched the ground and trampled the ashes, amidst mountains which shivered with fear then and continue to do so to this day, the ultimate desert where even Christ would have allowed Himself to be tempted by the same devil had He not already experienced the wiles of Satan, as one reads in the Bible. Joaquim Sassa and José Anaiço contemplate, what do they contemplate, the landscape, but this delightful word belongs to other worlds, to other languages, you cannot refer to what one sees here as being a landscape, we have called it an infernal abode, but we are not altogether sure, for in places of damnation we're almost certain to find men and women with the animals that keep them company until the moment comes to slaughter them in order to live, amidst disasters and misfortunes, this is the place of exile where the poet who never visited Granada must have written his verses. These are the lands of Orce, which must have soaked up so much Moorish and Christian blood, also again in the Dark Ages, but why speak of those who died so many years ago, if it is the land that is dead, buried by itself.

At Orce, the travellers met up with Pedro Orce, a pharmacist by profession, older than they would have imagined him, had they given the matter any thought. Pedro Orce did not appear on television, therefore we could not have known that he is a man in his sixties, thin in features and body, his hair almost entirely white, and were it not for his sober taste which shuns any artifice, he could make up dark and fair hair-dyes at will in the secrecy of his laboratory, for he is skilled in these chemical concoctions. When Joaquim Sassa and José Anaiço enter the pharmacy, he is filling capsules with quinine powder, an old-fashioned medicine which shuns the powerful concentrations of modern prescriptions, while astutely preserving the psychological effect of awkward deglutination, followed by immediate results as if by magic. In Orce, which one must inevitably pass through to reach Venta Micena, now that the commotion of excavations and discoveries has passed, travellers are rare, we do not even know where the skull of the town's oldest ancestor is kept, there in some museum awaiting a glass case with a label, normally any customers passing through buy aspirins, pills to help their digestion or to cure diarrhoea, as for the local inhabitants, they probably die from their first illness, so the pharmacist is never likely to get rich. Pedro Orce has finished sealing the capsules, just like a conjuring trick, after moistening the parts that will serve to seal the capsule, the two brass plates are pressed together, then opened, and the prescription is ready, one last capsule of quinine makes a dozen, and this done he asks them, What can I do for you gentlemen, We are Portuguese, a futile statement, one need only hear them speak to know at once where they come from, but, after all, it is only natural to declare who we are before saying why we have come, especially in situations of such importance, to travel hundreds of kilometres just to ask, although not necessarily with these dramatic words, Pedro Orce, do you swear on your honour and the excavated bones that you felt the earth shake when all the seismographs of Seville and Granada with a steady needle traced the straightest line you ever saw, and Pedro Orce raised his hand and said, with the simplicity of a just and honest man, I do, We should like to have a word in private, Joaquim Sassa added after they had revealed their nationality, and there and then, since there were no other clients in the pharmacy, they told him about their personal and collective experiences, about the stone, the starlings, crossing the frontier, they could not show him the stone, but as for the birds, you only need to pop your head outside the door and look, there, in this square or in the adjacent one, the inevitable flock of birds, all the inhabitants staring up at the sky amazed at this unusual spectacle, now the birds have disappeared, they have descended upon the Castle of the Seven Towers, Arabic in origin. Better not to speak here, Pedro Orce said, get into the car and drive out of town, In which direction, Drive straight ahead, in the direction of Maria, go for three kilometres beyond the last houses, there is a tiny bridge, near an olive tree, wait for me there, I'll join you shortly, Joaquim Sassa had the impression that he was about to relive a scene from his own life, that morning two days ago, when he had waited for José Anaiço, beyond the last houses.

They are seated on the ground, under a Cordoban olive tree, the one which, according to the popular quatrain, makes the oil yellow, as if olive oil weren't yellow, only occasionally slightly greenish, and the first words from José Anaiço, which he could not suppress were, This place is enough to put the fear of God into you, and Pedro Orce replied, It's much worse in Venta Micena, where I was born, an ambiguous formality which means what it appears to be saying as well as the exact opposite, depending more on the reader than on the reading, although the latter is entirely dependent on the former, which explains why we find it so difficult to know who is reading what has been read and the effect of what has been read on the person who reads it, let us hope that, in this case, Pedro Orce will not think that the curse on the place is the result of his having been born there. Then as their discussion got under way, they gradually started to compare their experiences as discus-thrower, bird-catcher and seismologist, and they came to the conclusion that all the events that had taken place had been, and continued to be, somehow connected, especially since Pedro Orce insists that the ground has not stopped shaking, I can feel it even at this very moment, and he stretched out his hand to show them what he meant. Drawn by curiosity, José Anaiço and Joaquim Sassa touched the hand which he kept outstretched, and they could feel, oh yes, without a shadow of doubt they could feel the tremor, the vibration, the drone, and although some sceptic might suggest that it is natural for people to start trembling at a certain age, Pedro Orce is not all that old, and trembling and tremor are not the same thing, whatever the dictionaries might tell us.

Anyone watching from afar would think that the three men had just pledged themselves to some commitment or other, what is certain is that they quickly shook hands, and nothing more. All around, the stones have intensified the heat, the white earth is dazzling, the sky is an open furnace blowing hot air, even in the shade beneath this Cordoban olive tree. So far, no olives have appeared, they are safe for the moment from the voracious starlings, but once December comes you will see such plundering, but since there is only one olive tree, the starlings are not likely to frequent these parts. Joaquim Sassa switched on his radio, for suddenly all three of them had nothing more to say, scarcely surprising, after all, they have not known each other for very long, the announcer's voice can be heard, grown nasal from all that broadcasting and because the batteries are flat, Judging from the latest measurements, the speed of the Peninsula's dislocation has stabilized at around seven hundred and fifty metres per hour, the three men started listening to the news, According to the latest reports to reach the newsroom, an enormous crack has appeared between La Línea and Gibraltar, the voice droned on and on, we shall be back with more news, unless anything unforeseen should happen, in an hour's time, at this very moment the starlings passed in a flurry, vruuuuuuuuu, and Joaquim Sassa asked, Are they yours, and José Anaiço didn't even have to look up before replying, They're mine, he has no difficulty in recognizing them, he knows them, Sherlock Holmes would be bound to say, Elementary my dear Watson, there isn't another flock like it in these parts, and he is right, for there are few birds in hell, only the nocturnal ones because of tradition.

Pedro Orce accompanies the flock's flight, initially out of mild curiosity, then his eyes light up with blue sky and white clouds, and, unable to hold back the words, he suddenly proposes, Why don't we go to the coast and see the rock as it passes. This may sound absurd, nonsensical, but it is not, even when we travel by train, we think we see trees passing which are firmly rooted in the soil, at this moment we are not travelling by train, we are travelling more slowly on a stone raft which is sailing the sea without any fetters, the only difference being that which exists between solid and liquid. So often we need a whole lifetime in order to change our life, we think a great deal, weigh things up and vacillate, then we go back to the beginning, we think and think, we dislodge ourselves on the tracks of time with a circular movement, like those clouds of dust, dead leaves, debris, that have no strength for anything more, better by far that we should live in a land of hurricanes. At other times, one word is all that is needed, Let's go and see the rock as it passes, and they get to their feet, eager for adventure, they don't even feel the scorching heat, like children given their freedom, they run laughing down the slope, Deux Chevaux is like a burning cauldron, within seconds the three men are bathed in sweat, but they scarcely take any notice of their discomfort, for from these same southern parts, men set out to discover the New World, and they too, rugged and fierce, sweating like pigs, advanced in armour, steel helmets on their heads, sword in hand, to fight the naked Indians, clad only in feathers and war-paint, an idyllic image.

They did not go back through the village, for people would

suspect if they were to see Pedro Orce and the two strangers travelling in the same car, either that he was being abducted or that the three of them were involved in some conspiracy, better to call the police, but an old man from among the veterans of Orce would say, We don't want the Civil Guard here. They went by other routes, along roads not marked on the average map, the person we need right now is the sphinx of tourism, to trace out the itinerary of these new discoveries, for she had turned out to be a sphinx, after all, rather than a sybil, for the latter have never been seen at crossroads, even if the latter and the former are both peninsular. Pedro Orce said, First I must show you Venta Micena, the place where I was born, the phrase came out, as if he were mocking himself or deliberately touching on a sore point. They passed through a village in ruins called Fuente Nueva, if there was ever any fountain here it has dried up and vanished, and on a wide bend on the road ahead, he called out, There it is.

They take a good look and see so little that they start searching for what must be missing and can no longer be found. There, asks José Anaiço, he has cause for doubt, because there are only a few scattered houses, they merge with the colour of the earth, a church tower below, what is unmistakably a cemetery, here at the edge of the road, with a cross and white walls. Under the volcanic sun, the countryside rolls like a petrified sea covered in dust, if this was already like this one million, four hundred thousand years ago, you do not have to be a palaeontologist to testify that Orce Man died of thirst, the world was then young, the stream that flows yonder would then have been a wide and generous river, there would have stood great trees, grasses taller than man, and all this took place before hell was located here. At the right season, when there is rain, some greenery will spread throughout these ashen fields, at present the low verges are cultivated with great effort, the plants dry up and die, then revive and flourish, it's man who still has not learned how cycles repeat themselves, with him it is once and nevermore. Pedro Orce makes a gesture that embraces the blighted village. The house where I was born no longer exists, and then, pointing to the left, in the direction of some hills which are flat on top, That's the Cueva de los Rosales, where the bones of Orce Man were discovered. Joaquim Sassa and José Anaiço looked at the livid landscape, one million, four hundred thousand years ago this place was inhabited by men and women who begot men and women who begot men and women, destiny, disaster, right up to the present day, one million, four hundred thousand years hence someone will come to carry out excavations in this poor cemetery, and since there is already an Orce Man, perhaps the skull that has just been found will now be returned to its rightful owner and be called Venta Micena Man. No one passes, no dog can be heard barking, the starlings have disappeared, Joaquim Sassa feels a shiver run all the way up his spine, as he tries in vain to suppress his uneasiness, and José Anaiço asks, What's the name of that mountain down there, That's the Sierra de Sagra, And this one here, on our right, That's the Sierra de Maria, When Orce Man died, that must have been the last vision he gazed upon, What would he have called it when he talked with other men from Orce, the ones who left no skull behind, Joaquim Sassa asked, At that time there were no names, José Anaiço said, How can you look at something without giving it a name, You have to wait for the name to be born. The three men stood there gazing, with nothing more to say, it was time to leave the past to its restless peace.

In order to lighten their journey, Pedro Orce repeated the story of the adventures he had experienced in greater detail, the scientists had been on the point of linking him up to a seismograph in the presence of the authorities, a desperate but useful measure, for then they would be able to establish whether he had been telling the truth, the needle on the dial immediately registered an earth tremor, the line becoming straight again once the guinea pig had been disconnected from the machine. The inexplicable has been explained, declared the Mayor of Granada who was looking on, but one of the experts corrected him, The inexplicable will have to wait a little longer, the statement wasn't strictly scientific but everyone understood what he meant and agreed. They sent Pedro Orce home, instructing him to remain at the disposal of science and the authorities, warning him that he should speak to no one of his extrasensory powers, a recommendation which didn't differ all that much from the decision taken by the French veterinary surgeons about the mysterious disappearance of the vocal cords of the dogs of Cerbère.

Deux Chevaux has finally turned in a southerly direction, the car is already travelling along frequented roads, there does not appear to be any shortage here of fuel, petrol, diesel oil, but little by little the car has been obliged to reduce its lively pace, in front there is an endless line of traffic, crawling at a snail's pace, other cars, lorries and buses carrying freight, motorbikes, bicycles, mopeds, scooters, horse-drawn carts, people mounted on donkeys, but no Roque

Lozano among them, and people on foot, lots of them, some asking for a lift, others clearly showing disdain for any means of transport as if they were doing penance, or fulfilling some dream, it is more likely to be some dream, and there is no point in asking them where they are going, you do not need to be called Pedro Orce to share the same thought and want to see Gibraltar pass in the distance, drifting off course, you need only be Spanish, and here Spaniards abound. They come from Cordoba, from Linares, from Jaén, from Guadix, all of them major cities, but also from Higuera de Arjona, from El Tocón, from Bular Bajo, from Alamedilla, from Jesús del Monte, from Almácegas, delegations appear to have been despatched from every region, these people have been extremely patient, ever since the year seventeen hundred and four, just imagine, if Gibraltar is not going to be ours, we who have become part of these waters, then why should it go to the English. The human river has grown so wide that the traffic police have to open wherever possible a third lane heading south, few vehicles are travelling north, only in an emergency, sickness or death, and even so they are looked at with mistrust, suspected of Anglophilia, perhaps they want to bury in some remote corner their distress at this geological and strategic separation.

But for most people, this is a day of great rejoicing, the week as holy as the official one, and there are lorries carrying statues of Christ, the Virgins of Triana and Macarena, brass bands, their instruments shining in the sun, and on the donkeys' backs can be seen bundles of firewood and mortars, if anyone were to put a lighted match anywhere near them, they would soar like Clavileño to the second and third regions of the atmosphere, and to that of fire, where they would singe Sancho Panza's beard, if, given his gullible nature, he should allow himself to be deceived yet again. The young girls are dressed in all their finery, with mantillas and shawls, and the elderly, when they can walk no further, are carried by the young on their backs, son you are, father you will be, you will reap as you have sown, until some vehicle stops, any vehicle, and the journey goes on, their weary limbs relaxed, everyone making for the coast, the beaches, better still if they can find some elevation looking out to sea, where they might be sure of a good view of that damned rock, what a pity one cannot hear from this distance the screeching of the monkeys, disorientated because there's no land in sight. As the sea gets closer, the traffic becomes more congested, some are already abandoning their vehicles and walking, or begging a lift from those travelling on horse-drawn carts or donkeys, the latter cannot abandon these creatures of nature, they have to tend them, to water them, put the baskets of straw and bean pods to their snouts, even the police are aware of the situation, they are all country-folk, therefore the orders are to leave the lorries and cars at the side of the road, the animals can go on, and motorbikes, bicycles, scooters and mopeds are also permitted, the latter have ways and means of manoeuvring smoothly in and out of traffic because they do not take up much space. The brass bands, on foot, rehearse the first paso dobles, an over-enthusiastic vendor of fireworks or ardent patriot prematurely lets off a mighty firecracker to the annoyance of his friends who were not prepared to waste their fireworks without good reason. Deux Chevaux has also come to a halt, it was the only Portuguese car in the procession, that is to say, with Portuguese registration, watching Gibraltar drifting past does not bother Deux Chevaux one way or the other, his historic sadness is called Olivença and this road does not lead there. You can see people who are already lost, women calling for their husbands, children calling for their parents, but fortunately for all of them, they will eventually be reunited, if this is not a day for laughter, it is not one for weeping either, God and that Cur of a Son willing. There are also dogs there sniffing around, few of them bark, except when they start fighting among themselves, not a single one of them from Cerbère. And when two donkeys appear on the loose, without any sign of their owners, Pedro Orce, Joaquim Sassa and José Anaiço unwisely decide to make use of them in turn, one walking, the other two riding, but their comfort is short-lived, the donkeys belonged to a band of gypsies who are travelling north, the latter could not care less about Gibraltar, and if Pedro Orce had not been Spanish, and of the most ancient and respected lineage, Portuguese blood would have been shed on the spot.

All along the coast the encampment stretches for miles, almost like a small village, thousands and thousands of people looking out to sea, some have clambered on to rooftops and up tall trees, not to mention all the other thousands who did not want to come so far and stayed behind, with spyglasses and binoculars, on the heights of the Sierra Contraviesa or on the slopes of the Sierra Nevada, here we are only interested in the more humble people, those who have to touch things in order to recognize them, they will not get all that close, but they are doing their utmost. José Anaiço, Joaquim Sassa and Pedro Orce have come with them, driven on by the enthusiasm of Pedro Orce and the good-natured friendliness of the others, now they are seated on some boulders facing the sea, the evening is drawing in, and Joaquim Sassa, the self-confessed pessimist, remarks, If Gibraltar should pass during the night, we have made the journey in vain. At least we'll be able to see her lights, Pedro Orce argued, and it might be even nicer to watch the rock moving away like a ship all lit up, then we'll have a real excuse for staging a fireworks display with pinwheels, silver rain, cascades, or whatever they're called here, while the rock fades away in the distance, disappears into the darkness of night, goodbye, goodbye, never to be seen again. But José Anaiço had opened out the map on his lap, and with pencil and paper he made some calculations, repeated them one by one to be absolutely certain, checked the scale once again, double-checked his figures, and finally declared, Gibraltar, my friends, it will take about ten days to get here, incredulous surprise on the part of his companions, then he showed them his arithmetic, he did not even need to invoke his authority as a certified teacher, knowledge of this kind, fortunately, is within reach of the simplest minds, If the Peninsula, or island, or whatever, is dislocated at a speed of seven hundred and fifty metres an hour, we believe it will cover eighteen kilometres each day, now then, in a straight line from the Bay of Algeciras to where we are standing, it is almost two hundred kilometres, so work that out, it's not difficult. Confronted with this irrefutable proof, Pedro Orce bowed his head in submission, And we have come running here with all these people thinking our day of glory has arrived, that today we could have mocked the Evil Stone, and now we shall have to wait for ten days, no fire lasts long. And suppose we were to go and meet it, taking the roads along the coast, Joaquim Sassa suggested, No, no, it isn't worth it, Pedro Orce replied, these things need to be at the right moment before one's enthusiasm flags, it's right now that the rock should be passing before our very eyes, while we're still feeling excited, we were in the right mood but not any more, Well what shall we do then, José Anaiço asked, Let's go, Don't you want to stay, You can no longer live your dream once the dream has gone, In that case, let's leave tomorrow, So soon, I have to get back to school, And I to my office, And I've always got my pharmacy.

They went to look for Deux Chevaux, but while they are searching and having some difficulty in finding the car, this is the moment to mention that many thousands of people who achieved neither voice nor vote in this story, who have not even made a brief appearance at the back of the stage, thousands of people who have not budged for the last ten days and nights, ate from the provisions they had brought, then, when they ran out on the second day, they went to buy whatever they could find locally, and they cooked in the open air, on great bonfires that were like firebrands from another age, and not even those who had run out of money went hungry, where there was food for one there was food for all, we are enjoying a revival of fraternity, if such a thing has ever been humanly possible or is likely to return. Pedro Orce, José Anaiço and Joaquim Sassa are not about to experience this admirable fraternity, they have turned their back on the sea, and now it is their turn to be looked at suspiciously by those hordes of people who are still descending.

Meantime darkness had fallen, the first lights went on. Let's go said José Anaiço. Pedro Orce would remain silent, sitting on the back seat, looking sad, his eyes closed, it has to be now or never, we shall never have a better opportunity to recall the Portuguese refrain, Where are you going, I'm off to the party, Where have you come from, I've come from the party, even without the help of exclamation marks and breaks, one can readily see the difference between the joyful anticipation of the first reply and the disillusioned weariness of the second, they only look alike on the page on which they're written. During the entire journey, only five words were spoken, You must dine with me, they came from the lips of Pedro Orce, he felt obliged to be hospitable. José Anaiço and Joaquim Sassa did not feel it was necessary to make any reply, some might think they were being impolite by remaining silent, but such people know very little about human nature, those better informed would testify that the three men had become close friends.

They reach Orce at dead of night. The roads at this hour are a desert of shadows and silence, Deux Chevaux can be left at the door of the pharmacy, and it is no bad thing that they should give it a rest, tomorrow the car will be back on the road carrying three men, a matter about to be decided indoors as they sit round the table enjoying a simple meal, for Pedro Orce also lives alone and there has not been enough time to prepare anything more elaborate. They switch on the television, the news bulletins are transmitted hourly, and they see Gibraltar, not simply separated from Spain, but already at a considerable distance, like an island abandoned in the middle of the ocean, transformed, poor thing, into a peak, a sugarloaf, or reef, with its thousand cannon out of action. Even if they should insist on opening new loopholes on the northern side, perhaps to gratify imperial pride, they would be throwing their money into the sea, both in the literal and the figurative sense. Those scenes undoubtedly made an impression, but were nothing when compared to the shock produced by a series of satellite pictures, showing the progressive widening of the canal between the Peninsula and France, flesh froze and hair bristled at the sight of this great catastrophe, beyond human powers, for that was no longer a canal but open sea, where ships sailed at will, over water which had truly never been sailed before. Obviously, the dislocation could not be observed, at this altitude a speed of seven hundred and fifty metres per hour cannot be captured by the naked eye, but, for anyone observing, it was as if the great mass of stone were being displaced in his head, sensitive people almost fainted, others complained of feeling dizzy. And there were pictures that had been taken from aboard the indefatigable helicopters, the gigantic Pyrenean escarpment, cut vertically, and the minute swarm of ants heading south, like a sudden migration, just to see Gibraltar adrift, an optical illusion, for it is we who are being carried off with the current, and also, to add a colourful detail, an entry worthy of a diary, a flock of starlings, thousands of them, like a cloud shutting out one's field of vision, darkening the sky. Even the birds are responding to the crowd's excitement, that was the verb the announcer used, responding, when we know from natural history that birds have their own good reasons for going wheresoever they choose or when the need arises, they do not aid either me or you, at most José, who ungratefully confesses, I'd forgotten about them.

They also showed shots of Portugal, taken on the Atlantic coast, with the waves beating on the rocks or swirling over the sands, and lots of people watching the horizon, with the tragic expression of someone who has been prepared for centuries for the unknown and fears that it may not come after all, or turn out to be no different from the common, banal experiences of everyday life. There they are now, as Unamuno described them, his swarthy face cupped in the palms of his hands, Fix your eyes where the lonely sun sets in the immense sea, all the peoples with the sea to the west do the same, this race is swarthy, there is no other difference, and it has sailed the seas. Lyrical, ecstatic, the Spanish announcer declaims, Look at the Portuguese, all along their golden beaches, once but no longer the prow of Europe, for we have withdrawn from the European quayside to sail once more the Atlantic waves, which admiral will guide us, which port awaits us, the closing shot showed a young lad throwing a pebble into the sea, practising the art of ricochet which requires no training, and Joaquim Sassa said, He has the strength of his years, the stone couldn't possibly go any further, but the Peninsula, or whatever it might be, appeared to be advancing with even greater vigour over the deep sea, so different from what it is normally like during summer. The final item of news was given by the announcer, in passing, as if he did not consider it very important, There seems to be some lack of stability among the population, lots of people are leaving their homes, not only in Andalusia, there we know the reason, and, bearing in mind that most of them are heading for the sea, it is believed that they are driven by natural curiosity, in any case we can assure our viewers that there is nothing to see on the coast, as we have just confirmed, all those Portuguese who were staring at the sea, stared and saw nothing, and we do not want to be like them. Then Pedro Orce said, If you have room for me, I'm coming with you.

Joaquim Sassa and José Anaiço remained silent, they could not understand why such a sensible Spaniard should want to visit the regions and beaches of Portugal. The question was worth raising, and as the owner of Deux Chevaux, it was up to Joaquim Sassa to ask, and Pedro Orce replied, I don't want to stay here, with the earth shaking under my feet all the time, and people telling me that I'm only imagining things, You might well feel the earth shaking in Portugal too, and very likely people there will say much the same thing, José Anaiço told him, and we have our jobs waiting for us. I won't be a burden to you, just take me with you and leave me in Lisbon, where I've never been, I'll come back here one day, And what about your family and your pharmacy, You must be aware by now that I have no family, I'm the last surviving member, the pharmacy will be all right, there is my assistant and he will look after things. There was nothing more to be said, no reason for refusing, We'll be glad of your company, was the phrase Joaquim Sassa used, The worst thing would be if they were to detain you at the frontier, José Anaiço reminded him, I'll tell them I've been touring Spain, so I couldn't possibly have known that anyone was looking for me, and that I'm just about to present myself to the civil governor, but it's unlikely there will be any need for explanations, they're sure to be paying more attention to those who are leaving than to those who are entering, Let's enter by some other frontier post because I'm worried about the starlings, José Anaiço reminded them, and, having spoken, he spread out on the table a map of the whole Iberian Peninsula, drawn and coloured at a time when everything was terra firma and the ossified callus of the Pyrenees discouraged any temptation to venture beyond, in silence the three men stood looking at the flat area representing this part of the world as if they failed to recognize it, Strabo used to say that the Peninsula is formed like the hide of an ox, Pedro Orce muttered these words earnestly, and despite the warm night, Joaquim Sassa and José Anaiço came out in goose pimples, as if suddenly confronted by the Cyclopean Beast which was about to be sacrificed and skinned in order to burden the continent of Europe with yet another carcass that would go on bleeding until the end of time.

The open map showed the two countries, Portugal indented, suspended, Spain unhinged to the south, and the regions, the provinces, the districts, the thick rubble of the major cities, the dust of the towns and villages, but not of all of them, for dust is often invisible to the naked eye, Venta Micena was merely one example. Their hands smoothed and stroked the paper, they passed over Alentejo and continued northwards, as if they were caressing a human face, from left to right, following the hands of the clock, the direction of time, the Beiras, Ribatejo before them, and then Trás-os-Montes and Minho, Galicia, Asturias, the Basque Country and Navarre, Castile and León, Aragón and Catalonia, Valencia, Extremadura, Spanish and Portuguese, Andalusia where we still find ourselves, the Algarve, then José Anaiço pointed with his finger to the mouth of the Guadiana and said, Let's enter through here.

Swept away by the volley of gunfire from Rosal de la Frontera of bitter memory, the starlings, prudent on this occasion, made a wide circle northwards and crossed to where the air was clear and the circulation free, some three kilometres from the bridge, which was already built by then, and not before time. The police on the Portuguese side expressed no surprise that one of the three travellers was called Joaquim Sassa, there were clearly more serious matters worrying the authorities and these soon became apparent from the following dialogue, Where are you gentlemen heading for, the guard enquired, For Lisbon, replied José Anaiço who was at the wheel, and he in turn asked, Why do you ask officer, You will come up against roadblocks along the motorway, strictly observe all instructions you may receive, under no circumstances should you try to force your way through or attempt any diversions, otherwise you'll be in trouble, Has there been some disaster, Depends what you mean by disaster, Don't tell us the Algarve is also breaking away, it had to come sooner or later, they've always thought of themselves as being a separate kingdom, No, there's another problem, and more serious, people are trying to occupy the hotels, they claim that if there are no tourists they ought to be given shelter, We've heard nothing about this, when did the occupation begin, Last night, Well I never, exclaimed José Anaiço, had he been French, he would have said Ça alors, everyone has his own way of expressing the surprise the next man also experiences, listen to Pedro Orce who gave a resounding Caramba, while from Joaquim Sassa you could scarcely hear the echo of that, Well I never.

The police instructed them to carry on, warned them for a second time, Look out for the roadblocks, and Deux Chevaux was able to

74

cross Vila Real de Santo António while the passengers went on discussing this extraordinary affair, Seriously, who would have believed it, there are two different types of Portuguese, those who take themselves off to the beaches and sand dunes to contemplate the horizon despondently, and others who advance intrepidly on those hotels-cum-fortresses defended by the police, by the Republican Guard and even, it would seem, by the army itself, already people have been wounded, this they were told secretly in a café where they decided to stop and gather some information. This was how they learned that in three hotels, one in Albufeira, one in Praia da Rocha, and the other in Lagos, the situation is critical, the forces of order are on the point of surrounding the buildings where the rioters have been stirring up trouble, barricading doors and windows, blocking all points of access, they are like besieged Moors, infidels without forgiveness who have renounced any creed, who heed neither appeals nor threats, they know that the white flag will be followed by tear gas, therefore they refuse to negotiate, and ignore the word surrender. Pedro Orce was shaken, went on repeating *Caramba* under his breath, and one could detect a hint of patriotic pique in his expression, deep regret that the Spanish should have failed to take the initiative.

At the first roadblock they were asked to turn off in the direction of Castro Marim but José Anaiço protested that he had some important business in Silves which must be dealt with urgently, he said Silves to allay any suspicions, Even so, you have to travel along country roads, and keep as far off the beaten track as possible, if you want to avoid complications, the officer in charge advised him, reassured by the harmless appearance of the three passengers and the jaded respectability of Deux Chevaux, But Officer, in a situation such as this, with the country going adrift, and the expression could not have been more apt, here we are worrying ourselves about some hotels being occupied, this isn't a revolution that warrants general mobilization, the masses are sometimes impatient, that's all, the comment came from Joaquim Sassa, scarcely diplomatic, fortunately the lieutenant was not a man to go back on his word but a soldier who upheld ancient traditions, otherwise they really would have found themselves obliged to go through Castro Marim. Joaquim Sassa's impertinence, nonetheless, was duly reprimanded, The army is here to carry out its orders, what would you say if we were to abandon our uncomfortable barracks and occupy the Sheraton or the Ritz, the officer must have been really caught off balance to condescend to giving explanations to a civilian. You're absolutely right, Lieutenant, just like my friend to speak without thinking, as I'm always telling him, Well he should think, because he's old enough, the officer retorted sharply. With an abrupt gesture he waved them on, he did not hear what Joaquim Sassa said, and just as well, otherwise they might have ended up behind bars.

They were detained at other roadblocks manned by the Republican Guard who were not quite so obliging, sometimes they were forced to make diversions along poor roads before being able to get back on to the main highway. Joaquim Sassa was angry and not without reason, he had been reprimanded twice, That the lieutenant should play the bully, I can accept, but you had no right to say that I don't think before speaking, Forgive me, I was only trying to prevent the conversation from turning sour, you were being ironic with the man and that was a mistake, you must never be ironic with the authorities, either they don't notice and then it is pointless, or they notice, and that makes matters worse. Pedro Orce asked them to explain, slowly, what they were arguing about, and the inevitable change of tone, the repetitions, revealed that it was a matter of no importance, when Pedro Orce understood everything, everything had been understood.

After the fork in the road at Boliqueime on a deserted stretch of road, José Anaiço, taking advantage of a shallow ditch and without warning, drove Deux Chevaux straight into an open field, Where are you going, Joaquim Sassa called out, If we keep to the road, like obedient little children, we'll never get close to any of those hotels and we want to see what's going on there, well do we or don't we, José Anaiço retorted between one jolt and another, struggling with the unsteady steering-wheel as the car bounced over the ruts like something demented. Pedro Orce, sitting on the back seat, was thrown from one side to another without pity or mercy, and Joaquim Sassa, who had burst out laughing, replied in fits and starts, That's really funny, that's really very funny. Fortunately, three hundred metres ahead they found a hidden path among the fig trees, behind a broken-down dry-stone wall, or one that had lost its mortar with time. They were, in a manner of speaking, in the field of operations. Taking every precaution they started approaching Albufeira, wherever possible they chose flat terrain, worst of all are the clouds of dust sent up by Deux Chevaux which is ill-equipped to act as beater and vanguard, but the police are already far away, guarding the crossroads, the major road junctions as they are called in the current terminology of communications, besides, the effective strength of the forces of order is not so great that it could strategically cover a province that is as rich in hotels as in locust trees, if such a comparison were permissible. In fact, anyone whose next destination is the city of Lisbon would not need to venture into these parts where subversion reigns, but we might as well confirm whether our information is correct, time and time again one has seen how stories get exaggerated in the telling, there might have been the odd, isolated incident, but the roadblocks might turn out in the end to be nothing more than the putting into practice of that wise proverb which warns us that prevention is better than cure. But there were already infiltrations. From among the sparse trees, eagerly tramping over the red soil, came men and women carrying sacks, suitcases and bundles on their shoulders, tiny children in their arms, their intention being to secure a place in a hotel, with these few belongings and the closest members of the family as a guarantee, wife, children, then, if all goes well, they will send for the rest of their relatives, and the bed, the chest and the table in the absence of any other belongings, no one seems to have remembered that there are plenty of beds and tables in hotels, and while there may not be all that many chests, there are wardrobes which serve the same purpose.

At the gates of Albufeira preparations were under way for the decisive battle. The travellers had left Deux Chevaux behind, parked tranquilly in the shade, in a situation of this kind once cannot rely on its assistance, a car is a mechanical entity, devoid of emotions, wherever you may drive it, it goes, it remains where it is parked, it does not care one way or another whether the Peninsula goes sailing off, the Peninsula's dislocation is not likely to make distances any shorter. The battle was preceded by a rallying speech, as was common in ancient warfare, with words of defiance and exhortation to the troops, prayers to the Virgin or their patron St James, words always sound fine at the outset, the outcome is invariably disastrous, at Albufeira, the harangue from the leader of the invading populace was to no avail, and how well he harangued, Guards, soldiers, friends, open your ears wide, and give me your attention, you are, and don't you forget it, sons of the people just like us, this much-sacrificed people which builds houses yet remains homeless, which erects hotels yet never earns enough money ever to stay in one, note that we have come here with our wives and children, but we didn't come here to ask for the moon, simply for a better and safer roof over our heads, for rooms where we can sleep with the privacy and respect we deserve as human beings, we're neither animals nor machines, we have feelings, now then, those hotels over there are empty, there are hundreds, thousands of rooms, they were built for tourists, now the tourists have gone and they're not coming back, so long as they were here we resigned ourselves to this miserable existence, now, we beg of you, let us in, we'll pay the same rent we paid for the houses we've abandoned, it wouldn't be right to ask us for more, and we swear, by all that is holy and profane, that you will always find everything clean and tidy, for when it come to cleanliness there have never been women to match ours, I know what you're going to say and you're quite right, there are our children, and grubby children create a lot of dirt, but ours will soon be washed and smartened up, there's no problem, each room, we've been told, has its own washing facilities, with a choice of shower or bath, and hot and cold water, this should make it easy to keep clean, and if any of our children have grown up with filthy habits and never got used to hygiene, these children, I promise you, will be the cleanest children in the world, all they need is a little time, besides, time is all that man needs, the rest is nothing but illusion, this was something no one was expecting, that the rebel leader should suddenly start playing the philosopher.

It is obvious from their features, and could be confirmed by their identity cards, that the soldiers are truly sons of the people, but their major has either disowned his humble upbringing on the benches of the military academy, or was born into the upper classes for whom the hotels at the Algarve were built. It was difficult to tell from his reply, Get back or I'll smash your face in, for this coarse language is not confined to the lower orders. The troops saw there in the crowd the beloved image of their father and mother, but the call of duty is stronger, You are the light of my eyes, the mother says to her son as he raises his hand to strike her. But the civilian leader of the rebels called out angrily, turning from pleas to invective in his exasperation, Race of bootlickers, who don't even recognize the breast that gave you milk, poetic licence, an accusation with no real meaning or purpose, for there is no son or daughter who remembers such a thing, although there are numerous authorities ready to affirm that deep down in our subconscious we secretly preserve these and other terrifying memories, and that our whole existence consists of these and other fears.

The major was not pleased that he should be accused of bootlicking, and, beside himself with rage, shouted, Charge, at the same moment as the fanatical general of the invaders called out, Get them, patriots, and they all surged forward together, fighting hand-to-hand, and there was a terrible clash. This was the moment when Joaquim Sassa, Pedro Orce and José Anaiço arrived on the scene, curious but innocent, and they walked straight into trouble, for once things got out of control the troops did not discriminate between actors and spectators, and one could say that the three friends who did not need a home suddenly found themselves obliged to fight for one. Pedro Orce, despite his years, fought as if this were his native land, the others did the best they could, perhaps a little less, belonging as they did to a peaceful race. People were injured and they either dragged themselves or were carried to the side of the road, the women burst into tears and cursed the enemy, the infants had been left in the safety of the chariots, for a battle of this nature can only be called medieval and described with the words of that age. A stone thrown from afar by a youth called David knocked Major Goliath to the ground, blood pouring from a deep gash on his chin, his steel helmet no protection, and this was the outcome when soldiers stopped using visors and nosepieces, and the worst thing was that, in the confusion of the onslaught, the rebels rushed past the troops, breaking through their ranks on all sides, in an instinctive but clever tactical move, only to disperse at once up steep roads and alleys, thus ensuring that the soldiers who were surrounding the occupied hotel could not rush to the aid of the defeated battalion with any real effect, no one could remember such humiliation since the time of the French agrarian revolts in the Middle Ages. One hotelier, perhaps because he was mentally disturbed, or had suddenly been converted to the popular cause, opened all the doors of his hotel, saying, Enter, enter, I'd rather have you than have the place deserted.

With this unexpected capitulation, Pedro Orce, José Anaiço and Joaquim Sassa found themselves occupying a room without any real struggle and two days later they gave it to one of the more needy families with a paralysed grandmother and wounded relatives who needed treatment. In the upheaval, the like of which had never been seen before, there were husbands who lost their wives, children who lost their parents, but the sequel of these traumatic separations, something no one could ever have invented, which, in itself, confirms the persuasive truth of the story, the sequel, as we were saying, was that the same family, broken up, but driven by the same dynamism even when divided, occupied rooms in different hotels, since it had proved extremely difficult to try and unite under one roof those who had been demanding that everyone should be under the same roof, and they usually finished up installing themselves in the hotel with the most stars on its signboard. The police commissioners, the army colonels and captains of the guard asked for reinforcements, armoured cars and instructions from Lisbon, the government, not knowing where to turn, gave orders and countermanded them, uttered threats and pleas, in fact, three ministers were believed to have resigned already. Meanwhile, from the sands and streets of Albufeira jubilant families could be seen at the hotel windows, those fine, spacious terraces with their breakfast tables and padded chaise-longues, Father was hammering the first nails into place, and putting up a clothesline, while Mother, singing to herself, was already doing her washing indoors in the bathroom. And the swimming pools were seething with bathers and divers, no one had remembered to explain to the children that they must take a shower before plunging into the blue water, it is not going to be all that easy to make these people change their habits now that they have left their slums.

Bad example has always prospered and borne more fruit than good advice, and who can tell by what rapid means bad example is transmitted, for within a few hours this popular movement of occupation had jumped over the border and spread throughout Spain, you can imagine what it must have been like in Marbella and Torremolinos, where the hotels are like cities and three are enough to form a megalopolis. Europe, upon receiving these alarming reports, began shouting Anarchy, Social Chaos, Invasion of Private Property, and a French newspaper, influential in forming public opinion, prophetically spelt out in bold print across its front page, You Can't Change Nature. These words, however unoriginal, struck a chord in the hearts of Europeans, whenever they spoke of the ancient Iberian Peninsula, they would shrug their shoulders and say to each other, What can you do, they're like that, you can't change human nature, the only exception to this accusing chorus has come from that modest but Machiavellian newspaper published in Naples, Housing Problem Solved in Portugal and Spain.

During the remaining days the three friends spent in Albufeira, the riot police, supported by a special squad, tried to clear one of the hotels by force, but the joint and co-ordinated resistance of the new arrivals and the owners, the former resolved to hold out to the last, the latter fearful of the havoc usually caused by the so-called rescuers, resulted in the operations being suspended, postponed until there might be another opportunity when time and promises might have weakened their vigilance. By the time Pedro Orce, Joaquim Sassa and José Anaiço resumed their journey to Lisbon there already existed democratically elected residents' committees in the occupied buildings with sub-committees responsible for matters such as hygiene and maintenance, kitchen and laundry, entertainment and recreation, cultural activities, education and counselling, gymnastics and sports, in short, all the essentials for the smooth and efficient running of any community. On their own improvised flagpoles the squatters hoisted banners and pennants of every conceivable colour, they used everything that came to hand, the flags of foreign countries, of sports clubs, of various associations, under the aegis of the symbol of the fatherland hoisted right at the top, there were even bedspreads hanging from the windows in admirable imitation of these decorations.

However, an adversative co-ordinating conjunction which invariably denotes opposition, restriction or difference, and which, applied to this situation, reminds us that even the things that are good for some are precisely those which disadvantage others, the savage occupation of these hotels was the drop of water which caused the disquiet gripping the rich and powerful from the outset to overflow. Many of them, afraid that the Peninsula might sink with great loss of property and life, had fled at once with the exodus of tourists, which obviously does not mean that the former were foreigners in their own country, although there are various degrees in which people can belong to the country which is naturally and administratively theirs, as history has shown time and time again.

Now, under the general condemnation of social outrages, universal more than general, leaving aside the incongruous attitude of that insignificant Neapolitan newspaper, there occurred a second emigration, massive, so much so that one feels justified in thinking that it had been carefully planned when it became clear to all that the wounds with which Europe had been inflicted would never heal, that the physical structure of the Peninsula, who would ever have believed it, had split just where it seemed strongest. The huge bank accounts suddenly dwindled to a bare minimum, a token sum remained, about five hundred escudos in Portugal, about five hundred pesetas in Spain, or perhaps a little more, current accounts were practically wiped out, deposit accounts cleared with some loss of interest, and everything, the whole lot, gold, silver, precious stones, jewels, works of art, bonds, everything was carried off by the strong gust of wind that swept over the sea, in the thirty-two directions of the compass, the personal property of the fugitives, in the hope of recovering the rest one day, with time and patience. Clearly these great removals could not be achieved within twenty-four hours, but a week was all that was needed for the social physiognomy of these two Iberian countries to be modified radically from top to bottom, from side to side. Any observer unaware of the facts and motives, who might have allowed himself to be deceived by superficial appearances, would have come to the conclusion that the Portuguese and Spaniards had suddenly been reduced to poverty from one minute to the next, when, strictly speaking, all that had really happened was that the rich had gone away, and without them the statistics soon showed a dramatic decline.

To those observers who can see an entire Olympus of gods and goddesses where there are nothing but passing clouds, or to those who have Thundering Jupiter before their eyes but refer to him as atmospheric vapour, we shall never tire of pointing out that it is not enough to speak of circumstances, with their bipolar division into precedents and consequences, as one does to reduce the mental effort, but rather that it is necessary to consider what is infallibly situated between the former and the latter, let us spell it out in the right order, time, place, motive, means, person, deed, manner, for unless we measure and ponder everything, we are bound to make some fatal mistake in the first opinion we offer. Man is undoubtedly an intelligent being, but not as intelligent as one would like, and this is a proof and confession of humility which should always begin at home, as one says of charity in the proper sense of the word, before you reproach us.

They arrived in Lisbon as night was falling, at that hour when the gentle light fills souls with sweet remorse, now one sees how right that admirable judge of sensations and impressions was when he affirmed that landscape was a state of mind, what he was not able to tell us was what it looked like in the days when there was nothing but Pithecanthropus in the world, as yet with little soul, and not just little but confused as well. Thousands of years later, and thanks to improvements, Pedro Orce could now recognize in the apparent melancholy of the city the faithful image of his own intimate sadness. He had grown accustomed to the company of these Portuguese who had come to look for him in those inhospitable parts where he was born and lived, soon they would have to go their separate ways, each man to his own destination, not even families can resist the erosion of necessity, so what are simple acquaintances to do, friends of recent vintage and tender roots.

Deux Chevaux crossed the bridge slowly, at the lowest speed permitted, to give the Spaniard time to admire the beauty of the views of land and sea, and also the impressive feat of engineering which links the two banks of the river, this construction, we are referring to the sentence, is periphrastic, used here to avoid repeating the word bridge, which would result in a solecism, of the pleonastic or redundant kind. In the various arts, and *par excellence* in that of writing, the shortest distance between two points, even if close to each other, has never been nor will be, nor is, what is known as a straight line, never, never, to put it strongly and emphatically in response to any doubts, and to silence them once and for all. The travellers were so absorbed in the wonders of the city and thrilled by this prodigious achievement that they did not even notice how

83

the starlings suddenly took fright. Inebriated by the altitude, dangerously skimming the enormous pillars that rose from the waters to support the sky, on this side the city with its windowpanes aflame, beyond the sea and the sun, and below the great river flowing past, like a sluggish current of lava burning beneath the ashes, the birds abruptly changed course, with a rapid, successive flapping of wings, and it was as if the earth were revolving round the bridge, the north becoming east and then south, the south west and then north, where in the world shall we end up one day when we ourselves are forced to move just as much or even more. As we have already stated, men, even when they see these things, fail to understand them, nor did they understand them on this occasion.

They were halfway across the bridge when Pedro Orce murmured, Nice city, words as amiable as these call for no reply, except perhaps for a modest, Yes, isn't it. There would still be enough time to leave Pedro Orce settled in a hotel and continue their journey, at least as far as the town in Ribatejo where José Anaiço lives, and where Joaquim Sassa could if he wished spend another night beneath the fig tree, but it would have been impolite to abandon their visitor, so the two Portuguese mutually agreed to remain there for a few days, sufficient time for the Spaniard to get to know the city and once back in Orce to make his own the words of that old saying which innocently boasts, Never to have seen Lisbon's fair city is to have missed something pretty, blessed be God for having given us rhymes without denying us His blessings.

Joaquim Sassa and José Anaiço are not short of money, they gathered what they had for their excursion across the border and back, and they were still able to economize, as we know, sleeping on one occasion under the moonlight, on another spending the night at the home of an Andalusian pharmacist, and, in the Algarve, by taking advantage of the anarchy and disorder, they were not presented with a bill for their stay in a hotel. In Lisbon, where we have already arrived, hotels have only been besieged and occupied on the outskirts of the city, while the more central hotels were protected by a combination of two discouraging factors, firstly, this being the capital, as in most countries this is where you are likely to find the greatest concentration of the forces of law and order, or repression, secondly, that timidity peculiar to the city-dweller, who often becomes uneasy and withdraws upon sensing that he is being observed by the neighbour who is judging him, and vice versa, the protozoa in the drop of water certainly disturb the lens and the eye

84

which from behind observes and disturbs them. Owing to the lack of clients, nearly all the hotels had closed their doors to carry out repairs, this was their excuse, but some continued to function, offering low-season tariffs and special reductions, to the point where some large families seriously considered abandoning their houses for which they were being charged colossal rents, and taking up residence in the Méridien or some such hotel. The aspirations of the three travellers did not rise to such a dramatic change of status, which is why they decided to install themselves in a modest hotel, at the bottom of the Rua do Alecrim, on the left as you go down, the name of which has no bearing on this story, once was enough and perhaps not even necessary.

Starlings are starlings, and that name is also used for people who are frivolous and giddy, in other words people who rarely reflect on their actions, who are incapable of foreseeing or imagining anything beyond the here and now, which is not incompatible with certain acts of generosity, even the sacrifice of their own lives, as we saw in the episode at the frontier, when so many tender little bodies dropped dead, shedding their blood for the cause of others, remember we're speaking about birds, not people. But frivolity and giddiness is the least one can say about those thousands of birds who foolishly go and perch on a hotel roof, attracting the attention of the crowd and the police, of the ornithologists and gourmets who relish a tasty meal of little fried birds, so betraying the presence of the three men who, despite having no guilt weighing on their conscience, have become the target of some unwelcome attention from the authorities. For unknown to the travellers, the Portuguese press, on the page that regularly features unusual events, had reported the irresistible attack waged by the starlings on the unsuspecting guards at the border, invoking, as one might have suspected, though scarcely original, the Hitchcock film about birds that we mentioned earlier. The newspapers, radio and television, informed immediately about the strange happenings at the Cais do Sodré, sent reporters, photographers and video technicians to the scene, which might have had no other consequences, beyond enriching the folklore at Lisbon, if the methodical and, why not say it, scientific mind of a journalist had not led him to consider a possible connection between the starlings outside on the roof, and the guests in the hotel, either permanent or simply passing through. Unaware of the danger which was literally hovering over their heads, Joaquim Sassa, José Anaiço and Pedro Orce, each in his own room, unpacked the little luggage they were carrying, within a few minutes they would be down on the street, having decided to take a quick look round the city, until it was time for dinner. Now then, at this precise moment the quick-witted journalist is consulting the guest list, he goes through the names registered there, and suddenly two of those names begin to set the wheels of memory in motion, Joaquim Sassa, Pedro Orce, he would not be much of a journalist had those names escaped his eye, the same thing might have occurred to him with another name, Ricardo Reis, but the book where that name was once registered many, many years ago, is stored away in the archives in the attic, covered in dust, written on a page that may never come to light, and if it should, probably the name will be illegible, because the line will be faded, or even the entire page, that's one of the effects of time, to blot out everything. To this present day there has been no greater achievement in the art of hunting than to kill two rabbits at one blow, from now on the number of rabbits within the scope of the hunter's skill will be increased from two to three, this will mean revising all the books of proverbs, so where you see two, read three, and perhaps we won't stop here.

Requested to come down to reception, then installed in the lounge, before the great mirror of truth, Joaquim Sassa and Pedro Orce, pressed by the journalists had no other choice but to confirm that they were, respectively, the one who threw the stone into the sea and the living seismograph. But there are the starlings, it's surely not by chance that so many starlings have gathered here, the observant reporter remarked, whereupon José Anaiço, loyal to his friends and true to the facts, made a statement, The starlings are accompanying me. Most of the questions addressed to Joaquim Sassa coincided, respectively, with the dialogue imagined between him and the civil governor, which explains why they aren't repeated here, nor the corresponding answers, but Pedro Orce, who hadn't exactly been a prophet in his own country, talked at length about recent events in his life, Yes sir, he could still feel the earth tremor, deep and intense, as if his bones were vibrating, and in Granada, Seville and Madrid he had undergone multiple tests to check his emotions and intellect, his sensory reactions and movements, and here he was, prepared to subject himself to similar or different checks if the Portuguese authorities should consider them necessary. Meanwhile, darkness had fallen, the starlings responsible for this investigation had dispersed into the trees of the nearby gardens, the journalists, having run out of questions and sated their curiosity, departed with their cameras and flashlights, but this did not restore peace in the hotel, waiters and porters invented excuses for coming to the reception desk and looking into the lounge to see what these freaks were like.

Worn out by the endless turmoil, the three friends decided not to go out but to dine in the hotel. Pedro Orce was worried about the consequences of having allowed himself to get carried away and having talked so much, After being warned repeatedly not to say a word about my situation, they won't like it in Spain when they find out, but perhaps if I stay on here for a few days they will forget all about me. José Anaiço was doubtful, Tomorrow our story will appear in all the newspapers, they might even give it out on television this evening, and those newscasters on the radio won't keep their mouths shut, they never get tired, and Joaquim Sassa retorted, Even so, among us three, yours is the best situation, you can always argue that you're not to blame if the starlings follow you, you don't whistle to them or feed them, but we're both in a tight spot, people stare at Pedro Orce as if he were some crank, the Portuguese scientists won't want to lose their guinea pig, and they won't give up on me with this story about the stone, You two have the car, Pedro Orce reminded them, you can leave at the crack of dawn, or even tonight, I'm staying on, if they ask me where you've gone, I'll say I don't know, Now it's far too late, the moment I appear on television someone will telephone from the town where I live just to say that they know me, that I'm the local schoolmaster, and that they've been suspicious for some time, some people thirst for glory, this is what José Anaiço had to say, and he added, It's preferable that we should stick together, we'll say very little and they'll soon get tired.

As predicted, there was a full report on the final news bulletin on television, they showed the starlings in flight, the façade of the hotel, the manager making statements we know to be false, as will soon become clear, These events are without precedence in the history of this hotel, and the three prodigies, Pedro, José and Joaquim, answering questions.

As always, when it is thought necessary to have the additional backing of some reliable authority, there was an expert in the studio, in this instance a specialist in the modern discipline of dynamic psychology, who, among other theories about the essence of the matter, declared that there was always the possibility that one was dealing with out-and-out charlatans. It's well known, he declared, that in moments of crisis such as this, you can always rely on some impostor or other turning up, individuals who tell tales and are out to take advantage of the gullible masses, often intent upon destabilizing the political status quo or assisting plans to gain power in the long term. If people believe him, we've had it, Joaquim Sassa observed, And what about the starlings, what's your opinion about the starlings, the announcer wanted to know, This is indeed a fascinating enigma, either the person the birds are following is carrying some irresistible bait, or it's a question of collective hypnosis, It can't be easy to hypnotize birds, On the contrary, a hen can be hypnotized with a simple piece of chalk, even a child can do it, But, here we have two or three thousand starlings all at once, how could they fly if they were hypnotized, Observe that the flock, for each bird that forms part of it, is already a hypnotic agent, agent and result simultaneously, Allow me to remind you that some of our viewers will have difficulty in following such technical jargon, Well, to put it more simply, I'd say that the entire group tends to constitute itself in homogeneous hypnosis, I doubt whether that will be any easier to understand, but I'd like to thank you just the same for coming along to the studio, there are certain to be further developments and then we shall have another opportunity to discuss the matter in greater depth, I'm at your disposal, the expert grinned. The one person who was not amused was Joaquim Sassa who muttered, The man's a fool, He certainly looks like one, but there are times when even fools have to be heeded, José Anaiço replied, and Pedro Orce confided, I didn't understand a word, this was the first time the Portuguese tongue had left him completely baffled, if we take the meaning of his words literally, what a splendid conversation there must have been between those ancient Portuguese warriors Viriato and Nuno Alvares Pereira, heroes of the same fatherland, as we're led to believe. While these grave matters were being discussed in the hotel lounge, in his private office the manager was receiving a delegation of restaurateurs from the vicinity who had come to offer him a deal. How much would you charge us to set up some nets on the roof, sooner or later the starlings will be back and settle up there again, we don't want to put nets on the trees, within everyone's reach, that would be just like getting other men's wives pregnant, these are the kind of men who believe that the only intimate sense of things is that they have no intimate sense, the manager wavers, he's afraid he might damage the roof-tiles, but he finally agrees, suggests a figure, That's a lot of money, the others say, and start haggling over the price.

Early next morning, another delegation of solemn-faced gentlemen, neatly turned out, extremely formal, came to ask Joaquim Sassa and Pedro Orce if they would be so good as to accompany them, they were acting on government orders, among the officials there was also a counsellor from the Spanish Embassy who greeted Pedro Orce, but with such manifest hauteur as could only stem from outraged patriotism. They wished to carry out a brief investigation, they explained, all very straightforward, the time it takes for a routine enquiry which will be added to the already voluminous dossier on the rupturing of the Peninsula, to all appearances irremediable, if we take into account its continuous displacement, fatal, in other words. They ignored José Anaiço, probably doubting that he could be endowed with powers of attraction and enticement comparable only with those of the Pied Piper of Hamelin, besides, the starlings are nowhere to be seen, they are flying back and forth, all together, getting to know the city, inside the nets that had been treacherously set up on the roof only four stray sparrows lay trapped awaiting another fate, but destiny decreed a different end to their life, What fate, asks an ironic voice, and thanks to this unexpected intervention we learn that there is more than one fate, contrary to what we are told, in *fados* and folk music, No one escapes his fate, it is always possible that some other person's fate might befall us, that's what happened to the sparrows, they met the fate of the starlings.

José Anaiço remained quietly in the hotel, awaiting the return of his companions, he ordered some newspapers, all the interviews were reported on the front page, with explosive photographs and dramatic headlines, Enigmas Baffle Science, The Unknown Forces of the Mind, Three Dangerous Men, The Mystery of the Hotel Bragança, we had been careful not to give any name, only to find it published by some treacherous reporter, Will the Spaniard Be Extradited, question mark, We're in a Fine Old Mess, this is not a headline but what José Anaiço was thinking. The hours passed, it was time for lunch, from Joaquim Sassa and Pedro Orce there was no news or message, have they been arrested, thrown into prison, a man loses his appetite with so much worry. I don't even know where they've taken them, how stupid of me, I should have asked, what am I talking about, what I should have done was to go with them, not to have left them on their own, calm down, even if I'd wanted to go, they probably wouldn't have let me, but how can one be sure, I was quite happy to be left out of it, cowardice is worse than an octopus, the octopus can contract and extend its arms, cowardice is only capable of contracting them, from these barbed words one can see just how annoyed José Anaiço is with himself, but who can tell where sincerity lies in these contradictory impulses and thoughts, best to wait, as in all human affairs, to see what he does. First he went to ask the manager whether he had heard any revealing remark, an address, a name, but the manager replied, Nothing at all sir, I didn't know any of the gentlemen, I was seeing them for the first time, and that goes for the two Portuguese as well as the Spaniard, suddenly José Anaiço had a brainwave, and about time too, he would go to the Spanish Embassy, the Embassy is bound to know, and then he had another brainwave, they never came singly, the press, of course, he need only turn to one of those newspapers and within a few hours all the sleuths of the press whether they be called Argos, Holmes or Lupin would trail the missing men, necessity is indeed the mother of invention, in this instance the father is called caution, but not always.

Wasting no time, José Anaiço went up to his room, he wanted to change his shoes, to brush his teeth, these mundane things are not incompatible with a resolute spirit, take Othello, for example, who, suffering from a cold and without realizing what he was doing foolishly blew his nose before killing Desdemona, who, for her part, notwithstanding her dark premonitions, didn't lock her door, for a wife never denies her husband even if she knows he is about to strangle her, and besides, Desdemona knew very well that the room only had three walls, now in this present drama José Anaiço is cleaning his teeth with a brush and rinsing out his mouth when he hears someone knocking, Who is it, he asks, although it doesn't sound like his voice the tone is one of happy anticipation, Joaquim Sassa is about to reply, We're back, but the deception was short-lived, May I come in, so it's the maid after all, One moment, he finished rinsing his mouth, wiped his hands and his mouth, dried them, and finally went to open the door. The maid is an ordinary hotel employee with such individual traits and so specific a role that this is the only moment in her life in which she will impinge ever so superficially, and only for as long as it takes to deliver a simple message, on the existence of José Anaiço and his companions, both present and future, this often happens in the theatre and in life, we need someone to come and knock on our door simply to tell us, There is a lady downstairs looking for you, sir. José Anaiço is taken aback and shows his surprise. Looking for me, and the maid adds what she had felt would be necessary, The lady asked to speak to all three of you, but since the others aren't here, She must be a journalist, José Anaiço thought to himself before replying, I'll be down at once. The maid retreated like someone withdrawing from life, we won't need her any more, there's no reason why we should remember her, not even with indifference. She came, knocked on the door, delivered the message, which for some strange reason wasn't given over the telephone, perhaps life enjoys cultivating from time to time this sense of the dramatic, if the telephone rings we think, What can it be, if someone's knocking at our door, we think to ourselves, Who can it be, and we give voice to our thoughts by asking, Who is it, We already know it was the maid, but the question was only half answered, perhaps not even that, which is why José Anaiço is pensive as he descends the staircase. Who can it be, he has forgotten his suspicion that it might be a journalist, some of our thoughts are like this, they serve only to occupy, out of anticipation, the place of others that would give us much more food for thought.

The hotel is so very peaceful, like an empty house bereft of restless activity, but it has not yet aged from neglect, there are still the echoes of footsteps and voices, a sob, a whispered farewell that lingers on the upper landing. The manager is on his feet, behind the counter hangs the key-rack with its pigeon-holes for messages, letters and bills, he is writing in a ledger or copying figures from it on to a sheet of paper, the type of man who keeps himself busy even when there is not much work to be done. As José Anaiço is about to pass, the manager nods in the direction of the lounge, and José Anaiço responds with an assenting nod, I know, is what this nod implies, while the first nod had implied at greater length, There's a lady in there waiting to see you. José Anaiço pauses in the entrance to the lounge, he sees a young woman, a mere girl, it can only be her, there's no one else here, although she's sitting in the shade of the curtains over the windows, she seems pleasant, even pretty, she is wearing blue slacks and a matching jacket, in a colour which might be described as indigo, she might or might not be a journalist, but beside the chair where she is sitting there is a small suitcase and on her lap a stick which is neither large nor small, somewhere between a metre and a metre and a half in length, the effect is disturbing, a woman dressed like this doesn't walk through the city carrying a stick in her hand, She can't be a journalist, José Anaiço thought to himself, at least there's no sign of the tools of that profession, notebook, ball-point pen, tape-recorder.

The woman got up, and this gesture was unexpected, for according to the rules of etiquette and good manners, a lady should remain seated until the gentleman approaches and greets her before extending her hand or offering her cheek, and depending on her confidence, degree of intimacy and disposition, the lady's smile will be polite, insinuating, conniving, or revealing. This gesture, well perhaps not so much the gesture as the fact that four paces away a woman is standing there waiting, or, rather the sudden awareness that time has stopped until someone makes the first move, it is true that the mirror is a witness, but of an earlier moment, in the mirror José Anaiço and the woman are still two strangers, not on this side, here, for they are about to know each other, know each other already. This gesture, this gesture which could not be fully described earlier, caused the wooden floor to sway like a deck, the pitching of a ship amidst the waves, slow and wide, an impression not to be confused with the familiar tremor that Pedro Orce talks about, José Anaiço's bones do not shake, but his whole body has felt, physically and materially felt, that the Peninsula, so called out of habit and convenience, is really and truly sailing away, before he only knew it from external observation, now he can actually feel it. And so, because of this woman, unless it were because of the hour she turned up, for most important of all is the hour when things happen, José Anaiço ceased to be merely the unwilling lure of demented birds. He goes up to her, and this movement, launched in the same direction, will be added to the force that pushes, without remedy or resistance, the image of the raft of which the Hotel Bragança, at this very moment, is the figurehead and forecastle, if you'll forgive the blatant inappropriateness of these terms. Is that too much to ask.

My friends aren't here, José Anaiço explains, Some scientists came this morning and took them away for questioning, I'm beginning to get worried at the delay, in fact I was just getting ready to go out and look for them, José Anaiço is aware that there was no need for all these words to say what mattered, but he can not restrain himself. She responds, and her voice is pleasing, low but clear. What I have to say can be said just as well to one of you as to all three, in fact this might make it easier to explain things more clearly. Her eyes are the colour of a new sky, What is a new sky, what colour might that be, where did I fish out that idea, José Anaiço thinks to himself, while saying in a loud voice, Please be seated, there's no need to stand. She sat down, he sat down, Are you called José

92

Anaiço, My name is Joana Carda, Delighted to meet you. They did not shake hands, that would look silly now that they were seated, besides, in order to shake hands they would both have to crane forward in their chairs, even sillier, or, only he would have to do so, which would halve the silliness, if being half silly were not exactly the same as being completely silly. She is indeed pretty, and her hair, which is almost black, shouldn't clash with her eyes, the colour of a new sky by day, the colour of a new sky by night, they go well together, What can I do for you, his intimate thoughts were translated by this polite enquiry. I'm not sure if it's safe to speak here, Joana Carda murmured, We're alone, no one can hear us, But people are watching, look out. Walking in a somewhat unnatural manner, the manager passed in front of the entrance to the lounge, he passed then passed once more, seemingly absorbed, as if he had just invented a new task, because the previous one had proved useless. José Anaiço glared at him but to no avail, he lowered his voice, making their conversation look even more suspicious, I can't invite you up to my room, besides attracting attention, it's almost certainly forbidden for guests to receive visitors in their rooms. That wouldn't bother me, I shouldn't feel threatened by someone who obviously has no intention of assaulting me, In fact, nothing could be further from my mind, especially when you're carrying a weapon. They both smiled, but there was something forced about their smile, a certain inhibition, a sudden disquiet, truly, the conversation had become much too intimate considering that they had only known each other for three minutes, and only by name. In an emergency this stick could be useful, Joana Carda observed, but that's not the reason why I carry it with me, to tell the truth, the stick is carrying me. This revelation, so unexpected, cleared the air, levelled the pressure, that of the atmosphere as well as that of the blood. Joana Carda rested the elm branch on her lap, waited for his reply, José Anaiço finally spoke, We'd better go out, we can chat on the street, in a café, or if you wish in a public park. She reached for her suitcase, he took it from her, We can leave this in my room, along with the stick, The stick stays with me, and the suitcase, too, it might be better not to come back here. As you wish, what a pity your suitcase is so small, otherwise you could have put the stick inside, Not everything is made to square with something else, Joana Carda replied, a somewhat obvious statement, which nonetheless embraces a world of meaning.

As they were leaving, José Anaiço said to the manager, If my friends should arrive, tell them I'll be back soon, Yes sir, leave it to me, the man replied, without taking his eyes off Joana Carda, but there was no desire in his eyes, only that vague suspicion one finds in all hotel managers. They went down the stairway, at the bottom, on the finial of the bannister, there was an ornamental statuette in bronze, modelled on a knight or a page from some opera, here is an effigy that would look right, with its illuminated globe, on any of the great Portuguese or Galician capes, that of São Vicente, Espichel, Roca, or Finisterre, and others of less importance, which nonetheless have just as much work to do breaking the waves, but the destiny of this knight is to be ignored, perhaps once upon a time someone may have looked at him closely, but not Joana Carda or José Anaiço, undoubtedly because they have greater worries on their mind, although, if asked, they probably wouldn't know what they are. Anyone in that hotel with its cool atmosphere and secular penumbra cannot imagine just how hot it is out in the street. This is August, as you may recall, the climate hasn't changed just because the Peninsula has travelled a mere one hundred and fifty kilometres, assuming that the speed has remained steady as reported by the National Radio of Spain, no more than five days have passed and it already seems like a year. José Anaiço remarked, as one would expect, To go around in this heat, carrying a suitcase in one hand and a stick in the other, isn't much fun, we'll be worn out in no time, better to go into a café and have a cool drink, Better still to find a park, a bench in some quiet, shady corner, There's a park nearby, at the Praça de Dom Luís, do you know it, I'm not from Lisbon, but I know it, Oh, you're not from Lisbon, José Anaiço repeated idly. They descended the Rua do Alecrim, he was carrying the suitcase and stick, people on the street wouldn't think much of him were he not to carry the suitcase or have much respect for her if she were to carry the stick, for we are all such relentless busybodies, malicious when we get the chance and for no good reason. Reacting to José Anaiço's cry of surprise, Joana Carda simply told him that she had arrived that same day, by train, and had gone straight to the hotel, the rest we are now about to learn.

They are seated, fortunately in the shade of some trees, and he has asked her, What then brought you to Lisbon, why did you come to look for us, and she told him, Because it must be true that you and your friends have something to do with what is happening, Happening, to whom, You know very well what I'm referring to, the Peninsula, the breaking up of the Pyrenees, this voyage, the like of which has never been seen before. Sometimes I think the same, that we're to blame, at other times I think we must all be mad, A planet that goes round a star, turning and turning, one minute day, the next night, one minute cold, the next hot, and an almost empty space where there are gigantic things that have no name other than the one we give them, and a time that no one can really fathom, all this too must be crazy, Are you an astronomer, José Anaiço asked her, suddenly remembering Maria Dolores, the anthropologist from Granada, I'm neither an astronomer nor a fool, Forgive my rudeness, we're all rather nervous, words don't express what they're meant to, we either talk too much or too little, do forgive me, You're forgiven, I probably strike you as being rather sceptical because nothing has ever happened to me except the starlings, although, Although, Not so long ago, in the hotel, when I saw you in the lounge, I felt as if I were on a ship at sea for the first time, Well I saw you as if you were coming from a distance, And yet you were only three or four paces away.

Appearing from everywhere on the horizon, the starlings suddenly flew on to the trees in the park. From the nearby streets, people came running, looking upwards, pointing, They're back again, José Anaiço sighed impatiently, and worst of all, we won't be able to speak with all these people around. At this moment, the starlings all took flight together, they covered the park with a great fluttering, a black cloud, people were shouting, some with annoyance, others with excitement, yet others with fear, Joana Carda and José Anaiço stared unable to grasp what was happening, then the huge flock dwindled away to form a wedge, a wing, an arrow, and after circling rapidly three times, the starlings disappeared in a southerly direction, crossed the river, vanished into the distance, over the horizon. The spectators gathered there, inquisitive and frightened, let out cries of amazement, of disappointment too, within minutes the park was deserted, the heat was back, on the bench sat a man and a woman all alone, they had an elm branch and a suitcase. José Anaiço said, I don't think they'll ever come back, and Joana Carda replied, Let me tell you what happened to me.

Once the seriousness of the facts related had been established, prudence decreed that Joana Carda should not lodge in that famous hotel where nets had been spread out on the roof, waiting in vain for the starlings to settle there. It was a wise decision on her part, and at least avoided any further modification to the proverb about killing two birds with one stone, in other words, it prevented this woman well versed in metaphysical skirmishing from falling into the same trap as the three suspects, if they have not already been incriminated. Putting what has been written into somewhat less baroque language and using less convoluted syntax, Joana Carda installed herself further up the road in the Hotel Borges, right in the heart of the Chiado, with her suitcase and elm branch, which unfortunately is neither telescopic nor easily packed away, so that people stare in amazement when she passes, and the receptionist at the desk, jesting to disguise his genuine curiosity, but without being impolite, makes a discreet reference to wands which are not walking sticks, Joana Carda responds with silence, after all, there is no law to prohibit guests from taking a branch of holm oak into their room, much less a thin little stick, not even two metres long, which fits easily into the lift and can be neatly stored away in a corner without even being noticed.

José Anaiço and Joana Carda carried on their conversation until well after sunset, can you imagine, they discussed the matter from every possible angle, and invariably came to the same conclusion, since it was all so unnatural, things were happening as if a new state of normality had taken the place of what once passed as normal, but without any convulsions, shocks or changes of colour, which, moreover, even were they to occur, would explain nothing. The mistake is entirely ours, with this taste for drama and tragedy, this need for the sublime and the theatrical, we marvel, for example, at the sight of a birth, all the moaning and groaning, and shouting, the body opening up like a ripe fig to expel another body, and this is undoubtedly marvellous, but no more marvellous than what we could not perceive, the burning discharge inside the woman, the fatal marathon, and then this protracted formation of a human being by itself, clearly with some assistance, who will that be, and to go no further, the one who is writing this, inevitably ignorant of what happened to him then, and let us be frank, not very clear about what is happening to him now. Joana Carda neither knows nor is able to say any more, The stick was lying there on the ground, I drew a line with it, if these things are happening because of what I did, who am I to swear it, you must go there and see for yourself. They went on debating and discussing and darkness was falling when they went their separate ways, she to the Hotel Borges up the road, he to the Hotel Bragança further down, and José Anaiço is smitten with remorse, he did not have the courage to try and find out what happened to his friends, ungrateful fellow, a woman has only to appear and tell him some fairy tale or other for him to spend nearly the entire afternoon listening to her, You should go there and see for yourself, she repeated, slightly modifying the phrase, perhaps to convince him once and for all, repeating oneself in a different manner is often the only solution. At the entrance to his hotel, José Anaiço raises his eyes, no sign of any starlings, the winged shadow that passed, fleeting and gentle as a discreet caress, a bat chasing mosquitoes and moths. The little nobleman on the bannister has his lamp lit, he is there to welcome guests, but José Anaiço does not even give him as much as a weary glance, he is certainly in for a bad night if Pedro Orce and Joaquim Sassa have not returned.

They have returned. They are waiting in the hotel lounge, seated in the same chairs in which Joana Carda and José Anaiço had sat, and to think that there are people who do not believe in coincidences, when one is constantly discovering coincidences in the world and begins to wonder if coincidences are not the very logic of this world. José Anaiço pauses in the doorway of the lounge, it's as if everything were about to be repeated, but no, not just yet, the wooden floor has remained firm, the distance of four paces is no more than a distance of four paces, there is no interstellar void, no leap of death or life, legs moved by themselves, then mouths spoke to say what one might expect, Were you out looking for us, Joaquim Sassa asked, but José Anaiço cannot give a simple answer to such a simple question, Yes or No, both answers would be true, both would be false, he would need a great deal of time to explain, so he replied with a question of his own, as reasonable and natural as the other, Where the devil have you two been all this time. One can see that Pedro Orce is tired, and little wonder, the years, whatever people might say to the contrary, take their toll, but even a young and vigorous man would have come away shattered from the hands of the doctors, one examination after another, analyses, X-rays, questionnaires, tiny hammer-blows on the tendons, hearing tests, eye tests, electroencephalograms, no wonder his eyelids feel as heavy as lead, I must lie down, he says, these Portuguese specialists have almost killed me off. It was decided there and then that Pedro Orce should retire to his room until dinnertime, when he could come down and have a little broth and breast of chicken despite his poor appetite, he felt as if his stomach were still full of X-ray pap, But you didn't have your stomach X-rayed, Joaquim Sassa reminded him, That's true, but I feel as if I had, Pedro Orce replied, his smile as wan as a withered rose. Have a good rest, José Anaiço suggested, Joaquim and I will dine at some nearby restaurant, we'll talk things over, and when we come back we'll knock on your door and see how you're feeling, Don't knock, I'll almost certainly be asleep, all I want right now is to sleep without any interruption until tomorrow morning, and off he went shuffling his feet. Poor fellow, what a nice mess we've got him into, this comment was made by José Anaiço, They've also been tormenting me with their cross-examining and endless questions, but that's nothing when compared with what they've done to him, shall I tell you what this reminds me of, a story I read years ago, entitled At The Mercy Of The Quacks, Do you mean the story by Rodrigues Miguéis, That's the one.

Once outside, they decided to go for a long drive in Deux Chevaux, they had plenty of time before dinner, and they could chat freely. People are totally bewildered, began Joaquim Sassa, and if they're latching on to us like this, that's because they've nothing else to go on, or rather, now they're beginning to have almost too much, probably because of the news on television yesterday, and today's reports in the press, did you see the headlines in the evening paper, people are taking leave of their senses, they're turning up from everywhere claiming to have felt the earth trembling, saying that they threw pebbles into the river and that a nymph came out from the water and that their pet budgies are making strange noises, It's always the same, news creates news, but we probably won't see our budgies again, Why not, what's happened, I think they've gone away, Simply gone away, just like that, after following you everywhere all week, So it would appear, Did you see them, Yes, I saw them, they crossed the river heading south and never returned, How did you know they were going away, were you standing near the window in your room, No, I was in a public park nearby, Instead of being there, you might have tried to find out where we were, That was the idea, but then I strolled into the park and stayed there, Taking the fresh air, Speaking to a woman, Well what about that, a fine friend you've turned out to be, here we are suffering the horrors of Calvary and you're chatting up a woman, having got nowhere with the archaeologist from Granada, you're making up for lost time, She wasn't an archaeologist, she was an anthropologist, What's the difference, This one is an astronomer, You're joking, To be honest, I don't know what she does, this business about her being an astronomer stems from something I said to her, Well, that's your affair, and I've no reason to interfere in other people's lives, You've every reason, what she told me concerns both of us, I know what you're going to tell me, she's also been throwing pebbles, No, Then she can feel the earth shaking, You still haven't got it, Her canary has changed its colour, If you start being ironic, you'll never find out, Forgive me, to tell you the truth, I feel very annoyed, I cannot forget that you didn't bother to come and look for us, I've already explained to you that that was my intention, but then this woman appeared just as I was getting ready to leave, my idea was to start making enquiries at the Spanish Embassy, then she appeared and she told me this story, she arrived carrying a stick in one hand, a suitcase in the other, she was wearing blue slacks and a jacket to match, she had black hair and the whitest of skin, her eyes strange and difficult to describe, These are interesting details for the history of the Peninsula, I suppose you're now going to tell me that the woman is beautiful, Yes, she is, Young, Yes, she does look young, although not exactly a girl. From the way you're talking, you've become infatuated, Infatuation is a big word, but it's true that I could feel the floor of the hotel lounge shaking, I've never heard it described like that before, Lay off, Unless you've been drinking and you don't remember, Lay off, will you, All right, I'll lay off, but what did Lady Strange Eyes want, and what kind

99

of stick was that, The branch of an elm tree, I know precious little about trees, what's an elm branch, The elm is the common word for *ulmus*, and if you'll allow me to digress for a moment, I must say you're pretty skilled when it comes to asking questions. Joaquim Sassa laughed, I must have learned something from those clever fellows who were pestering me earlier on, I'm sorry, do finish telling me about the woman, does she have any other name apart from Strange Eyes, She's called Joana Carda, Now that she's been introduced, let's get to the heart of the matter, Imagine that you find a stick on the road and in a moment of distraction, or without any conscious aim, you draw a line on the ground, As a boy I did that quite often, And what happened, Nothing, nothing ever happened unfortunately, Now imagine that by some magical effect or similar cause, this line produced a crack in the Pyrenees, and that the said Pyrenees split open from top to bottom and the Iberian Peninsula began to sail out to sea, Your Joana is mad, There have been other mad Joanas, but this one hasn't come to Lisbon to tell us that because she drew a line on the ground the Peninsula broke away from Europe, Thank God there's still some common sense left in the world. What she does say is that the line she drew can't be made to disappear, either with the wind or by pouring water over it, by scraping or sweeping it with a brush, or by trampling it underfoot, Nonsense, As nonsensical as your being the most powerful weight-putter of all time, six kilos hurled five hundred metres without cheating, even the great Hercules, demi-god that he was, couldn't have beaten your record, Are you trying to tell me that a line drawn on the ground, you said on the ground, didn't you, can resist wind, water, and a sweeping brush, And that even if you rake the soil, the line reappears, That's impossible, You're not being very original, I also used that word, and Little Joana Strange Eyes simply replied, You Must Go There And See For Yourself or You Should Go There And See For Yourself, I can't remember her exact words. Joaquim Sassa fell silent, at this point they were passing through Cruz Quebrada, which means Broken Cross. What sacrilege might these words conceal, words which have now become so innocuous, and José Anaiço said, All this would be absurd if it weren't happening, whereupon Joaquim Sassa asked, But is it really happening.

There was still some daylight, not much, barely enough to be able to glimpse the sea as far as the horizon, from this summit where one descends to Caxias you can judge the scale of these immense waters, perhaps that's why José Anaiço murmured, It's different, and Joaquim Sassa, who had no idea what he was referring to, asked him, What's different, The water, the water is different, life transforms itself like this, it has changed and we haven't even noticed, we were tranquil and thought we hadn't changed, an illusion, pure deception, we were moving on with life. The sea lashed with force against the parapet of the road, and no wonder, for these waves are also different, accustomed to having freedom of movement, without witnesses, except when some tiny vessel passes, not this Leviathan which is ploughing the ocean. José Anaiço suggested, Let's eat a little further on at Paço de Arcos, then we can return to the hotel, see how Pedro is, Poor chap, they would be the death of him. They parked Deux Chevaux in a side street, went in search of a restaurant, but, before entering, Joaquim Sassa said, During the enquiries and cross-examinations I heard something we'd never thought of, it was only a word but that was enough, the person who let it slip may have thought I wasn't listening, What are you talking about, Until now, the Peninsula, It isn't a peninsula, Then what the devil should we call it, it has virtually dislocated itself in a straight line, between the parallels thirty-six and forty-three, So what, You may be a good teacher in most subjects, but you're weak when it comes to geography, I don't understand, You'll understand at once if you remember that the Azores are situated between the parallels thirty-seven and forty, What the devil, Yes summon Old Nick, summon Old Nick, The Peninsula is about to collide with the islands, Precisely, It will be the greatest catastrophe in history, Perhaps, perhaps not, and, as you said yourself a short time ago, all this would be absurd if it weren't happening, now let's go and eat.

They found a place, sat down and ordered, Joaquim Sassa was starving, he pounced voraciously on the bread, the butter, the olives, the wine, with a smile that pleaded indulgence, This is the last meal of a man condemned to die, and some minutes passed before he asked, And the lady with the wand, where is she at this moment, She's staying at the Hotel Borges, the one on the Chiado, Oh, I thought she lived in Lisbon, No, she doesn't live in Lisbon, that much she did confide, without saying where she comes from, nor did I ask her, probably because I thought we would be accompanying her there, To do what, To examine the line on the ground, So you also have your doubts, I don't think I'm in any doubt, but I want to see the line with my own eyes, to touch it with my own hands, You're like the man with Platero the donkey, between the

Sierra Morena and the Sierra Aracena, If she's telling the truth, we'll see more than Roque Lozano, who discovers nothing but water when he reaches his destination, How do you know he was called Roque Lozano, I don't remember us asking him his name, the name of his donkey yes, but not his. I must have dreamed it, And what about Pedro, will he want to come with us, A man who can feel the ground trembling beneath his feet needs company, Like the man who felt the wooden floor swaying, Peace, Poor Deux Chevaux is becoming too small to carry so many people, four passengers with luggage even if they're only haversacks, and the car is old, poor thing, No one can hope to live beyond his last day, You're a prophet, About time you realized it, It looked as if our travels were over, that each of us would go home, back to our normal existence, Let's turn our back on these days and see what happens. So long as the Peninsula doesn't collide with the Azores, If that's the end that awaits us, until then our life is guaranteed.

They finished their dinner, resumed their journey without haste, at the slow pace of Deux Chevaux, there was little traffic on the road, probably because of the scarcity of petrol, they were fortunate in having a car with low consumption, But we could still run the risk of coming to a standstill somewhere or other, then our journey would really be over, Joaquim Sassa remarked, then suddenly remembering, he asked, Why did you say the starlings must have gone away, Anyone can tell the difference between farewell and goodbye, what I saw was a definite farewell, But I can't explain it, however there is a coincidence, the starlings went away the moment Joana appeared, Joana, That's her name, You could have said the lady, the woman, the girl, that's how male diffidence refers to the opposite sex, when to call them by their name might seem much too familiar, Compared with your wisdom, mine is rudimentary, but, as you've just seen, I spoke her name quite naturally, proof that my inner self has nothing to do with this matter, Unless, at heart, you're much more Machiavellian than you appear, trying to prove the opposite of what you really think or feel so that I may think what you think or feel is precisely what you only appear to be trying to prove, I don't know if I've made myself clear, You haven't, but no matter, clarity and obscurity cast the same shadow and light, obscurity is clear, clarity is obscure, and as for someone being able to say factually and precisely what he feels and thinks, don't you believe it, not because he doesn't want to, but because he cannot, Then why do people talk so much, Because that's all we can do, talk, perhaps not even talk, it's all a question of trial and error, The starlings went away, Joana arrived, one form of companionship went, another took its place, you should consider yourself fortunate, That remains to be seen.

At the hotel there was a message for Joaquim Sassa from Pedro Orce, his companion in torment, Don't disturb me, and another from Joana Carda, this time by telephone, for José Anaiço, So it is all true, he had not dreamed it. Over José Anaiço's shoulder, the voice of Joaquim Sassa seemed to be mocking him, Lady Strange Eyes assures you she's real, therefore don't waste your time dreaming about her tonight. They went upstairs to their rooms, José Anaiço said, Tomorrow, first thing in the morning, I'll call her to say we'll accompany her, if that's all right, Agreed, and don't pay too much attention to what I said, because as you've probably guessed, I'm jealous. To be jealous of what only appears to exist is a waste of effort. My wisdom secretly tells me that everything only appears to exist, nothing actually exists, we must be satisfied with that. Good night, prophet, Pleasant dreams, comrade.

People were neither aware nor even suspicious of what was going on, such was the secrecy with which governments and scientific institutions set about investigating the subtle movement that was carrying the Peninsula out to sea with enigmatic persistence and constancy. To discover how and why the Pyrenees had cracked was no longer a matter for discussion, any hope of redressing the situation was abandoned within days. Despite the vast amount of accumulated information, the computers coldly demanded fresh data or gave preposterous results, as in the case of the famous Massachusetts Institute of Technology, whose programmers blushed with embarrassment upon receiving on their terminals the peremptory decree, Too Much Exposure to the Sun, would you believe. In Portugal, perhaps because of the difficulty, even today, of ridding everyday speech of certain archaisms, the nearest conclusion we could reach was, The Pitcher Goes So Often to the Well that the Handle Finally Stays There, a metaphor that only served to confuse people, since one was not dealing with handles or wells or pitchers, but in which it is not difficult to perceive a factor or principle of repetition, which by its very nature, depending on the frequency, one never knows where it might end. Everything depends on the duration of the phenomenon, on the accumulated effect of these actions, something along the lines of A Steady Fall of Water Wears Away the Hardest Stone, a formula which curiously has never been output by a computer, as well it might, for between the one and the other there are similarities of every kind, in the first instance there is the heavy weight of the water in the pitcher, in the second instance there is water once more but this time drop by drop, dripping freely, and there is time, that other common ingredient.

These are popular philosophies we could go on discussing for-ever, but they are of no great interest to men of science, to geologists or oceanologists. For the sake of simple souls, the matter could even be put in the form of an elementary question which, in its ingenuousness, brings to mind that of the Galician confronted by the River Irati which was sinking into the earth, as you may recall, Where does this water go, he wanted to know, now we shall phrase it differently, What is happening beneath this water. Out here, with our feet firmly on the ground, looking at horizons, or from the air where observations go on indefatigably, the Peninsula is a mass of earth that seems, note the verb, seems to float on the waters. But obviously it cannot float. In order to do so it would need to have detached itself from the bottom, which means it would inevitably end up at the same bottom this time reduced to rubble, for even supposing that in the determining circumstances sufficient force could be applied without producing any greater deviation or dam-age, the disintegrating effect of the water and the maritime currents would progressively start reducing the thickness of the navigating platform until the surface layer was completely dissolved. Therefore, by a process of elimination, we must conclude that the Peninsula slides over itself at an unknown depth, as if it were divided horizon-tally into two layers, the lower one forming part of the earth's deep crust, the upper one, as already explained, sliding slowly through the darkness of the waters, amidst clouds of mud and startled fish, this is how the *Flying Dutchman*, of unhappy memory, must be navigating through the depths, somewhere in the ocean. The notion is intriguing and mysterious, with a little more imagination it could provide the most fascinating chapter of all for *Twenty Thousand Leagues under the Sea*. We live, however, in another age, science is much more exacting, and since it has not proved possible to discover what is causing the Peninsula to displace itself above the seabed, then someone should go down there to witness the phenomenon with his own eyes, to film the dragging of this great mass of stone, to record, perhaps, that cry made by the whale, that squeaking, that interminable laceration. For this is the moment for the deep-sea divers.

As everybody knows, divers holding their breath cannot go down very deep or for very long. The fisher of pearls, sponges, or coral, dives to fifty metres, and the best of them even to seventy, and they can stay under for three or four minutes, it's all a question of training and necessity. Here the depths are different and the waters much colder, even when the body is protected by one of those rubber wet-suits which transform anyone, man or woman, into a black triton, with yellow stripes and dots. So one must have recourse to diving-gear, to cylinders with compressed air, and, with these more recent techniques and apparatus, taking a thousand and one precautions, one can reach depths of the order of two or three hundred metres. Better not tempt providence by attempting to go any further down, but send down unmanned machines instead, equipped with film and television cameras, sensors, tactile and ultrasonic probes, all the appropriate instruments for the job in hand.

At the same hour, for the sake of comparing the results of their observations, operations began on the coasts to the north, south and west, discreetly passed off as naval manoeuvres within the scope of training programmes of the North Atlantic Treaty Organization, so that the announcement of these investigations should not provoke any fresh outbursts of panic, for inexplicably, it had not occurred to anyone so far that the Peninsula might be sliding over what had been its plinth for millions of years. The moment has come to reveal that the experts are about to conceal another nagging anxiety that stems, inevitably as it were, from this same hypothesis which supported the idea of a deep horizontal cut, and which can be summed up by this other question of terrifying simplicity, what will happen if a deep abyss should obstruct the path of the Peninsula, so that there is no longer any continuous surface over which to slide. Judging from experience, which is always desirable for a better understanding of the facts, in this case our experience as bathers, we shall understand perfectly what this must mean if we recall the panic and distress when one unexpectedly loses one's footing and does not have much idea about swimming. Should the Peninsula lose its footing or balance, it will inevitably sink, go to the bottom, suffocate, drown, who would have thought that after so many centuries of miserable existence we would be doomed to the fate of Atlantis.

Let us spare ourselves the details which will be divulged one day for the enlightenment of all those who are interested in submarine life and which, for the present surrounded by the utmost secrecy, are to be found in ships' logbooks, confidential reports and various records, some of them in code. All we shall say is that the continental platform was examined in detail without any results. No new crack was found, no abnormal grating was picked up by the microphones. This initial hypothesis having failed, they then proceeded to examine the abysses. The cranes lowered the instruments which had been built to withstand high pressures, and to scan and search the depths of the silent waters but found nothing. The *Archimedes*, a masterpiece of submarine research handled by the French who owned it, descended to the maximum peripheral depths, from the euphatic to the pelagic zone, and from there to the bathypelagic zone, used lamps, pincers, bathometers, sounding lines of various kinds scanned the subaquatic horizon with its panoramic sonar, to no avail. The extensive versants, the steep escarpments, the vertical precipices were exposed in their sombre majesty, in their unspoilt beauty, the instruments registered continuously with much clicking and switching on and off of lights, the ascending and descending currents, they photographed the fish, the shoals of sardines, the colonies of hake, the brigades of tunny and bonito, the flotillas of mackerel, the armadas of swordfish, and if the *Archimedes* were carrying in its belly a laboratory fitted out with the necessary reagents, solvents, and other chemical paraphernalia, it would be able to identify the natural elements which are dissolved in the waters of the ocean, namely, in diminishing order in terms of quantity, and for the cultural benefit of the masses who have not the faintest idea how much exists in the sea where they bathe, chlorine, sodium, magnesium, sulphur, calcium, potassium, bromide, carbon, strontium, boron, silica, fluorine, argon, nitrogen, phosphorus, iodine, barium, iron, zinc, aluminium, lead, tin, arsenic, copper, uranium, nickel, manganese, titanium, silver, tungsten, gold, such riches, dear God, and with all the things we lack on terra firma, the only thing we cannot trace is the crack that would explain the phenomenon which, after all, exists, and is plain for all to see. In desperation, a North American expert, and one of the most distinguished, went so far as to proclaim on the deck of the hydrographic ship, before the winds and horizon, I hereby declare that the Peninsula cannot possibly be moving, whereupon an Italian expert, who was much less knowledgeable, but armed with a historic and scientific precedent, muttered, but not so quietly that he could not be heard by that providential Being who hears all things, *Eppur si muove*. Empty-handed, chapped by all that salt, humiliated and frustrated, the governments simply announced that under the auspices of the United Nations, they had carried out an investigation of the eventual changes in the habitat of the ichthic species brought about by the Peninsula's dislocation. It was not the mountain that had conceived a mouse, but rather the ocean that had given birth to a tiny sardine.

The travellers heard this news as they were leaving Lisbon but did not consider it important, simply one more report among others referring to the separation of the Peninsula, which also seemed to be of no great importance. A person can get used to anything, nations with even greater ease and speed, when all is said and done it is as if we were now travelling in an immense ship, so big that it would even be possible to live aboard for the rest of one's life without ever seeing the prow or stern, the Peninsula was not a ship when it was still attached to Europe and there were still lots of people who knew no country other than that of their birth, so tell me, if you please, what's the difference. Now that Joaquim Sassa and Pedro Orce appear to be free at last from the obsessive prying of the scientists and there is nothing more to fear from the authorities, they can return to their respective homes, and José Anaiço too, for the starlings have unexpectedly lost interest in him, but the apparition, so to speak, of this woman, put everything back to square one, this being fairly characteristic of women, although not always in such a radical manner. It was after a meeting in that same garden, where Joana Carda and José Anaiço had been the day before, that the four of them decided, after re-examining the facts, to make the journey together that was to take them to the spot marked with a line on the ground, one of those lines we have all had to make in life, but with singular features, to judge from the agent and witness, coincidentally one and the same person. Joana Carda still hadn't revealed the name of the place or even that of the nearest city, but merely indicated the general direction. We're heading north along the motorway, then I'll show you how to get there. Pedro Orce had taken José Anaiço discreetly aside to ask him if he thought it was a good idea to venture forth like this, blindly falling in with the whims of an eccentric woman with a stick in her hand, suppose this were a snare, a plot to kidnap them, a cunning ruse, On whose part, José Anaiço wanted to know, That I can't tell you, perhaps they want to take us to the laboratory of some mad scientist, like you see in films, some Frankenstein or other, Pedro Orce replied smiling, No wonder people are always talking about the Andalusian imagination, it doesn't need much water to start boiling, José Anaiço commented, It's not because there isn't much water, it's because there's so much fire, Pedro Orce replied, Forget it, José Anaiço concluded, what must be, will be, and they rejoined the others, who had started a discussion more or less in this vein, I don't know how it happened, the stick was lying on the ground, I picked it up and drew a line, Did it ever occur to you that it might be a magic wand,

It seemed rather big for a magic wand and I've always heard it said that they are made of shimmering gold and crystal, with a star on top, Did you know it was an elm branch, I know very little about trees but in this case I'm sure a matchstick would have produced the same effect, Why do you say that, What has to be, has to be, and that carries a lot of weight which you can't resist, Do you believe in fate, I believe in what must be, Then you're just like José Anaiço, said Pedro Orce, he also believes in fate. The morning, with a light wind that blew like a playful puff of air, gave little promise of a warm day, Shall we go, José Anaiço asked, Let's go, they all replied, including Joana Carda who had come to look for them.

Life is full of little episodes that seem unimportant, while others at a certain moment absorbed all our attention, when we reappraise them later, in the light of their consequences, we find our memory of the latter has faded while the former have become decisive or, at least, the link in a chain of successive and meaningful events, to give the example one expects, there will not be any frenetic loading and unloading, apparently so justified in itself, as the luggage of four passengers is packed into a car as small as Deux Chevaux. This tricky operation engages everyone's attention, each of them makes some suggestion or proposal, tries to lend a hand, but the main question latent in all this upheaval, which may even determine the fortuitous grouping of the four people around the car, is to know at whose side Joana Carda will travel. That Joaquim Sassa should drive Deux Chevaux seems right, at the outset of the journey a car should always be driven by its owner, this is an undisputed fact which implies prestige, prerogative and a sense of possession. The alternative driver, at the right moment, will be José Anaiço, since Pedro Orce, not so much because of his age but because as someone living where excavations have taken place and whose job keeps him behind a counter, has never ventured into the complex mechanics of a steering wheel, or gear, and it is rather soon to be asking Joana Carda if she knows how to drive. In the light of these details, it seems inevitable that these two should travel on the back seat, with the pilot and co-pilot logically seated in front. But Pedro Orce is Spanish, Joana Carda is Portuguese, neither of them speaks the other's language, and besides, they've only just met, later on things will be different when they've had time to become acquainted. The seat beside the driver, although considered by the superstitious and proved by the statistics to be the dead man's seat, is generally regarded as a place of honour and should, therefore, be offered to Joana Carda, putting her on the right of Joaquim Sassa, with the other two men behind, and they should not have much difficulty in understanding each other after sharing so many experiences in common. But the elm branch is much too big to go in front, and Joana Carda has made it clear that she wouldn't part with it for anything. So, there being no alternative, Pedro Orce will sit in front for two explicable reasons, one more excellent than the other, firstly, as we have already said, because it is a place of honour, secondly, because Pedro Orce being the oldest person here, the one closest to death, on account of what we term, with black humour, the natural law of life. But what really counts, more than this bifurcated reasoning, is that Joana Carda and José Anaiço want to travel together on the back seat, and by means of gestures, pauses and feigned distractions they've managed it. Let us be seated then, and get on our way.

The journey was uneventful, that's what novelists in a hurry always say when they think that in the ten minutes or ten hours they are about to eliminate nothing has taken place that would warrant any special mention. Strictly speaking, it would be much more correct and honest to put it like this, As in all journeys, whatever their duration and length, there have been a thousand incidents, words and thoughts, and for a thousand you could read ten thousand, but the narrative is dragging, so I'm allowing myself to abbreviate, using three lines to cover two hundred kilometres, bearing in mind that four people inside the car have travelled in silence, without a thought or gesture, pretending that by the end of the journey they will have nothing to relate. In our case, for example, it would be impossible not to derive some meaning from the fact that Joana Carda had quite naturally accompanied José Anaiço when he took over from Joaquim Sassa, who wanted a rest from driving, and that she had managed, God knows how, to squeeze the elm branch into the front, without hampering the driver or blocking his vision. And needless to say, when José Anaiço returned to the back seat, Joana Carda went with him, and so wherever José happened to be Joana was there too, although neither of them, as yet, can say for what reason or purpose, or they already know but cannot bring themselves to say it, each moment has its own flavour and the flavour of this moment has not yet been lost.

There were few abandoned cars on the roads, and those they saw invariably had parts missing, having been stripped of their wheels, lamps, rear-view mirrors, windscreens, a door, sometimes all the doors, the seats, some cars were even reduced to mere shells like crabs without any meat inside. But due to the shortage of petrol, the traffic was thin and there were long gaps between one car passing and the next. Certain incongruities also hit one in the eye, such as a cart being drawn by a donkey along the motorway, or a squadron of cyclists who even at full speed were way below the minimum speed the respective road-signs foolishly continued to impose, indifferent to the dramatic meaning of reality. And there were also people travelling on foot, usually with a haversack on their back, or, in rustic fashion, with two sacks loosely tied together at the top and strung over one shoulder like a saddlebag, the women with baskets on their heads. Many people were travelling alone, but there were also families, to all appearances entire families with their old, young, and babes in arms. When Deux Chevaux had to leave the motorway further ahead, the number of pedestrians only diminished in proportion to the relative importance of the road. Three times Joaquim Sassa tried to ask people where they were going, and they all gave him the same answer, We're on our way to see the world. They must have known that the world, the immediate world, strictly speaking, was now much smaller than before, perhaps for this very reason their dream of knowing all of it had become much more feasible, and when José Anaiço asked, But tell me about your home and your job, they calmly replied, Our home will be waiting for us and work we can always find, these are the priorities of the past which must not be allowed to hinder the future. And perhaps it was just as well that people did not ask him the same question, either because they were too discreet or were absorbed in their own affairs, otherwise they would have been forced to explain, We're accompanying this woman to examine the line she drew on the ground with this stick, and as for the matter of work, they would have made a poor impression, perhaps Pedro Orce would have confessed, I've left my patients to look after themselves, and Joaquim Sassa argued, Let's face it, office clerks are ten a penny, I won't be missed, besides I'm enjoying a well-deserved vacation, and José Anaiço, I'm in the same situation, if I were to go back to school now I wouldn't find any pupils, until October my time is my own, and Joana Carda, I've nothing to tell you about myself, if I've revealed nothing so far to these men with whom I'm travelling, there's no reason why I should confide in strangers.

They had passed the town of Pombal when Joana Carda informed them, Just ahead there is a road to Soure, that's the one we have to follow, since leaving Lisbon this was the first indication she had given of a specific destination, until now they had felt as if they were travelling through mist, or, adapting this particular situation to general circumstances, they were ancient and ingenuous mariners, We are being carried along by the sea, where will she carry us. They would soon find out. They did not stop in Soure, they went through narrow roads that crossed, forked into two or three branches, and sometimes they seemed to be going round in circles, until they finally reached a village which had a road-sign at the access bearing the name Ereira, and Joana Carda announced, It's here.

Taken by surprise, José Anaiço who was driving Deux Chevaux at that moment, put his foot down sharply on the brake, as if the line were right there in the middle of the road and he were about to run over it, not that there was any danger of destroying this prodigious evidence which Joana Carda had described as indestructible, but because of that holy terror which strikes even the most sceptical of men when routine is broken like the thread that broke as we ran it through our hand, confident and without any responsibility, except that of preserving, strengthening, and prolonging this thread, and our hand too, as far as possible. Joaquim Sassa looked outside, saw houses, trees above the rooftops and low-lying fields, the marshes and rice-paddies are visible, it's the gentle Mondego, better that than arid rock. Had this been what Pedro Orce was thinking, then inevitably Don Quixote of the sad countenance would come into the story, the one he possesses and the one he presented when, stark naked, he began jumping up and down like a madman amidst the peaks of the Sierra Morena, it would be absurd to draw a comparison with similar episodes of knight errantry, therefore Pedro Orce, on getting out of the car and putting his feet on the ground, simply confirmed that the earth was still shaking. José Anaiço walked round Deux Chevaux, went to open, perfect gentleman that he is, the door on the other side, pretended not to notice the ironic, patronizing smile of Joaquim Sassa, and taking the elm branch from Joana Carda, he extended his hand to help her out, she gave him hers, they clasped hands for longer than was necessary for pledging support, but this was not the first time, the first and only time so far was on the back seat, an impulse, however they did not utter a word either then or now, in a louder or softer tone of voice which might embrace the word spoken by the other with equal force.

This is indeed the hour for explanations, but Joaquim Sassa's question demands others, like the ship's captain who opens sealed orders suspecting that he might find nothing except a blank page, Now where do we go, Now we take this road, Joana Carda replied, and on the way I'll tell you the rest of my story, not that it has anything to do with our coming here, but there's little point in continuing to act like strangers when we've travelled all this way together, You could have told us sooner, either in Lisbon or during the journey, José Anaiço remarked, Whatever for, either you came with me because you were convinced by a single word, or many more words would have been needed to convince you, and then it wouldn't have done much good, As a reward for having believed in you, It's for me to decide your reward and when it should be given, José Anaiço refrained from answering, he played for time, started looking at a row of poplars in the distance, but she heard Joaquim Sassa murmur, What a girl, Joana Carda smiled, I'm no girl, nor the harpy you take me for, I wouldn't call you a harpy, Domineering, stubborn, conceited, affected, Good heavens, what a list, why not say mysterious and leave it at that, For there is a mystery, and I wouldn't have brought anyone here who didn't believe without seeing, even you lot, in whom nobody believes, They're beginning to believe in us now, But I was more fortunate and only needed to say one word, Let's hope many more won't be needed now, This dialogue was conducted entirely between Joana Carda and Joaquim Sassa, given Pedro Orce's difficulty in understanding and the obvious impatience of José Anaiço, who had been excluded from the conversation through his own fault. But observe how this curious situation, with the differences that always mark situations, simply repeats that of Granada, when Maria Dolores conversed with a Portuguese but would have preferred to be conversing with another, in this particular case, however, there will be time to explain everything, the man who is really thirsty will have his thirst quenched.

They are now walking along the path which is narrow, Pedro Orce is obliged to follow, the others will explain matters to him later, if the Spaniard is truly interested in the fortunes of these Portuguese. I don't live here in Ereira, Joana Carda begins, my home was in Coimbra, I've only been here since separating from my husband about a month ago, for what reasons, why bother discussing the reasons, sometimes one is enough, at other times not even lumping them together, if your own lives haven't taught you this, poor things, and I repeat, lives not life, for we all have several, and fortunately they kill each other off, otherwise we wouldn't be able to survive. She leaps over a wide ditch, the men follow her, and when the group reassemble, now treading soft, sandy terrain where the earth has been waterlogged, Joana Carda continues speaking, I'm staying with some relatives, I wanted time to think, but not the usual self-questioning, have I done the right thing, have I done the wrong thing, what is done is done, I wanted time to think about life, what is its purpose, what's my purpose in life, yes, I reached a conclusion, the only possible conclusion, I simply do not understand life. The expression on the faces of José Anaiço and Joaquim Sassa is one of bewilderment, this woman who came down to the city carrying a stick in her hand to proclaim impossible feats of land-surveying, has now turned philosopher here in the fields of Mondego, a philosopher of the negative kind, and to complicate matters, in that special category which says yes after saying no, and that will say no after having said yes. Having been trained as a teacher, José Anaiço is better qualified to understand these contradictions, but this does not apply to Joaquim Sassa, he simply senses them and therefore finds them twice as bewildering. Joana Carda continues to speak, having come to a halt because they are now close to the spot she wants to show them, she still has something to say to them, other things will have to wait, I didn't go to Lisbon to find you because of the strange happenings which attracted so much attention but because I saw you as people detached from any apparent logic in the world, and that's precisely how I feel about myself, I should have been deeply disappointed if you hadn't accompanied me all this way, but you came, perhaps something still has some meaning, or will regain it after having lost all meaning, now come with me.

They enter a clearing away from the river, a circle surrounded by ash trees that appear never to have been cultivated, such places are less rare than one imagines, set foot in them and time appears to stand still, the silence seems different, you can feel the breeze all over your face and hands, no, no we're not talking about witchcraft and sorcery, this is not a witches' coven or a gate to the other world, that is simply the impression created by those trees in the form of a circle and the ground which appears to have been undisturbed since the beginning of time, the sand simply came and made it soft, but the soil is heavy beneath the humus, whoever planted the trees like this is entirely to blame. Joana Carda has nothing more to tell them. This is where I used to come to think things over, there can be no more peaceful place on earth, yet disturbing too, you don't have to tell me, but if you hadn't come here you wouldn't be able to understand, and one day, two weeks ago to be precise, as I was walking across the clearing to sit down under that tree over there, I found this branch lying on the ground, I was seeing it for the first time, I'd been here the day before and it wasn't here, it was as if someone had put it here deliberately, but there were no footprints to be seen, the marks you can see there are mine, or were left by people who passed this way a long, long time ago. They are standing on the edge of the clearing, Joana Carda detains the men further and these are her closing words, I picked up the stick from the ground, the wood seemed to be living as if it were the whole tree from which it had been cut, or this is what I now feel as it comes back to me, and at that moment, with a gesture more like that of a child than an adult, I drew a line that separated me forever from Coimbra and the man with whom I lived, a line which divided the world into two halves, as you can see from here.

They advance to the middle of the clearing, draw close, there is the line, as clear as if it had just been drawn, the earth piled up on either side, the bottom layer still damp despite the warmth of the sun. They remain silent, the men are at a loss for words, Joana Carda has nothing more to say, this is the moment for a daring gesture which could make a mockery of her wonderful tale. She drags one foot over the ground, smoothes the soil as if she were using a level, stamps on it and presses it down, as if committing an act of sacrilege. The next moment, before the astonished gaze of everyone, the line reappears, looks exactly as it was before, the tiny particles of soil, grains of sand, resume their previous shape and form, return to where they were before and the line is back. Between the part that was destroyed and the rest, on the one side and the other, there is no sign to be seen of the first or second separation. Her nerves on edge, Joana Carda says in a shrill voice, I've already swept away the entire line, I've covered it with water, yet it keeps reappearing, try for yourselves if you wish, I even put stones on top, and when I removed them the line was still there, why don't you have a go if you need any convincing. Joaquim Sassa bent down, buried his fingers in the soft earth, scooped up a handful of soil, threw it into the distance, and the line reconstituted itself immediately. Then it was José Anaiço's turn, but the latter asked Joana Carda to loan him her stick and he drew a deep line alongside the existing one, then pressed it down along its entire length. The line didn't come back. Now you do the same, José Anaiço told Joana Carda. The tip of the stick dug into the soil, was dragged along the ground, opened an extensive wound, which closed up at once like a defective scar when they pressed it down, and so it remained. José Anaiço said, It's got nothing to do with the stick or the person, it's the moment, it's the moment that counts. Then Joaquim Sassa did what had to be done, he lifted up from the ground one of the stones which had been used by Joana Carda, similar in weight and appearance to the one he had thrown into the sea, and gathering all his strength he hurled it as far as he could into the distance, it fell where one expected it to fall, several paces away, that's as much as human strength can achieve.

Pedro Orce had witnessed these trials and experiments without wishing to participate, probably he had enough to contend with as the earth went on shaking under his feet. He took the elm branch from Joana Carda's hands and said, You can break it, throw it away, burn it, it's no longer useful, your stick, Joaquim Sassa's stone, José Anaiço's starlings, no longer serve any purpose, they're like those men and women who were only useful once, José Anaiço is right, what counts is the moment, we only serve the moment, That may be so, Joana Carda retorted, but this stick will stay with me forever, moments give us no warning when they're coming. A dog appeared among the trees, on the far side. It gave them a long stare, then crossed the clearing, it was a large powerful animal, its tawny coat caught by a sudden ray of sunlight appeared to burst into flames. Taking fright, Joaquim Sassa aimed a stone, the first stone that came to hand, I don't like dogs, but he missed. The dog stopped in its tracks, not the least bit intimidated, not at all menacing, it simply stopped to look, not even barking. As it reached the trees, the dog turned its head, seemed much bigger when seen from a distance, then off it went, slowly, and disappeared. Joaquim Sassa tried to be humorous to relieve the tension, Joana might as well hold on to her stick, it might come in handy if such huge beasts are roving these parts.

They returned by the same route, now there were certain practical matters to settle, for example, since it was now too late to go back to Lisbon, where are the men going to spend the night. But it isn't all that late, said Joaquim Sassa, even without rushing we can get back to Lisbon in plenty of time for dinner, As far as I'm concerned, the best solution would be to stay here in Figueira da Foz, or in Coimbra, tomorrow we can come back this way, Joana might need something, José Anaiço said, and there was a note of deep concern in his voice. As you prefer, Joaquim Sassa said with a smile, and the rest of the sentence passed from words to a look, I know exactly how you feel, you want some time to think this evening, you want to decide what to say tomorrow, certain moments arrive without any warning. Pedro Orce and Joaquim Sassa are now leading the way, the afternoon is so peaceful that one is overcome with emotion not directed at anyone in particular, only at the light, at the pale sky, the inert trees, at the gentle river whose presence one senses before it looms into sight, a smooth mirror which the birds slowly traverse. José Anaiço takes Joana Carda by the hand, and says, We're on this side of the line, together, but for how long, and Joana Carda replies, We'll soon find out.

As they approached the car they saw the dog. Joaquim Sassa grabbed another stone, but decided not to throw it. The animal, despite this threatening gesture, did not stir. Pedro Orce went up to it, held out his hand as a gesture of peace, as if about to caress it. The dog remained impassive, its head raised. It had a chewed thread of blue wool hanging limply from its mouth. Pedro Orce stroked its back, then rejoined his companions. There are moments that warn you when they are coming, the earth is shaking beneath the dog's paws.

Man proposes, dog disposes, this very latest maxim is just as valid as the old one, we must give some name to whoever decides in the final analysis, for decisions don't always come from God, as is generally believed. There they took their leave of each other, the men heading for Figueira da Foz, which is nearest, the woman for the home of her hospitable relatives, but when Deux Chevaux had already released the brake and started moving, to everyone's astonishment the dog was seen to stand in front of Joana Carda, preventing her from passing. It didn't bark, it didn't bare its teeth, her gesture with the stick made no impression, after all, it was only a gesture. José Anaiço who was driving, thought his beloved might be in danger, and, once more the knight errant, he brought the car to a sudden halt, jumped out and ran to her assistance, a dramatic but somewhat ineffectual act, as he was soon to realize, for the dog simply lay down in the road. Pedro Orce drew near, Joaquim Sassa too, the latter disguising his antipathy with an air of detachment. What does the beast want, he asked, but no one could give him an answer, not even the dog itself. Pedro Orce, as he had done before, went up to the animal and laid his hand on its huge head. The dog closed its eyes in a wistful manner at this caress, should such an adjective be appropriate here, we are talking about dogs, not sensitive people who exercise sensibility, and then it got up, stared at them one by one, gave them enough time to understand and then started walking. It walked about ten metres, stopped, waited.

Now experience has taught us, movies and romances too are full of similar scenes, Lassie, for example, mastered the technique to perfection, experience tells us that a dog always behaves like this when it wishes us to follow. In this instance, the dog was obviously preventing Joana Carda from passing in order to oblige the men to get out of the car, and if, now that they are together, it is showing them the way which its canine instinct suggests they must follow, it is because, pardon these further repetitions, the dog wants them to follow it together. You don't have to be as intelligent as a man in order to grasp this, if an ordinary, simple dog can convey it so simply. But men, having been deceived so often, have learned to put everything to the test, principally by means of repetition, which is the easiest method of all, and when, as in this case, they have reached an average level of culture, they are not content with a second experience similar to the first, they introduce minor variations which do not radically alter the basic facts, to give an example, José Anaiço and Joana Carda got into the car while Pedro Orce and Joaquim Sassa stayed where they were, now we shall see what the dog does. Let us say that it did what it had to. The dog, which knows perfectly well that it cannot stop a car unless it gets in front of it, but that would mean certain death and there is not a single driver whose love for our animal friends is so great that he would stop to witness its last moments or move its pitiful corpse into the gutter, the dog prevented Joaquim Sassa and Pedro Orce from passing just as it had prevented Joana Carda before. The third and decisive proof came when all four of them got into the car, it started moving, and because Deux Chevaux happened to be facing in the right direction, the dog got in front of it, this time not to obstruct its progress, but to lead the way. All these manoeuvres took place without any inquisitive spectators looking on because, as on other occasions since this narrative began, certain important episodes have invariably taken place upon entering or leaving towns and cities, and not inside them, as happens in most cases. This undoubtedly warrants some explanation, but alas, we're unable to give one.

José Anaiço brought the car to a standstill, the dog stopped and looked round, and Joana Carda concluded, It wants us to follow. They were slow in seeing something which had been obvious from the moment the dog crossed the clearing, let us say that this was the crucial warning, but people do not always pay attention to these omens. And even when there is no longer any reason for doubt, they still persist in ignoring the warning, like Joaquim Sassa when he asks, And why should we follow it, how ridiculous for four grown-ups to go trailing after a stray dog which does not even have a disc on its collar, saying rescue me, or giving its identity, I'm called Pilot, if you should find me return me to my owners, Mr and

Mrs So-and-So, at such and such an address, Don't wear yourself out, José Anaiço told him, this episode is as absurd as all the others that have been happening and appear to make no sense, They don't make much sense to me, Don't worry about things not making sense, said Pedro Orce, a journey only makes sense if you finish it, and we're still only halfway there, or perhaps only at the beginning, who knows, until your journey on earth has ended I cannot tell you its meaning, Very well, and until that day arrives, what are we going to do. There was silence. The light faded, the day was drawing to a close, leaving shadows among the trees, the singing of the birds was already different. The dog went and lay in front of the car, three paces away, resting its head on its outstretched front paws and waiting patiently. Then Joana Carda said, I'm ready to go wherever the dog may lead us, we'll find out if that's what it came for when we reach our destination. José Anaiço took a deep breath, he was not sighing, although people do sigh with relief. So am I, was all he said. And you can count on me, Pedro Orce added, Now that you're all in agreement, I shan't be the killjoy to prevent you from walking behind the pilot, we'll go together, I might as well make the most of my vacation, concluded Joaquim Sassa.

Reaching a decision means saying yes or no, the merest whisper on one's lips, the difficulties come later when one puts that decision into practice, as we learn from human experience, gained with time and patience, with few hopes and even fewer changes. We'll follow the dog, yes sir, but one has to know how to, since our guide can't give explanations, it cannot travel inside the car, telling us to turn left, then right, go straight on until the third set of traffic lights, besides, and this is a real drawback, how could an animal this size fit into a car where all the seats are already occupied, not to mention the luggage and the elm branch, although the latter is scarcely noticeable when Joana Carda and José Anaiço are sitting side by side. And speaking of Joana Carda, her luggage has still to come, and what's more, before tackling the problem of finding room, her luggage has to be fetched, she must explain her sudden departure to her cousins, but three men, Deux Chevaux and a dog cannot suddenly appear on the doorstep, to say I'm going with them would be the innocent truth, but surely a woman so recently separated from her husband should give some explanation of her conduct, especially in a place as small as Ereira, a mere village, broken marriages are all very well in capitals and large cities and even then, God alone knows with what traumas and trials of body and soul.

The sun had already gone down, night was almost here, this was not an hour to be starting a journey into the unknown, and it would be wrong of Joana Carda to disappear without any warning, she told her relatives that she was travelling to Lisbon to attend to some business, she would go and come back by train. These are difficulties and complications we are led into by social conventions and family ties. No sooner had Pedro Orce got out of the car than the dog stood up and watched him approach, and there in the twilight they held a conversation, at least that's how we describe it, although we know this dog is not even capable of barking. When their dialogue ended, Pedro Orce went back to the car and told them, I think Joana Carda can go home now, the dog is staying with us, settle where we spend the night and decide how and where to meet tomorrow. No one doubted this assurance, Joaquim Sassa opened out the map and in three seconds they decided they would spend the night in Montemor-o-Velho, in some modest boarding-house. And if we don't find one, asked Joaquim Sassa, We'll go to Figueira, José Anaiço replied, besides, better to play safe, it's probably wiser to spend the night at Figueira, tomorrow you take the bus and we'll wait for you in the car park near the casino, needless to say these instructions were addressed to Joana Carda, who accepted them without questioning the competence of the person giving them. Joana said, See you tomorrow, and at the last moment, with one foot already on the ground, she turned and kissed José Anaiço on the lips, this was no little peck on the cheek or the side of the mouth, these were two lightning flashes, one of speed, the other of impact, but the effects of the latter lingered, something which wouldn't have happened if the contact between their lips, so heavenly, had been prolonged. Her cousins in Ereira would comment, You can't imagine the scandalous goings-on here, She's nothing but a trollop, and to think we believed her husband was to blame, he must have had the patience of a saint, a man you've only known since yesterday and you're already kissing him, you didn't even leave it to him to take the initiative as one would expect of a woman, for, when all is said and done, you have to think about your self-respect, and besides you said you were going and coming back on the same day but you spent the night in Lisbon away from home, what are people going to think, but when everyone's asleep, the wife gets out of bed and goes to Joana's room to ask her what happened, Joana tells her she doesn't really know, and it's the truth, Why did I do what I did, Joana Carda asked herself as she retreated

121

into the deep shadows beneath the trees, her hands were free so that she could lift them to her lips like someone trying to suppress her feelings. Her suitcase had remained in the car to reserve a place for the rest of her luggage, the elm branch was in safe keeping, guarded by the three men and a dog, the latter, summoned by Pedro Orce, got into the car and settled down in Joana Carda's seat, when everyone was already asleep in Figueira da Foz, two women would still be conversing in a house in Ereira at dead of night, How I'd love to go with you, Joana's cousin confided, her own marriage far from happy.

Next morning the sky was overcast, one cannot rely on the weather, yesterday afternoon was like a foretaste of paradise, bright and pleasant, the branches of the trees gently swaying, the Mondego as smooth as the surface of the sky, no one here would think this the same river under the low clouds, the sea throwing up spray, but the elderly shrug their shoulders, First of August, first day of winter, they say, most fortunate that the day should have come almost a month late, Joana Carda arrived early but José Anaiço was already waiting for her in the car, this had been agreed by the other two men so that the lovers could be alone and converse before they all set out on their journey, in which direction we still don't know. The dog had spent the night inside the car, but it was now strolling along the beach with Pedro Orce and Joaquim Sassa, discreet, rubbing its head against the leg of the Spaniard, whose company it already preferred.

In the car park, among the larger vehicles, Deux Chevaux looked insignificant, that's the first point, and moreover, as has already been explained, it was a wild morning, there was no one around, and that is the second point, therefore it is only natural that José Anaiço and Joana Carda should fall into each other's arms as if they had been separated for a whole year and had been longing for each other all that time. They kissed with passion and desire, this was no flash of lightning but one flash after another, there were fewer words, it is difficult to speak while kissing, but after several minutes they could hear each other at last, I like you, I believe I'm in love with you, said José Anaiço in all sincerity, I like you too, and I also believe I'm in love with you, that's why I kissed you yesterday, no, no, what I mean to say is that I wouldn't have kissed you if I hadn't felt that I loved you, but I'm capable of loving you much more, You know nothing about me, If one couldn't like another person before getting to know them, it would take a lifetime, Don't you believe that two people can get to know each other, Do you, I'm asking you, First you must tell me what you mean by knowing, I don't have a dictionary here, In this instance, to consult the dictionary is simply to discover what one already knew, Dictionaries only provide information which is likely to be useful to everyone, I must repeat the question, what do you mean by knowing, I'm not sure, And yet you can love, I can love you, Without knowing me, So it would appear, Where did you get the surname Anaiço from, One of my grandfathers was called Inácio, but back there in the village they got his name wrong, they started calling him Anaiço, after a while Anaiço became the family surname, and you, why are you called Carda, In the distant past, the family name was Cardo, which also means thistle, but when one of my grandmothers lost her husband and found herself with a family to support, people began to call her Carda, for she richly deserved the feminine form of that surname in her own right, I thought you might be a carder who combed wool for a living, I might have been, and something else too, for I once went to look the word up in the dictionary and saw that carder also meant an instrument of torture used for skinning animals, poor martyrs, skinned, burnt, beheaded and carded, Is that what awaits me, If I were to go back to using the name Cardo you wouldn't benefit from the change, Would you still prick me, No, I'm not the name I bear, Who are you then, I'm me, José Anaiço stretched out his hand, caressed her on the cheek, murmured, You, she did the same, repeated in a whisper, You, and her eyes filled with tears, probably because she is still conscious of her wicked past, now, as was only to be expected, she will want to know about his life, Are you married, do you have any children, what do you do for a living, I was married, I have no children, I'm a teacher. She took a deep breath or was it a sigh of relief, then she said smiling, We'd better call the others, poor fellows, they're dying of cold, José Anaiço said, When I told Joaquim about our first encounter, I tried to describe the colour of your eyes, but I couldn't, I told him they were the colour of a new sky, difficult to describe, and he latched on to that phrase, and started to call you just that, Just what, Lady Strange Eyes, of course he wouldn't dare to say it in your presence. I adore that name, I adore you, and now we'd better call the others.

One arm waving, another waving back in the distance, Pedro Orce and Joaquim Sassa came walking slowly across the sand, the large docile dog between them. Judging from the way you waved,

Joaquim Sassa said, their meeting went well, anyone listening who had experience of life would have no difficulty in detecting a note of subdued melancholy in those words, a noble sentiment, tinged with envy, or resentment, if you prefer a more refined word. Are you in love with the girl, too, Pedro Orce asked sympathetically, No, no it's not that, although it could be, my problem is that I don't know whom to love or how one goes on loving. Pedro Orce couldn't think of an answer to such a negative statement. They got into the car, good-day, how nice to see you, welcome aboard, where will this adventure lead us, good-natured platitudes, the last of them mistaken, it would have been more appropriate to enquire, Where will this dog lead us. José Anaiço switched on the engine, since he's at the wheel he might as well stay there, he manoeuvred the car out of the car park, now what, do I turn right, do I turn left, he pretended to hesitate, playing for time, the dog turned full circle and at a controlled but rapid trot, so regular as to appear mechanical, it started heading in a northerly direction. With the blue thread hanging from its mouth.

This was the memorable day on which the already distant Europe, according to the latest recorded measurements, had moved about two hundred kilometres away and found itself shaken from top to bottom by a psychological and social convulsion of nature which seriously endangered its identity, deprived at that decisive moment of its very foundations, of those individual nationalities so laboriously created throughout hundreds of years. Europeans, from top leaders to ordinary citizens, soon became accustomed, one suspects with an unspoken feeling of relief, to the lack of any territories to the extreme west, and if the new maps, rapidly circulated to bring the public up to date, still provoked some dismay, it could only have been for aesthetic reasons, that indefinable impression of disquiet people must have experienced and still experience today when they see that the arms are missing on the Venus of Milo, for this is the precise name of the island where the statue was found, So Milo is not the sculptor's name, No sir, Milo is the island where the poor creature was discovered, she rose from the depths like Lazarus, but no miracle occurred to make her arms grow again.

As the centuries pass, if they continue to pass, Europe will no longer remember the time when she was great and sailed the seas, just as we today can no longer imagine the Venus with arms. Obviously one cannot ignore the disasters and sorrows that continue to plague the Mediterranean with high tides, the coastal cities on their maritime fringe destroyed, hotels which once had steps leading down to the beach and now have neither steps nor beach, and Venice, Venice is like a swamp, a pile-dwelling under threat, the tourist boom is over, my friends, but if the Dutch were to work quickly, within several months the city of the Doges, the Aveiro of Italy, will be able to reopen its doors to the anxious public, much improved, no longer in danger of catastrophic flooding, for the systems of balancing sluice valves, dykes, locks, pressure and suction pumps will ensure a constant water level, now it's up to the Italians to assume responsibility for reinforcing the city's foundations, otherwise Venice will end up tragically and bury itself in the mud, the most difficult part, permit me to say, is being done, let us give thanks to the descendants of that brave lad who, with just the tender tip of his index finger, prevented the town of Haarlem from disappearing from the face of the earth through flooding and deluge.

By restoring Venice, a solution will also be found for the rest of Europe. This fascinating region has been stricken time and time again by plague and war, earthquakes and fires, only to rise again from dust and ashes, transforming bitter suffering into sweet existence, barbaric lust into civilization, a golf course and swimming pool, a sailing yacht in the marina and a convertible on the quayside, man is the most adaptable of creatures, especially when it is a question of moving up in the world. Although it may not be very polite to say so, for certain Europeans, to see themselves rid of baffling Western nations, now sailing adrift on the ocean, where they should never have gone, was in itself an improvement, the promise of happier times ahead, like with like, we have finally started to know what Europe is, unless there still remain some spurious fragments which will also break away sooner or later. Let us wager that ultimately we shall be reduced to a single nation, the quintessence of the European spirit, simple and perfect sublimation, Europe, that's to say, Switzerland.

However, if there are such Europeans, there are also others. The race of the restless, ferment of the devil, but not so easily extinguished, however much the soothsayers may tire themselves out with prophecies. It is she who watches the train passing and becomes sad with longing for the journey she will never make, it is she who cannot see a bird in the sky without feeling the urge to soar like an eagle, it is she who upon seeing a ship disappear over the horizon, gives a tremulous sigh from the heart, in her rapture she thought it was because they were so close, only to realize it was because they were so far apart. It was, therefore, one of those nonconformist and restless men who for the first time dared to write those scandalous words, *Nous aussi, nous sommes ibériques*, he wrote them on a corner of the wall, timidly, like someone who is still unable to express his desire but cannot bear to conceal it any longer. Having been written, as you can see, in the French language, you will think it happened in France, all I can say is, Let each man think what he will, it could also have been in Belgium or Luxembourg. This inaugural declaration spread rapidly, it appeared on the façades of the large buildings, on pediments, on pavements, in the corridors of subways, on bridges and viaducts, the loyal conservatives of Europe protested, These anarchists are mad, it is always the same, the anarchists are blamed for everything.

But the saying jumped frontiers, and after having jumped them it became clear that the same words had already appeared in other countries, in German *Auch wir sind iberisch*, in English We are Iberians too, in Italian, *Anche noi siamo iberici*, and suddenly it went off like a fuse, ablaze all over the place in letters of red, black, blue, green, yellow and violet, a holocaust that seemed inextinguishable, in Dutch and Flemish *Wij zijn ook Iberiërs*, in Swedish *Vi ocksa äro iberiska*, in Finnish *Me myöskin olemme iberialaisia*, in Norwegian *Vi ogsa er iberer*, in Danish *Ogsa vi er iberiske*, in Greek *Eímaste íberai ki emeís*, in Frisian *Ek Wv Binne Ibeariërs*, and also, although with ostensible reticence, in Polish, *My też jestesmy iberyjczykami*, in Bulgarian *Nie sachto sme iberytzi*, in Hungarian *Mi is ibérek vagyunk*, in Russian *Mi toje iberitsi*, in Rumanian *Si noi sîntem iberici*, in Slovak *Ai my sme ibercamia*. But the culmination, the climax, the crowning glory, a rare expression we're not likely to repeat, was when on the Vatican walls, on the venerable murals and columns of the Basilica, on the plinth of Michelangelo's *Pietà*, inside the dome, in enormous sky-blue lettering on the hallowed ground of St Peter's Square, that same declaration appeared in Latin, *Nos quoque iberi sumus*, like some divine utterance in the majestic plural, a *mene, mene, tekel upharsin* of the new eras, and the Pope, at the window of his apartments, blessed himself out of sheer terror, made the sign of the cross in mid-air to no avail, for this paint is guaranteed to last, not even ten whole congregations would suffice to erase those words even if they came armed with steel-wool, bleach, pumice-stones, scrapers, solvents for removing paint, and they will have plenty of work to keep them busy until the next Vatican Council.

From one day to the next, Europe was covered with these slogans.

What probably started out as being little more than the futile gesture of an idealist gradually spread until it became an outcry, a protest and public demonstration. Initially, these manifestations were dismissed with contempt, the words themselves treated with derision. But it wasn't long before the authorities became concerned about this course of events which could not be blamed on interference from abroad, where there was also much subversive activity going on, and this factor at least saved the authorities the trouble of investigating and naming the foreign power they had in mind. It had become the fashion for subversives to go out on to the streets with stickers in their lapels or, more daringly, stuck on their front or back, on their legs, on every part of their body and in every conceivable language, even in regional dialects, in various forms of slang, finally in Esperanto but this was difficult to understand. A strategy of counter-attack resolved by European governments consisted of organizing debates and round-table discussions on television, mainly with the participation of people who had fled the Peninsula when the rupture was complete and irreversible, rather than with people who had been there as tourists and who, poor things, still had not recovered from the fright, but the so-called natives, strictly speaking those who despite close ties of tradition and culture, of property and power, had turned their backs on this geological madness and opted for the physical stability of the Continent. Those people painted a black picture of the Iberian situation with deep compassion and knowledge of the facts, they offered advice to those restless spirits who unwisely were about to put Europe's identity at risk, and they ended their intervention in the debate with a definitive phrase, staring the spectator in the eye and assuming an attitude of utter sincerity, Follow my example, opt for Europe.

The result was not particularly productive, save for the protests of the partisans of the Peninsula who claimed that they had been the victims of discrimination, and who, if neutrality and democratic pluralism were not just empty words, should have been invited to appear on television to express their views if they had any to express. An understandable precaution. Armed with reasons which any discussion about reason always provokes, these youths, because it was chiefly they who were carrying out the most spectacular deeds, could have made their protests with greater conviction, whether in the classroom or in the street, not to mention in the home. It is debatable whether these youths, armed with reasons, would have dispensed with direct action, whereby the calming effect of their intelligence would have prevailed, contrary to what people have believed since the beginning of time. The question is debatable but scarcely worthwhile, for in the meantime the television studios were stoned, shops selling television sets were ransacked in the presence of the dealers, who cried out in despair, But I'm not to blame, their comparative innocence did not help them, lamps exploded like petards, the packing cases were piled up on the street, set alight, reduced to ashes. The police arrived and charged, the rebels dispersed and this test of strength has lasted for the past week right up until today when our travellers leave Figueira da Foz led by a dog, three men and the lover of one of them, who was his lover without yet being his lover, or who not yet being his lover was his lover, anyone with experience of the affairs and intrigues of the heart will understand this muddle. As the latter are heading north, and Joaquim Sassa has already suggested, If we pass through Oporto we can all stay at my house, hundreds of thousands, millions of youths throughout the Continent have taken to the streets, armed not with reasons but with clubs, bicycle chains, grappling-irons, knives, awls, scissors, as if driven insane with rage, as well as with frustration and the sorrow of things to come, they are shouting, We too are Iberians, with that same despair which has caused the shopkeepers to cry out, But we're not to blame.

When tempers have subsided, days and weeks from now, the psychologists and sociologists will come forward to prove that, deep down, those youths didn't really want to be Iberian, what they were doing, taking advantage of a pretext offered by the circumstances, was to give vent to that irrepressible dream, which lasts as long as life itself, but usually erupts for the first time in one's youth with an outburst of sentiment or violence, either the one or the other. Meanwhile battles were fought in the field, or in the streets and squares to be more precise, hundreds of people were injured, there were several deaths, although the authorities tried to suppress reports about serious casualties with confusing and contradictory bulletins, the Mothers of August never got to know for certain how many of their sons had disappeared, for the simple reason that they didn't know how to organize themselves, there are some who always remain outsiders, absorbed in their grief, or caring for the son who survived, or busy gratifying their menfolk in their efforts to conceive another son, which explains why mothers always lose out. Tear gas, water cannons, batons, shields and visors, stones dislodged from the pavements, cross bars from the road blocks, spikes from park railings, these are just some of the weapons used by both sides, while certain new strategies of persuasion with more painful effects are tried out by the different police forces, wars are like disasters, they never come singly, the first is a trial run, the second to improve performance, the third to secure victory, each of them being, according to where you start counting, third, second and first. For the catalogues of memoirs and reminiscences there remained those dying words of the handsome young Dutchman hit by a rubber bullet which turned out to be more deadly than steel because of a manufacturing fault, but legend will soon take this episode in hand and every nation will swear that the youth was theirs, on the other hand no one will be anxious to lay claim to the bullet, unlike those dying words, not so much for their meaning, but because they are beautiful, romantic, incredibly youthful, and nations relish such phrases, especially when they are dealing with a lost cause like this one, At last, I'm Iberian, and with these words he expired. This lad knew what he wanted, or thought he knew, which for want of anything better is just as good, he was not like Joaquim Sassa, who does not know whom he should love, but then he is still alive, perhaps his day will come if he watches out for the right moment.

Day turns to evening, evening will turn to night, along this winding road almost skirting the sea, the guide dog trots at a steady pace, but it's by no means a racing hound, even Deux Chevaux, decrepit as the car is, could travel more quickly as has been proved quite recently. And this pace does not suit it at all, Joaquim Sassa is at the wheel and feeling uneasy, if there should be engine failure, better that the car should be in his hands. The radio, its batteries renewed, reports the disastrous events in Europe, and refers to well-informed sources confirming that international pressure would be put on the Portuguese and Spanish governments to bring the situation to an end, as if it were in their power to achieve this desirable objective, as if controlling a peninsula adrift at sea were the same thing as driving Deux Chevaux. These protests are firmly rejected, with manly pride on the part of the Spanish and feminine haughtiness on the part of the Portuguese, without shaming or exalting either sex, with the announcement that the Prime Ministers will speak that same night, each addressing his own country, of course, by mutual agreement. What has caused a certain bewilderment is the cautious attitude of the White House, usually so ready to intervene in world affairs, whenever they sense it might be to their advantage, however, there are those who argue that the North Americans are not prepared to comment before seeing, literally speaking, where all this is going to end. Meanwhile, supplies of fuel have been coming in from the United States, with some irregularity, it is true, but we should be grateful that it is still possible to find the odd petrol pump in remote areas. Were it not for the North Americans, these travellers would have to go on foot, if they were determined to follow the dog.

When they stopped at a restaurant for lunch, the animal resigned itself to being left outside, it must have understood that its human companions needed to nourish themselves. As they finished their meal, Pedro Orce went out before the others, carrying some left-overs, but the dog refused to eat, and then the reason became clear, there were traces of fresh blood on its hair and around its mouth. The dog has been hunting, José Anaiço said, But it still has the blue thread in its mouth, Joana Carda pointed out, a much more interesting observation than the previous one, after all, our dog, if that's how we are to think of it, has been living this vagabond existence for nearly two weeks and has crossed the entire Peninsula on foot all the way from the Pyrenees to here, and who knows where else, and there couldn't have been anyone to fill his bowl regularly with water or console him with a bone. As for the blue thread, it can be dropped on the ground and picked up again, like the hunter who holds his breath to take aim and then starts breathing naturally again. Joaquim Sassa, who after all was a kind man, said, Dear little dog, if you're as capable of looking after us as you are of looking after yourself, we'll be well protected by your canine skills. The dog shook its head, a gesture we have not learned to interpret. It then went down on to the road and started walking again without once looking back. The afternoon turns out to be better than the morning, there is sunshine, and this devil of a dog, or dog of the devil, resumes its indefatigable trot, with head lowered, its nose protruding, its tail straight, its coat tawny. What breed can it be, asked José Anaiço, Were it not for the tail, it could be a cross between a setter and a sheepdog, Pedro Orce remarked, It's going faster, Joaquim Sassa observed with satisfaction, and Joana Carda, perhaps for the sake of saying something, asked, What shall we call it, sooner or later we inevitably come to this question of names.

The Prime Minister addressed the Portuguese and said, Citizens of Portugal, during recent days and most noticeably during the last twenty-four hours, our country has been subjected to pressures, which without exaggeration I consider unacceptable, from nearly all those European countries in which, as we know, public order has been severely disrupted, through no fault of ours, with vast numbers of demonstrators pouring on to the streets with great enthusiasm, anxious to show their solidarity with the nations and peoples of the Peninsula. These developments have exposed the serious contradiction in the debates between the governments of Europe, to which we no longer belong. Confronted with the profound social and cultural developments in these countries, they see in this historic adventure into which we find ourselves launched the promise of a happier future or, to put it in a nutshell, the hope of regenerating humanity. Now then, instead of supporting us as proof of their basic humanity and genuine awareness of European culture, those governments decided to make us the scapegoats of their internal problems, with their absurd demands that we must arrest the drifting Peninsula, although it would have been more fitting and accurate to describe it as navigating. Their attitude is all the more deplorable since everyone knows that with each passing hour we move a further seven hundred and fifty metres away from what are at present the western shores of Europe, and these European governments who in the past never showed any desire to have us with them are now trying to force us into doing what they don't really want and, moreover, know is beyond our powers. Unquestionably a place of history and culture, Europe in these troubled times has shown itself in the end to be lacking in common sense.

It is up to us as the legitimate and constitutional government, entrusted with preserving the peace of the strong and just, forcefully to reject pressures and interventions of every kind and from any quarter by declaring before the world that we shall only allow ourselves to be guided by the national interest and, in a wider context, by the peoples and nations of the Peninsula, and this I here solemnly affirm with the utmost conviction, now that the governments of Portugal and Spain have started working together, and will continue to do so in order to examine and discuss the necessary measures for a happy solution to the events set in motion after the historic separation of the Pyrenees. A word of acknowledgement is due to the humanitarian spirit and political realism of the United States of America, thanks to whom reasonable levels in supplies of fuel and also of foodstuffs have been maintained, which, within the framework of Community relations, we previously imported from Europe. Under normal conditions, such matters would obviously be dealt with through the competent diplomatic channels, however, in a situation of such gravity, the government over which I preside has decided that the people should be given the facts without delay, thereby expressing its confidence in the dignity of the Portuguese, who will respond, as on other historic occasions, by closing ranks around its legitimate representatives and the sacred symbol of the fatherland, presenting the world with the image of a united and determined people, at a particularly difficult and delicate moment in the nation's history, Long live Portugal.

The four travellers were already on the outskirts of Oporto when they heard this speech, they had gone into a café that served light refreshments and they lingered there long enough to see television coverage of the mass demonstrations and the attacks launched by the police, shivers ran up their spines when they saw those noble youths holding up placards and banners where one could read that formidable phrase written in their language. Why, asked Pedro Orce, should they be so concerned with us, and José Anaiço, echoing unknowingly but more directly the Prime Minister's sentiments, replied, All they're concerned about is themselves, and he probably couldn't have explained any better what he was thinking. They finished eating and left, this time the dog accepted the leftovers Pedro Orce brought him, and, having set Deux Chevaux in motion, now more slowly because the guide could scarcely be seen ahead, Joaquim Sassa said, Before crossing the bridge, let's try to coax the dog into the car, it can travel on the back in the laps of Joana and

José, for we can't go about the city as we've been doing so far, and the dog certainly won't want to go on travelling through the night.

The forecast turned out to be correct and Joaquim Sassa's wish was gratified, as soon as it understood what was required of it, the dog got into the car, slow and ponderous, it stretched out on the laps of the passengers on the back seat, rested its head on Joana Carda's forearm, but the dog did not fall asleep, it travelled with open eyes, the lights of the city danced over them as if over a surface of black crystal. Let's stay at my house, Joaquim Sassa suggested, I've got a wide bed and a sofa that opens out to sleep two people if they're not too fat. One of us, he was referring to the three men, of course, will have to sleep in a chair, but that's no problem, since it's my house, I'll use the chair or spend the night in a nearby boarding-house. The others made no reply, their respectful silence indicating that they agreed, or perhaps preferred to settle this delicate matter discreetly later on, the atmosphere had suddenly become tense, there was an awkward feeling of embarrassment almost as if Joaquim Sassa had done it on purpose and he was perfectly capable of doing such a thing simply to amuse himself. But within minutes Joana Carda spoke up and announced, We two are sticking together. Really, what is the world coming to when women start taking this kind of initiative, in the past there were rules, one always started at the beginning, a few warm, encouraging looks from the man, a subtle lowering of the woman's eyes, darting a furtive glance from under her eyelashes, and then, until that first touching of hands the courtship proceeded slowly, there were letters, lovers' tiffs, reconciliations, the waving of handkerchiefs, discreet coughs, naturally the final outcome was always the same, in bed with the wench on her back, the stud on top of her, in or out of wedlock, but never for a moment this outrageous behaviour, this lack of respect in the presence of an old man, and if anyone thinks the women of Andalusia are hot-blooded, they should take a look at this woman from Portugal, no woman has ever dared to say in Pedro Orce's presence, We two are sticking together. But times have changed, and not for the better if Joaquim Sassa was trying to tease them, the conversation had turned sour, unless Pedro Orce had misunderstood, perhaps the words sticking together do not mean the same thing in Castilian as in Portuguese. José Anaiço did not open his mouth, what could he say, he would look ridiculous if he were to play the lover, even more so if he were to appear scandalized, best to keep one's mouth shut, it does not take much to realize that only Joana Carda could have uttered those compromising words, imagine the bad impression he would have made if he had said those words without first consulting her, and even so, even if he had asked her if she agreed, there are certain attitudes that only a woman can adopt, depending on the circumstances and the moment, that's it, the moment, that precise second poised between two others which would result in confusion and disaster. Joana Carda and José Anaiço rest their clasped hands on the dog's back, Joaquim Sassa furtively watches the lovers through the rear-view mirror, they are smiling, the joke has been well received after all. This Joana is quite a girl and Joaquim Sassa feels another twinge of jealousy, but he admits he is to blame because he can never decide whom he should love.

The house is no palace, it has a tiny interior bedroom, and an even tinier sitting-room where there is a divan-bed, a kitchen, a bathroom, clearly a house for someone on their own, but he considers himself fortunate and at least he does not have to keep moving from one furnished room to another. The larder is empty, but they had satisfied their hunger at their last stop before arriving here. They watch television in the hope of catching up on the news, so far there have been no reactions from the European embassies, but just to remind them the Prime Minister has given another interview on the late news programme, Citizens of Portugal, he said, the rest we have already heard. Before they retire to bed there is a council of war, not that there has been any need to take decisions, those are left to the dog who is snoozing at Pedro Orce's feet, but they speculate in turn, Perhaps our journey ends here, Joaquim Sassa says hopefully, Or further north, José Anaiço suggests, thinking of something else, I think it will be further north, adds Joana Carda, who is thinking of the same thing, but Pedro Orce is right when he tells them, The dog is the only one who knows, whereupon he yawns and says, I feel sleepy.

Now there was no longer any uncertainty as to who would be sleeping with whom, Joaquim Sassa opened out the divan-bed assisted by Pedro Orce, Joana Carda retired discreetly, and José Anaiço lingered for a few minutes longer, embarrassed, as if none of this had anything to do with him, but his heart was thumping in his breast like the beating of a drum, causing the whole building to shake to its very foundations, although this tremor is quite different from the other one, finally he said, Goodnight, see you tomorrow, and withdrew. There is no doubt that words never match up to the grandeur of certain moments. The room was next door, the window almost at the height of the ceiling, one way of prolonging daylight, and it did not even have a curtain, this apparent lack of privacy is understandable, the house was only for one person, and even if Joaquim Sassa were to have such perverted tastes he could scarcely spy on himself, although it has to be said that it would be very interesting as well as revealing, if we could spy on ourselves from time to time, although we might not like what we should see. With these words of caution, we're not trying to insinuate that Joaquim Sassa and Pedro Orce are thinking of playing childish games in such poor taste, but that window, now the mere shadow of a window, barely visible in the darkness of the room, is disturbing, chills the blood, as if this were all one room, a dormitory, uncomfortably promiscuous, and Joaquim Sassa, lying on his back, preferred not to think, but raised his head from the pillow to create an aura of silence and be able to hear better, his mouth was dry but he stoically resisted the temptation to get up and go into the kitchen to drink some water and eavesdrop on the whispering on the way. As for Pedro Orce, he was so exhausted he fell asleep immediately, his face turned away from the wall, his arm reaching down to rest on the dog's back as it lay on the floor beside him, the trembling of the one is that of the other, their sleep probably one and the same. No sound comes from the bedroom, not even so much as an inaudible word, so much as a sigh, a stifled moan, Such silence, Joaquim Sassa thinks to himself, and he finds it strange, but he neither imagines nor is ever likely to suspect or know just how strange, for these things usually remain the secret of those who have experienced them, José Anaiço penetrated Joana Carda and she received him without any other movement, he hard, she most gentle, and there they stayed, their fingers clasped, their lips absorbing kisses in silence, as one mighty wave shakes the innermost fibres of their bodies, noiselessly, right to the very last vibration, to the last imperceptible drop, let us put it discreetly, so that no one may accuse us of crudely portraying scenes of coition, an ugly word which has fortunately become obsolete. Tomorrow, when Joaquim Sassa wakes up, he will think those two had the patience to wait, God knows at what cost, if God knows about these sublimations of the flesh, that they had waited until the others next door were asleep, he's deceiving himself, for just as he is about to fall asleep, Joana Carda receives José Anaiço once more, this time they will not be as quiet as before, certain feats cannot be repeated, The others must be asleep by now, one of them whispered, at last they could abandon themselves to passionate love, their patience rewarded.

Pedro Orce was the first to awaken, through a narrow chink in the window the ashen finger of morning touched his parched lips, then he dreamed that a woman was kissing him, oh how he struggled to make that dream last, but his eyes opened, and his mouth was dry, no mouth had deposited the truth of saliva or its fertile humidity in his. The dog lifted its head, raised itself on its paws, and gazed steadily at Pedro Orce in the dense shadows of the room, it was impossible to see where the light that shone in its eyes was coming from. Pedro Orce stroked the animal, and it responded only once by licking his bony hand. Disturbed by the noise, Joaquim Sassa woke up, initially without any idea of his whereabouts, even though he was in his own home, perhaps because he felt strange upon finding himself in a bed he rarely used, and because there was someone in the room beside him. Lying on his back, with the dog's head reclining on his chest, Pedro Orce said, Another day begins, what's going to happen, and Joaquim Sassa thought, Perhaps he's become confused after sleeping, it's not uncommon, people fall asleep and that in itself has changed everything, we are the same as before yet fail to recognize ourselves. In this case they did not appear to have changed. The dog had got to its feet, big, heavy, and had walked to the closed door. One could see its blurred outline, its shadowy form, the gleam in its eyes, The dog's waiting for us, said Joaquim Sassa, you better call him, it's still too early to get up. The dog came when Pedro Orce called and obediently lay down, the men were now conversing in a whisper, Joaquim Sassa was saying, I'm going to take out all the money I have in the bank, it isn't much but I can borrow some more, And what happens when that runs out, Perhaps our little adventure will come to an end before the money does, Who can tell what awaits us, We'll find some means of surviving, even by stealing if we have to, Joaquim Sassa said smiling. But perhaps it won't be necessary to resort to such drastic measures, José Anaiço will also pay a visit to the bank here in Oporto where he has his savings, Pedro Orce has brought all his pesetas, and as for Joana Carda we don't know anything about her financial situation, but to all appearances she is not the type of woman who lives off charity or is kept by some man. It is doubtful whether the four of them will find any work, if work requires permanency, stability, normal residential status, when their immediate destiny is to walk behind a dog who we can only hope knows something about its own destiny, but this is not the age when animals could speak and therefore, say where they wanted to go, so long as they had vocal cords.

In the next room, the exhausted lovers were asleep in each other's arms, sheer ecstasy but alas short-lived as one would expect, after all, one's body is this body and not the other, a body has a beginning and an end, it begins and ends with the skin, what's inside belongs to it, but the body needs its rest, independence, autonomy in its functioning, to sleep in each other's arms demands a harmony of tongue and groove which may be disturbed by the sleep of either partner, one of them may awaken suffering from cramp in the arm, or because there is an elbow sticking into their ribs, whereupon we say in a whisper, with all the tenderness we can muster, Dearest, move over just a little. Joana Carda and José Anaiço are asleep from exhaustion, for during the night they have had sexual intercourse three times, their love affair has only just begun therefore they respect the golden rule of never refusing the body what the body in its wisdom demands. Making as little noise as possible, Joaquim Sassa and Pedro Orce went out with the dog, they've gone to look for some provisions for breakfast, Joaquim Sassa refers to it as *pequeno almoço* rather like the French *petit dejeuner*, Pedro Orce as *desayuno* in the Spanish, but their common hunger will resolve the linguistic differences. By the time they return, Joana Carda and José Anaiço will be out of bed, we can hear them in the bathroom, the shower is running, a blissful pair, and such great walkers for in a very short time they have come a long way.

When it is time to set out and resume their journey, the four of them start looking at the dog with the perplexed air of someone awaiting orders, who is as uncertain of their reliability as of the wisdom of obeying them. Let us hope that in order to get out of Oporto the dog entrusts itself to us as it did when we came in, says Joaquim Sassa, and the others understood the reason for that observation, just imagine if the dog Faithful, faithful to its instinct to head north, were to start taking one-way streets here in the city where north was precisely the direction you couldn't follow, there would be endless trouble with the police, accidents, traffic jams, with the entire population of Oporto turning out to enjoy the fun. But this dog isn't any old sheepdog of suspect or clandestine paternity, its genealogical tree has its roots in hell, which, as we know, is the place where all knowledge ends up, ancient knowledge which is already there, modern and future knowledge which will pursue the same path. For this reason, and perhaps also because Pedro Orce has repeated the trick of whispering into the dog's ear words which we still have not been able to make out, the dog gets into the car as if it were the most natural thing in the world, as if it has always travelled like this all its life. But, look out, this time the dog hasn't rested its head on Joana Carda's forearm, this time it sits up attentively as Joaquim Sassa drives Deux Chevaux along curves and bends on the road, in every direction, anyone who happened to be there watching would think, They're heading south, but soon they would change their mind and decide, They're going west, or, They're going east, and these are the main or cardinal directions but if we were to mention the entire compass-card we would never get out of Oporto or this confusion.

There is an agreement between this dog and these travellers, four rational beings consent to being led by brute instinct, unless they are all being drawn by some magnet located in the north or being pulled by the other end of a blue thread identical to this one the dog won't let go. They leave the city, one knows that despite the curves, the road is going in the right direction, the dog gives signs of wanting to get out of the car, they open the door and off it goes, refreshed after a night's rest and the large meal it had been given at the house. The dog goes at a brisk trot, Deux Chevaux cheerfully accompanies it, feels no need to keep a tight rein. The road no longer skirts the sea, it wends inland, and for this very reason we won't see the shore where Joaquim Sassa acquired more strength than Samson at a given moment in his life. Joaquim himself remarks, What a pity the dog decided not to follow the coastline, then I could have shown you where the episode of the stone took place, not even the Samson mentioned in the Bible could have done what I did, but out of modesty he would say no more. What was and continues to be a much greater feat was that of Joana Carda there in the fields of Ereira, and even more enigmatic is the tremor felt by Pedro Orce, and if our guide here on earth is a dog from the underworld, what shall we say of the thousands of starlings that accompanied José Anaiço for so long and only abandoned him when it was time to take flight once more.

The road slopes upwards, descends, then starts rising again, and goes on rising, and whenever it goes down, it is only to take a short pause, these mountains are not all that high, but they affect Deux Chevaux's heart, causing it to struggle for breath on the slopes while the dog travels on at a nimble pace. They stopped to have lunch at a snack bar on the roadside, once more the dog disappeared in search of its own food and when it returned there was blood on its mouth, but we already know why, there's no mystery, if no one is around to fill the bowl, a dog has to make do with what it can find. Back on the road, they kept heading north, at one point José Anaiço quipped to Pedro Orce, If we carry on like this we'll find ourselves in Spain, in your native country. My native land is Andalusia, Country and land are one and the same thing, No they're not, we may not know our country but we always know our own land, Have you ever been to Galicia, No, I've never been to Galicia, Galicia is the land of others.

Whether they would get there remains to be seen, because they were to spend the night in Portugal. José Anaiço and Joana Carda signed the hotel register as man and wife, in order to economize Pedro Orce and Joaquim Sassa shared a room, and the dog had to sleep with Deux Chevaux, the huge beast terrified the landlady, I don't want a monster like that in my hotel, it can sleep outdoors where dogs belong, the last thing I need is to have the place infested with fleas, The dog hasn't got any fleas, Joana Carda protested to no avail, for that was not the main point. In the middle of the night Pedro Orce got out of bed, hoping to find that the front door wasn't locked and it was not in fact, so he went to sleep for a couple of hours in the car with the dog in his arms, when one has no one to love, in this case for obvious impediments of nature, friendship is the next best thing. It seemed to Pedro Orce as he got into the car that the dog was whimpering, but he must have been hallucinating, as we often do when we dearly want something, our wise body takes pity on us, simulates within itself the satisfaction of our desires, this is what dreaming means, what do you think, If it weren't so, tell me how we could ever bear this intolerable life, comes the commentary from the unknown voice which intervenes from time to time.

When Pedro Orce returned to the bedroom, the dog followed him, but when told not to enter, it lay down in the doorway and there it remained. There are no words to describe the terror and outcry at first light of day, when the landlady arrives early to begin her daily chores, opens the shutters to the freshness of the dawn, and lo and behold, here on the door-mat the Nemean lion springs to its feet with bared fangs, it was simply the yawn of a dog that hadn't had enough sleep, but even yawns should be treated with caution when they expose formidable teeth and a tongue so red that it appears to be bleeding. Such was the uproar that the guests' departure had all the appearance of expulsion rather than peaceful withdrawal, Deux Chevaux was already at some distance, almost turning the corner, and the landlady was still yelling on the doorstep at the silent beast, for these are the worst beasts of all if one is to believe the proverb which says, Dogs that bark don't bite, it's true that this one hasn't bitten yet, but if those powerful jaws are in direct proportion to its silence, God protect us from the beast. Once on their way, the travellers laugh at the episode, Joana Carda, out of feminine solidarity, didn't find it amusing, Had I been in that woman's position, I'd also have been terrified, and you lot needn't think yourselves such heroes or, worse still, feel obliged to show how brave you are, her words made a deep impression, each man quietly pondered his own cowardice, the most interesting case was that of José Anaiço who decided he would confess his fear to Joana Carda at the first possible opportunity, for real love means keeping no secrets from one's beloved, the worst comes later when the romance is over and the lover who has confided his secrets regrets having spoken while the beloved abuses his confidence, it's up to Joana Carda and José Anaiço to arrange their affairs so as to avoid anything like this happening.

The frontier isn't far away. Having got accustomed to the scouting talents of their guide, the travellers have not even noticed the speedy manner, without a moment's hesitation or pause for thought, with which Faithful or Pilot, he'll have to be given some name or other one day, chooses the right fork in the road he must follow, and to make things more awkward, this is not simply a fork but a cross-roads. Even if this cunning animal has covered this same route from north to south, and of this no one can be sure, the experience will not be of much help, if we bear in mind the difference in the point of view, on which, as we are fortunately aware, everything depends. It is all too true that people live alongside things wondrous and prodigious, but they do not even fathom half of these marvels, they nearly always deceive themselves about the half they know, mainly because they desire with all their might, like Our Lord God, that this and other worlds should be made in their own image and likeness, not that it matters who created them. This dog is guided by instinct, but we have no way of telling what or who guides instinct, and if we should ever be able to start explaining the strange episode narrated here, in all probability any such explanation would be no more than the semblance of an explanation, unless from that explanation we can derive another and then another, until there comes a moment when there would be nothing left to explain the primary source of the things explained, presumably beyond that there is nothing but chaos, but we are not speaking about the formation of the universe, we do know about that, we are only discussing dogs.

And people. These people who are following a dog and heading for the frontier just ahead. They are about to leave Portuguese territory at sunset, and suddenly, perhaps because of the approaching twilight, they realize that the animal has disappeared, and they suddenly feel like children lost in the forest, now what are we going to do, Joaquim Sassa seizes the opportunity to express his disdain for canine loyalty, but Pedro Orce's serene judgment, based on his experience of life, prevailed. The dog has probably swum across the river to wait for us on the opposite side, if these people had really paid attention to the ties and bonds which link existence and alchemy they would have realized it at once, we are referring to José Anaiço and Joaquim Sassa, for the dog's motives may be the same as those of a thousand starlings, if Faithful came from the north and passed this way, perhaps it may not wish to repeat the experience, without collar or muzzle, it could be suspected of having rabies and might even find itself being riddled with bullets.

The customs officers examine their papers distractedly, wave them on, it is obvious that these officials are not exactly overworked, as we have seen, people travel a great deal, but for the moment it is more within frontiers, they seem to be afraid of straying from their home in the wider sense, namely their native land, even if they have abandoned the family home where they have lived their humdrum lives. On the other side of the Minho there is the same boredom, all one detects is a glimmer of detached curiosity as they watch these Portuguese arrive with a Spaniard of another generation, were this a period of greater traffic to and fro they wouldn't even be noticed. Joaquim Sassa drives for a kilometre, draws Deux Chevaux on to the side of the road and comes to a halt, Let's wait here, if the dog, as Pedro claims, knows what it is doing, it will come to look for us. They did not even have time to become impatient. After ten minutes, the dog appears in front of the car, its coat still damp. Pedro Orce had been right, and if we had not been quite so sceptical, we should have waited on the riverbank to witness the dog's heroic crossing which we could have described with such relish, instead of this banal crossing of frontiers with guards whose only difference is their uniforms, Carry on, You may pass, this summed up the episode, even the glimmer of curiosity was no more than a feeble invention to fill out the narrative.

Further and somewhat better inventions would now be timely to enhance what remains of the journey, with two nights and two days in between, the former spent in rural lodging-houses, the latter on old roads that once went north, always towards the north, the land of Galicia and mist, with light showers announcing the arrival of autumn, this is all one feels like saying and no invention was needed. The rest would be the nocturnal embraces of Joana Carda and José Anaiço, the intermittent insomnia of Joaquim Sassa, Pedro Orce's hand resting on the dog's back, for here the dog was allowed inside the bedrooms where it could spend the night. And the days on the road, heading right towards a horizon which seemed to move further and further away. For the second time, Joaquim Sassa said that this was utter madness, trailing after a stupid dog to the ends of the earth without knowing why or for what purpose, to which Pedro Orce replied abruptly, betraying his annoyance, Scarcely to the ends of the earth since we'll reach the sea before then. The dog is clearly beginning to tire, its head is drooping, its tail has dropped, and the pads on its paws, despite their hard skin, must be hurting by now after all that rubbing against soil and gravel, that same night Pedro Orce will examine them and find open sores which are bleeding, no wonder he responded so sharply to Joaquim Sassa, who looks on and says as if trying to excuse himself, Some compresses with hydrogen peroxide should do them good, it's rather like teaching your grandmother how to suck eggs, Pedro Orce is familiar with all the skills of pharmacy, he doesn't need any advice from Joaquim Sassa. Nevertheless, this conciliatory gesture was enough to restore the peace.

In the vicinity of Santiago de Compostela the dog veered in a northeasterly direction. It must be nearing its destination, this could be seen from the renewed vigour with which it was now trotting along, from its firm gait, the way it held its head, its bristling tail. Joaquim Sassa was forced to accelerate a little so that Deux Chevaux could keep up with the dog, and they got so close that they were almost touching the animal. Joana Carda exclaimed, Look, look at the blue thread. They all turned round. The thread didn't look the same. The other one had become so dirty that it could have been mistaken for blue or black, but this one was as blue as blue could be, and quite unlike the blue of the sky or sea, who could have dyed and combed it, who could have washed it, if it was the same thread, and put it back into the dog's mouth with the words, Off you go. The road has become narrow, it's almost like a footpath skirting the hills. The sun is about to set over the sea which still cannot be seen from here, nature is masterly when it comes to composing spectacles attuned to human circumstances, this morning and all afternoon the sky had been overcast and sombre as it sprinkled the land with Galician drizzle, and now the countryside is bathed in a coppery light, the dog glows like a jewel, an animal made of gold. Even Deux Chevaux no longer looks the worse for wear and the passengers inside are suddenly transformed, the light is shining on them and they go forth like the beatified. José Anaiço observes Joana Carda and shudders at the sight of such beauty, Joaquim Sassa lowers the rear-view mirror in order to gaze into his own sparkling eyes, and Pedro Orce contemplates his wrinkled hands, they are no longer wrinkled, no, they've been restored by alchemy, they've become immortal, even if the rest of his body should die.

Suddenly the dog stops. The sun is level with the summit of the mountains, the sea can be glimpsed on the other side. The road goes winding down, two hills appear to cut it off down below, but this is an optical illusion at a distance. In front, halfway down the slope, there is a large house, an austere building with an air of neglect, very old, despite signs that the surrounding fields have been cultivated. Part of the house is already in the shade, the light is waning, the whole world appears to be sinking into inertia and solitude. Joaquim Sassa brings the car to a halt. They all get out. The silence can be heard vibrating like one last echo, perhaps it is only the distant thrashing of the waves against the rocks, that is always the best explanation, the interminable memory of the waves echoes even inside the shells, however this is not the case, what can be heard here is silence, no one should die before experiencing it, silence, have you heard it, now you may go, you know what it sounds like. But that hour still has not arrived for any of these four. They know that their destination is that house, this amazing dog has brought them here, mute as a statue, waiting. José Anaiço is at Joana Carda's side but he does not touch her, he knows that he must not touch her, she knows it too, these are moments when even love must resign itself to its own insignificance, forgive us for reducing the greatest of affections to almost nothing, that affection which on other occasions can be almost everything. Pedro Orce is the last to get out of the car, he puts his feet on the ground and feels the earth vibrating with terrifying force, here every seismograph needle would snap, and these hills appear to sway with the movement of the waves which surge one upon the other in the sea beyond, pushed by this stone raft, throwing themselves against it with the reflux of the powerful currents we are cutting through.

The sun had disappeared. Then the blue thread fluttered in the air, almost invisible in its transparency, searching for some support, and grazing hands and faces, Joaquim Sassa held it, was this a coincidence or destiny, let us leave these hypotheses aside, even though there are a number of reasons for not giving credence either to the one or the other, and now what will Joaquim Sassa do, he cannot travel in the car, with one hand outside holding and accompanying the thread, for a thread at the mercy of the wind does not necessarily follow the line of the road. What should I do with this, he asked, but the others could not give him an answer while the dog could, it left the road and began to descend the gentle slope, Joaquim Sassa followed it, his raised hand followed the blue thread as if it were stroking the wings or the breast of a bird above his head. José Anaiço went back to the car with Joana Carda and Pedro Orce, put it into gear, and, keeping a watchful eye on Joaquim Sassa, slowly began descending the road, he did not want to arrive before him, or for that matter much after him, the potential harmony of things depends on their equilibrium and the time when they occur, not too soon, not too late, which explains why it is so difficult for us to attain perfection.

When they stopped in the square in front of the house, Joaquim Sassa was ten paces from the door, which was ajar. The dog gave a sigh that seemed almost human and lay down, stretching its neck over its paws. It removed the thread from its mouth with its claws and shook it on to the ground. A woman emerged from the dark interior of the house. She had a thread in her hand, the same as the one Joaquim Sassa was still holding. She descended the last step at the front door and said, Come in, you must be tired. Joaquim Sassa was the first to move, his end of the blue thread tied round his wrist.

One day, Maria Guavaira told them, about this hour and with much the same light, the dog appeared, looking as if it had come from afar, its coat was filthy, its paws bleeding, it came and knocked on the door with its head, and when I went to open it, thinking it might be one of those beggars who travel from place to place, who arrive tapping their stick and plead, Some alms for a poor man, good woman, what do I find but the dog, panting as if it had come running from the end of the world and the blood stained the ground under its paws, the most surprising thing of all was that I didn't feel frightened, though there was every reason to take fright, anyone who didn't know just how harmless the dog is would think they were looking at the wildest of beasts, poor creature, the moment it saw me, the dog lay down on the ground as if it had been waiting until it reached me before attempting to rest, and it seemed to be crying, as if trying to speak but unable to, and all the time the dog was here I never ever heard it bark. It's been with us now for six days and it hasn't barked once, Joana Carda said, I took it in, cleaned it up, nursed it, it's not a stray, you can tell from its coat, and the dog's owners obviously fed it properly, showed it love and affection, if you want to see the difference you need only compare it with Galician dogs, who are born hungry and die from starvation after a lifetime of being deprived, beaten and stoned, that's why the Galician dog can't lift its tail, but hides it between its legs in the hope of not being noticed, its revenge when it gets the chance, is to bite. This one doesn't bite, Pedro Orce assured them, As for knowing where it came from, we shall probably never know, José Anaiço remarked, perhaps it's not all that important, what surprises me is that it should have come to look for us to bring us here, you

145

cannot help wondering why. I don't know, all I know is that one day it went off with a piece of thread in its mouth, looking at me as if to say, Don't move from here until I return, and off it went up the hill there from which it has just descended, What is this thread, Joaquim Sassa asked, as he wound then unwound from his wrist the end of the strand which still tied him to Maria Guavaira. I wish I knew, she replied, winding her end between her fingers and stretching the thread like the taut string of a guitar, but neither he nor she appeared to notice that they were tied together, but the others did as they stood there looking on, what they were thinking they kept to themselves although it wouldn't be all that difficult to guess. For I did nothing except unpick an old sock, one of those socks people used to keep their money in, but the sock I unpicked would have given only a handful of wool, while the amount of wool here is what you would get from shearing a hundred sheep, not to say a thousand, and how is one to explain such a thing. For days, two thousand starlings kept following me, said José Anaiço, I threw a stone into the sea that weighed almost as much as me and it landed way in the distance, Joaquim Sassa added, aware that he was exaggerating, and Pedro Orce simply said, The earth is trembling, and has trembled.

Maria Guavaira got up and opened a door and said, Look, Joaquim Sassa was standing beside her, but it was not the thread that had drawn him, and what they saw was a blue cloud, of a blue which darkened and became almost black in the middle, If I leave this door open there are always ends sticking out, just like the one that went up the road and brought you here, Maria Guavaira said, addressing Joaquim Sassa, and the kitchen where they had all gathered was now deserted, except for those two, joined together by a blue thread, and the blue cloud which appeared to be breathing, wood could be heard crackling in the hearth where some cabbage soup was on the boil flavoured with scraps of meat, not as heavy as the Galician recipe.

Joaquim Sassa and Maria Guavaira must not remain tied together like this for too long otherwise this union will begin to look suspicious, so she winds up all the thread and on reaching his wrist she pulls the thread round it as if she were invisibly attaching him to her once more, and then holds the tiny ball of wool against her breast, only a fool would be in any doubt about the gesture, and he would be an even bigger fool not to be in doubt. José Anaiço moves away from the fire burning in the hearth, Although it may seem absurd, we've come to the conclusion that there is some connection or other between what has happened to us and the separation of Spain and Portugal from Europe, you must have heard about it, Yes, I have but in these parts no one gave it another thought, if we go over the mountains and down to the coast the sea is always the same. It was shown on television, I don't have television, It was broadcast in the news bulletin, News is nothing but words, and you can never really tell if words are news.

On this sceptical note the conversation was interrupted for several minutes. Maria Guavaira went to fetch some bowls from the shelf, ladled out the soup, the last but one for Joaquim Sassa, the last one of all for herself, for a moment everyone thought there would be one spoon short, but no, there were enough to go round, so Maria Guavaira did not have to wait for Joaquim Sassa to finish his soup. Then he asked her if she was living alone, for so far they hadn't seen anyone else in the house, and she told him that she had been a widow for three years, and that hired labourers came to work the land, I'm between the sea and the mountains, without children or family, my brothers emigrated to Argentina, my father died, my demented mother is in an asylum in La Coruña, there can't be many women as lonely as me in this world, You could have remarried, Joana Carda pointed out, but immediately regretted having spoken, she had no right to say such a thing, she who only a few days ago had broken up her marriage and was already keeping company with another man, I was worn out, and if a woman remarries at my age, it's because of any land she may own, men are more interested in marrying land than some woman, You're still young, I was young once but I can scarcely remember that time, and with these words she leaned over the hearth so that the flames lit up her face, she looked up at Joaquim Sassa as if to say, This is what I'm like, take a good look at me, you turned up on my doorstep tied to a thread I was holding in my hand, I could, if I so wished, draw you to my bed, and I'm certain you would come, but beautiful I shall never be, unless you can transform me into the most desirable woman who ever lived, that's something only a man can do, and does, but what a pity it can't last forever.

Joaquim Sassa watched her from the other side of the fire and saw that the flames as they danced kept on changing her expression, one moment making her cheeks look sunken, the next moment smoothing away the shadows, but the gleam in her dark eyes did not change, perhaps a suspended tear had become transformed into a membrane of pure light. She isn't pretty, he thought, nor is she ugly, her hands are rough and worn, quite unlike mine, the smooth hands of an office clerk enjoying paid leave, which reminds me that tomorrow, unless I'm mistaken, is the last day of the month, the day after tomorrow I'm due back at work, but no, how can I, how can I possibly leave José and Joana, Pedro and the Dog, they've no reason for wanting to come with me, and if I take Deux Chevaux they're going to find it extremely difficult to get back to their respective homes, but they probably don't want to go back, the only real thing that exists at this moment on earth is our being here together, Joana Carda and José Anaiço conversing in whispers, perhaps about their own life, perhaps about each other's life, Pedro Orce with his hand on Pilot's head, no doubt measuring vibrations and tremors no one else can feel, while I watch and go on watching Maria Guavaira who has a way of looking which isn't exactly looking but a way of showing her eyes, she is dressed in black, a widow whom time has consoled but whom custom and tradition restricts to wearing black, fortunately her eyes shine, and there is the blue cloud which doesn't seem to belong to this house, her hair is brown, and she has a rounded chin and full lips, and her teeth, I caught a glimpse of them a moment ago, are white, thank God, this woman is pretty after all and I didn't even notice, I was tied to her and didn't realize, I must decide whether to return home or remain here, even if I arrive back at work a few days late I'll be excused, with all this upheaval in the Peninsula who's going to pay any attention to employees who are a few days late in returning to work, one can always say there was no transport. One minute she looked common, the next quite pretty, and now, right now, standing beside Maria Guavaira, Joana Carda looks terrible, my girl is much more attractive Senhor José Anaiço, how can you compare your city dame and her affectations with this wild creature who clearly tastes of the salty air the breeze carries over the mountains and whose body must be white underneath that black dress, if I could, Pedro Orce, I'd tell you something, What would you tell me, That I now know whom I should love, Congratulations, there are people who have taken much longer, or have never come to know, Do you know any such person, Take me, for example, and with this reply, Pedro Orce then said in a loud voice, I'm going to take the dog for a walk.

Darkness has not yet fallen, but it is cold. In the direction of the mountain which is hiding the sea there is a path that begins to wend its way up the slope ahead in one bend after another, to the left and right like a winding thread until it disappears from sight. Soon the valley will be plunged into darkness as on the night of the blackout, although it would be more accurate to say that in the valley where Maria Guavaira lives every night is like a blackout, so there was no need for all the electric cables of civilized and cultured Europe to break down. Pedro Orce leaves the house because he is not needed there. He walks on without looking back, at first as quickly as his strength permits, then as he begins to tire, he slows down. He does not feel the least bit nervous in this silence amidst the great walls formed by the mountains, he's a man who was born and bred in a desert, in a land of dust and stones, where one is never surprised to find a horse's skull, a hoof with the metal shoe still attached, there are some who say not even the horsemen of the Apocalypse could survive there, the Warhorse died in war, the infected horse died of infection, the starved horse of starvation, death is the supreme *raison d'être* of all things and their infallible conclusion, what deceives us is this line of the living in which we find ourselves, which advances to what we call the future simply because we had to give it a name, from where we constantly gather new beings while constantly leaving old ones behind which we were obliged to refer to as the dead lest they should emerge from the past.

Pedro Orce's heart is already starting to grow old and weary. He now has to rest more often and for longer, but he does not give up, the dog's presence consoles him. They exchange signs with each other, like a code of communications which even though undeciphered is enough, for the simple fact of existing is enough, the animal rubs its back against the man's thigh, the man's hand strokes the soft skin inside the dog's ear, the world is filled with the sound of footsteps, breathing, friction, and now the muffled clamour of the sea can unmistakably be heard behind the summit of the mountain and growing louder, louder, getting clearer and clearer, until the immense surface looms up before one's eyes, vaguely sparkling beneath the night sky bereft of moonlight and with few stars, and below, like the living line separating night and death, the dazzling whiteness of spume constantly dissolving and renewing itself. The rocks are blacker where the waves are lashing, as if the stone there had greater density or had been soaked in water since the beginning of time. The wind comes in from the sea, in part it is blowing naturally, in part it can scarcely be felt, this must be due to the Peninsula's displacement in the water, it is no more than a breeze, as we well know, and yet there has never been such a typhoon since the world began.

Pedro Orce measured the dimension of the ocean and at that moment found it small, because on taking a deep breath his lungs expanded so much that all the chasms of liquid could rush in and still leave space for the raft which with its stone battering-rams started forcing its way through the waves. Pedro did not know if he was man or fish. He went down to the sea, the dog racing ahead to sniff out and choose the path, and this prudent and astute guide was much needed, for without daylight, Pedro Orce on his own could not have found the entrance or exit of this labyrinth of stones. At last they reached the great slabs of rock which descend to the sea, there the roar of waves breaking is deafening. Beneath this pitch-black sky and the cries of the sea, should the moon now appear, a man could die of rapture, believing himself to be dying of anguish, fear and solitude. Pedro Orce no longer felt cold. The night became clearer, more stars have appeared and the dog, which had been gone for a moment, came running back, it had not been trained to tug its master's trousers, but we know it well enough to be certain that it is perfectly capable of making its wishes known, and now Pedro Orce must accompany it to examine its discovery, a castaway swept up on to the shore, a treasure chest, some vestige of Atlantis, the wreckage of the *Flying Dutchman*, an obsessive memory, and when he arrived he saw that they were nothing but stones, but since this was a dog not easily fooled, there had to be something unusual there, that was when he noticed that he was actually standing on it, the thing, an enormous stone, roughly in the form of a boat, and there was another one, long and narrow like a mast, and yet another, this must be the helm with its tiller, although broken. Thinking that the dim light was deceiving him, he started walking round the stones, touching and probing them, and he was no longer in any doubt, this side, tall and pointed, is the prow, this other flat one is the stern, the mast is unmistakable, and the helm could only be made for a giant, for example, were it not for the fact that this is definitely a stone ship which is standing here. A geological phenomenon, to be sure. Pedro Orce knows more than enough about chemistry to be able to explain the discovery to himself, an ancient wooden vessel brought here by the waves or abandoned by mariners, stranded on these rocks since time immemorial, then they were covered by earth, their organic material petrified, once more the earth has retreated, until today, thousands of years will be needed to blunt the edges and reduce these volumes, wind, rain, the erosion of cold and heat, the day will come when one stone won't be distinguishable from another. Pedro Orce sat right inside the boat, from where he's sitting he can see nothing but sky and the distant sea, if this ship were to pitch ever so slightly he would imagine himself to be sailing, and then, which shows you what the imagination can do, he absurdly began to imagine that this petrified ship was indeed sailing and towing the Peninsula, one cannot trust these flights of fantasy, obviously it is not impossible, one has witnessed even more difficult feats, but as it happens the ship's stern is ironically facing out to sea, no reputable vessel would ever sail backwards. Pedro Orce stood up, he now feels cold, and the dog has jumped on to the parapet, Time we were going home, Master, you're rather old for these late nights, if you didn't go in for them when you were young, it's too late now.

When they reached the summit of the mountains, Pedro Orce could scarcely walk, and his poor lungs, which only a short time ago could have inhaled the entire ocean, gasped like punctured bellows, the harsh air chafed his nostrils, parched his throat, these mountain tracks are not for a pharmacist getting on in years. He sank on to a boulder, had to rest, with his elbows resting on his knees, holding his head in his hands, the perspiration glistening on his forehead, the wind ruffling loose strands of hair, he was a physical wreck, weary and dejected, alas no one has yet discovered ways of petrifying a human being in the flower of youth and transforming him into an eternal statue. His breathing was more relaxed, the air had softened, it came and went without that grating noise like sandpaper. Aware of these changes, the dog, which had been waiting, stretched out, made as if to get up. Pedro Orce raised his head, looked down into the valley where the house stood. There seemed to be an aura hovering over it, a diffused radiance, a kind of light without any luminosity, if this phrase, which like all others can only be formed with words, is understood with only one meaning. Pedro Orce suddenly remembered that epileptic back in Orce who, in the wake of those fits which left him prostrate, tried to explain the confused sensations which preceded them, it could be a vibration of the invisible particles of air, the radiation of energy like heat in the distance, the distortion of luminous rays just beyond his reach, this night was truly filled with wonders, the thread and cloud of blue wool, the stone ship grounded on the rocks on the shore, and now this house which is shaking tremendously, or so it appears to us, seen from here. The image flickered, the outlines merged, it appeared to recede until it became an almost invisible point, then it returned, slowly vibrating. For an instant, Pedro Orce was afraid of being left abandoned in this other desert, but the fear passed, just enough time to realize that down there Maria Guavaira and Joaquim Sassa had got together, times have changed a lot, nowadays a man no sooner sets eyes on a woman than he is poking the fire, if you'll pardon this crude plebeian and obsolete comparison. Pedro Orce had got up to start descending the slope, but sat down again and patiently waited, shivering with cold, for the house to return to his image of home, where there would be no flames other than that final one, which still burned in the hearth, if he lingers here too long he is much more likely to find nothing but ashes instead of the fire.

Maria Guavaira woke up with the first light of morning. She was in her room, in bed, and there was a man asleep at her side. She could hear him breathing deeply, as if he were drawing renewed strength from the marrow of his bones, and semi-conscious, she wanted her own breathing to accompany his. It was the different rhythm of her breast that made her feel that she was naked. She ran her hands over her body, from her thighs to around her pubes, then over her belly up to her breasts, and suddenly she remembered her cry of surprise when her orgasm had burst inside her like a sun. Now completely awake, she bit her fingers in order to suppress that same cry, but in that stifled sound she would have liked to recognize those sensations, to capture them forever, or perhaps it was reawakened desire, perhaps remorse, the anguish which utters that familiar phrase, Now what is to become of me, thoughts cannot be isolated from other thoughts, impressions are not untainted by other impressions, this woman lives in the country, remote from the amatory arts of civilization, and any moment now, two men will arrive who have come to work on Maria Guavaira's land, what is she going to say to them, her house filled like this with strangers, there is nothing like the light of day to alter the appearance of things. But this man sleeping beside her threw a stone into the sea, and Joana Carda cut the earth in two, and José Anaiço became the king of starlings, and Pedro Orce can cause the earth to tremble with his feet, and the Dog has come from who knows where to bring these people together, And it brought me closer to you than to the others, I pulled the thread and you came to my door, to my bed, you even penetrated my body, even my soul, for only from there could that cry have come. She closed her eyes for several minutes, when she opened them she saw Joaquim Sassa had woken up, she could feel his firm body and sobbing with desire, she opened herself to him, she did not cry out, but wept smiling, and day broke. There is no point in making indiscreet revelations about the words they spoke, let people form their own idea, try to imagine it for themselves, they are unlikely to succeed, however limited the language of love may appear to be.

Maria Guavaira got up and her body is as white as Joaquim Sassa had dreamt, she told him, I didn't want to wear these widow's weeds, but now I haven't got time to look for something else to wear, the farmhands will be here any minute. She dressed, returned to the bed, covered Joaquim Sassa's face with her hair and kissed him, then rushed out of the bedroom. Joaquim Sassa rolled over on the bed, closed his eyes, he's going back to sleep. There's a tear on one of his cheeks, it could have been shed by Maria Guavaira or by him, for men also weep, there's nothing to be ashamed of and weeping only does them good.

This is the room where Joana Carda and José Anaiço spent the night, the door is closed, they are still asleep. The other door is ajar, the dog comes to look at Maria Guavaira, then goes back inside and lies down again, keeping vigil over the sleeping Pedro Orce who is resting from his adventures and discoveries. One can tell from the atmosphere that it will be a hot day. The clouds are coming in from the sea and appear to be moving more swiftly than the wind. Near Deux Chevaux are two men, they are the hired labourers who have arrived for work, they are commenting to each other that the widow, who is always complaining about how little she earns from farming, has finally bought herself a car, Once the husband is out of the way, these women manage very nicely, this sarcastic remark came from the older man. Maria Guavaira calls out to them, and as she sets about lighting the fire and heating up the coffee she explains that she has offered shelter to some travellers who lost their way, poor things, You aren't safe living here all on your own, the younger man said, but this phrase, so full of concern, is simply a variant of many others which have been spoken with somewhat different intentions, You should have remarried, you need a man to keep an eye on the house, Without a word of exaggeration, You couldn't have found a better man than me, when it comes to work and all the rest, Believe me when I say I'm very fond of you, One day you'll see me come through that door and mark my words I'll be here to stay. You're driving me out of my wits, you think men have no feelings and are made of wood, whereupon Maria Guavaira threatens him, If you come any closer, I'll soon find out for you'll get a live coal in your face, and the younger man had no choice but to rephrase his opening sentence, You should have a man living here to look after you, but even expressing it like this has not helped him to get what he wants.

The labourers go into the fields and Maria Guavaira returns to the bedroom. Joaquim Sassa is fast asleep. Slowly, so as not to awaken him, she opens her trunk and begins sorting out clothes in the light colours she used to wear before going into mourning, shades of pink, green, blue, white and red, orange or lilac, and those other colour combinations popular with women, not that this was any stage wardrobe or that she was a wealthy landowner, but as everyone knows, two dresses are enough to strike a festive note, and two skirts with two blouses create a rainbow. The clothes smell of mothballs and staleness, Maria Guavaira will hang them out in the sun to allow the miasma of chemicals and the musty smell to evaporate, and just as she is about to go down, her arms a riot of colour, she bumps into Joana Carda who has also left her man tucked up snugly between the sheets and who, seeing at once what is happening, offers to help. The two of them laugh at the display, the wind blows their hair about, the clothes make a smacking sound and flutter like flags, one feels like shouting, Long live liberty.

They went back into the kitchen to prepare food, the place smelled of freshly-brewed coffee, there was milk, bread which was no longer fresh but edible, some hard cheese, jam, these appetizing odours would rouse the men, first José Anaiço appeared, then Joaquim Sassa, next to appear was not a man but a dog, it appeared in the doorway, had a good look and went away. It's gone to call its master, said Maria Guavaira, who in theory has more claims to ownership, but she has already given them up. Pedro Orce finally appeared, said good-morning and sat down in silence, there is a hint of resentment in his expression when he observes the still very discreet gestures of affection with which the four express themselves, whether as couples or all together. The world of contentment has its own distinctive sun.

Pedro Orce's resentment may look bad for he knows he is an old man, but we must try to understand his feelings if he still is not resigned to the idea. José Anaiço tried to include him in the conversation, asked if he enjoyed his nocturnal stroll, if the dog had been good company, and Pedro Orce, already mollified, was inwardly grateful for the olive branch offered, it came just at the right moment before any bitterness could complicate further the feeling of privation, I walked as far as the sea, he said, and this caused great surprise, greatest of all that of Maria Guavaira who knows perfectly well where the sea lies and how difficult it is to get there. But if I hadn't taken the dog with me I couldn't have managed, Pedro Orce explained, and suddenly the stone ship came to mind, he felt uneasy, incapable of deciding for a few seconds if he had seen it in a dream or whether it had been concrete and real, If I wasn't dreaming, if it wasn't some vision in a dream, it exists, it's there at this precise moment, I'm sitting here drinking coffee and the ship is there, and, such are the powers of imagination, despite his only having seen it under the feeble light of the odd star, that he could now visualize it mentally in full daylight with the sun and the blue of the sky, the black rock beneath the petrified ship. I've found a ship, he said, and without thinking he might be deceived, he expounded his theory, explained the chemical process without always knowing the precise terms, but little by little words began to fail him, Maria Guavaira's look of disapproval had disturbed him, and he finished off defensively with another cautious theory, Of course, this could also be an unusual effect caused by erosion.

Joana Carda said she wanted to go and take a look, José Anaiço and Joaquim Sassa agreed at once, only Maria Guavaira remained silent, she and Pedro Orce looked at each other. Gradually, the other fell silent, they realized that the last word remained to be said, if there really exists a last word for everything, which raises the delicate question of knowing how things will stand after everything has been said about them. Maria Guavaira held Joaquim Sassa's hand as if she were about to take an oath, It's a stone ship, you said, That's right, it turned to stone with time, perhaps through petrification, but perhaps it is just a coincidence that it has taken on this form because of the wind and other atmospheric agents, the rain, for example, and even the sea, for there must have been a time when the sea level was higher, It's a stone ship that was always of stone, it's a ship that came from afar, and there it remained after all the persons sailing in it had disembarked. Persons, asked José Anaiço, Or person, of this I can't be sure, And of what you claim as being certain, what certainty is there, Pedro Orce asked sceptically, The ancients used to say, for their forefathers had told them, as their forefathers in turn had told them, some saints landed on this coast from ships of stone, coming from the deserts on the other side of the world, some arrived alive, others dead, as in the case of St James, the ships have been stranded since that time and this is only one of them. Do you believe in any of what you're saying, It's not a question of believing or not believing, everything we go on saying is added to what is, to what exists, first I said granite, then I say ship, when I get to the end of what I'm saying, I have to believe in having said it, that's often all that's needed, just as water, flour and yeast make bread.

Joaquim Sassa now saw her as a wise shepherdess, a Minerva from the Galician mountains, we generally fail to notice, but the truth is that people know much more than we think, the majority of people do not even suspect the knowledge they possess, the trouble is that they try to pass for what they are not, they lose their knowledge and wit, they would do better if they were like Maria Guavaira who simply says, I've read a number of books in my life, the wonder is that I profited so much from them, this woman is not so presumptuous that she should say this of herself, it is the narrator, a lover of justice, who cannot resist making this comment. Joana Carda is about to ask when they will go to see the stone ship when Maria Guavaira, perhaps so as to cut short this discussion which is above her head, when as we were saying, Maria Guavaira switched on the radio she keeps in the kitchen, the world must have some news to report, it is like this every morning, and the news is always startling, even when one has not caught the opening words which can be reconstructed later. Since last night the speed of the Peninsula's displacement has inexplicably altered, the latest measurement registers more than two thousand metres per hour, practically fifty kilometres each day, that is, three times the distance recorded since the drift began.

At this moment there must be silence everywhere in the Peninsula, people are listening to the news in their homes and in the public squares, but there are some who will only find out later what has happened, such as those two men who are working for Maria Guavaira, they are way out in the fields, remote from everything, I'll bet the younger one will forget the compliments and flattery and think of nothing except his own life and safety. But there's worse to come, when the announcer reads a bulletin from Lisbon, the news had to be leaked sooner or later, the secret has lasted for a long time, There is grave concern in official and scientific circles in Portugal, since the archipelago of the Azores is situated precisely on the route the Peninsula has been following, the first signs of the population's anxiety are already in evidence, for the moment one cannot speak of panic, but it is expected that within the next few hours steps will be taken to evacuate people living in those cities and towns along the coast which are at greatest risk in the event of a collision, as for us here in Spain, we can consider ourselves safe from any immediate effects, in so far as the Azores are distributed between the thirty-seventh and fortieth parallel, while the entire region of Galicia lies north of the forty-second parallel, it is fairly obvious that unless there are modifications in the route, only our neighbouring country, ever unfortunate, will suffer the direct impact, without forgetting, of course, the no less unfortunate islands themselves, which, because of their reduced dimensions, run the risk of disappearing under the great mass of stone which is now being displaced, as we mentioned, at the terrifying speed of fifty kilometres each day, although it is just possible that those very same islands could form a providential barrier which would halt this approaching peril which so far has proved relentless, we are all in the hands of God, since human might is not sufficient to avoid the catastrophe should it happen, fortunately, we repeat, we, the Spaniards, are more or less safe, however, there's no place for excessive optimism, the secondary consequences of the collision are always to be feared, so the utmost vigilance is called for and only those whose duties and obligations prevent them from moving inland should remain on the Galician coast. The announcer broke off, then there was music composed for an altogether different occasion, and José Anaiço, suddenly remembering, said to Joaquim Sassa, You were right when you spoke of the Azores, and such is human vanity, even when one's life is at such serious risk, that Joaquim Sassa felt very pleased that his judgment should be publicly acknowledged in the presence of Maria Guavaira, albeit without any merit on his part for it was something he picked up when he was taken round a number of laboratories with Pedro Orce.

As in a recurring dream, José Anaiço made some calculations, he had asked for paper and pencil, this time he would not say how many days Gibraltar would take to pass in front of the battlements of the Serra de Gádor, that had been a time of festivity, now it was necessary to ascertain how many days lay ahead before the Cabo da Roca crashed into the island of Terceira, one shudders just to think of that horrendous moment, once the island of São Miguel has been buried like a spike in the soft earth of Alentejo, truly,

truly I tell you, nothing but evil can come of it. Having made his calculations, José Anaiço told them, So far we've gone about three hundred kilometres, now then, since the distance from Lisbon to the Azores is more or less one thousand two hundred kilometres, we still have nine hundred to go, and nine hundred kilometres at fifty kilometres a day, in round figures makes eighteen days, in other words, we'll reach the Azores around the twentieth of September, perhaps even sooner. The blandness of this conclusion was a forced and bitter irony which did not bring a smile to anyone's face. Maria Guavaira reminded him, But we're here in Galicia, beyond its reach, You can't rely on it, Pedro Orce cautioned her, it only needs to change course ever so slightly towards the south, and we are the ones who will take the full impact, the best thing, the only thing to do is to escape inland, as the announcer said, and even then we can't be sure, Abandon our homes and lands, If what they're telling us should happen, there won't be any homes or lands. They were seated, for the time being they could remain seated, they could remain seated for eighteen days. The fire was burning in the hearth, the bread was on the table, there were other things too, milk, coffee, cheese, but it was the bread that attracted everyone's gaze, half of a large loaf, with a thick crust and firm in the centre, the taste lingered on their palate, even after some time, but their tongues recognized the crumbs that were left after chewing, when the last day of the universe comes we shall look at the last ant with the painful silence of someone who knows that they are taking their leave for the last time.

Joaquim Sassa said, My vacation finishes today, if I'm going to stick to the rules, I should be back at work in Oporto tomorrow morning, these objective words were only the beginning of a statement, I don't know if we'll carry on together, that's a matter we must decide here, but speaking for myself, I want to be with Maria, if she agrees and wants to be with me. Well now, so that everything should be said at the right moment and each piece be fitted into the right order and sequence, they waited for Maria Guavaira, who had been summoned, to speak first, and she said, That's what I want too, without any needless elaboration. José Anaiço said, If the Peninsula should collide with the Azores, the schools won't reopen all that soon, in fact they might never open again, I shall stay with Joana and with the rest of you if she decides to remain. Now it was the turn of Joana Carda, who like Maria Guavaira said no more than four words, women have so little to say for themselves, I'm staying with you, these were her words for she was looking straight at him, but everyone understood the rest. Last of all, because someone had to be last, Pedro Orce said, Wherever we go, I go, and this phrase which obviously offends grammar and logic with its excess of logic and very likely of grammar too, must stand uncorrected, exactly as it was said, perhaps there is some special meaning which will justify and absolve it, anyone who knows anything about words knows to expect anything from them. Dogs, as everyone knows, do not speak, and this one cannot even give a loud bark as a sign of jovial approval.

That same day they walked all the way to the coast to see the stone ship. Maria Guavaira was wearing her brightest clothes, she had not even bothered to iron them, the wind and light would smooth out the creases after years of being committed to darkest limbo. Pedro Orce, their experienced guide, led the way, although he trusts the dog's instinct and scent more than his own eyes, to which everything in the light of day looks like a new route. While we cannot expect any guidance from Maria Guavaira, her route is another, everything with her is an excuse to hold hands with Joaquim Sassa and draw near to him until their bodies touch long enough to steal a kiss, a variable time span as we know, which explains why they do not so much accompany the expedition as trail behind it. José Anaiço and Joana Carda are more discreet, they have been together for a week now, have sated their initial hunger, slaked their initial thirst, desire comes to them when they summon it, and if truth be told, they do so frequently. Even last night, when Pedro Orce saw that splendour in the distance, it was not just Joaquim Sassa and Maria Guavaira who were making love, there could have been ten couples sleeping in that house and all making love at the same time.

The clouds come from the sea and speed away in haste, they form and disintegrate rapidly as if each moment lasted no more than a second or a fraction of a second, and all the gestures of these men and women are, or appear to be, at the very same instant, both slow and swift, one would think the world had gone crazy, if one could ever fully grasp the meaning of such an impoverished but popular expression. They reach the top of the hill and the sea is tempestuous. Pedro Orce scarcely recognizes these places, the enormous rounded boulders that are piled up, the almost invisible ox-cart descending in stages, how could he have taken this route by night, even with the dog's guidance, this is a feat he simply cannot explain. He tries to scan the stone ship but it is nowhere to be seen, now it is Maria Guavaira who leads the group, and not before time because she knows these paths better than anyone. They arrive at the spot, and Pedro Orce is about to open his mouth to say, It's not here, but he has stopped himself in time, he has before his eyes the stone of the helm with its broken tiller, the great mast looks even thicker in daylight, and as for the ship, this is where he finds the greatest change, as if the erosion of which he had been speaking that morning had accomplished in one night the work of thousands of years, where is it, for I cannot see it, the tall pointed prow, the concave belly, the stone certainly has the broad outline of a ship, but not even the brightest of saints could work the miracle of keeping such a precarious vessel afloat without bulwarks, there is no doubt it is made of stone, but somehow it seems to have lost the form of a ship, after all, a bird only flies because it looks like a bird, Pedro Orce thinks to himself, but now Maria Guavaira is saying, This is the ship in which a saint came from the east, here you can still see the marks of his feet when he disembarked and started walking inland, the marks were some cavities in the rock, now tiny puddles which the ebb and flow of the waves at high tide would constantly renew, clearly any doubts are legitimate, but things depend upon what one accepts or refutes, if a saint came from afar sailing on a slab of stone, then why should it not be possible for his feet of fire to have fused the rock up to the present day. Pedro Orce has no choice other than to accept and confirm, but keeps to himself the memory of another ship which he alone saw on a night almost without stars yet inhabited by sublime visions.

The sea splashes over the rocks as if struggling against the advance of this irresistible tide of stones and earth. They no longer look at the phantom ship, they look at the threshing waves, and José Anaiço says, We're on the road, we know it yet don't feel it. And Joana Carda asked him, The road to where. Then Joaquim Sassa said, There are five of us and a dog, we won't fit into Deux Chevaux, this is a problem we must solve, one solution would be for us two, José and me, to go and search for a bigger car among the vehicles abandoned all over the place, the difficulty will be finding one in good condition, the ones we've seen always had some part missing, We can decide what we're going to do once we get home, José Anaiço said, there's no hurry, But what about the house, the land, Maria Guavaira muttered, We have no choice, either we get away from here or we all die, these words were spoken by Pedro Orce and they were final.

After lunch Joaquim Sassa and José Anaiço set off in Deux Chevaux in search of a bigger car, preferably a jeep, an army jeep would be fine, or, better still, one of those freight lorries, a removal van which might be transformed into a house on wheels with sleeping accommodation, but just as Joaquim Sassa had more or less surmised, they found nothing suitable, and besides this region where we are is not particularly well provided with car parks. They returned in the late afternoon along the roads which little by little became congested with vehicles travelling from west to east, it was the beginning of the exodus of the population living on the coast, there were cars, carts, once more these traditional donkeys, and bicycles, although there were not many of them on the bumpy roads, and motorcycles, and long-distance buses with seats for fifty or more passengers and which were transporting entire villages, it was the greatest migration ever in the history of Galicia. Some people stared in amazement at these travellers going in the opposite direction, they even tried to stop them, didn't they know what had happened, Yes we know, many thanks, we're only going to look for some people, meanwhile there's no real danger, and then José Anaiço said, If it's like this here, what must it be like in Portugal, and suddenly the perfect way out occurred to them, How stupid we are, the solution is very simple, let's make the journey twice, or three times, as many times as is necessary, we can choose some place in the interior to install ourselves, a house, it shouldn't be difficult, people are leaving everything behind. This was the good news they brought, and it was deservedly given a warm welcome, next day they would start to sort out and put aside what they thought they should take, and to speed up the task they held a full discussion after dinner, made an inventory of their needs, drew up lists, chopping and changing as they went along, Deux Chevaux had a long journey ahead and a heavy load to transport.

The following morning, the labourers didn't appear and Deux Chevaux's engine wouldn't start. Expressed like this, we might give the impression there is some connection between the two facts, for instance, that the absentee farmhands have stolen some essential part from the car, either out of desperate need or sudden malice. Not so. Both the older and younger man had been swept off in the exodus which was depopulating the entire region along the coast for more than fifty kilometres inland, but three days from now, when the inhabitants of the house have already departed, the younger man will return to this spot, the one who coveted Maria Guavaira and her land, in this order or the other way round, and we shall never know if he is returning to attain his dream of becoming a landowner, even if only for a few days before being killed in a geological disaster which will carry off both the land and his dream, or if he has decided to stay here on guard, fighting loneliness and fear, risking everything to gain everything, the hand of Maria Guavaira and her possessions, if the terrifying threat should somehow fail to materialize, Maria Guavaira may come back here one day, if she should return she will find a man digging the soil or sleeping soundly after all that labour, in a cloud of blue wool.

All day long Joaquim Sassa struggled with the unwilling engine, José Anaiço helped as best he could, but what they knew between them was not enough to solve the problem. There were no parts missing, there was no lack of power, but somewhere deep down in the engine something had been damaged or broken, or it had gradually worn out, it happens to people, it can also happen to machines, one day, without any warning, the body says, No, or the soul, or the spirit, or the will, and nothing will move it, Deux Chevaux had also reached this point, it had brought Joaquim Sassa and José Anaiço all this way, it did not dump them in the middle of the road, so let them at least be grateful, there is no point in losing their temper, punches do not solve anything, putting the boot in gets you nowhere. Deux Chevaux was finished. When they arrived indoors feeling discouraged, covered in grease, their hands filthy after struggling, practically without tools, with nuts, bolts and gears, and went to clean themselves up lovingly assisted by their womenfolk, the atmosphere was tense. How are we going to get out of this place now, asked Joaquim Sassa who, as the owner of the car, not only felt himself responsible, but at fault, he saw it as an ungrateful act of destiny, a personal affront, certain susceptibilities about one's honour do not irritate any less because they happen to be absurd.

Then a family council was summoned, it looked like being a troubled session, but Maria Guavaira immediately took the initiative and made a proposal, I've got an old wagon here that we could use and a horse that's seen better days, but if we handle it carefully perhaps it'll get us there. Several moments of bewilderment followed, a natural reaction on the part of people accustomed to travelling by car and suddenly finding themselves obliged in a crisis to revert to old-fashioned means of transport. Is the wagon covered, Pedro Orce enquired, being a practical man and of an older generation, The awning must be worn by now but it can be patched up if necessary, I've got some strong material that will do the job, And if we need to, said Joaquim Sassa, we can always strip away the canvas from Deux Chevaux since it won't be needed any more and that'll be the last favour I owe it. They were all on their feet, cheerful, this promised to be an exciting adventure, travelling round the world in a wagon, the world in a manner of speaking, and they said, Let's go and see the horse, let's go and inspect the wagon, Maria Guavaira had to explain that the wagon was not a carriage, it had four wheels, an axle for pulling it in front, and under the awning that would shelter them from the weather there was enough room for a family, with a little planning and making the best of their resources, this wouldn't be so very different from living in a house.

The horse is old, it saw them coming into the stable and turned round to stare at them with its enormous black eyes, startled by the light and commotion. The wise man's saying is true, While there's life, there's hope, so do not despair.

Being far away, we know little about the knots and entanglements of the crisis which, latent since the breaking away of the Peninsula, has become more serious in government circles, especially since the celebrated invasion of the hotels when the ignorant masses trampled on law and order, in so far as they are unable to foresee how the situation can be resolved in the immediate future, restoring what is theirs to the rightful owners as the higher interests of morality and justice prescribe. Above all, because no one knows if there will be any immediate future. The news that the Peninsula is rushing at a speed of two kilometres per hour in the direction of the Azores was used by the Portuguese government as a pretext for resigning because of the seriousness of the situation, the imminence of collective danger, which leads one to believe that governments are only capable and effective at times when there is no real need to put their ability and effectiveness to the test. The Prime Minister, in his speech to the nation, saw the one-party system of his government as an obstacle to the broad national consensus which he considered indispensable if this terrible crisis were to be overcome and a state of normality restored. In keeping with this line of thought, he had proposed to the President of the Republic the formation of a government of national salvation with the participation of all political forces, with or without parliamentary representation, bearing in mind that one could always find a position as deputy under-secretary to some deputy secretary to some deputy minister to be given to political cronies who in normal circumstances would not even be entrusted with opening the door. Nor did he forget to make it quite clear that he and his ministers considered themselves at the service of the nation so that in any new or different capacity they might collaborate in the salvation of the fatherland and contribute to the prosperity of the nation.

The President of the Republic accepted the government's resignation and, complying with the constitution and the norms established for the democratic functioning of institutions, he invited the resigning Prime Minister, as the leader of the party most often elected and which, so far, had governed without any alliances, he invited him, as we were saying, to form the proposed government of national salvation. Because there can be no doubt that governments of national salvation are also perfectly valid and one could even go so far as to say they are the best governments of all, the sad thing is that countries need them only very rarely, therefore we do not normally have governments who know how to govern nationally. On this most delicate issue there have been interminable debates between constitutionalists, political analysts and other experts, and in all this time precious little has been added to the obvious meaning of these words, namely that a government of national salvation, because it is national and concerned with salvation, is one of national salvation. That is how any simpleton would put it, and he could not do better. The most interesting thing about all of this is that the moment the formation of the aforesaid government was announced, the masses suddenly felt they had been saved, or soon would be, although certain manifestations of innate scepticism are inevitable when the list of ministerial appointments is announced and their photographs appear in the newspapers and on television. At the end of the day they are the same old faces, and why should we have expected otherwise, since we are so unwilling to put ourselves forward.

We have already mentioned the danger Portugal is facing should she collide with the Azores, and also the secondary consequences, unless they turn out to be direct, which threaten Galicia, but the situation of the population on the islands is obviously much more serious. After all, what is an island. An island, in this instance an entire archipelago, is the emergence of submarine cordilleras and very often just the sharp peaks of rocky needles which miraculously remain upright at depths of thousands of metres, an island, in short, is the most fortuitous of events. And now here is something which, although no more than an island, is so enormous and fast that we are in great danger of witnessing, let us hope from a distance, the decapitation of São Miguel followed by that of the islands of Terceira, São Jorge and Faial, and other islands of the Azores, with widespread loss of life, if the government of national salvation which is due to take office tomorrow does not come up with a solution very soon for the evacuation of thousands and millions of people to regions of reasonable safety, if such places exist. The President of the Republic, even before the new government started to function, has already appealed for international solidarity, thanks to which, as we are reminded, and this is only one of the many examples we could give, famine was once avoided in Africa. The countries of Europe, where fortunately a certain lowering of the tone in their voice has been noted whenever they refer to Portugal and Spain following the serious crisis of identity they underwent when millions of Europeans resolved to declare themselves Iberian, received the appeal sympathetically and have already enquired how we would like to be helped, although, as usual, everything depends on our needs being satisfied from whatever surplus they may have at their disposal. As for the United States of North America, which should always be named in full, despite their having sent word that the plan for a government of national salvation is not to their liking, they have declared that given the circumstances, they are willing nonetheless to evacuate the entire population of the Azores, which is just under two hundred and fifty thousand people, although there is still the problem of where to settle all those people, certainly not in the philanthropic United States because of their strict immigration laws. The ideal solution, if you want to know, and this is the secret dream cherished by the State Department and the Pentagon, would be for the islands to halt the Peninsula, whatever the destruction, for then it would be stuck in the middle of the Atlantic and benefit world peace and Western Civilization with obvious strategic advantages. The people will be told that the North American squadrons have received orders to head towards the region of the Azores, upon arrival they will pick up many thousands of islanders and the rest will have to wait for the air lift which is at present being organized, Portugal and Spain will have to deal with any local problems, the Spanish less so than we Portuguese, for history and fortune have always treated the former with all too obvious partiality.

Leaving aside the case of Galicia, a case and region which are purely peripheral, or, adopting other criteria, appendicular, Spain is protected from the more fatal consequences of the collision, since Portugal essentially acts as a screen or buffer. There are problems of a certain logistic complexity to be resolved, such as the important cities of Vigo, Pontevedra, Santiago de Compostela and La Coruña but, as for the rest, the people who live in villages are so accustomed to a precarious existence that, almost without waiting for orders, advice or information, they started retreating further inland, peaceful and resigned, using the means of transport already described, and others, starting with the most primitive means of all, their own feet.

Portugal's situation, however, is quite different. Note that the entire coast, excepting the southern part of the Algarve, finds itself in danger of being stoned by the islands of the Azores, the word stoned is used here because the outcome is much the same whether a stone hits us or we hit against a stone, it is all a question of speed and inertia, not forgetting that in this case, the head, even though wounded and cracked, will reduce all those stones to splinters. Now then, with a coastline like this, nearly all of it flat, and with the larger cities by the sea, and taking into account the unpreparedness of the Portuguese for the slightest catastrophe, earthquake, flood, forest fire or persistent drought, it is doubtful whether the government of salvation will know how to do its duty. The solution would be to actually stir up panic, to rush people into abandoning their homes and force them to seek refuge further inland. The worst thing of all will be if people start to run out of food either during the journey or wherever they decide to settle, then there will be so much indignation and frustration that all hell will break loose. Naturally, we are worried but frankly we would be much more worried if we happened to be in Galicia watching the travel preparations of Maria Guavaira and Joaquim Sassa, Joana Carda and José Anaiço, Pedro Orce and the Dog, the relative importance of topics is variable, it is the point of view, the humour of the moment, one's personal sympathies, the objectivity of the narrator is a modern invention, we need only reflect that Our Lord God didn't want it in His Book.

Two days have passed, the horse has been given extra rations of food, as much oats and beans as it likes, after being almost starved, Joaquim Sassa even suggested giving it soup pepped up with wine, and the wagon, now that the holes have been patched with the canvas removed from Deux Chevaux, is not only more comfortable inside but will protect them from the weather as the light showers give way to constant rain, for September is here and we're in a region which is invariably wet. Meanwhile, one can reckon that the Peninsula has sailed about a hundred and fifty kilometres since José Anaiço made precise calculations, so there are still seven hundred and fifty kilometres to go, or fifteen days, for those who prefer more empirical measurements, at the end of which, give or take a minute, the first collision will take place, Jesus, Mary and Joseph, those poor wretches in Alentejo, just as well they are used to disasters, they are like the Galicians, their skin is so tough that we would be fully justified in using another word, let us put leather instead of skin and dispense with any further explanation. Here in these northern territories, in the Elysian valleys of Galicia, there is plenty of time for our travellers to get out of harm's way. The wagon is already equipped with mattresses, sheets and blankets, all the luggage has been loaded together with basic utensils for cooking, food already prepared for the first few days, omelettes to be precise, and various foodstuffs, plain and simple fare such as white and red beans, rice and potatoes, a barrel of water, a cask of wine, two laying hens, one of them mottled and its neck bald, salt cod, a pitcher of olive oil, a bottle of vinegar, and some salt, for we cannot live without it, unless we refuse baptism, pepper and saffron, all the bread they had in the house, a bag of flour, hay, bran and bean pods for the horse, the dog does not present any problem, it knows how to look after its own needs, when it accepts any help, it is only to please others. Maria Guavaira, without any explanation, but then perhaps she could not have explained even if asked, wove bracelets for everyone with the blue thread, and collars for the horse and dog. There is such a pile of wool there that no one noticed any difference. Besides, one has to say that even if they'd wanted to take it with them, there's no room for the wool in the wagon, nor was it ever foreseen that there would be, otherwise where would that young farmhand, who is about to arrive, sleep.

On the last night in the house, they were late in getting to bed, they sat up chatting for hours on end, as if the following morning was to be one of sad farewells, with each of them going their separate ways. But staying together like this was one way of keeping up their spirits, it is a well-known fact that canes start to break the moment they separate from the bundle, everything breakable has already been broken. They spread out the map of the Peninsula on the kitchen table, as drawn here it is still incongruously joined to France, and they marked out the first day's itinerary, the inaugural route, taking care to choose the least bumpy roads given the feeble strength of their scraggy horse. But they would have to make a diversion more to the north, as far as La Coruña where Maria Guavaira's demented mother was in a mental institution, daughterly love would decree that she should go and rescue her from that pandemonium, for one can imagine the panic in that bedlam, an enormous island bursting through the front door, hurling itself on to the city and sweeping before it the anchored boats, and all those glass-paned windows on the avenue on the waterfront shattering to smithereens at the same time, and the demented inmates thinking, if they are capable of thinking in their lunacy, that the Day of Judgment has finally come. Maria Guavaira will have the honesty to say, I don't know what life is going to be like with my mother in the wagon, even if she isn't really violent, bear with me, it's only until we reach a place of safety. They promised to be patient, they would arrange things as best they could, but as we know very well not even the greatest love can withstand its own madness so how will it cope with another's madness, in this case the insane mother of one of the insane. Just as well that José Anaiço had the fortunate idea of telephoning from the first place where it was possible to get some information, the health authorities might well have transferred or be about to transfer the inmates to a place of safety, for this is not one of your classical shipwrecks, the first to be rescued here are those who are lost.

The couples finally withdraw to their rooms, they do what people normally do on these occasions, who knows if we shall ever return here, so let the vibrations of carnal love between humans remain, that love which has no equal among the species because made of sighs, murmurings, impossible words, saliva and sweat, anguish, implored martyrdom, Not just yet, one is dying of thirst yet refuses the water of freedom, Now, now, my love, and this is what old age and death will steal from us. Pedro Orce, who is old and already bearing the first sign of death which is solitude, leaves the house once more to go and take a look at the stone ship, accompanied by the dog which has every name and none, and just in case you are about to say that if the dog accompanied him then Pedro Orce is no longer alone, do not forget the animal's remote origins, the hounds of hell have already seen everything, and because they have such a long life they accompany no one, it is the humans who live for such a short time who accompany dogs. The stone ship stands there, and the prow is tall and pointed as on the first night, Pedro Orce is not surprised, each of us sees the world with the eyes we possess, and eyes see what they choose to see, eyes create the world's diversity and fabricate its wonders, even if they're only made of stone, and tall prows, even if they're only an illusion.

The morning awoke overcast and drizzly, a manner of speech which is used, but incorrect, because mornings do not awaken, it is we who awaken in the mornings, and then going to the window, see that the sky is covered with low clouds and the rain is drizzling down, tiresome for anyone caught in it, however, such is the power of tradition that if there were a ship's logbook on this journey of ours, the clerk would inscribe his first paean as follows, The morning awoke overcast and drizzly, as if the skies were gazing down with disapproval on this adventure, the skies are always invoked in these instances, no matter whether it rains or shines. Deux Chevaux, with one mighty heave, replaced the wagon under the tiled roof, that's to say the thatch, for this is not a garage but a lean-to, exposed to the elements. Abandoned like this and without its canvas hood which was used to patch the awning of the wagon, the car already looks a wreck, the same thing happens to objects as to people, when they have outlived their usefulness they are discarded, they are discarded once they no longer serve any purpose. The wagon on the other hand, despite being ancient, has been rejuvenated after being taken out into the open air, and as the rain washes it down, the wagon is restored, being put into action has always had this admirable effect, just look at the horse, covered with an oil-cloth to protect its back and looking almost like a charger in a joust, caparisoned for battle.

These descriptive interludes should cause no surprise, they're ways of showing how difficult it is to uproot persons from places where they were happy, all the more so as the persons here are not preparing to flee in panic, Maria Guavaira is now closing the doors carefully, she sets free the hens that are being left behind, releases the rabbits from their hutch, the pig from the sty, these are animals accustomed to being fed, now left to God's mercy if not to the wiles of Satan, for the pig is quite capable, should the mood take it, of attacking the other animals. When the younger of the two farmhands arrives he will have to break a window to enter the house, there is no one for leagues around to see him break in. If I broke in, there was good reason for doing so, these are his words, and perhaps it is true.

Maria Guavaira climbed into the driver's seat, beside her sat Joaquim Sassa with open umbrella, his duty is to accompany the woman he loves and to protect her from the inclement weather, but he cannot do her job for her, because of the five persons here only Maria Guavaira knows how to drive a wagon and horse. Later in the afternoon when the sky clears, she would teach them. Pedro Orce would insist upon being the first to receive some basic training, a thoughtful gesture on his part, so that the two couples may relax under the awning without any unwelcome separations, the driver's seat is spacious enough for three, an ideal solution so that the other two may be together even if it only means being able to sit quietly side-by-side in silence. Maria Guavaira shook the reins, the horse, hitched between the shafts of the wagon, without any partner at its side, gave the first pull, felt the harness tugging, then the weight of the load, memories came flooding back to its old bones and muscles, and the almost forgotten sound returned of the earth being crushed beneath the rotating metal rims of the wheels. You can learn, forget and learn everything anew, when forced by necessity. For several hundred metres the dog accompanied the wagon in the rain. Then it saw that it could travel, even though on foot, sheltered by that great encumbrance. It got under the wagon, fell into step with the horse's rhythm, and that is how we shall see the dog for the rest of the journey, come rain or shine, since it does not fancy acting as guide or amusing itself with all that coming and going bereft of any apparent meaning which makes men and dogs so very much alike.

That day they did not travel far. They had to conserve the horse's strength, all the more so since the bumpy road demanded constant effort, whether it was pulling on the way up or braking as it came down. There was not a living soul as far as the eye could see. We must have been the last people to leave these parts, Maria Guavaira said, and the clouded sky, the leaden atmosphere, the gloomy landscape were like the dying breath of a world at its end, desolate, expiring after so much sorrow and weariness, so much living and dying, so much resolute life and successive death. But new loves travel in this wagon and new loves, as those who have observed them know, are the greatest force in this world, they fear no misfortune, since new loves by their very nature are themselves the greatest misfortune of all, a sudden flash of lightning, joyful surrender, disquieting confusion. However one must not put too much trust in first impressions, this almost funereal departure from a deserted country in the depressing rain, it would be better, were we not so discreet, to listen carefully to the conversations between Joana Carda and José Anaiço, between Maria Guavaira and Joaquim Sassa, Pedro

Orce's silence is even more discreet, it is almost as if he were not here at all.

The first village they passed through had not been abandoned by all its inhabitants. Some of the elderly had reassured their worried children and relatives that to die for the sake of dying was preferable to dying of hunger or some malignant disease, if a person has been so gloriously chosen to die with his own world, even though he may be no Wagnerian hero, sublime Valhalla awaits him where all great catastrophes finish up. Elderly Galicians and Portuguese, for they belong to the same race, know nothing about such matters, but for some strange reason were capable of saying, I'm staying put, you can leave if you're frightened, and this doesn't mean that they felt all that courageous, simply that at this point in their lives they have finally come to realize that courage and fear are the two oscillating pans on the scale while the pointer remains still, paralysed by amazement at the useless invention of emotions and feelings.

As the wagon crossed through the village, curiosity, which is probably the last human trait to disappear, brought the elderly out on to the road, they waved slowly, and it was as if they were bidding themselves goodbye. Then José Anaiço suggested that it would be wise to grab this opportunity to get some sleep by making use of one of the empty houses, here or in some other village, or in some deserted spot, they were certain to find beds, greater comfort than in the wagon, but Maria Guavaira announced that she would never set foot in a strange house without the owner's consent, some people have such scruples, while others if they see a locked window smash it in and then say, It was all for the best, and whether it is for their own good or that of someone else, there will always be some doubt about the first and ultimate motive. José Anaiço regretted having made the suggestion, not because it was a bad one, but because it was absurd, Maria Guavaira's words were enough to define a code of self-respect, Try to be self-sufficient as far as you can, then confide in someone deserving of your trust, better still if it be someone deserving of you. As matters stand, these five appear to deserve each other, reciprocally and in all other respects, so let them stay in the wagon, eat their omelettes, chat about the journey they have made so far and the journey that lies ahead of them. Maria Guavaira will reinforce the practical driving lessons she has given with a little theory, beneath a tree the horse goes on munching its ration of hay, the dog satisfies itself on this occasion with domestic provisions, it prowls around sniffing and startling the nightjars. It has stopped raining. A lantern illuminates the inside of the wagon, anyone passing this way would say, Look, a theatre, they are certainly characters but not actors.

When Maria Guavaira finally succeeds in contacting the asylum in La Coruña by telephone tomorrow, she will be told that her mother and the other inmates have already been transferred inland, And how is she, As mad as ever, but this response could refer to anyone. They will continue their journey until the land becomes populated once more. There they will remain waiting.

The government of national salvation was formed in Portugal and got down to business without delay, the Prime Minister himself had appeared on television and uttered a phrase that will certainly go down in history, words such as Blood, sweat and tears, or, Burying the dead and cherishing the living, or, Honour your country for your country is relying on you, or, The sacrifice of our martyrs will sow the seed of future harvests. In this instance and bearing in mind the peculiar circumstances of the situation, the Prime Minister thought it best simply to say, Sons of Portugal, Daughters of Portugal, salvation lies in retreat.

But to find accommodation way back in the interior for the millions of people who live along the coastal strip was a task of such extreme complexity that no one had the presumption, absurd to say the least, to put forward a national plan of evacuation, comprehensive and capable of integrating local initiatives. With regard, for example, to the city and region of Lisbon, the analysis of the situation and the ensuing measures started from a preconception, both objective and subjective, which could be summed up as follows, The great majority, let us be frank, the overwhelming majority of Lisbon's inhabitants were not born there, and those who were find themselves united to the others by family ties. The consequences of this fact are broad and decisive, the first being that both the former and the latter will have to transfer themselves to their places of origin where many still have relatives, some of whom they had lost touch with through various circumstances, and taking advantage of this enforced opportunity they restore harmony in their families, healing old wounds, patching up quarrels caused by contentious inheritances and unfair distributions which resulted in brawling and cursing. This great misfortune which has befallen us will have the merit of bringing hearts together again. The second consequence, which naturally stems from the first, touches on the problem of feeding the people evacuated. For here too, without any need for State intervention, the family community will have an important role to play, which, translated into numbers, one could express with a macroeconomic updating of the old saying, Three can eat as cheaply as two, the well-known arithmetic of resignation in any family where a child is expected, now one can say with even greater authority, Ten million can eat as cheaply as five, and with a quiet smile, A nation is nothing other than one big family.

Those living on their own, without any family, or misanthropists, would be without any recourse, but even they would not be excluded automatically from society, one has to have confidence in spontaneous solidarity, in that irrepressible love for one's neighbour which manifests itself at all times, take train journeys for example, especially in the second-class compartments, when the moment comes to open the basket of provisions, the mother of the family never forgets to offer some food to the other passengers occupying the adjacent seats, Would you care for something to eat, if someone accepts she does not mind, even though she may be counting on everyone replying in chorus, Not for me, thank you, but do enjoy your meal. The most awkward problem will be that of accommodation, it is one thing to offer someone a fish cake and a glass of wine, but it is quite a different matter to have to give up one half of the bed we are sleeping in, yet if we can get it into the heads of people that these solitary and abandoned people are reincarnations of Our Lord, as when He wandered the world disguised as a beggar in order to test the generosity of mankind, then someone will always find them a cupboard under the stairs, a corner in the attic, or, in rustic terms, a loft and a bundle of straw. God, this time, however much He may multiply Himself, will be treated as someone responsible for creating humanity deserves to be treated.

We have spoken of Lisbon, with only a quantitative difference in the terms we could have used in speaking of Oporto or Coimbra, or of Setúbal and Aveiro, of Viana or Figueira, without forgetting those innumerable little towns and villages one finds everywhere, although in some cases it may raise the perplexing question of knowing where those people must go who live exactly in the place where they were born, and also those who, living somewhere on the coast, were born somewhere else on the coast. After these difficulties had been discussed by the cabinet of ministers, their spokesman brought the reply, The government is confident that private initiative will find a solution, perhaps something truly original that will ultimately benefit everyone, for those matters which are not included in the national programme for the evacuation and resettlement of the population. So having been authorized from on high to put aside these individual destinies, we shall simply mention with regard to Oporto, the case of Joaquim Sassa's employers and colleagues. Suffice it to say that if he, respecting discipline and professional integrity, had rushed from the Galician mountains at the drop of a hat, abandoning love and friends to fate, he would have found his office closed and a notice pinned on the door with the latest instructions from the management, Employees returning from vacation should report for work at our new premises at Peñafiel, where we hope to continue to satisfy the needs of our esteemed clients. And Joana Carda's cousins, the ones from Ereira, now find themselves in Coimbra, at the home of their deserted cousin, who was not exactly overjoyed to see them, it stands to reason, after all he is the one who is aggrieved, he still had a glimmer of hope, he thought that his cousins had gone ahead to prepare the ground for the returning fugitive, but when nothing happened he asked them, And what about Joana, his cousins confessed sorrowfully, We don't know, She was there in our house, but disappeared even before the commotion began, we heard no more from her, what the cousin knows about the rest of the story she cautiously keeps to herself, for if he was astonished at what little he was told, what would he say if he were to learn everything.

And so the world is in a state of suspense, anxiously awaiting what is or is not about to happen to the western shores of Portugal and Galicia. But we must repeat, tiresome though it may be, that it is an ill wind that blows nobody any good, that at least is the attitude of the governments of Europe, because from one moment to the next, on a par with the salutary results of the repression mentioned earlier, they saw the revolutionary fervour of youth fade and almost disappear, youngsters who are now being told by their wise parents, Do you see, my boy, what you were risking if you had insisted on being Iberian, and the repentant son dutifully replies, Yes Papa. As these scenes of domestic reconciliation and social appeasement are enacted, the geostationary satellites, regulated to maintain a constant relative position, transmit photographs and measurements to earth, the first of these naturally invariable regarding the form of the object displaced, the second registering with every passing moment a reduction of almost thirty-five metres in the distance that separates the large island from the small ones. In an age such as ours with its acceleration of particles, thirty-five metres per minute as a cause for concern would be laughable, but when we remind ourselves that behind these pleasant, sandy beaches, this outlined and picturesque coastline, these jagged promontories overlooking the sea, five hundred and eighty thousand square kilometres of surface area are approaching and an incalculable, astronomical number of millions of tons, if we only count the sierras, cordilleras and mountains, let us try to visualize what the inertia of all the orographic systems of the Peninsula now set in motion will be like, not to mention the Pyrenees, despite their having been reduced to half their former size, then we can only admire the courage of these peoples with so much mixed blood and applaud their fatalist sense of existence, which, with the experience of centuries, has become condensed into that most notable precept, From among the dead and wounded, someone must get away.

Lisbon is a deserted city. Army patrols are still going around, with support from the air provided by helicopters, just as in Spain and France when the breakaway occurred and during the turbulent days that followed. Until they are withdrawn, which is expected to happen twenty-four hours before the anticipated moment of collision, the soldiers' mission is to be vigilant and on the alert, although they were really wasting their time since all the valuables had already been removed from the banks. But no one would forgive a government for abandoning a city as beautiful as this one, perfect in its proportions and harmony, as will inevitably be said of it once the city has been destroyed. That's why the soldiers are here as the symbolic representatives of the people in their absence, the guard of honour that would fire the customary salvos if there should still be time at that sublime moment when the city sinks into the sea.

Meanwhile, the soldiers start firing a few shots at the looters and thieves, they offer advice and guidance to the odd person who refuses to abandon his home or who has finally decided to get out, and when, as happens from time to time, they meet a harmless madman wandering through the streets, who has had the misfortune to be allowed out of the asylum on the day of the exodus and, not having known about or understood the order to return, ended up being left to his fate, two courses of action are generally adopted. Certain officers argue that the madman is always more dangerous than the looter, bearing in mind that the latter, at least, is as rational as himself. In such a case they don't think twice, but order the troops to open fire. Other officers who are less intolerant and, above all, aware of the desperate need to relieve nervous tension in time of war or catastrophe, order their men to have a bit of fun at the expense of the idiot before sending him on his way in peace, unless it happens to be a madwoman rather than a madman, who is exactly in the same state, for there is always someone, whether it's in the army or elsewhere, who is prepared to abuse the elementary and obvious fact that sex, instrumentally speaking, is not in the head.

But there is no longer a living soul to be seen in this city, along the avenues, in the roads and squares, in the neighbourhoods and public parks, when faces no longer appear at the windows, when the canaries that haven't already died of hunger and thirst sing in the deathly silence of the house or on the verandah overlooking the empty courtyards, when the waters of the fountains and springs sparkle in the sunlight and no hand is moistened there, when the vacant eyes of the statues look round in search of eyes that might be looking at them, when the open gates of cemeteries show that there is no difference between one absence and another, when the city, at last, is on the brink of that anguished moment as it waits for an island to come from the sea and destroy it, then the wonderful story and miraculous salvation of the lonely navigator will unfold.

For more than twenty years the navigator had been sailing the seas of the world. He had inherited or bought his ship, or it had been given to him by some other navigator who had also sailed in it for twenty years, and before him, if the memory does not end up becoming confused after such a long time, yet another solitary navigator apparently ploughed the oceans. The history of ships and the seamen who sail them is full of unexpected adventures, with terrible storms and sudden lulls as terrifying as the worst hurricanes, and, to add a touch of romance, it is often said, and songs have been composed on the theme, that there is a woman waiting for her sailor in every port, a somewhat optimistic picture which the realities of life and the betrayals of women nearly always contradict. When the lonely navigator disembarks, it is usually to get a fresh supply of water, to buy tobacco or some spare part for the engine, or to stock up with oil and fuel, medicine, sewing needles for the sails, a plastic raincoat to keep out the rain and drizzle, hooks, fishing tackle, the daily newspaper to confirm what he already knows and is not worth knowing, but never never never did the lonely navigator set foot on land in the hope of finding a woman to accompany him on the voyage. If there really is a woman waiting for him in port, it would be foolish to turn her down, but it is usually the woman who makes the first move and decides for how long, the lonely navigator has never said to her, Wait for me, I'll come back one day, that's not a request he would permit himself to make, Wait for me, nor could he guarantee that he will be back on this or any other day, and, on returning, how often he would find the harbour deserted, or should there be a woman waiting there, she is waiting for some other sailor, although it often happens that if he does not turn up, any sailor who appears will do just as well. One has to admit that neither the woman nor the sailors are at fault, solitude is to blame which can sometimes become unbearable, it can even drive the sailor into port and bring the woman to the harbour.

These considerations, however, are spiritual and metaphysical, we could not resist making them either before or after these extraordinary events, which they do not always help to make clearer. To put it simply, let us say that far away from this Peninsula which has turned into a floating island, the lonely navigator sails with his sail and engine, his radio and binoculars, and with the infinite patience of someone who one day decided to divide his life into one part sky and one part sea. The wind suddenly stopped blowing and he lowered the sail, the breeze suddenly dropped, and the great billow carrying the ship gradually starts losing its force, no longer soars, within the hour the sea will be smooth and calm, we find it incredible that this chasm of water, thousands of metres deep, should be able to maintain its balance, without falling to one side or the other, the observation will only seem foolish to those who believe everything in the world can be explained by the simple fact that they are as they are, something one obviously accepts but it is not enough. The engine is running, chug-chug chug-chug, nothing but sea as far as the eye can see, it corresponds sparkle for sparkle to the classical image of the mirror, and the navigator, despite having mastered a strict routine of sleep and vigil many years ago, closes his eyes, drugged by the heat of the sun, and falls fast asleep, perhaps thinking he has slept for several minutes or hours but they were only seconds, he wakes up shaken by what seemed to be a mighty blast, in that fleeting moment of sleep he has dreamt that he collided with the corpse of an animal, with a whale. Startled, his heart beating furiously, he tries to discover where the sound was coming from, but did not immediately notice that the engine has stopped. The sudden silence has woken him, but in order to awaken more naturally, his body has invented a sea-monster, a collision, thunder. Broken-down engines, on land and sea, are much more common, we know of one for which there is no remedy, it has a broken heart and has been dumped under a lean-to and exposed to the elements up north where it is gathering rust. But this navigator is not like those motorists, he's experienced and knowledgeable, he stocked up with spare parts the last time he touched land and woman, he intends to dismantle the engine as far as possible and to examine the mechanism. Such a waste of effort. The damage is right down in the piston rod, the horsepower of this engine is mortally wounded.

Despair, as we all know, is human, there is no evidence in natural history that animals despair. Yet man, inseparable from despair, has become accustomed to living with it, endures it to the extreme limits, and it will need more than an engine breaking down in mid-ocean for the sailor to start tearing out his hair, to implore the heavens or rail at them with curses and abuse, one gesture being as useless as another, the solution is to wait, whoever carried off the wind will bring it back. But the wind that went did not come back. The hours passed, serene night came, another day dawned, and the sea remains motionless, a fine thread of wool suspended here would drop like a plumb line, there isn't the tiniest ripple on the surface of the water, it is a stone ship on a stone slab. The navigator is not greatly concerned, this is not the first lull he has experienced, but now the radio has stopped working for some inexplicable reason, all one can hear is a buzzing sound, the carrier wave, if such a thing still exists, which is carrying nothing but silence, as if beyond this circle of stagnant water the world has become silent in order to witness, unseen, the navigator's mounting agitation, his madness, perhaps his death at sea. There is no lack of provisions or drinking water, but the hours are passing, each one increasingly prolonged, silence tightens its grip on the ship like the coils of a slippery cobra, from time to time the navigator taps the gunwale with a grappling iron, he wants to hear a sound unlike that of his own thick blood coursing through his veins, or the beating of his heart which he sometimes forgets, and then he awakens after having thought he was already awake, for he was dreaming that he was dead. The sail is raised against the sun, however the still air retains the heat, the lonely navigator is sunburnt, his lips are cracked. The day passes, and the following day is no different. The navigator finds refuge in sleep, he descends into the tiny cabin despite its being like a furnace, there is only one bunk there, narrow, proof that this navigator is truly alone and he is stark naked, the sweat first pouring off him, then with his skin dry, covered in goose pimples, he struggles with his dreams, a row of very tall trees swaying beneath a wind that pushes the leaves backwards and forwards, and then dies away before returning to attack them once more, endlessly. The navigator gets up to drink some water and the water is finished. He goes back to sleep, the trees no longer stir, but a seagull has come to settle on the mast.

From the horizon there advanced an enormous, dark, solid mass. As it got closer, houses could be seen along its shores, lights resembling white fingers outstretched in mid-air, a thin line of spume, and beyond the wide mouth of a river a great city built on hills, a red bridge joining both margins, and from this distance it looked like an etching done with a fine brush. The navigator went on sleeping, had sunk into a state of extreme torpor, but the dream suddenly came back, a sudden breeze shook the branches of the trees, the ship swayed in the choppy waters of the channel, and, swallowed up by the river, it ran aground, rescued from the sea, still immobile, while the earth is still moving. The lonely navigator could feel the swaying in his bones and muscles, he opened his eyes and thought, The wind, the wind's come back, and, almost without strength, he slipped down from his bunk, dragged himself out, he felt as if he were dying with each moment and with each moment being reborn, the light of the sun hurt his eyes, but it was the light of earth, bringing whatever it could extract from the green foliage of the trees, from the obscure depths of the countryside, from the soft colours of the houses. He was safe, and at first he did not know how, the air was still, the breath of wind had been an illusion. It took him some time to understand that a whole island had saved him, the former Peninsula which had sailed to meet him and opened the river's arms to receive him. This all seemed so unlikely that the lonely navigator himself, who so many years ago had heard rumours about the geological rupture, while knowing that he was on the route of the terrestrial ship, had never imagined that he might be saved in this way, for the first time ever in the history of shipwrecks and losses at sea. But on land there was no one to be seen, on the decks of the anchored and moored ships no face appeared, the silence was once more that of the cruel sea, This is Lisbon, the navigator murmured, but where are the people. The windows of the city are gleaming, cars and buses can be seen at a standstill, a great square surrounded by arcades, a triumphal arch at the far end with figures in stone and crowns in bronze, they must be bronze because of the colours. The lonely navigator who was familiar with the Azores and knew how to find them whether on the map or at sea, then remembered that the islands are on a collision course, what saved him will destroy them, what is about to destroy them will destroy him too, unless he gets away from these parts without delay. With no wind and a broken engine, he could not go upriver, the only way out was to inflate the rubber dinghy, to lower the anchor to secure the boat, a useless gesture, to row ashore. Strength always returns with one's hopes.

The lonely navigator had dressed to go ashore, shorts, vest, a cap on his head, sandals, everything a dazzling white, it's a point of honour with sailors. He hauled the rubber dinghy up the harbour steps, stood there watching for several seconds, also waiting to get his strength back, but, above all, to allow time for someone to appear from the shadows of the arcades, for the cars and buses suddenly to start moving again, and for the square to fill up with people, who knows, perhaps some woman might approach smiling, gently swaying her hips as she walks, without overdoing it, simply that insinuating appeal which affects a man's sight and speech, mainly because he has just come ashore. But the desert remained a desert. The navigator finally understood what had to be understood. Everyone had left because of the collision with the islands. He looked back, saw his boat in the middle of the river, he felt certain he was seeing it for the last time, not even a battleship could withstand the tremendous head-on collision, so what chance would there be for a sailing nutshell abandoned by its owner. The navigator crossed the square, his legs still stiff from lack of exercise, he looked like a scarecrow with his tanned skin, his hair sprouting out of his cap, his sandals hanging off his feet. He looked up as he approached the great arch, read the Latin inscription *Virtutibus Majorum ut sit omnibus documento P.P.D.*, he had never studied Latin, but vaguely understood that the monument was dedicated to the virtuous ancestors of the people who live here, and he proceeded along a narrow street with identical buildings on either side until he came out into another square, smaller, with a Greek or Roman building at one end, and in the middle of the square there were two fountains with naked women cast in iron, the water was playing, and suddenly he felt very thirsty, felt the urge to plunge his mouth into that water and his body into those naked forms. He walked with outstretched arms, as if delirious, sleepwalking or in a trance, he muttered as he went, had no idea what he was saying, only knew what he wanted.

The patrol appeared on the corner, five soldiers under the command of a second lieutenant. They spotted the madman twitching in his madness, they heard him rambling like a madman, there was no need to give any order. The lonely navigator lay stretched out on the ground, there is still some way to go before reaching the water. The women, as we know, are made of iron.

These were also the days of the third exodus. The first, which was fully reported at the appropriate moment, was of the foreign tourists when they fled in terror from what then, how time passes, still seemed no more than the possible danger of a crack opening up in the Pyrenees as far as sea level, and what a pity this unexpected misfortune didn't stop there, just imagine how proud Europe would have felt to find itself to all intents and purposes with a geological canyon compared with which the one in Colorado would look no bigger than a tiny ditch. The second exodus was that of the rich and powerful when the fracture became irreparable, when the Peninsula's course, although still slow, seemed to be gathering speed, showing in a manner we believe definitive, the precariousness of established structures and ideas. It then became clear how the social edifice, with all its complexity, is no more than a house of cards, solid merely in appearance, we need only shake the table on which it stands and the house collapses. And the table in this instance, and for the first time in history, had moved by itself, Dear God, let's save our precious possessions and precious lives and get away from here.

The third exodus, the one we were discussing before summing up the first two, had as it were, two components or parts, which some believe should be referred to as the third and fourth exodus in view of their essential differences. Tomorrow, that's to say in the distant future, those historians who will devote themselves to the study of events which have changed the face of the earth, both in an allegorical and a literal sense, will decide, let us hope with the reflection and impartiality of whoever dispassionately observes the phenomena of the past, whether or not this division should be made, as some people now uphold. The latter claim that it betrays a serious lack of critical judgment or sense of proportion to equate the retreat of millions of people from the coastal regions inland and the flight of a few thousand people abroad, just because there was an undeniable coincidence in the timing of the one exodus and the other. And whereas we have no intention of taking sides in the debate nor of expressing any opinions, it does not cost us anything to recognize that while both groups of people might have experienced the same fear, their methods and means of remedying this fear were quite different.

In the first case, they were nearly all people with few possessions, who on finding themselves forced to move elsewhere by the authorities and the hard facts of their situation, hoped, at most, to save their lives by trusting in some miracle, luck, chance, fate, good fortune, prayer, faith in the Holy Ghost, the Star of David, by wearing an amulet round their neck or a holy medal, and all those other traditional beliefs and customs too numerous to mention here but which can be summed up in that other well-known saying, My hour has not yet come. In the second case, the refugees were people with assets and wealth at their disposal who had held out to see how things would go, but now there was no longer any doubt, the planes operating the new shuttle service were full, the mail-boats, cargo vessels and other smaller craft carried their maximum load. Let us cast a discreet veil over certain unedifying episodes, bribes, intrigues and treacherous betrayals were common, even crimes, and some people were murdered for a ticket, it was a sorry sight, but, the world being what it is, we would be ingenuous to expect anything better. In short, all things considered, most likely the history books will record a fourfold rather than a triple exodus, not for the sake of precise classification but lest we should confuse the wheat with the chaff.

Excluding, nevertheless, anything in the summary analysis given here which may reflect, however involuntarily, a certain mental attitude tainted by Manichaeism, in other words, a tendency to give an idealized picture of the lower orders and a superficial condemnation of the upper classes, readily but not always correctly labelled as being rich and powerful, which naturally provokes hatred and dislike on a par with base feelings of envy, the source of all evils. Of course the poor exist, and their presence cannot be ignored but we must not overrate them. Especially since they are not and never have been models of patience, of resignation, of the self-imposed discipline needed in this crisis. Anyone remote from these events and locations, who imagined that the Iberian refugees, crammed into houses, shelters, hospitals, barracks, warehouses, or whatever army tents or huts it was possible to requisition, along with those relinquished and set up by the military, and that an even greater number of people without accommodation and huddled here and there under bridges and trees, inside abandoned cars, or even out in the open, anyone who imagined that God came to live with these angels may know a great deal about angels and God, but he knows little about mankind.

Without fear of exaggeration one can say that the inferno distributed uniformly throughout the entire Peninsula in mythical times, as we recalled in the opening of this narrative, is now concentrated into a vertical strip about thirty kilometres wide, extending from northern Galicia to the Algarve, with the uninhabited lands to the west which few people regard as effective buffers. For example, if the Spanish government didn't need to leave Madrid, so comfortably positioned inland, anyone wishing to locate the Portuguese government will now have to travel to Elvas which is the city furthest from the coast, if you draw a straight line, more or less horizontal and meridian, from Lisbon. Among the starving refugees, exhausted from lack of sleep, with old people dying, children screaming and crying, the men without work, the women supporting the entire family, quarrels inevitably break out, insults are exchanged, there is disorder and violence, stealing of clothes and food, people are ousted and assaulted, and also, would you believe, there is so much loose living that these settlements are transformed into collective brothels, quite shameful, an appalling example for the older children who may still know their father and mother but have no idea what children they themselves will beget, nor where nor by whom. Clearly this aspect of the question is less important than it appears at first sight, consider how little attention today's historians give to periods which, for one reason or another, were somewhat similar, especially to this one. When all is said and done, perhaps indulging the flesh in moments of crisis is what best serves the deeper interests of humanity and human beings, both habitually harassed as they are by morality. But since this hypothesis is controversial, let's move on, the mere allusion is enough to satisfy the scruples of the impartial observer.

Amidst this tumult and confusion, however, there exists an oasis of peace, these seven creatures who live in the most perfect harmony, two women, three men, a dog and a horse, although the last of these may have to suppress several reasons for complaint regarding the distribution of labour, having to pull on its own a loaded wagon, but even this will be remedied one day. The two women and two of the men constitute two happy couples, only the third man is without a partner, perhaps he does not mind this privation given his age, at least so far there have not been any of those unmistakable signs of edginess which betray an excess of blood in the glands. As for the dog, whether it seeks and finds other pleasures when it goes in search of food, we cannot say, for even though the dog in this context is the greatest exhibitionist among animals, certain species are discreet. Let us hope no one takes it into his head to follow this one, certain unwholesome pryings must be curbed in the name of hygiene. Perhaps these considerations about relationships and forms of behaviour wouldn't be so marked by sexuality if the couples who have formed, out of intense passion or because their love is so new, were not so exuberantly demonstrative, which, let it be said before anyone thinks evil, does not mean that they kiss and embrace each other all over the place, they are restrained to this extent, what they cannot conceal is the aura that surrounds them or that they exude. Only a few days ago Pedro Orce saw the glow of the brazier from the summit of the mountain. Here on the edge of the forest where they now live, sufficiently remote from the settlements to imagine themselves alone, but sufficiently close to ensure supplies of provisions, they might believe in happiness were they not living for who knows how many days yet under the threat of a cataclysm. But they are taking advantage, they would claim as the poet exhorted, *Carpe diem*, the merit of these old Latin quotations is that they contain a world of secondary and tertiary meanings, without counting the latent and undefined ones, so that when one starts to translate, Enjoy life, for example, it sounds feeble and insipid, and doesn't warrant the effort. Therefore we insist on saying *Carpe diem*, and we feel like gods who have decided not to be eternal in order to be able, in the precise meaning of the expression, to take advantage of their time.

What time still remains, one cannot say. Radios and television sets are going twenty-four hours a day, there are no longer news bulletins at certain hours, programmes are interrupted every second to read the latest newsflash, and there are endless announcements, We're now at a distance of three hundred and fifty kilometres, We're now at a distance of three hundred and twenty-seven, We're able to report that the islands of Santa Maria and São Miguel have been completely evacuated, the evacuation of the remaining islands has been stepped up, We're at a distance of three hundred and twelve kilometres, A small team of North American scientists have remained at the base in Lajes and they will leave, by plane of course, only at the last minute in order to witness the collision from the air, let's use the word collision without any adjectives. A request from the government of Portugal that a Portuguese should be included as an observer in the aforesaid team went unheeded. There are three hundred and four kilometres to go, those responsible for the recreational and cultural programmes on television and radio discuss what should be transmitted, some insist on classical music given the seriousness of the situation, others argue that classical music is depressing, that it would be preferable to transmit some light music, French *chansons* of the Thirties, Portuguese *fados*, Spanish *malagueñas* and other popular airs from Seville, and lots of rock and folk music, the top tunes from the Eurovision Song Contest. But surely such cheerful music will shock and upset people who are living through this terrible crisis, retort the classical buffs. It would be worse if we were to play funeral marches, the modern buffs allege, and the argument raged on with neither side giving an inch, two hundred and eighty-five kilometres to go.

Joaquim Sassa's radio has been used sparingly, he has some batteries in reserve, but is reluctant to use them, no one can tell what tomorrow will bring, a popular saying which tells us a good deal, here we could almost bet on what tomorrow will bring, death and destruction, millions of corpses, half the Peninsula going under. But those moments when the radio is switched off soon become unbearable, time starts becoming tangible, viscous, it grips one's throat, you sense that you are about to feel the impact at any moment although we are still far away, the tension is intolerable, Joaquim Sassa switches on the radio, *É uma casa portuguesa com certeza é com certeza uma casa portuguesa*, the delightful voice sings of life, *Dónde vas de mantón de Manila dónde vas con el rojo clavel*, the same delight, the same life, but in another language, then they all sigh with relief, they're twenty kilometres closer to death, but what does that matter, death has yet to be announced, the Azores are not in sight, Sing, girl, sing.

Seated under the shade of a tree, they have just finished eating, and they could pass for nomads in their habits and dress, they have changed so much in such a short time, the result of having no

189

comforts, their clothes are creased and stained, the men are unshaven, but let us not reproach them or the women whose lips are now their natural colour, turned pale from anxiety, perhaps when their last hour comes, they will put on some lipstick and prepare themselves to receive death with dignity, ebbing life does not warrant so much effort. Maria Guavaira is leaning against Joaquim Sassa's shoulder, she grips him by the hand. Several tears appear between her eyelashes, but not because she is afraid of what is about to happen. These are tears of love which come springing to her eyes. And José Anaiço cradles Joana Carda in his arms, kisses her on the forehead, then her eyelids close, if only I could take this moment with me where I am going, I should ask no more, only one moment, not this moment as I am speaking, but that previous one, and the one before that, now almost vanished, I failed to grasp it as I experienced it and now it is too late. Pedro Orce has got up and walks away, his white hair gleams in the sun, he too carries the aura of cold light. The dog has followed him with lowered head. But they won't go very far. They now keep together as much as possible, neither of them wishes to be alone when the disaster occurs. The horse, as the experts claim, is the only animal that does not know it is going to die, it feels contented despite the great trials it has endured on its long, long journey. It munches the hay, shakes off the gadflies with a shudder, sweeps its grizzled flank with the long hair of its tail, probably unaware that it had been about to end its days in the semi-darkness of a dilapidated stable, among cobwebs and dung, its infected lungs gasping for breath, how true that the misfortune of some is the fortune of others, however short-lived.

The day passed, another came and went, one hundred and fifty kilometres to go. You can sense the terror growing like a black shadow, the panic becomes a flood seeking out weak spots in the dyke, corroding the stone foundations until they finally give way, and those who so far had remained more or less peacefully in their camps, began to move further eastwards now realizing that they were far too close to the coast, only some seventy or eighty kilometres away, they could visualize the islands tearing through the land up to where they were, and the sea inundating everything, the mountain on the island of Pico like some ghostly presence, who knows, perhaps with the impact the volcano will become active again, But there is no volcano on Pico, though no one listened to this or any other explanation. Naturally, the roads became congested, every crossroads became a knot impossible to untie, at one point neither advance nor retreat was possible, people were trapped like mice, but scarcely any were willing to give up the few possessions they were carrying for the sake of trying to save their lives by taking to the fields. In order to arrest this influx with good example, the Portuguese government abandoned the security of Elvas and installed itself at Evora, while the Spanish government settled more conveniently at León from where they issued communiqués which the President of our Republic and the Sovereign of their Realm also signed, for we should have mentioned that our President and their King have accompanied their respective ministers at every stage of the crisis, even offering to go and confront the hysterical mobs with extended arms, exposing themselves to some act of violence or aggression, and to address them once more as, Friends, Romans, countrymen, and so on and so forth. No Your Majesty, no Mr President, crowds in a state of panic, and ignorant crowds to boot, would not understand, people have to be extremely cultured and civilized to meet a king or a president with extended arms in the middle of a road and stop to ask him what he wants. But there was also one who in an outburst of anger turned round and shouted, Better to be dead than to survive so briefly, let's put an end to this once and for all, and they stayed there waiting, contemplating the serene mountains in the distance, the rosy morning, the deep blue of the hot afternoon, the starry night, perhaps the last, but when my hour comes, I won't look away.

Then it happened. About seventy-five kilometres away from the easternmost point of the island of Santa Maria, without any warning, without anyone feeling the slightest shock, the Peninsula began to sail in a northerly direction. For several minutes, while observers in all the geographical institutes of Europe and North America analysed in disbelief the data received from the satellites and hesitated about making them public, millions of terrified people in Portugal and Spain were already safe from death without knowing it. During those minutes, some tragically began quarrelling in the hope of being killed and perhaps had their wish granted, and some frightened out of their wits committed suicide. Some implored pardon for their sins, while others, thinking there was no time for repentance, enquired of God and the Devil what new sins they might still commit. There were women who gave birth hoping that their offspring would be still-born, and others who knew they were carrying children they would never deliver. And when a universal cry echoed throughout the world, They're saved, they're saved, some would not believe it and went on lamenting the approaching end until there could be no more doubt, governments swore to it in every tone, the experts started giving explanations, the reason given for their salvation was a mighty sea-current artificially produced, and a great debate ensued as to whether the North Americans or the Russians were responsible.

Rejoicing spread like wildfire, filling the entire Peninsula with laughter and dancing, especially on that great strip of land where millions of displaced persons had gathered. Fortunately this occurred at midday when those who still had some provisions were about to eat, otherwise the confusion and chaos would have been dreadful, claimed the responsible authorities, but they were soon to regret this hasty judgment, for no sooner had the news been confirmed than thousands and thousands of people began the long trek home. It became necessary to circulate the cruel hypothesis that the Peninsula might revert to its original route, now a little further north. Not everyone believed the news, especially since another worry was quietly creeping into people's thoughts, in their mind's eye they could see abandoned cities, towns and villages, their own native city, town or village, the street and house where they once lived, their home ransacked by opportunists who didn't believe in old wives' tales or accepted the hypothetical risk with the naturalness of the acrobat who has to attempt a triple somersault night after night, these visions were not the fantasies of a sick mind, for throughout all those deserted places, thieves, robbers and scoundrels of every age were warily mustering, ready to pounce, and passing the word from one to the other. The first to arrive helps himself and anyone who comes later must look for another house to loot, don't start bickering for there's plenty for everyone. Let no one, say we, be tempted to break into Maria Guavaira's house, it's the worst thing anyone could do, for the man inside is armed with a shotgun, and he will open the door only to the mistress of the house to assure her, I've guarded your property, now marry me, unless, dazed and exhausted after so many nights of vigil, he might have fallen asleep on a pile of blue wool, and thus have wasted the best years of his manhood.

Exercising prudence, the inhabitants of the Azores still had not returned to their homes on the islands, let us try to imagine ourselves in their shoes, it is true that any immediate danger has passed, yet it continues to lurk there, this is like a new version of the tale about the iron pan and the clay pan, with the important difference that the clay in this case was only good for making the mugs typical of these islands, there was not enough to make the pan of a continent, which, if it ever existed, sank to the bottom and was called Atlantis. We would be very foolish were we not to learn from experience or our memory of it, however false both may be. But the sentiment that causes the five persons under that tree to linger is not prudence, now that everyone has set off in the direction of the coasts of Portugal and Galicia, in triumphant re-entry, as it were, bearing branches and flowers, with bands playing, fireworks exploding, bells pealing as they pass in procession, families return to their homes, perhaps there are things missing, but they have brought life with them and that is the most important thing, life, the table where we eat, the bed where we sleep and where this night, out of sheer happiness, they will make the most wonderful love in the world. Underneath the tree, their wagon waiting and the horse's strength restored, the five who have remained behind look at the dog as if expecting some sign or mandate, You who came from we know not where, you who turned up one day so weary from your travels that you collapsed into my arms, you who passed and stared as I was showing the men where I drew a line on the ground with a stick, you who waited for us beside the car we parked beneath the lean-to, you who had a blue thread hanging from your mouth, you who guided us along so many roads and paths, you who accompanied me to the sea where we found the stone ship, tell us by some movement, gesture or sign, since you cannot even bark, tell us where we must go, for none of us wishes to return to the house in the valley, for all of us it would mean the beginning of that final return, the man who wants to marry me would say, Marry me, the office manager where I work would tell me, I need that invoice, my husband would say to me, So you've finally come back to me, the father of my worst pupil would inform me, Schoolmaster I've given him a few strokes with the cane, the notary's wife who complains of headaches would plead, Give me some pills for my headache, so do tell us where we should go, arise and walk and that will be our destination.

The dog, who was lying under the wagon, lifted its head as if hearing voices, jumped up briskly and ran to Pedro Orce who held its head between his hands, Would you like to come with me, he asked the dog and these were the only words he spoke. Maria Guavaira owns the horse and wagon and she still has not made up her mind, but Joana Carda looked at José Anaiço, who read her thoughts, Whatever you may decide, I'm not going back. Then Maria Guavaira said in a loud, clear voice, There's a time for staying and a time for leaving, the time hasn't yet come to return, and Joaquim Sassa asked, Where do we want to go. Nowhere in particular. Let's go to the other side of the Peninsula, Pedro Orce suggested, for I've never seen the Pyrenees. Nor are you likely to see them now, half of them were left behind in Europe, José Anaiço reminded them. What does it matter, you can recognize a giant by looking at his finger. They were delighted with this decision, but Maria Guavaira warned them, The horse has carried us all this way on its own, but it won't make the rest of the journey alone, the horse has seen better days and the wagon ought to be drawn by a pair of horses, with only one, it's a one-armed wagon. So what are we going to do, asked Joaquim Sassa. We'll need to find another horse, It can't be easy to find horses around here, besides a good horse costs a lot of money, and we probably can't afford it.

The problem appears to be without any solution, but here we shall see further evidence of how adaptable the human spirit can be. Only a few days ago, Maria Guavaira flatly rejected the idea of spending the night in an abandoned house, her words still echo in the ears of those who remember, yet such is the force of circumstance that Maria Guavaira is about to condemn a lifetime of moral integrity, let us hope no one will taunt her with this lapse from grace, We won't buy it, we'll steal it, those were her very words, and now Joana Carda tries to ease their conscience indirectly, so as not to offend sensibilities, I've never stolen anything in my life. There was an awkward silence, people need time to adapt to new codes of morality, here the first move was made by Pedro Orce, contrary to the custom of the elderly who are staunch believers in traditional values, We've never stolen anything in our life, it's always in the lives of others, this could be the maxim of a cynical philosopher, but is merely a statement of fact, said Pedro Orce with a smile, but the words had been spoken. Very well, we've decided, let's steal the horse, but how do we go about it, let's toss a coin to see who should go on this expedition, I'd better go, said Maria Guavaira, for you don't know anything about horses, and you'd never be able to get it here. I'll come with you, said Joaquim Sassa, but perhaps we should take the dog with us to protect us from any danger we might encounter.

That night the three of them left the encampment and headed east, a region which had remained relatively tranquil and where there was greater likelihood of finding what they wanted. Before departing, Joaquim Sassa said, We don't know how long we'll be, wait for us here. Thinking it over, perhaps we should have brought a bigger car with room for everyone including the luggage and the dog, commented José Anaiço. There are no such cars, what we need is a lorry, besides, don't forget that we didn't find a single vehicle in working order and fit to put on the road, and now that we have a horse we can't just dump it anywhere. In their time the musketeers declared, One for all and all for one, they were four, now they are five, without counting the dog. Or the horse.

Maria Guavaira and Joaquim Sassa set off, the animal trotting in front, sniffing out the winds and investigating the shadows. The expedition is faintly absurd, chasing off in search of a horse. A mule would do just as well, Maria Guavaira had said, without knowing if such an animal existed within five leagues, perhaps it would be easier to find an ox, but you don't hitch an ox and a horse together to a wagon, or a donkey, with such a load to carry it would be like trying to make something strong from combined weakness, something which only happens in parables, like the one about the rushes we quoted earlier. They walked and walked, left the road whenever they glimpsed any dwellings or farmhouses amidst the fields, if there were any horses around that is where they would find them, for what we need are beasts of burden rather than horses for parading or performing in the arena. The moment they approached dogs started barking, but they soon quietened down, one will never know what secret powers the Dog possessed for even the loudest and most excitable watchdog suddenly fell silent, and not because some wild beast from the underworld had savaged it, otherwise there would have been signs of a struggle, cries of pain, the silence is not sepulchral simply because no one is dying.

By the early hours of morning, Maria Guavaira and Joaquim Sassa could scarcely lift their feet they were so tired, he had said, We must go on searching, and they searched so hard that they found rather than discovered what they were looking for, and it came about in the simplest way imaginable. Dawn was already breaking, the night sky to the east had turned a deep blue, when they heard a muffled neigh coming from a hollow on the road, a sweet miracle, I'm here, they went to look and found a tethered horse, it was not the Good Lord who had put it there to enhance His catalogue of miracles, but the beast's rightful owner whom the blacksmith had instructed, Put this ointment on the sore and leave the horse out to catch the morning dew, do this for three consecutive nights starting on a Friday, and if the horse isn't cured, I'll give you back your money and stake my reputation. A fettered horse, unless one has a sharp knife to cut the rope, cannot be carried off on one's shoulders, but Maria Guavaira knew how to deal with animals and despite the beast's nervousness at being handled by a stranger, she succeeded in coaxing it into the shadows of the trees where at the risk of being trampled or receiving a mighty kick, she managed to untie the awkward knot. Usually in such cases one makes a simple knot which can easily be undone, but perhaps that's a skill people do not practise in these parts. Fortunately the horse also realized that they were trying to free it, and freedom is always welcome, even when we're facing the unknown.

They returned by roads way off the beaten track, trusting more than ever in the dog's ability to foresee anything suspicious coming in their direction and its effectiveness in dealing with any inopportune visitors. When day broke, already remote from the scene of the crime, they began meeting people in the fields and along the roads, but no one appeared to recognize the horse, and even if they did, perhaps they would not have given it another thought for they made such a lovely and innocent picture, to put it in medieval terms, the damsel riding side-saddle on the palfrey, and the knight errant walking ahead, tediously leading the horse by the reins which fortunately they had remembered to bring. The mastiff completed this heavenly vision, which some mistook for a dream, others as a sign of a change in life, the former and latter unaware that all they are seeing go past are two wicked horse-thieves, how true that appearances can deceive, what is generally overlooked is that they can deceive twice, perhaps a reason for trusting first impressions and not enquiring any further. That's why some will be claiming before the day is out, Why this morning I saw Amadís and Oriana, she on horseback, he on foot, and they had a dog with them, It can't have been Amadís and Oriana, for they were never seen with a dog, Well I saw it, and that's a fact, one witness is as good as a hundred, But in the lives, loves and adventures of those two, no dog is ever mentioned, Well let their stories be rewritten, and as often as may prove necessary until nothing has been left out, Nothing, Well, almost nothing.

They reached the encampment early that evening and were received with much hugging and laughter. The grey horse looked askance at the sorrel which was gasping for breath. It had a sore on its back which was almost dry, they'd obviously rubbed on some ointment and left it outdoors for three nights, starting on a Friday, an infallible remedy.

As the people return to their homes and life gradually gets back, as one is wont to say, to normal, the arguments rage on among the scientists about possible causes for the Peninsula's deviation at the very last minute, just when it appeared that nothing could avert the catastrophe. The theories vary, nearly all of them in conflict, thus contributing mathematically to the irreducibility of experts locked in controversy.

A first theory supports the sheer coincidence of the new route inasmuch as it forms a perfect right angle with the previous one, thereby ruling out any explanation that might assume, shall we say, an act of volition. Besides, to whom could such an act be attributed since no one is likely to suggest that an enormous mass of stone and earth, on which tens of millions of people swarm restlessly, could produce merely by reciprocal addition or multiplication an intelligence and power capable of acting with a precision one can only describe as diabolical.

Another theory maintains that the Peninsula's advance or, to put it more accurately, its progression, and we shall soon see why this is the better word, will result time and time again in another right angle, which *ipso facto* allows for the amazing possibility of the Peninsula returning to its point of departure after a succession or, we repeat, progression of impulses which after a certain point could be less than a millimetre until it finally settles in precisely the right place.

The third theory advances the possibility of a magnetic field on the Peninsula, or some such force, which on approaching an alien body of sufficient volume may react and unleash a process of repulsion of a quite specific nature, since that repulsion, as we have seen, does not proceed in a reverse direction from that of the initial or final movement, but rather goes into a skid, to borrow an example from the routine practice of driving a car, and why this should be to the north or south is something the experts forgot to consider.

Finally, a fourth and more heterodox theory has recourse to what it terms metapsychic powers, affirming that the Peninsula has been diverted from collision by a vector formed within a tenth of a second from the concentration of the desire for salvation and the sheer terror of the stricken population. This explanation gains wide popularity mainly because the author of the theory in his efforts to make it accessible to simple minds has borrowed a comparison from physics by demonstrating how the incidence of solar rays in a biconvex lens causes those rays to converge on an actual point of focus resulting, as one would expect, in heat, combustion, and fire, so that the intensifying effect of the lens has an obvious parallel in the power of the collective mind, which would be the chaotic sun, stimulated, concentrated and worked up in a moment of crisis to a state of paroxysm. The incongruity of this explanation does not bother anyone, on the contrary, lots of people begin proposing that henceforth all the problems of the psyche, spirit, soul, will, and creation, should be explained in physical terms, even if only by simple analogy or dubious conclusion. The theory is being studied and developed with a view to applying its fundamental principles to daily life, in particular to the functioning of political parties and in competitive sports, to quote two common examples.

Some sceptics argue, however, that the real proof of all these hypotheses, since that is all they are, will be seen in a few weeks' time, if the Peninsula continues to follow its present route which will cause it to get stuck between Greenland and Iceland, inhospitable territories for Portuguese and Spaniards who are normally accustomed to the mildness and languor of a temperate climate which tends to be warm for the greater part of the year. If this were to happen, the only logical conclusion to be drawn from all we have witnessed so far is that the journey was not worthwhile. Which, on the other hand, would or will be much too simple a way of confronting the problem, for no journey is but one journey, each journey comprises a number of journeys, and if one of them seems so meaningless that we have no hesitation in saying it was not worthwhile, our common sense, were it not so often clouded by prejudice and idleness, would tell us that we should verify if the journeys within that journey were not of sufficient value to have justified all the trials and tribulations. If we take all these factors into account we shall refrain from making any final judgments or assumptions. Journeys succeed each other and accumulate like generations, between the grandson you were and the grandfather you will be, what father will you have been. Therefore a journey, however futile, is necessary.

José Anaiço studied the details of the journey they are about to make, along paths that will not be direct if they are to avoid the great slopes of the Cantabrian mountains, and he explained what he had worked out, From Palas de Rei, which is about where we are now, to Valladolid must be about four hundred kilometres, and from there to the frontier, forgive me, but on this map I still have a frontier, there are another four hundred, making eight hundred kilometres altogether, a long journey at a horse's pace, Not a horse's pace, that's over and done with, and it won't be so much a pace as a trot, Maria Guavaira corrected him. Then Joaquim Sassa spoke, With two horses pulling, he broke off in mid-sentence with the expression of someone who sees a light inside his own head, and then bursts out laughing, Isn't it ironic, we've abandoned Deux Chevaux and now we're travelling with two horses, I suggest we call the wagon Deux Chevaux, *de facto et de jure*, not that I've ever studied Latin, but I've heard others use the expression, as one of my grandfathers used to say who also didn't know the language of his ancestors. The Deux Chevaux are munching hay behind the wagon, the sore on the sorrel's back is now completely healed, and the grey horse, if not exactly rejuvenated, looks fitter and stronger, it can't lift its head as high as the sorrel, but they don't make a bad pair. Joaquim Sassa repeated his question once the laughter had subsided. As I was saying, with two horses pulling, how many kilometres on average shall we cover in an hour, and Maria Guavaira replied, About three leagues, So about fifteen kilometres as calculated nowadays, Correct, Ten hours at fifteen kilometres an hour makes one hundred and fifty, within three days we'll be in Valladolid, and three days after that we'll reach the Pyrenees, it doesn't take long. Looking dismayed Maria Guavaira replied, That's quite a schedule unless we're trying to work the horses to death in no time, But you said . . ., I said fifteen kilometres, but that was on flat land and in any case the horses will never keep going for ten hours each day, But they can rest, Just as well you haven't forgotten they need to rest. From the sarcastic tone in her voice it was clear that Maria Guavaira was close to losing her temper.

At such moments, even when horses do not come into it, men become submissive, a fact women generally ignore, they only notice what has struck them as male resentment when their authority is challenged, that is how mistakes and misunderstandings come about, perhaps the root of the problem lies in the inadequate hearing of human beings, of women in particular, who nevertheless pride themselves on being good listeners. I must admit, I know nothing about horses, I belong to the infantry, Joaquim Sassa muttered. The others listened in on this duel of words, they smiled because it was not to be taken seriously, the blue thread was the most powerful bond in the universe, as we would soon see. Maria Guavaira said, Six hours per day is the most we can hope for, at best we'll cover three leagues in an hour, or whatever the horses can manage. Do we leave tomorrow, José Anaiço asked her, If everyone agrees, Maria Guavaira told him, and softening her tone she enquired of Joaquim Sassa, Is that all right, and taken by surprise he smiled and said, That's fine by me.

That night they counted their money, so many escudos, so many pesetas, some foreign currency belonging to Joaquim Sassa who had acquired it when they left Oporto, only a few days ago and yet centuries seem to have passed, scarcely an original thought but as irresistible as most banal statements. The provisions they brought with them from Maria Guavaira's house have almost run out, their supply of food will have to be replenished and that will not be easy, given the chaos and disruption and the marauding horde who did not even leave the cabbage stalks in their wake, not to mention the plundered chicken-coops, the angry response of people who were starving when they were asked to pay a fortune for a scraggy chicken. Once the situation began to return to normal, prices fell a little, but not to what they were before, for as we know, they never do. And now there is a shortage of everything, even finding anything to steal would be a problem, if anyone should want to resort to such wickedness. The horse's situation was special. Had it not been for that sore, it would still be adorning the stables and assisting the labours of its former owner who knows nothing of the beast's fate except that it was taken away by two scoundrels and a dog who left their traces behind. People say time and time again that out of evil comes good. It has been said so often and by so many that it might well be a universal truth so long as we take the trouble to distinguish evil from good, and those who have experienced the one or the other. Then Pedro Orce said, We'll have to work to earn some money, it seemed a sensible idea but after taking stock of their skills they arrived at the depressing conclusion one might have expected. For Joana Carda, after graduating in humanities, never taught but married and became a housewife, here in Spain there is not a great deal of interest in Portuguese literature and, besides, the Spaniards have more important things on their minds right now, Joaquim Sassa, as he declared with some annoyance, belongs to the infantry, which, coming from his lips, meant that he belongs to the lowly rank of office clerk, a useful profession undoubtedly, but only in times of social stability and normal trading, Pedro Orce has spent his life making up prescriptions, when first we met him he was preparing capsules filled with quinine, what a pity he didn't remember to bring his pharmacy with him, he could now be offering consultations and earning good money, for in these rural districts the pharmacist and doctor are one and the same thing, José Anaiço is an elementary-school teacher, and that tells us everything, without forgetting that he is in a country with a different geography and history, and how could he explain to Spanish children that the Battle of Aljubarrota was a victory when they are usually taught to forget that it was a resounding defeat. Maria Guavaira is the only person in the group who could look for work on one of these farms and be up to it in proportion to her strength and experience which are limited.

They look at each other without knowing what to do and Joaquim Sassa says hesitantly, If we have to stop every five minutes to make some money we'll never reach the Pyrenees, money made like this never lasts, it's no sooner made than spent, the ideal solution for us would be to travel like gypsies, I mean those who wander from country to country, they must live on something, he was asking a question, expressing his doubt, perhaps manna fell from heaven on the gypsies. Pedro Orce answered him, hailing as he did from the south where the gypsy race abounds, Some of them trade in horses, others sell clothes in the market, others hawk their wares from door to door, the women tell fortunes, We don't want to hear any more about horses, we'll never live this one down, besides, it's a profession we know nothing about, and as for telling fortunes, let's hope ours won't give us cause for concern. And without taking into account that in order to sell horses one has to start by buying them, their money would not stretch that far, when even the horse they have had to be stolen. Silence fell, no one knew how it happened and when it passed, Joaquim Sassa, who is beginning to reveal that he has a practical mind, told them, I can only see one way out of this situation, let's buy clothes from one of those wholesalers, there are bound to be some in the first big town we come to, and then we can sell them in the villages at a reasonable profit, I can look after the accounts. It seemed a good idea for the want of a better one, and they might as well give it a try. Since they could not be farmers or pharmacists or teachers or landlords, they might as well be pedlars and travelling salesmen, they could sell clothes for men, women and children, which is no dishonour, and with sound book-keeping they'd be able to live.

Having drawn up this plan for survival, they settled down for the night, the moment having arrived to decide how all five should accommodate themselves in the wagon, now called Deux Chevaux, which is as follows, Pedro Orce sleeps in front, lying crosswise on a narrow pallet which is just big enough for him, then Joana Carda and José Anaiço lengthwise in an empty space amid some of the luggage they are carrying with them, and the same for Maria Guavaira and Joaquim Sassa further back. Improvised curtains create imaginary compartments and some semblance of privacy, if Joana Carda and José Anaiço who sleep in the middle of the wagon need to go outside during the night, they pass alongside Pedro Orce who does not mind, here they share discomfort as they share everything else. And what about the kisses, embraces and sexual intercourse, inquisitive spirits will enquire whom nature has endowed with a perverse interest in malice. Let us say that the lovers had two ways of satisfying the sweet impulses of nature, either they go through the fields in search of some lonely and pleasant spot, or they take advantage of the temporary and deliberate absence of their companions to do what need not be spelt out, the signs speak for themselves unless we choose to ignore them, and while they might lack money they are not without understanding.

They do not set out at break of day, as poetry would demand, for why get up early when they have all the time in the world now, but this is not the only or most persuasive reason, they take their time in getting ready, the men shaved, the women neat and tidy, their clothes carefully brushed, in some suitable corner of the wood where they have carried a bucket to draw water from the stream, the couples wash one after the other, perhaps naked for there is no one to look on. Pedro Orce is the last to wash and he takes the dog with him, they look like two animals, I'm tempted to say the one laughed as much as the other, the dog pushing Pedro Orce and

Pedro Orce splashing water on the dog, a man of his age should not make such a fool of himself in public, anyone passing there would have said at once, The fellow ought to show more self-respect, he is certainly old enough to know better. Few traces have been left of the encampment, nothing except the trampled ground, the water splashed from their ablutions under the trees, ashes among blackened stones, the first gust of wind will sweep everything away, the first heavy shower will flatten the soil and dissolve the ashes, only the stones will reveal that people have been here, and if needed they will serve for another campfire.

It is a nice day for travelling. From the slope of the hillock where they had taken shelter they descend the road, Maria Guavaira is in the driver's seat for she does not trust anyone with the reins, one has to know how to talk to horses, there are boulders and potholes on the road and if one of the axles should break that would be the end of all their endeavours, God protect us from any such misfortune. The chestnut sorrel and the grey horse still make an ill-matched pair, Chess seems uncertain about the steadiness of Grizzly's legs, and Grizzly once harnessed and yoked tends to pull outwards, as if trying to get away from its companion and forcing Chess to make an even greater effort. Maria Guavaira is watching their goings-on, once they are on the road she will bring Chess under control with a skilful combination of whipping and tugging on the reins.

Joaquim Sassa had invented the names Chess and Grizzly, bearing in mind that these Deux Chevaux are not like those of the car, the former were so closely knit that they were indistinguishable and wanted the same thing at the same time, while these two differ in everything, colour, age, strength, size and temperament, so it seems right and proper that each should have a name. But Grizzly in English usually refers to bears, Chess is a game, complained José Anaiço, whereupon Joaquim Sassa retorted, We're not in England, the grey horse has been baptized Grizzly and the sorrel Chess and I'm their godfather. Joana Carda and Maria Guavaira exchange smiles at the men's childishness. And Pedro Orce unexpectedly joins in, If those were a mare and a horse and they had a foal, we might end up with a chess-playing bear.

On the first day they travelled no more than seventy kilometres, firstly because it did not seem right to put pressure on the horses after they had been rested for so long, one of them because suffering from malaria, the other because awaiting certain decisions that were slow in coming, and secondly because they had to go through the town of Lugo which lay off the beaten track to the northeast where they had gone to stock up with the merchandise from which they hoped to earn their living. They bought a local newspaper to catch up with the latest news, the most interesting item of all was a photograph taken yesterday of the Peninsula. After one day the displacement to the north, away from its previous route, could be seen clearly indicated by the editor with a dotted line. There was no doubt, it was unmistakably a right angle. But the conflicting theories we summarized earlier made little progress, and as for the views held by the newspaper itself, one could detect a note of caution and scepticism, perhaps justified because of previous disappointments but also typical of the narrow-mindedness one tends to find in the provinces.

In the wholesale warehouses the women, for naturally it was left to them to choose the clothes with Joaquim Sassa on hand to do the costing, could not decide what to buy, whether they should select garments for the approaching winter, or plan ahead for the following spring. Joaquim Sassa referred to mid-term planning but Joana Carda insisted it should be mid-season whereupon Joaquim Sassa told her curtly, Back in the office that was the expression we used, we always referred to short-, mid- or long-term planning. The final choice was dictated by their own needs for they were all badly in need of some new clothes for the autumn, besides it was inevitable that Maria Guavaira and Joana Carda should be tempted to buy what they themselves wanted. On balance, they were able to complete their purchases to everyone's satisfaction and there were healthy profits in store if demand should match up to the stock they now had to offer. Joaquim Sassa expressed some disquiet. We've tied up more than half our money and unless we recoup half of what we've spent within a week, we'll be in trouble, In our situation, with no funds in reserve or possibility of obtaining a bank loan, we must regulate our stock so that we maintain a steady turnover and bring our income into line with our investment. Joaquim Sassa delivered this little speech, in his capacity as book-keeper, at the first stop they made after leaving Lugo, and it was benevolently received by the others.

They soon realized this business would not be a bed of roses when a woman who knew how to strike a bargain obliged them to lower the price of two skirts to the extent of depriving them of any profit. As it happened, Joana Carda was doing the selling and she later apologized to her trading partners and promised that in future she would be the most intransigent saleswoman operating in the Peninsula. Repeating his warning, Joaquim Sassa told them, Unless we're cautious from the outset, we'll find ourselves bankrupt and without any money or goods, and besides, it's not just a question of our livelihood, we have three more mouths to feed, the dog and the horses. The dog looks after itself, interrupted Pedro Orce. So far it has managed to look after itself, but should it ever be unable to hunt for its own food, it will come back to us with its tail between its legs, and if we have nothing to give it, what then. Half of everything I own is for the dog. That's a kind thought but our main concern should be to share wealth instead of poverty. Wealth and poverty is one way of expressing it, José Anaiço observed, but at this moment in our lives we find ourselves poorer than we really are, it's an odd situation, we're living as if we had chosen to be poor. Were it a matter of choice, I don't believe it would be in good faith, it was a question of circumstances of which we only accepted some, those which served our personal aims, we're like actors, or mere characters, said Joana Carda before asking, For example, if I were to go back to my husband, who would I be, the actor outside the character, or a character playing the part of an actor, and where would I stand between the one and the other. Maria Guavaira had been listening in silence and now she began speaking like someone beginning another conversation, perhaps she had not fully grasped what the others had said, People are reborn each day, only they can decide whether they go on living the previous day or make a fresh start. But there is experience, all that we've learnt, Pedro Orce pointed out. Yes, you're quite right, Joaquim Sassa said, but we usually live our lives as if we had no previous experience, or make use only of that part of life which allows us to go on making mistakes, quoting examples and the fruits of experience, I've just thought of something which you may find absurd and nonsensical, perhaps experience has a greater effect on society as a whole than on individuals, society takes advantage of everyone's experience, but no one wishes, knows, or is able to take full advantage of their own experience.

They debate these interesting problems under the shade of a tree while having their lunch, frugal as befits travelling salesmen who have not yet finished their day's work, and lest anyone should find this discussion unsuitable in these circumstances and in such a place, we must remind them that taken as a whole, the learning and culture of pilgrims permit, without any blatant impropriety, a conversation whose drift should, from the exclusive point of view of literary composition in search of strict verisimilitude, in fact betray some flaws. But everyone, independent of any skills they may possess, has at some time or other said or done things way above their nature and condition and if we could remove those people from the dull humdrum existence in which they gradually lose their identity, or if they were to throw off the fetters and chains, how many more wonders would they be able to perform, how many fragments of deep knowledge would they be able to communicate, for we all know infinitely more than we think and everyone else infinitely more than we are prepared to acknowledge. Five individuals are assembled here for the most extraordinary reasons and it would be most surprising if they were not to say some astonishing things.

In these parts there is rarely a car to be seen. Now and then a big lorry goes by carrying provisions, mainly foodstuffs, to the villages. With all the things that have happened local food supplies have been disrupted, shortages are common, suddenly followed by a glut, but there is always some excuse, remember, the human race has never experienced a similar situation. As for sailing, man has always sailed, but in small ships. Lots of refugees are on foot, others ride donkeys and if the road were not so uneven there would be more bicycles around. People here are usually good-natured and peaceable but envy is probably the one trait you find in every social class and more often than not in most human beings, so it was no surprise that the sight of Deux Chevaux passing along the road, when nearly everyone was without transport, should have provoked some jealousy. Any determined and violent gang of brigands would soon have disposed of the occupants, one is an old man, the others could hardly be mistaken for Samson or Hercules, and as for the women, once their menfolk had been overpowered, they would be easy prey, true, Maria Guavaira is a woman who can stand up to any man, but not without a firebrand in her hand. It might well have happened, therefore, that our travelling salesmen should be suddenly attacked and be left to their fate, the poor women raped, the men injured and humiliated, but the dog was there and if anyone appeared it came out from under the wagon and whether in front or behind, stationary or walking, its nose down like that of a wolf-hound, it transfixed the passers-by, who were nearly always harm-less, with an icy stare, but they felt every bit as afraid as any assailants. If we consider everything this dog has done so far, it would deserve to be called guardian angel, despite the continuous innuendo about its infernal origins. Objections will be raised, citing the traditional teaching of Christian and non-Christian doctrine whereby angels have always been depicted with wings, but in all those cases where the necessary angel would not be required to fly, what harm would be done if it were to appear now and then in the guise of a dog, without being obliged to bark which in any case would be quite unfitting for a spiritual being. At least let us acknowledge that dogs which do not bark are just as good as angels.

They set up camp that evening on the banks of the River Minho, near a village called Portomarín. While José Anaiço and Joaquim Sassa untied and attended to the horses, kindled the fire, peeled the potatoes and prepared the salad, the women, accompanied by Pedro Orce and their guardian angel, took advantage of the remaining twilight to call at some houses in the village. Because of the language barrier, Joana Carda did not say a word, it was probably the problem of communication which had foxed her last time, but she is gaining experience for the future which is the only place where mistakes can be corrected. Business was not bad and they sold their goods at the right price. When they got back the camp looked homely, the campfire crackled among the stones, the lamp hanging from the wagon cast a semi-circle of light in the open space, and the smell coming from the pot on the boil was as consoling as the Lord's presence.

As they chatted around the fire after they had eaten, it suddenly occurred to Joaquim Sassa to ask, Where did you get this name Guavaira, what does it mean, and Maria Guavaira told him, As far as I know there is no one else with this name, my mother dreamt it when I was still inside her, she wanted me to be called Guavaira and nothing else, but my father insisted that I should be called Maria, so I ended up with a name I was never meant to have, Maria Guavaira. So you don't know what it means, My name turned up in a dream. Dreams always have some meaning. But not names that turn up in dreams, now the rest of you tell me your names. They told her one by one. Then, poking the fire with a stick, Maria Guavaira said, The names we possess are dreams, who shall I be dreaming about if I should dream your name.

The weather has changed, an expression of admirable concision which informs us in a soothing and neutrally objective manner that having changed, it has changed for the worse. It is raining, a gentle rain now that autumn is here, and until the ground becomes muddy we will be tempted to stroll through the countryside in rubber boots and raincoats receiving that gentle spray of moisture on our faces, and absorbing the melancholy of the distant haze, the first trees shedding their leaves, looking bare and cold, as if they were about to plead to be caressed, there are some one would like to press to one's bosom with tender pity, we rest our cheek against the moist bark and it feels as if the tree were covered in tears.

But the canvas of the wagon goes back to the origins of such coverings which were solidly woven and made to last rather than to keep out the rain. It dates from an age when people were accustomed to letting their clothes dry out on their bodies, their only protection, if they were lucky, was a glass of aquavit. Then there was the effect of the seasons, the drying out of the fibres, the fraying of the stitches, it is easy to see that the canvas removed from the car is not enough to patch up all the damage. And so the rain continually leaks into the wagon despite Joaquim Sassa's reassurances that the soaking and enlarging of the threads, with the consequent tightening of the weave, will help if only they would be patient. In theory nothing could be truer, but in practice it clearly does not work. If they had not taken the trouble to roll up the mattresses to protect them, it would have been some time before they could sleep on them.

When the rain turns heavy and there is an opportunity, the travellers take shelter under any viaduct they encounter, but these are rare, this is only a country road, off the main highways which, to avoid crossings and permit high speeds, are bridged by the secondary roads. One of these days it will occur to José Anaiço to buy some waterproofing varnish or paint, and he will get some, but the only suitable paint he has found is a bright red and not even enough to cover a quarter of the canvas. If Joana Carda had not come up with the better and more feasible idea of sewing large strips of plastic together to make a cover for the wagon and then a second one for the horses, when they realized they probably would not find any waterproof paint in the same shade of red for the next thirty kilometres, the wagon might well have found itself travelling the wide world with a multicoloured hood, with stripes, circles and squares, in green and yellow, orange and blue, violet, white on white, brown, and perhaps even black, according to the artist's whim. Meanwhile it is raining.

After their brief, inconclusive dialogue about the meaning of names and the significance of dreams, they begin discussing what name they should give to the dream which this dog is. Opinions are divided, which, as we ought to know, are simply a matter of preference, we might even say any opinion is to all appearances the reasoned expression of preference. Pedro Orce suggests and upholds rustic and traditional names such as Faithful or Pilot, both very suitable if we consider the animal's character, an infallible guide and utterly loyal. Joana Carda wavers between Major and Rookie, names with military overtones which don't quite fit the temperament of the woman making the suggestion, but the feminine soul possesses unfathomable depths, Goethe's Marguerite will struggle all her life at the spinning wheel to repress the urge to behave like Lady Macbeth, and to her dying hour she will not be certain of having won. As for Maria Guavaira, although unable to explain why, and not for the first time, she proposes, somewhat embarrassed by her own suggestion, that they should call the dog Guardian Angel, and she blushes as she speaks, aware of how ridiculous it would sound, especially in public, to summon one's guardian angel, and instead of some heavenly being, garbed in white robes descending with a flutter of wings, there should appear, covered in mud and the blood of some poor rabbit, a ferocious mastiff which only respects its masters, if they deserve that name. José Anaiço is quick to silence the laughter provoked by Maria Guavaira's suggestion, and proposes that the dog should be named Constant, for if I've understood the meaning of that word, it embraces all the qualities evoked by those other names, Faithful, Pilot, Major, Rookie and even Guardian Angel, for if any of them should not be constant, all trust is lost, the pilot loses his way, the major abandons his post, the rookie surrenders his arms, and the guardian angel allows himself to be seduced by the young girl he was supposed to be shielding from temptation. They all applaud, although Joaquim Sassa feels that it would still be preferable simply to call the animal Dog, for as the only dog around, there was little danger of mistaking any summons or response. So they've decided to call the dog Constant, but they needn't have taken so much trouble christening it because the animal answers to whatever name they care to use once it knows it's being called, though there is another name that lingers in its memory, Ardent, but no one here remembers that one. The man who once said that a name is nothing, not even a dream, was right, even if Maria Guavaira believes otherwise.

Unknown to them, they were following the old route of Santiago, they passed through places that bear names of hope or past misfortune, depending on what travellers experienced there in bygone days, Sarriá, Samos, or the privileged Villafranca del Bierzo, where any sick or weary pilgrim who might knock on the door of the apostle's church was dispensed from making the journey to Santiago de Compostela, and gained the same indulgences as if he had gone all the way. So even in those days faith made concessions, although nothing like today when the concessions are more rewarding than faith itself, the Catholic faith or any other. At least these travellers know that if they wish to see the Pyrenees, they will actually have to arrive there and lay their hand on the summit, a foot is not enough, since it is less sensitive, and the eyes are more easily deceived than one imagines. Little by little, the rain has started to abate, the odd drizzle now and then, until it finally stopped altogether. The sky had not cleared, night was rapidly falling. They camped under some trees to shelter from any further showers, although Pedro Orce could quote the Spanish proverb which goes something like this, Shelter under a tree and you'll get soaked twice. The fire wasn't easy to light, but Maria Guavaira's know-how finally conquered the damp twigs which crackled and flared up at the ends as if the sap were spilling out. They ate as best they could, enough to prevent their stomachs from rumbling with hunger during the night, for as another proverb tells us, Go to bed without a bite, you'll be restless all the night. They had their meal inside the wagon, by the light of the smoking oil-lamp, the atmosphere heavy, their clothes damp, the mattresses rolled up and stacked away, their remaining possessions in a heap, any houseproud wife would have had a fit at such untidiness. But since there's no evil that lasts forever or rain that never stops, let's wait for a ray of sunshine to appear and then they'll tackle the washing, the mattresses opened out so that they can dry down to the last fine wisp of straw, and the clothes spread over the bushes and boulders, when we gather them in they'll give off that fresh, warm smell the sun always leaves behind and all this will be done while the women, creating a cosy domestic scene, adjust and sew the long strips of plastic which will solve all their problems with leaking rain, blessed be whoever invented progress.

They remained there chatting with the ease and indolence of people whiling away the hours until it was time to go to bed and then Pedro Orce interrupts what he was saying and starts telling them, I once read somewhere that the galaxy to which our solar system belongs is heading towards a constellation of which I can't remember the name, and that constellation is heading in its turn to a certain point in space, I wish I knew more but the details escape me, but what I wanted to say is this, look here, we're on a peninsula, the peninsula is sailing on the sea, the sea goes round with the earth to which it belongs, and the earth turns on itself but also goes round the sun, and the sun also turns on itself, and the whole lot heads in the direction of the aforesaid constellation, so I ask myself if we're not the last link in this chain of movements within movements. And what I'd like to know is what moves inside us and where does it go, no, no I'm not talking about worms, microbes and bacteria, those living creatures that inhabit us, I'm referring to something else, to something that moves and perhaps moves us at the same time, just as constellation, galaxy, solar system, sun, earth, sea, Peninsula and Deux Chevaux move and move us with them, what is the name, after all, of the thing that moves all the rest, from one end of the chain to the other, or perhaps there is no chain and the universe is a ring at once so thin that apparently only we and what is inside us fit into it and so thick that it can accommodate the maximum dimension of the universe which is the ring itself, what is the name of what follows after us. The non-visible begins with man, came the surprising answer of José Anaiço, who spoke without thinking.

From leaf to leaf, large drops of water come trickling down on to the canvas. Outside, Grizzly and Chess can be heard stirring under their plastic sheets which do not quite cover them, this is where total silence can be useful, allowing us to hear the slightest noise. Everyone here believes it to be his or her duty to make a contribution to this solemn council with whatever knowledge they possess, but they are all terrified that if they open their mouths, even if those little toads in the fable don't pop out, they will trot out various banalities about existence, ontological pronouncements, however doubtful the relevance of that word in the context of wagon, drops of rain and horses, without forgetting the dog that is fast asleep. Maria Guavaira, having the least education, is the first to speak, Perhaps we should call the non-visible God, but it is curious how a certain note of interrogation was introduced into the phrase, Or willpower, suggests Joaquim Sassa, Or intelligence, adds Joana Carda, Or history, and this closing remark is made by José Anaiço. Pedro Orce has no suggestion to make, he simply comments, Anyone who thinks this is easy is much mistaken, there are endless answers just waiting for questions.

Prudence cautions us that any investigation of such complex matters should stop here lest those participating start saying something different from what they said before, not because it is necessarily wrong to change one's mind but because the difference can sometimes be so great that the discussion often goes back to the beginning without those who are debating the issue even noticing. In this instance, that first inspired statement by José Anaiço, after having circulated among his friends, ended up trivially with the more than obvious evidence of the invisibility of God, or willpower, or intelligence, and, perhaps a little less trivial and obvious, of history. Putting his arms around Joana Carda, who complains of feeling cold, José Anaiço tries not to fall asleep, he wants to reflect on his idea, to ponder whether history is really invisible, if the visible witnesses of history confer sufficient visibility on it, if the visibility of history, which is so relative, is anything more than a covering like the clothes worn by the invisible man, even while continuing to be invisible himself. He could not bear to have these thoughts going round and round in his head for much longer and it was just as well that during those final moments before falling asleep, his mind had foolishly concentrated on distinguishing the difference between what is invisible and non-visible, which, as will be obvious to anyone who stops to think about it, had no particular bearing on the case. In the light of the day all these entanglements seem much less important, God, the most famous example of all, created the world because it was night when He thought about it. At that sublime moment He felt that He couldn't stand the darkness any longer, but had it been day God would have left everything as it was. And just as the sky here dawned bright and clear and the sun came out unhindered by clouds and so remained, all the nocturnal philosophizing dissipated and all attention is now concentrated on the smooth passage of Deux Chevaux over a peninsula, no matter whether it is drifting or not, for even if my life's journey should lead me to a star, that has not excused me from travelling the roads of this earth.

That afternoon, as they were selling their wares, they learned that the Peninsula, after having reached in a straight line a point due north of the northernmost island of the Azores, the island of Corvo, and from this summary description it should be clear that the extreme south of the Peninsula, the Punta de Tarifa, found itself on another meridian to the east, north of the northernmost point of Corvo, the Ponta dos Tarsais, now then, the Peninsula, after what we have tried to explain, immediately resumed its displacement to the west in a direction parallel to that of its initial route, that is to say, let us see if we are making ourselves clear, pursuing it some degrees higher. When this happened, those who had put forward and defended the theory of displacement in a straight line broken into right angles were fully vindicated. And if no movement had yet been confirmed which might support the hypothesis of a return to its point of departure, stated, moreover, as a demonstration of the sublime rather than as a foreseeable confirmation of the general thesis, which did not rule out the possibility of return, there was even a possibility that the Peninsula might never come to a halt again but drift for ever more across the seas of the world, like the much-quoted *Flying Dutchman*, and now the Peninsula goes under another name, tactfully suppressed here to avoid any outbursts of nationalism and xenophobia, which would be a tragedy in present circumstances.

The village where the travellers found themselves had not heard of these matters, the only news they had received was that the United States of America had promised in a statement made by the President himself that the approaching countries could count on the support and solidarity, both moral and material, of the North American people, If they continue to move in this direction they will be received with open arms. But this declaration of remarkable perception, as much from a humanitarian as a geostrategic view-point, faded somewhat with the sudden bedlam in tourist agencies throughout the world, besieged by clients who wanted to travel to Corvo without delay regardless of means or expense, and why, because unless it should change course the Peninsula was about to pass within sight of the island of Corvo, a spectacle not to be compared with the insignificant parade of the Rock of Gibraltar when the Peninsula broke away from the Rock and left it there abandoned to the waves. Now it is a huge mass about to pass before the eyes of those privileged enough to find a little spot on the northern half of the island, but despite the vastness of the Peninsula, the event will last only for a few hours, two days at the most, for bearing in mind the peculiar outline of this raft, only the extreme southern part will be visible and only if it is a clear day. The rest, because of the earth's curvature, will pass well out of sight, just imagine what it would be like if instead of that angular shape, the Peninsula's southern coast formed a straight line, I hope you can visualize my drawing, it would take sixteen days to watch it pass, an entire vacation, if the speed of fifty kilometres daily were to be maintained. Be that as it may, in all likelihood more money will flow into Corvo than has ever been seen before, obliging the island's inhabitants to order locks for their doors and to hire locksmiths to fit them with crossbars and alarm systems.

From time to time there are still light showers, at worst a rapid cloudburst, but for most of the day it is sunny with blue skies and high clouds. The great plastic cover has been put up, sewn and reinforced, and now that it looks like rain their progress is arrested, and, in three stages, first the cover is unfolded, then stretched and finally tied down, the awning is finally protected. Inside the wagon are the driest mattresses you ever saw, the musty smell and dampness have gone, the interior, neat and tidy, things could not be cosier. But now one can see just how much rain there has been in these parts. The land is waterlogged and one has to be careful with the wagon, testing the soft ground at the edge of the road before passing, otherwise it would be a devil of a job to move it, two horses, three men and two women are not as effective as a tractor. The landscape has altered, they have left the mountains and hills behind, the last undulations are disappearing from sight and looming up before one's eyes is what looks like an endless plain with such a vast sky overhead that one begins to doubt that the sky is all one, more likely each location, if not each person, has its own sky, greater or smaller, higher or lower, and this has been an amazing discovery, yes sir, the sky like an infinite succession of encrusted domes, the contradiction in terms is only apparent, you need only look. When Deux Chevaux reaches the summit of the last hill one thinks the world will come to an end before the earth rises again and since it is quite common for different causes to have the same effect, we have to struggle for breath up here as if we had been carried to the top of Everest, as anyone will tell you who has also been there, unless he has had the same experience as we have had on this flat ground.

Pedro reckons without his host. However, let it be said at once that this Pedro is not Orce, nor does the narrator know who he is, even if he admits that behind the aforementioned is that apostle of the same name who denied Christ three times, and these are also the same calculations made by God, probably because he was Tri-une, and not very good at arithmetic. In Portugal it is customary to say that Pedro knows his sums when the sums done by all Pedros come out wrong, this is a popular and ironic way of saying that some people should leave decisions to others, in other words, Joaquim Sassa was wrong when he estimated they would cover one hundred and fifty kilometres each day. Maria Guavaira was also wrong when she reduced it to ninety. The trader knows about trading, horses know about pulling a wagon, and just as one says or used to say, Bad money drives out good, so the pace of the old horse moderated that of the young one, unless the latter was show-ing pity, kindness, human respect, because for the strong to brag about their strength in the presence of the weak is a sign of moral perversion. All these words have been considered necessary in order to explain that we have been travelling more slowly than was pre-dicted, but concision is not a definitive virtue, on occasion one loses out by talking too much, it is true, but how much has been gained by saying more than was necessary. The horses go at their own pace, they had set off at a trot and they obey the whims or demands of the driver, but little by little so subtly that no one even notices, Grizzly and Chess start reducing their pace, how they can manage it so harmoniously is a mystery, for no one heard the one say to the other, Slow down, or the other reply, When we get past that tree.

Fortunately the travellers are not in a hurry. In the beginning, when they left the already distant lands of Galicia, they felt that they had dates to meet and itineraries to respect, there was even a certain feeling of urgency, as if each of them had to save a father from the gallows or reach the scaffold before the executioner dropped the hatch. Here it is not a question of father or mother, for we know nothing about the one or the other, except for Maria Guavaira's mother, who is senile and no longer lives in La Coruña, unless she returned there once the danger had passed. About the other mothers and fathers, ancient and modern, nothing has been revealed, when children fall silent, questions must also be silenced and enquiries suspended, for when all is said and done, the world begins and ends with each one of us, although this statement might deeply offend the family spirit, and show disrespect for one's heritage and lineage. Within several days, the road became a world outside the world, like any man who on finding himself in the world discovers that he himself is a world, nor is it difficult, one only needs to create a little solitude around oneself, like these travellers who while travelling together travel alone. That is why they are not in a hurry, that is why they stopped counting the distance they have covered, any stops are for selling or taking a rest and they often feel tempted to stop for no other reason than that same appetite, for which there may always be reasons but generally we do not really waste much time looking for them. We all end up where we want to be, it is only a question of time and patience, the hare goes faster than the tortoise, perhaps it will arrive first, so long as it does not cross the path of the hunter and his shotgun.

We have left the barren plain of León, have entered and are travelling through Tierra de Campos where that famous preacher Fray Gerúndio de Campazas was born and flourished, whose words and deeds were recounted in detail by the no less celebrated Padre Isla, as an example to long-winded orators, relentless bores who never stop quoting, compulsive rhymers and tiresome scribblers who go on and on, what a pity we have not learned from their example which could not be clearer. Therefore let us prune this rambling exordium from the outset and say quite simply that the travellers will spend the night in a village called Villalar, not far from Toro, Tordesillas and Simancas, all of them touching closely on Portuguese history in terms of a battle, a treaty and archives. Being a teacher by profession, José Anaiço finds these names evocative, but little else, because his knowledge of history being general, it consists of rudimentary facts furnished with a few more details than that of his Spanish and Portuguese audience who must have learned something or can't have forgotten everything about Simancas, Toro and Tordesillas, given the wealth of information and national interest in the history books of both countries. But no one here knows anything about Villalar except Pedro Orce who, although a native of Andalusia, has the enlightenment of someone who has travelled throughout the Peninsula, the fact that he said he did not know Lisbon when he arrived there two months ago does not rule out this hypothesis, perhaps he simply did not recognize the place, just as the city would no longer be recognized today by its Phoenician founders, its Roman colonizers, its Visigothic rulers, perhaps the Muslims would with a glimmer of recognition, and the Portuguese with increasing bewilderment.

They are sitting in pairs around the bonfire, Joaquim and Maria, José and Joana, Pedro and Constant, the night is a little chilly, but the sky is serene and clear, there are scarcely any stars to be seen for the moon which came out early floods the flat countryside with light, and the nearby rooftops of Villalar, whose friendly mayor raised no objections to this band of Spanish and Portuguese migrants camping so close to the village despite their being vagrants and pedlars and therefore likely to steal trade from local shopkeepers. The moon is not high but has already taken on that appearance we enjoy admiring, that luminous disc which inspires trite verses and even more trite sentiments, a silken sifter sprinkling white dust over the submissive landscape. Then we exclaim, What lovely moonlight, and we try to forget the shudders of fear we experience when the heavenly body appears, enormous, red, threatening, over the curving earth. After thousands and thousands of years, the nascent moon continues even today to appear like some threat, like a sign of the approaching end, fortunately the anxiety lasts only for a few minutes, the moon has risen, become small and white, we can breathe more easily. The animals, too, are fretful, a short time ago when the moon appeared the dog stood there staring at it, tense, rigid, perhaps it might have howled had it not been without vocal cords, but the dog bristled all over as if a frozen hand had stroked its back ruffling its coat. There are moments when the world leaves its axis, we sense that nothing is secure, and if we could fully express what we are feeling, we should say with an expressive absence of rhetoric, That was a close shave.

What Pedro Orce knows about the history of Villalar we are now about to find out once they finish their meal. As the flames of the bonfire dance in the still air, the travellers look at them pensively, stretch out their hands as if they were imposing them or surrendering them to the flames, there is an ancient mystery in this relationship between us humans and fire, even when under the open sky, as if we and the fire were inside the original cave, grotto or matrix. Tonight it is José Anaiço's turn to wash up, but there is no hurry, the hour is peaceful, almost gentle, the light of the flames flickers on their weather-beaten faces, the colour of sunrise, the sun is of another order and alive, not dead like the moon, that is the difference.

And Pedro Orce tells them, You may not know this but many, many years ago in fifteen twenty-one there was a great battle here in Villalar, greater for its consequences than for the number of dead, because had it been won by him who lost it, those of us who are alive today would have inherited a very different world. José Anaiço is well-informed about the great battles in history, and if the question were fired at him, he would be able to run off without a moment's hesitation some ten names beginning classically with Marathon and Thermopylae, and disregarding chronology, Austerlitz, and Borodino, Marne and Monte Cassino, Ardennes and El Alamein, Poitiers and Alcácer Quibir, and also Aljubarrota, which means nothing to the world and everything to us, they've been paired for no special reason, But I've never heard of the Battle of Villalar, concluded José Anaiço, Well, that battle, explained Pedro Orce, took place when the communes of Spain rebelled against Emperor Charles the Fifth, a foreigner, but not so much because he was a foreigner, for in past centuries it was the most natural thing in the world for nations to find a king being brought in through the back door, who spoke another language, the whole business was left to Royal Houses who gambled away their own countries along with those of others, I wouldn't say dice or cards, but for dynastic interests, with fake alliances and marriages of convenience, which is why one cannot say that communes rebelled against the unwanted King, nor let anyone imagine it was the great war of the poor against the rich, if only things were that simple, the fact is that the Spanish nobility did not approve, not in the slightest, of the Emperor having conferred appointments on so many foreigners, and one of the first measures taken by these new masters was to raise taxes, an infallible means of paying for luxuries and further ventures, well the first city to rebel was Toledo and others soon followed its example, Toro, Madrid, Avila, Soria, Burgos, Salamanca, and so on and so forth, but the motives of some were not the motives of others, sometimes they coincided, yes sir, but at other times they were in conflict, and if this was true of the cities it was even more true of the people living in them, certain nobles simply defended their own interests and ambitions and therefore changed sides depending on how the wind was blowing and what would benefit them. Now, as always happens, the people were involved in this for their own reasons, but especially for those of others, this has been the case since the world began, if people were all one, that would be fine, but people are not all one, that's something we cannot get into our heads, not to mention that the masses are generally deceived, how often their representatives have taken their vote to parliament and once they got there, through bribes and threats, have voted contrary to the will of those who sent them, and strange as it may seem, despite all these divergencies and contradictions, the communes were able to organize militias and fight the King's army, needless to say battles were won and lost, the last battle was lost here in Villalar, and why, habit, mistakes, incompetence, betrayals, people got tired of waiting to be paid and deserted, battle ensued, some won, others lost, it was never discovered exactly how many members of the communes died here, by modern statistics not all that many, some put the figure at two thousand, others swore that there had been less than a thousand casualties, perhaps even as few as two hundred, one doesn't know nor is one ever likely to know, unless the graves are moved elsewhere one day and the skulls are counted because to count the other bones would only add to the confusion, three of the commune leaders were tried the following day, sentenced to death and beheaded in the main square of Villalar, their names were Juan de Padilla, born in Toledo, Juan Bravo from Segovia, and Francisco Maldonado from Salamanca. This was the Battle of Villalar and had it been won by those who lost, Spain's destiny would have changed course. With moonlight such as this, one can imagine what the night and day of battle must have been like, it was raining, the fields were flooded, they fought up to their knees in mud, undoubtedly by modern standards few lost their lives, but one is tempted to say that the few who lost their lives in the wars of old had greater influence on history than the hundreds of thousands and millions who died in the twentieth century, the moonlight is the one thing that doesn't change, it covers Villalar just as it covers Austerlitz or Marathon, or ... Or Alcácer Quibir, interrupted José Anaiço, What battle was that, Maria Guavaira asked, If that, too, had been won instead of lost, I can't imagine what Portugal would be like today, replied José Anaiço, I once read in a book that your King Dom Manuel fought in this war, said Pedro Orce, In the textbooks I use for teaching there's no mention of the Portuguese having gone to war with Spain at that time, It wasn't fought by the Portuguese in flesh and blood, but by fifty thousand crusaders loaned by your King to the Emperor, I see, said Joaquim Sassa, with fifty thousand crusaders in the royal forces the communes were bound to lose for the crusaders always win.

This night Constant dreamed that it went to unearth bones on the battlefield. It had already gathered one hundred and twenty-four skulls when the moon went down and the earth turned dark. Then the dog went back to sleep. Two days later, some boys playing at soldiers in the fields reported to the mayor that they had found a heap of skulls in a field of wheat, and no one ever discovered how they came to be there, gathered into a pile. But the housewives of Villalar have nothing but good to say of those Portuguese and Spaniards who came with a wagon and have already left, For price and quality they were the most honest pedlars who had ever passed this way.

Overcome evil with good, the ancients used to say and with good reason, at least they put their time to good use by judging facts that were then new in the light of facts that were already old. Nowadays we make the mistake of adopting a sceptical attitude to the lessons of antiquity. The President of the United States of America promised that the Peninsula would be welcome, and Canada, as we shall see, was not pleased. As the Canadians pointed out, Unless the Peninsula changes course, it is we who will be acting as hosts and then we shall have two Newfoundlands here instead of one, little do the people on the Peninsula know, poor devils, what awaits them, biting cold, frost, the only advantage for the Portuguese is that they will be close to supplies of cod which they are so fond of. They will lose their summers but have more to eat.

The spokesman at the White House hastened to explain that the President's speech had been prompted fundamentally by humanitarian considerations without aspiring to political supremacy, especially since the countries of the Peninsula had not ceased to be sovereign and independent just because they had gone floating off over the waters, they will have to come to a halt one day and be like every other country, and then added, For our part, we solemnly guarantee that the traditional spirit of good neighbourliness between the United States and Canada will not be affected by any eventuality, and as proof of North America's desire to maintain friendly relations with the great Canadian nation, we propose setting up a bilateral committee to examine the various problems which, within the ambit of this dramatic transformation of the political and strategic physiognomy of the world, will certainly constitute a first step towards the birth of a new international community, comprising the United

States, Canada and the Iberian countries, who will be invited to participate as observers at this meeting since they are still not physically close enough for any immediate prospect of specifying some form of integration.

Canada publicly expressed its satisfaction with this explanation but let it be known that it considered an early meeting to be inopportune, arguing that any terms proposed might well offend feelings of patriotism in Portugal and Spain, and suggesting as an alternative a quadripartite conference to examine what measures should be taken to deal with any violent opposition once the Peninsula reached the Canadian coast. The United States agreed forthwith, and their leaders silently thanked God for having created the Azores. For if the Peninsula had not veered northwards and moved consistently in a straight line after breaking away from Europe, the city of Lisbon would definitely have remained with its windows facing towards Atlantic City, and after much reflection they came to the conclusion that the more they veered north the better, just imagine what it would be like if New York, Boston, Providence, Philadelphia or Baltimore were to be transformed into inland cities with the inevitable lowering of their standard of living. There is no doubt that the President had been much too hasty when he made that initial statement. In a subsequent exchange of confidential diplomatic notes, followed by secret meetings between officials from both governments, Canada and the United States agreed that the best solution would be to arrest the Peninsula, if at all possible, en route at a point sufficiently close to keep it outside the sphere of European influence and sufficiently remote not to cause any immediate or indirect damage to Canadian and North American interests, and to set up a committee without delay, to introduce timely changes in their respective immigration laws which would strengthen discretionary clauses and discourage the Spanish and Portuguese from thinking that they can enter our countries at will with the pretext that we are now close neighbours.

The governments of Portugal and Spain protested at the discourtesy of these powers who were presuming to dispose of their interests and destinies, the Portuguese government with greater vehemence in view of its pledges as a government of national salvation. Thanks to initiatives on the part of the Spanish government, contact will be established between the two Peninsular countries to decide on a joint plan aimed at taking full advantage of the new situation, but in Madrid it is feared that the Portuguese government will enter these negotiations quietly hoping that some time in the future it will derive special benefits from its greater proximity to the coasts of Canada and North America, but that depends. And it is known, or believed to be known, that in certain Portuguese political circles there is a campaign in favour of a bilateral agreement, although of a non-official nature, with the region of Galicia which evidently won't please the central powers in Spain at all, intolerant as it is of any irredentism, however disguised. There are even some who cynically claim and spread the word that none of this would have happened if Portugal had been on the other side of the Pyrenees and, better still, had clung on to the Pyrenees when the rupture occurred. That would have been one way of ending once and for all this reduction to a single country, with this problem of being Iberian, but the Spaniards are deceiving themselves, for the problem will persist and we need say no more. The days before reaching the shores of the New World are counted, a plan of action is under way so that negotiations may get under way at the right moment, neither too soon nor too late which, after all, is the golden rule of diplomacy.

Unaware of these political intrigues behind the scenes, the Peninsula continues sailing westwards, so steadily and easily that the various observers, whether millionaires or scientists, have already withdrawn from the island of Corvo where they have positioned themselves in the front rows, as it were, to watch the Peninsula passing. The spectacle is breathtaking, suffice it to say that the extreme tip of the Peninsula passed less than five hundred metres away from Corvo, with a great seething of waters. It was like watching the climax of a Wagnerian opera or, better still, like being at sea in a tiny vessel and seeing the enormous hulk of an unladen oil-tanker passing a few metres away with most of its keel out of the water, in short, enough to strike terror into us and make us dizzy, to send us on to our knees to beg a thousand pardons for our heresies and evil deeds and exclaim, God exists. Such is the power of primitive nature over the spirit of man, however civilized.

But while the Peninsula is playing its part in the movements of the universe, our travellers are already proceeding beyond Burgos, so successful with their trading that they have decided to put Deux Chevaux on the motorway which is unquestionably the fastest route. Further ahead, after passing Gasteiz, they will go back on to the roads serving the smaller villages, there the wagon will be in its element, a cart drawn by horses on a country road rather than this unusual and startling exhibition of dawdling along a road designed for high speeds, this lazy trot at fifteen kilometres an hour, provided they are not going uphill and the animals are in a good mood. The Iberian world is so greatly altered that the traffic police who witness this do not order them to stop, impose no fine, mounted on their powerful motorcycles they give them a nod wishing them a good journey, at most they ask about the red paint on the awning if they happen to be on the side where the patch is visible. The weather is good, there has been no rain for days, you would think summer had returned were it not for the autumnal wind which can sometimes be extremely cold, especially since we are so close to high mountains. When the women started complaining about the chill in the air, José Anaiço remarked, as if in passing, about the consequences of getting too close to high latitudes, telling them, If we end up in Newfoundland, our journey is finished, to live out of doors in that climate you have to be an Eskimo, but the women paid no attention, perhaps they weren't looking at the map.

And perhaps because they were talking not so much about the cold they were feeling as about a greater cold that someone else, but who, might be feeling, not they themselves who had the comfort of their partners every night, even during the day when the circumstances were favourable. Many a time one couple kept Pedro Orce company in the driver's seat, while the other couple lay down inside the wagon allowing themselves to be lulled by the swaying of Deux Chevaux, then semi-naked, both man and woman satisfied their sudden or postponed desire. Knowing that five people were travelling in that wagon thus divided by sex, anyone with experience of life would have a good idea of what was going on under that awning simply by looking to see who was up there in the driver's seat, for example, if there were three men there, you could be sure that the women were doing their household chores, especially the mending, or if, as we said before, there were two men and a woman in the seat together, the other woman and man would be enjoying intimacy, even if dressed and simply chatting. Clearly, these were not the only possible combinations, but neither of the women ever sat in the driver's seat except with her own partner, while the other woman was with her man under the awning, for they didn't want people to start gossiping. This tactful behaviour came about of its own accord. There was no need to convene a family council to decide on ways and means of safeguarding morality inside and outside the awning and worked out mathematically, it was inevitable that Pedro Orce nearly always had to travel in the driver's seat, except on the rare occasion when the three men rested at the same time while the women took the reins, or when, all their urges having been satisfied, one couple sat up in front while the other, their privacy restricted, refrained from engaging in any acts under the awning which might embarrass or disturb Pedro Orce who lay stretched out on his narrow pallet arranged sideways. Poor Pedro Orce, Maria Guavaira murmured to Joana Carda when José Anaiço spoke of the frost in Newfoundland and of the advantages of being an Eskimo, and Joana Carda agreed, Poor Pedro Orce.

They nearly always set up camp before nightfall, they liked to choose a nice spot with water nearby, if possible within sight of some village, and if a place took their fancy they stopped there even if there were two or three hours of sunshine left. The lesson of the horses had been well learnt to the advantage of all, now the animals enjoyed a longer rest, the travellers lost that human trait of haste and impatience. But ever since that day when Maria Guavaira said, Poor Pedro Orce, a different atmosphere surrounds the wagon on its journey and the people inside. This gives food for thought if we recall that only Joana Carda heard those words being spoken and when she repeated them only Maria Guavaira was listening, and since we know they kept them to themselves, for this was not a matter for amorous dialogue, then we can only conclude that a word, once spoken, lasts longer than the sound and sounds that formed it, the word remains, invisible and inaudible, in order to be able to keep its own secret, a kind of hidden seed below the earth that germinates out of sight until suddenly it pushes the soil aside and emerges into the light, a coiled stem, a crumpled leaf slowly unfolding. They set up camp, unhitched the horses, released them from their harness, lit the fire, everyday actions and gestures which all of them were now capable of doing with equal skill, depending on whatever tasks they were assigned each day. But contrary to their behaviour since the outset, they now conversed very little and they themselves would be taken by surprise were we to tell them, Not one of you has uttered a word in the last ten minutes, then they would be aware of the special nature of that silence or they would reply like someone unwilling to acknowledge an obvious fact and looking for some futile justification. It sometimes happens, and frankly one cannot be talking all the time. But were they to look at each other at that moment, they would see on each other's faces, as if in a mirror, the reflection of their own disquiet, the

226

embarrassment of someone who knows that explanations are but empty words. Although it has to be said that the looks exchanged between Maria Guavaira and Joana Carda convey such explicit meanings for them that they cannot stand it for very long and soon turn their eyes away.

After finishing his chores Pedro Orce was in the habit of going off with the dog Constant, telling the others that he was off to get to know the neighbourhood. He was always gone for some time, perhaps because he walked slowly, perhaps because he wandered off the main road, or, remote from the gaze of his companions, ended up resting on a boulder watching the evening draw to a close. One day recently, Joaquim Sassa had said to him, You want to be alone, are you feeling unhappy, and José Anaiço commented, If I were in his shoes, I'd probably do the same. The women had finished washing some clothes and had hung them up to dry on a rope stretched between the frame of the awning and the branch of a tree, they listened and kept silent, for they were not included in the conversation. This was some days after Maria Guavaira, because of the frosts of Newfoundland, had said to Joana Carda, Poor Pedro Orce.

They were alone, how strange that four people should give the impression of being alone, they were waiting for the soup to be ready, there was still daylight and rather than waste time, José Anaiço and Joaquim Sassa checked the harnesses while the women read out and make a note of the day's takings which Joaquim Sassa as book-keeper was later to transfer into the ledger. Pedro Orce had wandered off, disappeared among the trees about ten minutes ago, accompanied by Constant the dog, as usual. He no longer felt cold and the breeze that was blowing was probably the last tepid waft of autumn, at least that's what it feels like after the cold we've experienced recently. Maria Guavaira says, We must buy aprons, we haven't many left in stock, and as she spoke she looked up at the trees, she stirred as she sat there, as if repressing some urge before giving way, only the harsh noise of the horses champing could be heard, then Maria Guavaira stood up and walked towards the trees where Pedro Orce had disappeared. She did not look back, not even when Joaquim Sassa asked her, Where are you going, but in fact, he did not even finish the question, but left it suspended in mid-air as it were, for the reply had already been given and could not be amended. A few minutes later the dog appeared, went and lay down under the wagon. Joaquim Sassa was standing some metres away, appeared to be scanning some hills in the distance. José Anaiço and Joana Carda avoided looking at each other.

Maria Guavaira finally returned with the first shadows of evening. She arrived alone. She walked up to Joaquim Sassa but he turned away abruptly. The dog came out from under the wagon and disappeared. Joana Carda lit the oil-lamp. Maria Guavaira removed the soup from the fire, poured some oil into a frying pan which she then placed on the trivet, waited for the oil to sizzle, meantime she had cracked some eggs which she scrambled, added some slices of sausage, soon a smell would fill the air which at any other time would have made mouths water. But Joaquim Sassa did not come to eat. Maria Guavaira called him but he refused to come. There was food left over. Joana Carda and José Anaiço didn't feel hungry and when Pedro Orce returned the camp was already in darkness apart from the dying embers of the bonfire. Joaquim Sassa had lain down underneath the wagon, but it was a bitterly cold night, the chill comes from the mountains, there is no wind, just a mass of cold air. Then Joaquim Sassa told Joana Carda to go and sleep beside Maria Guavaira, he didn't refer to her by name, but said, Lie down beside her, I'll stay with José, and since it seemed a good moment for a bit of sarcasm, he added, There's no danger, we're decent people, there's nothing promiscuous about us. When he returned, Pedro Orce climbed into the driver's seat, who knows how but the dog Constant managed to get up there beside him. It was the first time this had happened.

All the next day Pedro Orce travelled in the driving seat. José Anaiço and Joana Carda sat beside him and Maria Guavaira remained alone in the wagon. The horses were driven at a steady pace. When they tried to please themselves by breaking into a trot, José Anaiço restrained their impetuous speed. Joaquim Sassa travelled on foot, lagging way behind the wagon. They covered only a few kilometres that day. It was still mid-afternoon when José Anaiço brought Deux Chevaux to a halt in a place that looked exactly like the other, it was as if they had never got around to leaving or had come full circle, even the trees looked the same. Joaquim Sassa only appeared much later as the sun was setting over the horizon. On seeing him approach, Pedro Orce withdrew, the trees soon concealed him and the dog went after him. The campfire sent up great flames, but it was still too early to prepare supper. Besides, the soup was ready and there were sausages and eggs left over. Joana Carda remarked to Maria Guavaira, We didn't buy any aprons and we only have two. Joaquim Sassa told José Anaiço, I'm leaving tomorrow, I'll need my share of the money, show me where we are on the map, there ought to be some sort of railway around here. Then Joana Carda got up and headed towards the trees where Pedro Orce had disappeared with the dog. José Anaiço didn't ask her, Where are you going. The dog reappeared after a few minutes and went and lay down under the wagon. Time passed, and Joana Carda returned. Reluctantly, Pedro Orce came with her, but she led him gently as if there was no need for much force or it was another kind of force. They arrived in front of the campfire, Pedro Orce with lowered head, his white hair dishevelled, and the flickering light of the flames appeared to dance on top of his head. And Joana Carda, whose blouse was unbuttoned and outside her slacks, said quite openly and naturally, tucking her blouse in when she realized how untidy she looked, The stick with which I drew a line on the ground has lost its power but it can still be used to draw another line here, then we shall know who is to remain on this side and who on the other, if we cannot all be together on the same side. As far as I'm concerned, I couldn't care less, I'm leaving tomorrow, Joaquim Sassa told her. I'm the one who is going tomorrow, said Pedro Orce. Just as we came together, we can go our separate ways, said Joana Carda, but if someone has to be blamed to justify our separation, don't make Pedro Orce the scapegoat. If anyone is to blame, we are, Maria Guavaira and I, and if you think what we did calls for an explanation, then we've been wrong about each other since the day we met. I'm leaving tomorrow, Pedro Orce repeated. Don't go, said Maria Guavaira, for if you leave, it's almost certain that we'll all separate, for the men won't be able to stay with us nor we with them, not because we don't love each other, but because we don't understand each other. José Anaiço looked at Joana Carda, suddenly stretched out his hands to the fire as if they had suddenly become cold, and said, I'm staying. Maria Guavaira asked, And what about you, are you leaving or staying, Joaquim Sassa did not reply at once, he caressed the dog's head as it stood beside him, then, with his fingertips, he stroked its blue woollen collar, then the bracelet round his arm before saying, I'll stay, but on one condition. He didn't need to spell it out, Pedro Orce began speaking, I'm an old man, or at least, getting on. I've reached that age when one isn't too sure, but let's say I'm old rather than young. Obviously not all that old, smiled José Anaiço and his smile was somewhat bitter. Sometimes things happen in life which can never be repeated, he appeared to be about to continue, but sensed that he had said enough. Nodding his head, he withdrew to weep alone. Whether he wept a lot or little, one cannot say, but to weep he had to be alone. That night they all slept inside the wagon, but their wounds were still bleeding, the two women slept together, also the two betrayed men, and Pedro Orce, out of sheer exhaustion, slept soundly throughout the night. He had wanted to mortify himself with insomnia but nature proved stronger.

They awoke early with the little birds. As dawn broke, the first to emerge was Pedro Orce from the front of the wagon, then Joaquim Sassa and José Anaiço from the back, and finally the women, as if they were all coming from different worlds and were about to meet here for the first time. To begin with they scarcely looked at each other, nothing but furtive glances as if to confront another face would have been intolerable, too much to bear in their weak state after the recent crisis from which they had emerged. Having drunk their morning coffee, the odd word could be heard, words of advice, a request, an order cautiously phrased, but the first delicate problem now had to be tackled, how were the travellers to accommodate themselves in the wagon given the various complications of the way in which they were grouped together as we mentioned before. They were all agreed that Pedro Orce must travel in the driver's seat, but the men and women in open conflict could not go on being separated. Try to imagine this distasteful and equivocal situation. If Joaquim Sassa and José Anaiço were to sit up in front with Pedro Orce what conversation could they possibly hold with the driver, or more embarrassing still, were Joana Carda and Maria Guavaira to travel in the driver's seat, what would they talk about to the driver, what memories would they evoke and meantime, under the awning, what biting of nails would there be, the two male partners asking each other, What can they be saying. These are situations that make us laugh when seen from outside, but any temptation to laugh soon disappears if we imagine ourselves in the anguished predicament in which these men find themselves. Fortunately, there's a remedy for everything. Death alone has still to find one. Pedro Orce was already seated in his place, holding the reins and waiting for the others to make up their mind when José Anaiço said, as if addressing the invisible spirits of the air, The wagon can go ahead, Joana and I will walk for a bit. And we'll do the same, Joaquim Sassa announced. Pedro Orce shook the reins, the horses gave the first sharp tug, the second one was more convincing, but even had they wanted to, they could not have gone quickly this time, the road is uphill all the way, amidst mountains which loom higher to the left. We're in the foothills of the Pyrenees, Pedro Orce thinks to himself, but it's so peaceful up here that it's hard to believe this is the place where those dramatic ruptures we've described took place. Trailing behind come two couples, apart obviously, for what they have to discuss is between man and woman without any witnesses.

The mountains are no good for selling wares, especially these ones. In addition to the sparse population one usually finds in these mountainous regions, one has to consider the terror of the local inhabitants who still haven't got used to the idea that this side of the Pyrenees is no longer complemented or supported on the other side. These villages are almost deserted, some completely abandoned. As the wagon passes between doors and windows that remain firmly closed, the impression conveyed by the sound of Deux Chevaux's wheels on the stony roads is lugubrious. I'd rather be in the Sierra Nevada, thinks Pedro Orce, and these magical and entrancing words filled his heart with longing or *añoranza* as the Spanish would say. If there is any advantage to be gained from such desolation, it will be that the travellers after so many nights of discomfort and some promiscuity will be able to get a good night's sleep. We are not referring to the recent and particular manifestation of promiscuity about which opinion is divided and which the interested parties have been discussing, but simply pointing out that they will be able to sleep in the houses abandoned by their owners. For while possessions and valuables were carried off in the general exodus, the beds were normally left behind. How remote that day now seems when Maria Guavaira vigorously turned down the suggestion of sleeping in someone else's house, let us hope this ready complacency isn't an indication of a lowering in moral standards but simply the outcome of lessons learnt from hard experience.

Pedro Orce will sleep alone in a house of his choice with the dog for company. Should he decide to go for a nocturnal stroll, he's free to go out and return whenever he wishes, and this time the other men will not sleep separated from their women, Joaquim Sassa will finally be back sleeping with Maria Guavaira and José Anaiço with Joana Carda, they've probably already said all they had to say to each other and they might go on conversing into the night but human nature being what it is, out of weariness and displeasure, out of tender sympathy and sudden love, it's only natural for a man and woman to come together, to exchange a first, uncertain kiss and then, blessed be whoever made us so, the body awakens and desires the other body, it might be madness, it might, for the scars still throb, but the aura grows, if Pedro Orce should be walking along these slopes at this hour, he will see two houses lit up in the village, perhaps he'll feel jealous, perhaps tears will come to his eyes once more, but he will not know that at this moment the reconciled lovers are sobbing for joyful sorrow and in an outburst of passion. Tomorrow will truly be another day, it will no longer be important to decide who should travel inside the wagon or in the driver's seat, all combinations are now possible and none of them ambiguous.

The horses were tired, the slopes were never-ending and ever upwards. José Anaiço and Joaquim Sassa went to have a quiet word with Pedro Orce, using the utmost tact so that their motives should not be misunderstood. They wanted to know if he thought they had seen enough of the Pyrenees or if he wanted to carry on until they reached the uppermost summits, and Pedro Orce replied that it was not so much the summits that attracted him as the end of the earth, although he was aware that from the end of the earth one always sees the same sea. That's why we didn't go in the direction of Donostia, what was the attraction of looking at a beach which had been severed, of finding oneself on the edge of the sand with water on either side. But for us to see the sea from such a height, I'm not sure that the horses can make it, rejoined José Anaiço. We don't need to climb two or three thousand metres, assuming there are tracks on the peaks, but I'd rather we went on climbing up until we see for ourselves. They opened the map. Running his finger between Navascués and Burgui, and then pointing in the direction of the frontier, Joaquim Sassa said, We must be about here. There don't appear to be great heights on this side, the road follows the River Esca, then moves away to continue on climbing, here's where things start to get difficult, on the other side there's a peak of more than one thousand seven hundred metres. There isn't any longer. There was, said José Anaiço. Yes of course there was, agreed Joaquim Sassa, I must ask Maria Guavaira for some scissors to cut the map along the frontier. We could try this path and if it becomes too hard on the horses we can always turn back, suggested Pedro Orce.

They took two days to reach where they wanted to be. At night they could hear the wolves howling in the hills and felt apprehensive. People from the lowlands, they now suddenly became aware of the danger they were facing. Should wild beasts invade the encampment, they would first savage the horses, then attack any human beings. If only they had a gun with which to defend themselves. Pedro Orce confessed, It's my fault that we're running these risks, let's turn back, but Maria Guavaira replied, Let's go on, the dog is here to protect us. A dog can't do much when confronted by a pack of wolves, Joaquim Sassa reminded her. This one can, and however strange this may seem to anyone who knows more about these things than the narrator, Maria Guavaira was right. One night the wolves came fairly close, the terrified horses began neighing, such anguish, and pulling at the ropes with which they were tethered, the men and women looked around to see where they might take shelter from any attack, only Maria Guavaira insisted, though trembling, They won't come, and she repeated, They won't come. The bonfire was blazing and they kept it like this throughout that sleepless night, and the wolves drew no closer. Meanwhile, the dog appeared to grow bigger in the circle of light. The flickering shadows created the impression that heads, tongues and teeth were multiplying, nothing but optical illusion, human forms expanded, swelled out of all proportion and the wolves went on howling, but only because of their fear of other wolves.

The road had been severed, truly severed in the literal sense of the word. To both left and right, the mountains and valleys were suddenly cut off in a clean line, as if sliced with a blade or cut out of the sky. The travellers were now some way from the wagon which was being guarded by the dog, and they advanced cautiously and in dread. About a hundred metres from the scission there was a customs post. They went inside. Two typewriters still stood there, one with a sheet of paper stuck in the roller, a customs form with some words typed on it. The cold wind penetrated an open window and rustled the papers which were lying on the floor. There were birds' feathers. The world is coming to an end, Joana Carda exclaimed. Let's go then and see how it's ending, suggested Pedro Orce. They left. They trod cautiously, worried in case cracks might suddenly appear in the ground, a clear sign when the land is unstable. José Anaiço was the one who remembered this, but the road looked smooth and even, with only the odd bump caused by wear and tear. Ten metres from the gap, Joaquim Sassa said, Better not get too close on foot in case we get dizzy, I'm going to crawl

233

there. They got down on all fours and advanced, at first by crawling on their hands and knees, then by dragging themselves along the ground, they could hear their hearts beating with fear and uneasiness, their bodies sweating profusely despite the intense cold, asking themselves whether they would be brave enough to reach the edge of the abyss, but none of them wished to appear cowardly and almost in a trance they found themselves looking out to sea at an altitude of about one thousand eight hundred metres, the escarpment a sheer vertical cut and the sea shimmering below, the tiniest waves in the distance and white spume where the ocean waves thrashed against the mountain as if trying to dislodge it. Pedro Orce cried out, exalted in jubilant grief. The world is coming to an end, he was repeating Joana Carda's words and they all repeated them. My God, happiness exists, said the unknown voice, and perhaps that's all it is, sea, light and vertigo.

The world is full of coincidences, and if one thing does not coincide with another which may be close to it, that is no reason for denying coincidences, all it means is that what is coinciding is not visible. Precisely at the moment when the travellers were leaning over the sea, the Peninsula came to a halt. No one there noticed what had happened, there was no jolt as it braked, no sudden sign of loss of balance, no impression of rigidity. It was only two days later, after descending from the magnificent heights and on arriving at the first inhabited place that they heard the astounding news. But Pedro Orce said, If they affirm that the Peninsula has come to a halt, it must be true, but speaking for myself and Constant, I swear to you that the earth is still shaking. As he spoke, Pedro Orce's hand was resting on the dog's back.

Newspapers throughout the world, some with a banner headline on the front page, published the historic photograph showing the Peninsula, which perhaps we should now definitively call an island, sitting out there quietly in the middle of the ocean, maintaining its position to the nearest millimetre in relation to the cardinal points by which the earth is ruled and guided, with Oporto as far north of Lisbon as ever, Granada as far south of Madrid as it has been since Madrid came into being, and the rest with the same familiar contours. The journalists concentrated their imaginative powers almost exclusively on bold, dramatic headlines, inasmuch as the geological displacement, or rather, the tectonic enigma, continued to unfold secrets as indecipherable now as on the first day. Fortunately the pressure of public opinion, for want of a better expression, had diminished, people had stopped asking questions, they were satisfied with the stimulus of direct and indirect suggestions aroused by striking comparisons, The Birth of a New Atlantis, A Stone Has Moved on the Universal Chessboard, A Link between America and Europe, An Apple of Discord between Europe and America, A Battlefield for the Future, but the headline which made the deepest impression was the one in a Portuguese newspaper which read The Need for a New Treaty of Tordesilla, this is truly the simplicity of genius, the author of the idea looked at the map and verified that, give or take a kilometre, the Peninsula would be situated on the line which in those glorious days had divided the world into two parts, one to me, one to you, one to me.

In an unsigned editorial it was proposed that the two Peninsular countries should adopt a joint and complementary strategy which would make them the pointer on the scales of world politics,

Portugal facing west, towards the United States, Spain turned to the east, towards Europe. A Spanish newspaper, anxious to come up with something equally original, advocated the administrative theory whereby Madrid would become the political centre of this entire strategy, under the pretext that the Spanish capital is situated, as it were, at the geometric centre of the Peninsula, which is not even true if one looks at the map, but there are people who have no qualms about the means used to achieve their objective. The chorus of protests did not come only from Portugal, the autonomous Spanish regions also rebelled against the proposal which they saw as further proof of Castilian centralism. On the Portuguese side, as one might have expected, there was a sudden revival of interest in the occult and in esoteric sciences, which did not go further simply because the situation changed radically, nevertheless it lasted long enough to sell out every copy of Padre António Vieira's *History of the Future* and *The Prophecies of Bandarra*, as well as Fernando Pessoa's *Mensagem*, but that goes without saying.

From the standpoint of practical politics, discussion of the problem in European and American foreign ministries centred on spheres of influence, in other words, whether despite the question of distance, the Peninsula, or island, should preserve its natural ties with Europe, or whether without entirely severing them it should orientate itself rather towards the ideals and destiny of the great North American nation. With no hope of having any clear influence in the matter, the Soviet Union pointed out time and time again that nothing should be decided without its participation in the discussions, and meantime reinforced its fleet which from the outset had been accompanying the errant voyage under the watchful eye, needless to say, of the fleets of the other powers, the Americans, the British and the French.

It was within the ambit of those negotiations that the United States informed Portugal, during an audience urgently requested of the President of the Republic by Ambassador Charles Dickens, that the continuance of a government of national salvation made no sense whatsoever once the reasons no longer existed which, In the most dubious fashion, Mr President, if you will allow me to express an opinion, led to its institution. This tactless intervention was leaked indirectly, not because the competent ministries of the Presidency had made any public announcement, or through any statements made by the Ambassador as he left the Palace of Belém, in fact he simply remarked that his discussions with the President had been very frank and constructive. But that was enough for the parties who would inevitably have to go, were the government to be reshuffled or a general election called, to launch an attack on the Ambassador's intolerable meddling. The internal problems of Portugal, they declared, must be solved by the Portuguese, and they added with spiteful irony, Just because the Ambassador has written *David Copperfield* doesn't entitle him to come and give orders in the land of Camoës and *The Lusiads*. At this point, the Peninsula, without any warning, started moving again.

Pedro Orce had been right when he said there at the foot of the Pyrenees, It may have stopped, yes sir, but it's still trembling and so as not to be the only one to say so, he had put his hand on Constant's back, the dog was also trembling, as the two men and women were themselves able to confirm, repeating the unique experience of Joaquim Sassa and José Anaiço in the arid lands between Orce and Venta Micena beneath the Cordoban olive tree. But now, and the shock was general and universal, the movement was neither to west nor east, nor south nor north. The Peninsula was turning on itself, withershins, that's to say anti-clockwise which, once made public, immediately caused the Portuguese and the Spaniards to suffer from dizziness although the speed of rotation was anything but vertiginous. Faced with this decidedly unusual phenomenon which threatened to jeopardize absolutely all the laws of physics, especially the mechanical ones, by which the earth had governed itself, political negotiations, alliances made behind closed doors and in corridors, diplomatic manoeuvres, whether direct or step by step, were broken off. Besides, we must agree that it could not have been easy to keep calm, when one knew, for example, that the table at the council of ministers, along with the building, the street, the city, the country and the entire Peninsula was like a carousel, going round and round as if in a dream. Those who were more sensitive swore they could feel a circular displacement while admitting that they could not feel the earth itself going round in space, but to show what they meant, they held out their arms to hold on, often they did not succeed, they even fell and finished up on their backs on the ground, watching the sky slowly turn, at night the stars and the moon, and during the day, with a smoked lens, the sun, too. Some doctors were of the opinion that these were nothing other than manifestations of hysteria.

Obviously, there was no lack of more radical sceptics, Get away with you, the Peninsula turning on itself, quite impossible, that it might be sliding one could believe, for we know about landslides and that what happens to an escarpment when there is a heavy rainfall can also happen to a peninsula even without rain, but all this talk about rotation would imply that the Peninsula was wrenching itself from its own axis, and not only is such a thing objectively impossible, but it would result in the central nucleus breaking sooner or later, and then we should certainly be adrift without any moorings and at the mercy of the whims of fate. These sceptics were forgetting that the rotation might simply be like that of a plate revolving on top of another, this lamellar schist, take note, composed, as the name implies, of thin layers of shale placed one over the other. If the adhesion between them should loosen, the one could revolve quite easily on top of the other thus maintaining, theoretically speaking, a certain degree of union between them which would prevent total separation. That's precisely what's happening, asserted those who defended the theory. And in order to be able to confirm this, they sent divers once more to the bottom of the sea, as far down as possible into the bowels of the ocean, and with them went the *Archimedes*, the *Cyana* and a Japanese machine with an unpronounceable name. As a result of all these efforts, the Italian investigator repeated those famous words, he emerged from the water, opened the hatch and spoke into the microphones of television stations throughout the world, It cannot move and yet it moves. There was no central axis coiled like a rope, there were no layers of shale, yet the Peninsula turned majestically in the middle of the Atlantic, and as it turned, it became less and less recognizable, Is this really where we've spent our lives, people asked themselves. The Portuguese coast veered to the southeast and what had formerly been the easternmost point of the Pyrenees was pointing in the direction of Ireland. Observing the Peninsula had become an obligatory part of transatlantic commercial flights, although frankly, to little advantage, for there was no indispensable fixed point to which the movement might be related. In fact, nothing could replace the image captured and transmitted by satellite, the photograph taken from a great altitude which really gave some idea of the magnitude of the phenomenon.

This movement continued for a month. Seen from the Peninsula, the universe transformed itself little by little. Every day the sun emerged from a different point on the horizon and one had to search for the moon and the stars in the sky, their own movement, tracking around the centre of the system of the Milky Way, was no longer enough, now that there was this other movement which transformed space into a frenzy of flickering stars, as if the universe were being reorganized from one end to the other, perhaps on discovering that it had not turned out right first time round. Until one day the sun set in the same place where it had risen in normal times and there was no point in saying that it was not true, that it was a mere impression, that the sun was following its normal path and was incapable of any other. The man in the street simply retorted, Allow me to tell you, kind sir, that the morning sun used to come through my front window and now it comes in at the back of the house, so perhaps you could explain that in simple language. The expert explained it as best he could, he brought out photographs, made drawings, opened a map of the sky, but the pupil could not be persuaded and the lesson ended with him asking the good doctor to please arrange for the rising sun to go back to coming through his front window. Seeing that he could not convince him with scientific arguments, the expert told him, Don't worry, if the Peninsula turns right round you will see the sun as before, but the suspicious pupil rejoined, So Mr Know-All, you believe this is happening so that things can go back to being the same as before. And in fact they did not.

It should already have been winter, but winter which appeared to have arrived suddenly backed away, that is the only verb to describe it. It was neither winter nor autumn, certainly not spring nor remotely like summer. It was a season in suspension, without a date, as if the world were just beginning and the seasons or their timing had still to be decided. Deux Chevaux proceeded slowly along the foothills and the travellers now stopped from time to time, astonished, above all, at the spectacle of the sun, which no longer appeared over the Pyrenees but rose from the sea, casting its first rays on the uppermost slopes of the mountain as far as the snow-covered peaks. Here, in one of these villages, Maria Guavaira and Joana Carda realized that they were pregnant. Both of them. There was nothing surprising about their situation, one might even say that these women had done their utmost to become pregnant during these months and weeks, giving themselves to their men whole-heartedly without the slightest precaution on either side. Nor should anyone be surprised at both women being pregnant at the same time, this was simply another of those coincidences which constitute life on this earth, the good thing being that they can sometimes be clearly identified to enlighten the sceptics. But the situation was embarrassing, as it hit one in the eye, and the embarrassment stemmed from the difficulty of ascertaining two dubious paternities. The fact is, that were it not for the false step taken by Joana Carda and Maria Guavaira who, moved by pity or some other more obscure sentiment, went into the woods and forests in search of the solitary Pedro whom they almost had to beg to penetrate and impregnate them with his last seeds, such was his confusion and disquiet, were it not for this lyrical and far from erotic episode, Maria Guavaira's child would undoubtedly be accepted as that fathered by Joaquim Sassa and Joana Carda's child as that efficiently fathered by José Anaiço. But then Pedro Orce had to cross their path although it might be truer to say that the temptresses waylaid him, and decency overcome by shame concealed its face. I don't know who the father is, said Maria Guavaira who had set the example, Nor do I, said Joana Carda who later followed her example for two reasons, firstly to prove that she was no less heroic, and secondly to amend error with error, making exception the rule.

But neither this argument nor any even more subtle, could help them to evade the main problem. José Anaiço and Joaquim Sassa had to be told. How they would react and what expression would come into their faces when their respective women told them, I'm pregnant. Were the situation more harmonious, they would be, as one is wont to say, overcome with joy, and perhaps with the initial shock their faces and expressions would betray the sudden jubilation that springs from the soul, but their faces would soon cloud over, their eyes would darken, foretelling a dreadful scene. Joana Carda suggested that they should say nothing, with the passing of time and the swelling of their bellies, the fact of the matter would soothe susceptibilities, offended honour, and reawakened resentment. Maria Guavaira, however, did not agree. She felt it was sad that the courage and generosity shown on all sides should end up in feeble deception, in cowardice worse than tacit complacency. You're right, Joana Carda conceded, but we must take the bull by the horns, she answered, without realizing what she was saying, that is the danger of using certain expressions without paying enough attention to the context.

That same day the two women called their men aside, went for a stroll with them into the countryside, there where the wide-open spaces reduce the most choleric and rending cries to mere whispers, that unfortunately is the reason why human voices fail to reach heaven, and there, without beating about the bush, as they had agreed, the women told them, I'm pregnant and I'm not sure whether you're the father or Pedro Orce. Joaquim Sassa and José Anaiço reacted as one might have expected. There was the most furious outburst, a violent waving of arms, the most poignant sorrow, they were not within sight of each other, but their gestures were identical, their words equally bitter, Not satisfied with what has happened, you have the nerve to come and tell me you're pregnant and you don't know who's responsible, How can I be expected to know, and in any case when the child is born there won't be any doubt, What on earth are you talking about, There will be some resemblance, Of course, but do you imagine it will only resemble you. If it only resembles me then it will be my child and no one else's, Are you trying to make a fool of me, I'm not making a fool of anyone, that's something I never do, So how are we supposed to solve the problem, If you could accept that I might have slept with Pedro Orce for one night, then you can put up with waiting for nine months before making any decision, if the child resembles you then it's yours and if it resembles Pedro Orce then it's his and you can disown it and me as well, if that's what you want, and as for only resembling me, don't you believe it, there's always some physical trait that belongs to the other partner. And what about Pedro Orce, how do we deal with him, are you going to tell him, No, for the first two months nothing will show, especially dressed in these large blouses and loose jackets, I think it's best to say nothing, I must say that it would anger me to see Pedro Orce looking at you, at both of you, with the smug expression of a regular stud, that was the expression José Anaiço used with his superior command of language. Joaquim Sassa was much more down to earth, I'd hate to see Senhor Pedro Orce strutting around like the Cock of the Walk. So the two men resigned themselves in the end to this affront, encouraged by the thought that their worst fears might be proved groundless once the mystery was cleared up and nature took its course.

It does not even dawn on Pedro Orce, who has never known what it meant to have children, that his semen might be germinating in the wombs of the two women. How true that man never gets to know all the consequences of his deeds, here is an excellent example, the memory of the happy moments he enjoyed begins to fade, and their possible effect, little as yet, but more important in itself than all the rest, should it come to pass and be confirmed, is invisible to his eye and concealed from his knowledge. God Himself made men, yet does not see them. Pedro Orce, however, is not entirely blind, he can see that something has upset the harmony between the couples, a certain remoteness has crept in, not exactly coldness, more a note of reserve without hostility, but causing long periods of silence, the journey had begun so well and now it is as if they had nothing more to say to each other or they were too frightened to utter the only words that would have made any sense. It is over and done with, what had been alive is now dead, if that is what it is all about. It could also be that the fire of those first jealous moments had rekindled with the passage of time. And perhaps because no one saw me passing, Pedro Orce has started going for long strolls again into the surrounding neighbourhood whenever they set up camp. It is almost incredible just how much this man can walk.

One day, after they'd already left behind the first foothills which announce the Pyrenees from afar, Pedro Orce had gone ahead along secluded roads, feeling almost tempted never to go back to the camp, these are thoughts that come into one's head in moments of weariness, when he came across a man resting by the roadside. He looked about his own age, if not older, but worn-out and tired. Beside him stood a donkey with pack-saddle and load, nibbling at the sun-bleached grass with its yellow teeth, for the weather, as we mentioned earlier, is not very favourable for fresh growth and causes any new shoots to sprout out of place and season, nature has lost its way, as any lover of metaphors would say. The man was chewing a lump of stale bread and nothing else, obviously in a bad way, a tramp without food or shelter, but he seemed peaceful and harmless and, besides, Pedro Orce is not easily intimidated as he has clearly shown on those long walks through deserted countryside. The dog hasn't left him for a moment, that's to say it has left him twice, but in better company and out of sheer discretion.

Pedro Orce greeted the man, Good afternoon, and the other replied, Good afternoon, the hearing of both men registered familiar pronunciation, a southern accent, that of Andalusia, to put it in a nutshell. But the man eating the stale bread found it mighty suspicious to come across a man and a dog in these parts, remote from any habitation, and looking as if they had been dropped there by a flying saucer, and as a precaution, without trying to conceal it, he reached out for his stick which had a metal tip and was lying on the ground. Pedro Orce observed this gesture and the tramp's uneasiness, he was probably afraid of the dog as it stood there watching him, its head lowered, without moving a muscle. Don't worry about the dog, it's quite gentle, well not exactly gentle, but it won't attack unless it thinks there's some danger of being harmed. How can the dog tell when someone is going to harm it. Now there's a good question and I wish I knew the answer, but neither I nor my travelling companions have been able to discover the dog's breed or where it came from. I thought you were on your own and lived nearby, I'm travelling with some friends, we have a wagon and because of what's happened we've set out along the road and have never left it. You're from Andalusia, I can tell from your accent. I'm from Orce in the province of Granada. I hail from Zufre in the province of Huelva. Pleased to meet you. The pleasure's mine. May I join you for a moment. Make yourself comfortable, I'm afraid all I can offer you is some stale bread. Many thanks, but I've already eaten with my companions, Who are they, Two friends and their womenfolk, the two men and one of the women are Portuguese, the other woman is Galician, And how did you all meet up. Ah, that's a long story.

The other did not insist, saw that he should not, and said, You must be wondering how someone from the province of Huelva landed up here. In times like these, you rarely find people where you would expect to find them. I come from Zufre and I've relatives living there unless they've gone elsewhere, but when the rumour spread that Spain was about to break away from France, I decided to go and see for myself. No, not Spain, the Iberian Peninsula. Yes, of course. And it wasn't from France that the Peninsula broke away but from Europe, that may sound like the same thing but there's a difference. I don't understand these niceties, I only wanted to go and see for myself. And what did you see. Nothing, I reached the Pyrenees and only saw the sea. That was all we saw. There was no France and there was no Europe, now in my opinion, something that isn't there is the same as something that has never been and I wasted my time travelling league after league in search of something that didn't exist. Well, that's where you're wrong. Wrong in what way. Before the Peninsula separated from Europe, Europe did exist, naturally there was a frontier, and you had to cross from one side to the other, the Spanish passed, the Portuguese passed, foreigners came, have you never seen tourists in your region. Sometimes, but there was nothing to see there. They were tourists coming from Europe, But if I never saw Europe when I was living in Zufre, and if I've now left Zufre and I still haven't seen Europe, where's the difference. Nor have you been to the moon, yet it exists. But I can see it, at the moment it's off course, but I can still see it. What's your name. I'm called Roque Lozano and I'm at your service. I am Pedro Orce, Are you named after the place where you were born. I wasn't born in Orce, I was born in Venta Micena which is nearby. That reminds me that when I began my journey I met two Portuguese who were travelling to Orce. Perhaps they are the same two. I'd dearly like to know. Come with me and you'll find out. If that's an invitation, I'll willingly accept it, I've been travelling alone for such a long time. Get up slowly in case the dog thinks you're going to attack me, I'll hand you your stick. Roque Lozano put his bundle on his back, pulled the donkey's rein and off they went, the dog at Pedro Orce's side, perhaps this is how it should always be, wherever there is a man there should be an animal with him, a parrot perched on his shoulder, a snake coiled round his wrist, a beetle in his lapel, a scorpion curled up, we might even say a louse in his hair, if this bug did not belong to that detested species of parasites which is not even tolerated by insects, although they, poor creatures, are not to blame, for God willed them as they are.

Travelling at the same aimless pace, they penetrated into the depths of Catalonia. Business flourished, it was a brilliant idea to have launched themselves into this branch of commerce. Fewer people are now to be seen on the roads which means that, although the Peninsula is still rotating, people are returning to their normal habits and pursuits if that is the right word to describe their former habits and pursuits. Villages are no longer deserted although one cannot be sure that all the houses are now lived in by their previous occupants, some men are now with other women and some women with other men and their children are thrown together. This is the inevitable outcome of all great wars and migrations. That very morning José Anaiço suddenly announced that they must decide about the group's future since there no longer appeared to be any danger of collisions and clashes. The most likely or at least plausible hypothesis, in his opinion, would be for the Peninsula to go on rotating on the same spot, which would not inconvenience people's everyday existence, and although it might no longer be possible to know where the different cardinal points are, what does it matter, for there's no law which says that we cannot live without the north. But now they had seen the Pyrenees, and what a wonderful thrill they'd experienced looking down at the sea from such a height, Just like being in an aeroplane, Maria Guavaira had exclaimed, only to be corrected by the experienced José Anaiço, They cannot be compared, after all, no one feels dizzy looking out of the window of an aeroplane but up here, unless we cling on with all our might, we'd be tempted to throw ourselves into the sea. Sooner or later, said José Anaiço, respecting the warning he had given that morning, we shall have to decide about our future unless we mean to spend the rest of our lives on the road. Joaquim Sassa agreed but the women were reluctant to express any opinion, they suspect there may be some ulterior motive in this sudden haste, only Pedro Orce timidly reminded them that the earth was still trembling, and if this was not a sign that the journey had not reached its end, then perhaps they could explain to him why they had made it in the first place. At some other time, the wisdom of this argument, even if hypothetical, would have made some impression but one must take into account that the wounds of the soul are deep, otherwise they would not be of the soul, now whatever Pedro Orce may say, he is suspected of some ulterior motive, this is the thought one can read in the eyes of José Anaiço as he says, Immediately after dinner, each person will say what he thinks ought to be done, whether we should return home or carry on, and Joana Carda simply asked, Which home.

Now here comes Pedro Orce bringing another man with him. From this distance he looks old, just as well, we have quite enough problems of cohabitation already. The man is leading a donkey harnessed with saddle-pack and load, as old-fashioned a donkey as you have ever seen but this one is an unusual, silvery colour, were it called Platero, like the scraggy Rocinante, it would be worthy of its name. Pedro Orce comes to a halt on the invisible line that marks out the terrain of the encampment, he must observe the formalities of presenting and introducing the visitor, something which must always be done on the other side of the threshold, these are rules we do not have to learn, the historic man within us observes them, one day we tried to enter the castle without permission and we were taught a lesson. Pedro Orce says emphatically, I came across this fellow countryman and I've brought him along to have a bowl of soup with us, there is obvious exaggeration in the term fellow countryman, but it is understandable at a time like this in Europe, a Portuguese from Minho and one from Alentejo feel nostalgia for the same fatherland, even though five hundred kilometres separated the one from the other, and now they are both six hundred kilometres from home.

Joaquim Sassa and José Anaiço did not recognize the man, but the same cannot be said of the donkey. There was something unmistakable and familiar about it, in a manner of speaking, which is not surprising, for a donkey does not change in appearance within a few months, while a man, if he is dirty and unkempt, if he has let his beard grow, has become thin or fat, or has lost his hair, would need his own wife to strip him to see if that special mark is in the same place, sometimes much too late, when all has been consummated and repentance will not gather the fruit of pardon. Observing the rules of hospitality, José Anaiço said, You are welcome, do join us and if you'd like to unload the donkey and give it a rest, there's enough fodder there for both the donkey and the horses. Without its saddle-pack and load the donkey looked much younger and its coat was now seen to be in two tones of silver, the one dark, the other light and both quite striking. The men went to tether the beast, the horses looked askance at the newcomer and doubted whether it could be of much assistance to them with that scraggy frame which would be difficult to harness. The man returned to the campfire and before pulling over the stone on which he would sit, he introduced himself, My name is Roque Lozano, and as for the rest, the elementary techniques of narrative demand that it should avoid repetition. José Anaiço was about to ask if the donkey had a name, if it was named by any chance Platero or Silver, but the final words uttered by Roque Lozano which in the end always repeat themselves, I came to see Europe, caused him to fall silent, his memory was suddenly jolted and he muttered to himself, I know this man, just as well he remembered in time, it would be nothing less than offensive were a donkey needed for people to recognize each other. Similar thoughts must have been stirring in Joaquim Sassa's head too when he said hesitantly, I have the impression that we've met before, Me too, replied Roque Lozano, you remind me of two Portuguese I met at the beginning of my journey, but they were travelling by car and they didn't have any women with them, Life takes so many turns, Senhor Roque Lozano, and one gains and loses so much that one could just as easily lose a Deux Chevaux car as find a wagon with two horses, two women and yet another man, quipped Maria Guavaira, And there's more on the way, interrupted Joana Carda. Neither Pedro Orce nor Roque Lozano had any idea what she was talking about, but José Anaiço and Joaquim Sassa knew and did not much like this allusion to secrets of the human body, especially women's bodies.

They had recognized each other. Any doubts had disappeared.

Roque Lozano was the man they had encountered between the Sierras Morena and Aracena, travelling with his donkey Platero towards Europe, which he had not seen in the end, although that was still his intention and hope of salvation. And now where are you heading for, Joana Carda asked him, I'm going back home because, despite all these turns the earth has taken, it's bound to be in the same place. You mean the earth. No, my home, one's home is always where the earth is. Maria Guavaira started to ladle the soup into bowls after adding a little water to ensure there would be enough for everyone. They ate in silence, except for the dog which methodically gnawed a bone and the beasts of burden that munched and chewed the hay. Now and then you could hear a dry bean-pod snap. These animals cannot complain about their rations when one considers the difficulties at the present time.

Some of the more personal difficulties will be resolved by the family council convened for tonight. The presence of a stranger will be no impediment. On the contrary, for now that Roque Lozano has said he is returning home, what are we going to do, wander at random like gypsies, buying and selling clothes off the peg, or shall we return home, go back to work, to a normal existence, for even if the Peninsula should never again come to a halt, everyone will start getting used to it, just as mankind got used to inhabiting the earth which is constantly moving. We're not even capable of imagining how much it must have upset everyone's balance to go whizzing round an aquarium with a sun-fish inside. Forgive me for correcting you, said the unknown voice, but there's no such thing as a sun-fish, there's a moon-fish but no sun-fish. In that case I won't argue with you, but if there isn't one there ought to be. Alas, you can't have everything, José Anaiço concluded, comfort and freedom are incompatible, this wandering existence has its charms but four solid walls with a roof overhead give more protection than a wagon covered with canvas and bouncing along over potholes. Joaquim Sassa suggested, Let's start by taking Pedro Orce home, and then, he broke off in mid-sentence unable to finish it and at this point Maria Guavaira intervened and said clearly what had to be said, Very well, let's drop Pedro Orce off at his pharmacy and then go on to Portugal, José Anaiço can return to his school at a place unknown to me, while we continue in a direction once referred to as north, Joana Carda will have to decide whether she prefers to stay behind in Ereira with her cousins or go back to her husband in Coimbra, once this matter has been settled we can head for Oporto and drop Joaquim Sassa off outside his office, his bosses must be back from Peñafiel by now, and finally I'll make my own way home where a man is waiting to marry me, he'll say he's been guarding my property while I've been away, Now marry me, Mistress, and with a firebrand I'll set this wagon alight as one burns a dream and perhaps finally succeed in pushing the stone vessel out to sea and embark.

Such a long speech leaves the person speaking breathless not to mention those who are listening. For a moment they all remained silent, then José Anaiço reminded her, We're already travelling on a stone raft. But it's much too big for us to feel like sailors, rejoined Maria Guavaira and Joaquim Sassa observed smiling, How true, nor has travelling through space above the world turned us into astronauts. There was further silence, then it was Pedro Orce's turn to speak. Let's do one thing at a time, Roque Lozano can join us and we'll take him to his family who must be waiting for him in Zufre and then we can decide about our own future. But there isn't any room for anyone else to sleep inside the wagon, José Anaiço insisted. Don't let that worry you, if that's the only reason why I shouldn't accompany you, I'm used to sleeping out in the open, just so long as it doesn't rain, and if I can sleep under the wagon that will be as good as having a roof over my head at night, I was beginning to get tired of being on my own, believe me, Roque Lozano confided.

Next day they resumed their journey. Grizzly and Chess grumbled at the good fortune of donkeys, this one is trotting behind the wagon, comfortably attached with a rope and relieved of any burden, as naked as it came into the world, with its nice silvery sheen, its master is in the driver's seat, chatting about the past with Pedro Orce, the couples talk under the canvas, the dog walks ahead, on patrol. From one moment to the next, almost miraculously, harmony has been restored to the expedition. Yesterday, after their final deliberation, they drew up an itinerary, nothing very precise but so as not to go blindly. First they would descend to Tarragona, then travel along the coast as far as Valencia, move inland through Albacete as far as Cordoba, go down to Seville, and finally, less than eighty kilometres away, arrive at Zufre where we shall say, Here comes Roque Lozano, returned safe and sound from his great adventure, he left poor and poor he returns, he has discovered neither Europe nor Eldorado, not everyone who has gone in search of them has found them, nor is the traveller always to blame. Time and time again, there are no riches whatsoever where, out of malice or ignorance, we were promised we would find them. Then we will look on and see how he is received, Beloved grandfather, Dear father, Beloved husband, What a pity you've returned, I thought you might have perished in the wilderness or been devoured by wolves, not everything can be said aloud.

Then at Zufre the family council will convene once more, now where are we going and what will they say about us when we arrive, where, for what, for whom, your questions are false if you already know the answer. Within such a short time, the unknown voice had spoken twice.

After turning from east to west until a perfect semi-circle had been completed, the Peninsula began to incline. At that very moment, and in the most rigorous sense, if metaphors as a vehicle of literal sense can be rigorous, Portugal and Spain were two countries with their legs up in the air. Let us leave to the Spaniards, who have always disdained our assistance, the task and responsibility of evoking as best they know how, the structural changes of the physical space in which they live, and let us say here with the modest simplicity that has always characterized primitive peoples, that the Algarve, a southern region on the map since time immemorial, became in that supernatural moment the most northerly part of Portugal. Incredible but true, as a Father of the Church has preached to the present day, not because he's alive, for all the Fathers of the Church have died, but because people are constantly borrowing the phrase and using it indifferently, as much for spiritual profit as for human expediency. If the fates had decreed that the Peninsula should be immobilized once and for all in that position, the consequences, social and political, cultural and economic, not to mention the psychological aspect which people tend to overlook, the various consequences, as we were saying, and their aftermath would have been drastic, radical, in a word, earth-shattering. One need only remember, for example, that the famous city of Oporto would find itself stripped, without any hope of logical and topographical recourse, of its precious title of capital of the north, and if this reference in the eyes of some cosmopolites smacks of provincialism and lack of vision, then let them imagine what would happen if Milan were suddenly to end up in Calabria in southern Italy, and the Calabrians were to prosper from the commerce and industry of the north, a transformation not entirely impossible, if we bear in mind what happened to the Iberian Peninsula.

But it lasted, as we were saying, only for a minute. The Peninsula was falling but went on rotating. Therefore, before proceeding any further, we must explain what we mean by the verb to fall in this context. The meaning here is clearly not the immediate one of falling bodies which would literally imply that the Peninsula had started to sink. Well now, if throughout all those days at sea, often deeply troubled and with the imminent threat of catastrophe, no such calamity, or anything like it, occurred, it would be the greatest misfortune for the odyssey to end now in total submersion. However much it may cost us, we are now resigned to the possibility that Ulysses may not reach the shore in time to encounter sweet Nausicaa, but may the weary sailor at least be allowed to touch the coast of the island of the Phaeacians and failing that one, some other, so that he may rest his head on his own forearm, if no woman's breast awaits him. Let us be calm then. The Peninsula, we promise, is not about to sink into the cruel sea where, should such havoc ensue, everything would disappear, even the highest summit of the Pyrenees, such is the depth of these chasms. Yes, the Peninsula is falling, there is no other way of describing it, but southwards, for that is how we divide the planisphere, into top and bottom, upper and lower, white and black, figuratively speaking, even if it should cause some surprise that the countries below the Equator do not use maps of a different kind which might justly give the complementary image of the world which is lacking. But things are what they are, they have that irresistible virtue, and even a schoolchild understands the lesson first time round without the need for further explanation. Even the dictionary of synonyms, so lightly dismissed, confirms as much, one descends or falls downwards, fortunately for us this stone raft does not go sinking to the bottom, gurgling through a hundred million lungs, blending the sweet waters of the Tagus and the Guadalquivir with the bitter swell of the infinite ocean.

There is not and never has been any lack of those who affirm that poets are truly superfluous, and I ask myself what would become of us if poetry were not there to help us to understand how little clarity there is in the things we describe as clear. Even at this point, after so many pages have been written, the narrative material can be summed up as the description of an ocean voyage, although not altogether banal, and even at this dramatic moment when the Peninsula resumes its route southwards, while continuing to go round its imaginary axis, we certainly would not know how to surpass and enhance the simple statement of facts were it not for the inspiration of that Portuguese poet who compared the revolution and descent of the Peninsula to a child in its mother's womb taking its first tumble in life. The simile is magnificent, although we must deplore this yielding to the temptations of anthropomorphism which sees and judges everything in an obligatory rapport with human beings, as if nature had nothing better to do than to think about us. It would all be much easier to understand if we were simply to confess our infinite fear, that fear which leads us to people the world with images resembling what we are or believe ourselves to be, unless this obsessive effort is nothing other than feigned courage or sheer stubbornness on the part of someone who refuses not to be where there is emptiness, who decides not to give meaning where no meaning exists. We are probably incapable of filling emptiness, and what we call meaning is no more than a fleeting collection of images which once seemed harmonious, or where the intelligence in panic tried to introduce reason, order and coherence.

Generally speaking, the poet's voice is not understood and while this is the rule there are, nevertheless, some exceptions, as can be seen in the lyrical episode where the felicitous metaphor has been glossed in every manner and repeated on everyone's lips, even if one cannot include in this popular enthusiasm the majority of the other poets, something which needn't surprise us if we bear in mind that they are not exempt from all these human feelings of spite and envy. One of the most interesting consequences of that inspired comparison was the resurgence of the maternal spirit, of maternal influence, however mitigated by the changes modernity brought to family life. And if we reconsider the known facts, there are many reasons for believing that Joana Carda and Maria Guavaira were precursors of that influence out of natural subtlety rather than deliberate premeditation. The women undoubtedly triumphed. Their genital organs, if you'll pardon the crude reference to their anatomy, finally became the expression, simultaneously reduced and enlarged, of the expulsive mechanism of the universe, of all that machinery which operates by extraction, that nothingness which will become everything, that uninterrupted progression from the small to the large, from the finite to the infinite. It's nice to see that at this point the commentators and scholars got into deep water, but no surprise, for experience has taught us all too well how inadequate words become as we get closer to the frontiers of the inexpressible, we try to say love and the word will not come out, we try to say I want and we say I cannot, we try to utter the final word only to realize that we have gone back to the beginning.

But in the reciprocal action of cause and effect, another consequence, at once fact and factor, has come to alleviate the graveness of these discussions and to leave everyone, as it were, smiling and embracing each other. It so happened that from one moment to the next, allowing for the exaggeration that these simplified formulae always imply, all, or nearly all the fertile women declared themselves pregnant, although no significant change in the contraceptive practices of the women and men had been verified, we are referring, of course, to the men with whom they cohabited regularly or by chance. As things stand, people are no longer surprised. Several months have passed since the Peninsula separated from Europe, we have travelled thousands of kilometres over this violently open sea, the leviathan just missed colliding with the terrified islands of the Azores, or perhaps was never meant to collide with them, as later emerged, but the men and women did not know as they found themselves obliged to flee from one side to the other, these were only some of the many things that happened, such as waiting for the sun to rise on the left only to see it appear on the right, and as for the moon, as if its inconstancy were not enough since breaking away from the earth, and also the winds which blow on all sides and the clouds which shift from all horizons and circle above our dazzled heads, yes dazzled, for there is a living flame overhead, as if man needn't emerge after all from the historic sloth of his animal state and might be placed once more, lucid and entire, in a newly-formed world, pure and with its beauty intact. All of this having happened, and the aforementioned Portuguese poet having declared that the Peninsula is a child conceived on a journey and now finds itself revolving in the sea as it waits to be born in this watery womb, why should we be astonished that the human wombs of women should be swollen, perhaps the great stone descending southwards fertilized them and how do we know if these new creatures are really the daughters of men, or whether their father is that gigantic prow pushing the waves before it, penetrating them, murmuring waters, the blowing and sighing of winds.

The travellers were informed of this collective pregnancy from the news on the radio and in press reports, and television programmes spoke of nothing else. Journalists only had to catch a woman on the street and they were shoving a microphone into her face and bombarding her with questions, how and when did it happen, what name was she going to give the baby, poor woman, with the camera devouring her alive, she blushed and stammered, the only thing she did not do was to invoke the Constitution because she knew they would not take her seriously. Between the travellers on the wagon there was renewed tension, after all, if all the women of the Peninsula have fallen pregnant, these two women here are not saying a word about their own mishap and one can understand their silence, if they were to confess that they are pregnant, Pedro Orce would include himself on the paternity list and the harmony they restored with such difficulty last time might not survive a second blow. So, one evening as Joana Carda and Maria Guavaira were serving dinner to the men, they said with a wry smile, Just imagine, all the women in Spain and Portugal are pregnant and here we are without any hope. Let us accept this momentary pretence, let us grant that José Anaiço and Joaquim Sassa may disguise their annoyance, the annoyance of the male who sees his sexual potency called into question and the worst of it is that the women's feigned sarcasm might well have struck a chord, for if it is true that they are both pregnant, it is also true that nobody knows by whom. With so many unanswered questions, this pretence certainly didn't relieve the atmosphere, in the fullness of time it will become clear that Maria Guavaira and Joana Carda were pregnant, after all, despite their denial, what explanation will they offer, the truth always awaits us, the day arrives when it has to be faced.

Visibly embarrassed, the Prime Ministers of both countries appear on television, not that there is any reason to feel awkward when speaking of the demographic explosion which would be evident in the Peninsula nine months hence, twelve or fifteen million children born almost at the same hour, crying out in chorus to the light, the Peninsula transformed into maternity, happy mothers, smiling fathers, in those cases where there appears to be sufficient certainty. It is even possible to gain some political advantage from this aspect of the question by pointing to the population figures, by appealing for austerity in the name of our children's future, by going on about national cohesion and comparing this fertility with the sterility in the rest of the Western world. One cannot but rejoice at the thought that in order to have this demographic explosion there must certainly have been a genetic explosion since no one believes that this collective fecundity is of a supernatural order. The Prime Minister now speaks of the health measures to be taken, of maternity services on a national scale, of the teams of doctors and midwives who will be hired and deployed at the appropriate time, and his face betrays conflicting emotions, the solemnity of his official statement vies with the urge to smile, he appears to be on the point of saying at any minute, Sons and daughters of Portugal, the benefits we shall reap will be great and I trust that the pleasure has been just as great, for to beget children without indulging the flesh is the worst punishment of all. The men and women listen, exchange smiles and glances, they can read each other's thoughts, recall that night, that day, that hour, when driven by a sudden urge they came together and did what had to be done, beneath a sky which slowly began turning, a demented sun, a demented moon, the stars in turmoil. The first impression is that this might be some illusion or dream, but when the women appear with swollen bellies, then it will be clear that we have not been dreaming.

The President of the United States of America also addressed the world. He declared that notwithstanding the Peninsula's diversion towards some unknown place lying to the south, the United States would never abdicate its responsibilities to civilization, freedom and peace, although the nations of the Peninsula cannot count, now that they were penetrating contested areas of influence, They cannot count, I repeat, on aid equal to that which awaited them when it seemed likely that their future would become inseparable from that of the American nation. These were more or less his pronouncements to the wide world. In private, however, in the secrecy of the Oval Office at the White House, as an ice-cube clinked in his Bourbon, the President would have confided to his advisers, If they were to become stranded in the Antarctic our worries would be over, where should we finish up with the world roaming from one side to another, no strategy could cope with it, take for example the bases we still have on the Peninsula, what good would they be to us except for firing missiles at the penguins. One of his advisers then pointed out that if one considered it carefully, the new route really was not all that bad. They are moving down between Africa and Latin America, Mr President, Yes, the route could be advantageous, but it could also encourage further insubordination in the region, and perhaps because of this annoying reminder, the

President thumped the table, upsetting the smiling portrait of the First Lady. An elderly adviser jumped with fright, looked round and said, Do be careful Mr President, you can never tell what a thump like that might do.

It's no longer the flayed skin of the bull but a gigantic stone in the shape of one of those flint artefacts used by men in prehistoric times, chipped out patiently blow by blow until it becomes a working tool, the upper part compact and rounded to fit into the palm of the hand, the lower part pointed for the tasks of scraping, digging, cutting, marking and designing, and also, because we have not yet learnt to resist the temptation, to wound and kill. The Peninsula has stopped rotating and is now descending vertically in a southerly direction between Africa and Central America, as the President's adviser should have explained, and its form, to the surprise of anyone who might still have in mind or on their map its former position, matches that of the two continents on either side, we see Portugal and Galicia to the north, occupying the entire width from west to east, then the great mass starts becoming narrower, with Andalusia and Valencia still jutting out on the left and the Cantabrian coast on the right, and on the same line, the great wall of the Pyrenees. The tip of the stone, the cutting edge, is the Cape of Croesus, carried from Mediterranean waters to these threatening seas, so far from his native sky, he who was the neighbour of Cerbère, that little French town so often mentioned at the beginning of this narrative.

The Peninsula is descending, but descending slowly. The experts, although with the utmost caution, predict that the movement is about to stop, trusting in the universal evidence that if the whole, as such, never stops, the constituent parts must stop at some time, this axiom being demonstrated by human life itself, which abounds as we know in potential comparisons. With this scientific statement, the game of the century got under way, an idea which must have emerged practically at the same time throughout the world, and which consisted of establishing a system of placing a double wager on the time and place in which the suspension of movement would be verified, let's take a hypothetical case to clarify the point, at five thirty-three and forty-nine seconds local time of the person betting, obviously, and the day, month and year, and the position restricted to indicating the meridian in degrees, minutes and seconds, the aforementioned Cape of Croesus serving as a point of reference. There were trillions of dollars at stake, and if someone were to guess both answers correctly, that is to say, the precise moment and the exact place, which according to the calculation of probabilities was little short of unthinkable, that person endowed with almost divine foresight would find himself in possession of greater wealth than has ever been gathered on this earth which has seen so many riches. Do not forget that there has never been a more terrible game than this one because with each passing moment, with each kilometre covered, the number of gamblers with any chance of winning is gradually reduced, although one should note that many of those eliminated come back again to wager, thus increasing the prize money to an astronomical figure. Of course not everyone manages to raise enough money to place another bet, clearly many of them find no other way out of their financial ruin except by committing suicide. The Peninsula is descending southward leaving behind a trail of deaths of which it is innocent, while in the wombs of its women are being conceived millions of infants which it innocently generated.

Pedro Orce goes around looking restless and ill at ease. Scarcely speaks, spends hours away from the encampment, comes back exhausted and refuses to eat, his companions enquire if he's feeling ill and he tells them, No, no I'm not ill, without further explanation. Any conversation he makes is reserved for Roque Lozano, they are always reminiscing about their native parts as if there were no other topic of conversation. The dog accompanies him everywhere and one senses that the man's restlessness has affected this animal which was once so placid. José Anaiço has already commented to Joana Carda, If he thinks that history is about to repeat itself, the poor man alone and abandoned who finds compassionate women ready to comfort him and bring him sexual relief, he's much deceived, and she answered with a wan smile, You're the one who must be deceived, Pedro Orce's trouble, if that's the right word, is something quite different. What trouble. I don't know, but I can assure you he's not craving for us this time, a woman is never in any doubt about these things. Then we should talk to him, oblige him to speak, perhaps he really is ill. Perhaps, but even that isn't certain.

They travel along the Sierra de Alcaraz, today they will set up camp near a village which, according to the map, is called Bienservida. At least in name it is indeed well served. Perched in the driver's seat, Pedro Orce tells Roque Lozano, From here we should soon be arriving in the province of Granada, if that's where we're heading. But my land is still far away. You'll get there. Oh yes, I'll get there, but the question is whether there's much point. These are things we only discover afterwards, give the grey horse a prod, for it's slowing down. Roque Lozano shook the reins, flicked his whip over the horse's rump, the merest graze, whereupon Grizzly obediently adjusted its trot. The couples travel inside the wagon, they converse in whispers and Maria Guavaira says, Perhaps he'd rather go back home but doesn't like to say so in case we take offence. You could be right, replied Joaquim Sassa, we'd better ask him straight out, tell him we understand, and that there are no hard feelings, after all, no oath or contract need last a lifetime, friends we are and friends we remain, one day we'll come back and visit him. God forbid, Joana Carda muttered under her breath. Have you something else in mind. No, not at all, just a premonition. What premonition, Maria Guavaira asked her. That Pedro Orce is going to die. We can all expect to die sooner or later. But he'll be the first to go.

Bienservida lies off the main road. They had gone there to sell their wares, they bought some provisions, renewed their supply of water, and still early, they returned on to the road. However they did not get far. A little further on there was a small country church known as Turruchel, a pleasant spot to spend the night, so they decided to stop. Pedro Orce started to get down from the driver's seat and, contrary to habit, José Anaiço and Joaquim Sassa jumped down from the wagon as it came to a halt and went to his assistance, causing him to say as he held on to their outstretched hands, What's this my friends, I'm not an invalid, He failed to notice that the word friends immediately brought tears to the eyes of these men who harbour the sorrow of mistrust in their hearts even while receiving that weary body as it falls into their arms despite the old man's proud statement, for there comes a time when pride has nothing but words, is nothing but words. Pedro Orce puts his feet on the ground, takes a few steps and pauses with an expression of amazement on his face, in his every gesture, as if intense light were paralysing and blinding him. What's wrong, asked Maria Guavaira who had drawn near. Nothing, it's nothing. Do you feel unwell, Joana Carda asked him. No, it's something else. He bent down, spread out his hands on the ground, then summoned the dog Constant, placed one hand on its head, ran his fingers along its neck, its spine, back and croup. The dog did not move, it stood stock-still as if trying to dig its paws in the earth. Now Pedro Orce had stretched out, his head resting on a clump of grasses, his white hair mingling with fresh shoots, flowering at a time when it should have been winter. Joana Carda and Maria Guavaira knelt down beside him and held his hands, What's the matter, tell us what you feel, for he was clearly suffering some great pain judging from the expression on his face. He opened his eyes wide and stared at the sky, at the passing clouds. Maria Guavaira and Joana Carda did not need to look up to see them, they floated slowly in Pedro Orce's eyes just as the streetlamps of Oporto had played in the dog's eyes, so long ago perhaps, in some other existence, and now they are together, reunited with Roque Lozano who has as much experience of life as of death, the dog appears to be hypnotized by Pedro Orce's expression, it stares at him, its head lowered and hairs bristling, as if it were about to confront all the wild beasts in the world, and then Pedro Orce said distinctly, word by word, I no longer feel the earth, I can no longer feel it, his eyes darkened, a grey cloud, the colour of lead, passed slowly across the sky, slowly, very slowly. With the utmost delicacy Maria Guavaira lowered his eyelids and told them, He's dead, whereupon the dog came running and let out a howl that was almost human.

A man dies and what then. His four friends weep, even Roque Lozano whom he has known for such a short time, rubs his eyes furiously with clenched fists, and the dog has only howled once, it now stands beside the corpse, soon it will lie down and rest its enormous head on Pedro Orce's chest. But we must decide what to do with the body, José Anaiço remarked. Let's take it to Bienservida and inform the authorities, we can do no more for him, then Joaquim Sassa reminded him, You once told me that the poet Machado must have been buried under a holm oak, let's do the same with Pedro Orce, but Joana Carda had the last word, Neither to Bienservida nor underneath a tree, let's take the body to Venta Micena, let's bury him in the place where he was born.

Pedro Orce is lying on the bier laid out crosswise. Beside him kneel the two women holding his cold hands, those same eager hands which scarcely became familiar with their bodies, and in the driver's seat are the two men. Roque Lozano leads the horses by the reins, they thought they were going to have a rest, and they are on the road, after all, and in the middle of the night, such a thing has never happened to them before, perhaps the sorrel remembers another night, perhaps it was asleep and dreaming that it was shackled so that a painful sore might be cured with ointment and the morning dew, a man and a woman came looking for it accompanied by a dog, they untied it from its trappings and the horse did not know if the dream began or ended there. The dog walks underneath the wagon and below Pedro Orce as if it were carrying him, such is the weight it feels pressing down on its collar. There is a burning oil-lamp hanging from the steel arch that supports the canvas in front. They still have one hundred and fifty kilometres to go.

The horses can feel death pursuing them and need no other whip. The silence of night is so deep that the wagon's wheels can scarcely be heard as they turn on the rough surface of these old roads, and the horses' trot sounds muffled as if their hooves were clad in rags. No moon will appear. They travel among shadows, there is a total blackout, an *apagón* or *negrum*, the first night of all before those words were spoken, Let there be light, and there was no great wonder, for God knew that the sun would inevitably appear two hours hence. Joana Carda and Maria Guavaira have been weeping since they set out. They had given their bodies out of compassion to this man whose corpse they all now escort, with their own hands they had drawn him to them, shown him what to do and perhaps the infants forming inside their wombs and being made to tremble by their sobs are his offspring, my goodness, how everything in this world is linked together and here we are thinking that we have the power to separate or join them at will, how sadly mistaken we are having been proved wrong time and time again, a line traced on the ground, a flock of starlings, a stone thrown into the sea, a blue woollen sock, but we are showing them to the blind, preaching to the deaf with hearts of stone.

The sky was still covered in darkness as they reached Venta Micena. Along the entire route stretching almost thirty leagues they hadn't met a living soul. And slumbering Orce was a ghost, its houses like the walls of a labyrinth, their windows and doors firmly closed. Rising above the rooftops, the Castle of the Seven Towers was like some mirage. The streetlamps flickered like stars about to disappear, the trees in the square reduced to trunks and thick boughs might well have been the remnants of a petrified forest. The travellers passed in front of the pharmacy, this time there was no need to stop, the details of the route were still fresh in their memories, Carry straight on in the direction of Maria, continue for three kilometres after the last houses, there you'll come to a little bridge, nearby there's an olive tree, I'll catch up with you shortly. He has already arrived. After the last bend they saw the cemetery with its whitewashed walls and enormous cross. The gate was locked, they had to force it open. José Anaiço went in search of a lever, pushed the claw between the gate and the post, but Maria Guavaira grabbed him by the arm, We're not going to bury him here. She pointed to the white hills towards the Cueva de los Rosas where the skull of the most ancient man in Europe had been excavated, the one who had lived more than a million years ago, and she said, The body will rest over there, that's the spot Pedro Orce himself might have chosen. They took the wagon as far as possible, the horses could scarcely walk, their hooves dragging in the loose dust. There's no one living in Venta Micena to attend the funeral, all the houses have been abandoned, nearly all of them are in ruins. On the horizon the shadowy outline of the mountains can scarcely be seen, those same mountains that Orce Man must have watched as he lay dying. It is still night, Pedro Orce is dead, in his eyes only a dark cloud has remained and nothing else.

When the wagon could go no further, the three men removed the corpse. Maria Guavaira helps them. Joana Carda carries the elm branch in one hand. They climb a hill which is flat on top. The dry soil crumbles under their feet, goes scattering down the slope, the corpse of Pedro Orce sways, almost slips, taking those carrying it with them, but they manage to hoist it to the top where they rest it on the ground. They are bathed in perspiration, covered in white dust. Roque Lozano starts digging the grave, having asked the others to leave the job to him. The soil comes away easily, the lever serves as a spade and their hands as shovels. Light begins to dawn to the east, the blurred form of the sierra has turned black. Roque Lozano emerges from the hole, shakes the soil from his hands, kneels and starts to lift the corpse assisted by José Anaiço who takes it by the arms. They lower the body slowly into the ground, the grave is not deep, should anthropologists ever return to these parts they would have no difficulty in finding it. Maria Dolores will say, Here's a skull, and the leader of the expedition will take a quick look, It's of no interest, we have plenty of those. They covered the body, levelled out the earth until it merged with the rest of the terrain, but they had to remove the dog which was trying to scratch at the grave with its claws. Then Joana Carda stuck the elm branch into the ground where Pedro Orce's head lay buried. It is not a cross, as one can see, nor a sign of mourning, it is only a branch which has lost any value it ever had, yet can still be put to this simple use, a sundial in a fossilized wilderness, perhaps a resuscitated tree, if a piece of dry wood stuck in the ground is capable of working miracles, of creating roots, of ridding Pedro Orce's eyes of that dark cloud. Tomorrow the rain will fall over these fields.

The Peninsula came to a halt. The travellers will rest here today, tonight and tomorrow. It is raining as they are about to leave. They have called the dog which hasn't left the grave during all this time, but it hasn't come. It's only to be expected, observed José Anaiço, dogs cannot bear to be separated from their master, sometimes they even pine away. He was mistaken. The dog Ardent looked at José Anaiço, then moved off slowly with lowered head. They would never see it again. The journey continues. Roque Lozano will remain in Zufre, he will knock on the door of his house saying, I've come back, that's his story and perhaps someone will tell it one day. As for the other men and women, they will travel on their way, who knows what future awaits them, how much time, what destiny. The elm branch is green. Perhaps it will flower again next year.